'[A] ren... erature, ... absurdist tour de ... or Genet'

New York Times Book Review

'Extraordinary ... Surely a new classic of war fiction ... [Nguyen] has written a cerebral thriller around a desperate expat story that confronts the existential dilemmas of our age ... I haven't read anything since Orwell's *Nineteen Eighty-Four* that illustrates so palpably how a patient tyrant, unmoored from all human constraint, can reduce a man's mind to liquid'

Washington Post

'This debut is a page-turner (read: everybody will finish) that makes you reconsider the Vietnam War ... Nguyen's darkly comic novel offers a point of view about American culture that we've rarely seen'

Oprah.com (Oprah's Book Club Suggestions)

'The satire is delicious'

New Yorker

'*The Sympathizer* reads as part literary historical fiction, part espionage thriller and part satire. Nguyen knows of what he writes'

Los Angeles Times

'An important new perspective on the Vietnam War . . . *The Sympathizer* will both startle and grip you'

BuzzFeed

'An early front-runner for debut novel of the year'

Flavorwire (10 Must-Read Books for April)

'I cannot remember the last time I read a novel whose protagonist I liked so much. Smart, funny, and self-critical, with a keen sense of when to let a story speak for itself … [Nguyen] proves a gifted and bold satirist'

Barnes & Noble Review

'Arresting . . . One of the best pieces of fiction about the Vietnam war – and by a Vietnamese. . . . Stunning . . . Could it be that Nguyen has captured the shape of the devolution of war itself, from grand ambition to human ruin? . . . One of the finest novels of the Vietnam War published in recent years'

Daily Beast

'Read this novel with care; it is easy to read, wry, ironic, wise, and captivating, but it could change not only your outlook on the Vietnam War, but your outlook on what you believe about politics and ideology in general. It does what the best of literature does, expands your consciousness beyond the limitations of your body and individual circumstances'

Karl Marlantes, author of *Matterhorn* and *What It Is Like to Go to War*

'Magisterial. A disturbing, fascinating and darkly comic take on the fall of Saigon and its aftermath, and a powerful examination of guilt and betrayal. *The Sympathizer* is destined to become a classic and redefine the way we think about the Vietnam War and what it means to win and to lose'

T.C. Boyle, author of *The Tortilla Curtain*

'[A] dark and exciting debut novel … Black humour seeps through these pages'

Wall Street Journal

THE
SYMPATHIZER

VIET THANH NGUYEN

corsair

CORSAIR

First published in the United States of America in 2015 by Atlantic Monthly Press,
an imprint of Grove/Atlantic, Inc.
First published in Great Britain in 2015 by Corsair
This edition published in 2016

27 29 30 28

A CIP catalogue record for this book
is available from the British Library.

ISBN: 978-1-4721-5136-0 (paperback)
ISBN: 978-1-4721-5138-4 (eBook)

Printed and bound in Great Britain by Clays Ltd, Elcograf S.p.A.

Papers used by Corsair are from well-managed forests
and other responsible sources.

Corsair
An imprint of
Little, Brown Book Group
Carmelite House
50 Victoria Embankment
London EC4Y 0DZ

An Hachette UK Company
www.hachette.co.uk

www.littlebrown.co.uk

For Lan and Ellison

Let us not become gloomy as soon as we hear the word 'torture':
in this particular case there is plenty to offset and mitigate that
word – even something to laugh at.
—Friedrich Nietzsche, *On the Genealogy of Morals*

THE
SYMPATHIZER

CHAPTER 1

I AM A SPY, a sleeper, a spook, a man of two faces. Perhaps not surprisingly, I am also a man of two minds. I am not some misunderstood mutant from a comic book or a horror movie, although some have treated me as such. I am simply able to see any issue from both sides. Sometimes I flatter myself that this is a talent, and although it is admittedly one of a minor nature, it is perhaps also the sole talent I possess. At other times, when I reflect on how I cannot help but observe the world in such a fashion, I wonder if what I have should even be called talent. After all, a talent is something you use, not something that uses you. The talent you cannot *not* use, the talent that possesses you—that is a hazard, I must confess. But in the month when this confession begins, my way of seeing the world still seemed more of a virtue than a danger, which is how some dangers first appear.

The month in question was April, the cruelest month. It was the month in which a war that had run on for a very long time would lose its limbs, as is the way of wars. It was a month that meant everything to all the people in our small

1

part of the world and nothing to most people in the rest of the world. It was a month that was both an end of a war and the beginning of . . . well, "peace" is not the right word, is it, my dear Commandant? It was a month when I awaited the end behind the walls of a villa where I had lived for the previous five years, the villa's walls glittering with broken brown glass and crowned with rusted barbed wire. I had my own room at the villa, much like I have my own room in your camp, Commandant. Of course, the proper term for my room is an "isolation cell," and instead of a housekeeper who comes to clean every day, you have provided me with a baby-faced guard who does not clean at all. But I am not complaining. Privacy, not cleanliness, is my only prerequisite for writing this confession.

While I had sufficient privacy in the General's villa at night, I had little during the day. I was the only one of the General's officers to live in his home, the sole bachelor on his staff and his most reliable aide. In the mornings, before I chauffeured him the short distance to his office, we would breakfast together, parsing dispatches at one end of the teak dining table while his wife oversaw a well-disciplined quartet of children at the other, ages eighteen, sixteen, fourteen, and twelve, with one seat empty for the daughter studying in America. Not everyone may have feared the end, but the General sensibly did. A thin man of excellent posture, he was a veteran campaigner whose many medals had been, in his case, genuinely earned. Although he possessed but nine fingers and eight toes, having lost three digits to bullets and shrapnel, only his family and confidants knew about the condition of his left foot. His ambitions had hardly ever been thwarted, except in his desire to procure an excellent bottle of Bourgogne and to drink it with companions who knew better than to put ice cubes in their wine. He was an epicurean and a Christian, in that order, a man of faith who believed in gastronomy and God; his wife and his children; and the French and the Americans. In his view, they offered us far better tutelage than those other foreign Svengalis who had hypnotized our northern brethren and some of our southern ones: Karl Marx, V. I. Lenin, and Chairman Mao. Not that he ever read any of those sages! That was my job as his aide-de-camp and junior officer of intelligence, to provide him with cribbed notes on, say, *The Communist Manifesto* or Mao's *Little Red Book*. It was up to him to find occasions to demonstrate his knowledge of the enemy's thinking, his favorite being Lenin's question, plagiarized whenever the need arose: Gentlemen, he would say, rapping the relevant table with adamantine knuckles, *what is to be done?* To tell the General that Nikolay Chernyshevsky actually came up with the question in his novel of the same title seemed irrelevant. How many remember Chernyshevsky now? It was Lenin who counted, the man of action who took the question and made it his own.

In this gloomiest of Aprils, faced with this question of what should be done, the general who always found something to do could no longer do so. A man who had faith in the *mission civilisatrice* and the American Way was at last bitten by the bug of disbelief. Suddenly insomniac, he took to wandering his villa with the greenish pallor of a malarial patient. Ever since our northern front had collapsed a few weeks before in March, he would materialize at my office door or at my room in the villa to hand off a snatch of news, always gloomy. Can you believe it? he would demand, to which I said one of two things: No, sir! or Unbelievable! We could not believe that the pleasant, scenic coffee town of Ban Me Thuot, my Highlands hometown, had been sacked in early March. We could not believe that our president, Thieu, whose name begged to be spit out of the mouth, had inexplicably ordered our forces defending the Highlands to retreat. We could not believe that Da Nang and Nha Trang had fallen, or that our troops had shot civilians in the back as they all fought madly to escape on barges and boats, the death toll running to the thousands. In the secret privacy of my office, I dutifully snapped pictures of these reports, which would please Man, my handler. While they pleased me, too, as signs of the regime's inevitable erosion, I could not help but feel moved by the plight of these poor people. Perhaps it was not correct, politically speaking, for me to feel sympathy for them, but my mother would have been one of them if she were alive. She was a poor person, I was her poor child, and no one asks poor people if they want war. Nor had anyone asked these poor people if they wanted to die of thirst and exposure on the coastal sea, or if they wanted to be robbed and raped by their own soldiers. If those thousands still lived, they would not have believed how they had died, just as we could not believe that the Americans—our friends, our benefactors, our protectors—had spurned our request to send more money. And what would we have done with that money? Buy the ammunition, gas, and spare parts for the weapons, planes, and tanks the same Americans had bestowed on us for free. Having given us the needles, they now perversely no longer supplied the dope. (Nothing, the General muttered, is ever so expensive as what is offered for free.)

At the end of our discussions and meals, I lit the General's cigarette and he stared into space, forgetting to smoke the Lucky Strike as it slowly consumed itself in his fingers. In the middle of April, when the ash stung him awake from his reverie and he uttered a word he should not have, Madame silenced the tittering children and said, If you wait much longer, we won't be able to get out. You should ask Claude for a plane now. The General pretended not to hear Madame. She had a mind like an abacus, the spine of a drill instructor, and the body of a virgin even after five children. All of this was wrapped up in one of those exteriors that inspired our Beaux Arts–trained painters to use the most pastel of watercolors and the fuzziest of brushstrokes. She was, in short, the ideal Vietnamese woman. For this good fortune, the General was eternally grateful and terrified. Kneading the tip of his scorched finger, he looked at me and said, I think it's time to ask Claude for a plane. Only when he resumed studying his damaged finger did I glance at Madame, who merely raised an eyebrow. Good idea, sir, I said.

Claude was our most trusted American friend, our relationship so intimate he once confided in me to being one-sixteenth Negro. Ah, I had said, equally smashed on Tennessee bourbon, that explains why your hair is black, and why you tan well, and why you can dance the cha-cha like one of us. Beethoven, he said, was likewise of hexa-decimal descent. Then, I said, that explains why you can carry the tune of "Happy Birthday" like no one's business. We had known each other for more than two decades, ever since he had spotted me on a refugee barge in '54 and recog-nized my talents. I was a precocious nine-year-old who had already learned a decent amount of English, taught to me by a pioneering American missionary. Claude supposedly worked in refugee relief. Now his desk was in the American embassy, his assignment ostensibly to promote the develop-ment of tourism in our war-stricken country. This, as you might imagine, required every drop he could squeeze from a handkerchief soaked with the sweat of the can-do American spirit. In reality, Claude was a CIA man whose time in this country dated back to the days when the French still ruled an empire. In those days, when the CIA was the OSS, Ho Chi Minh looked to them for help in fighting the French. He even quoted America's Founding Fathers in his declara-tion of our country's independence. Uncle Ho's enemies say he spoke out of both sides of his mouth at the same time, but Claude believed he saw both sides at once. I rang Claude from my office, down the hall from the General's study, and informed him in English that the General had lost all hope. Claude's Vietnamese was bad and his French worse, but his English was excellent. I point this out only because the same thing could not be said of all his countrymen.

It's over, I said, and when I said it to Claude it finally seemed real. I thought Claude might protest and argue that

American bombers might yet fill our skies, or that American air cavalry might soon ride on gunships to our rescue, but Claude did not disappoint. I'll see what I can arrange, he said, a murmur of voices audible in the background. I imagined the embassy in disarray, teletypes overheating, urgent cables crisscrossing between Saigon and Washington, the staff working without respite, and the funk of defeat so pungent it overwhelmed the air conditioners. Amid short tempers, Claude stayed cool, having lived here so long he barely perspired in the tropical humidity. He could sneak up on you in the dark, but he could never be invisible in our country. Although an intellectual, he was of a peculiarly American breed, the muscular kind who rowed crew and who flexed substantial biceps. Whereas our scholarly types tended to be pale, myopic, and stunted, Claude was six-two, had perfect vision, and kept himself in shape by performing two hundred push-ups each morning, his Nung houseboy squatting on his back. During his free time, he read, and whenever he visited the villa, a book was tucked under his arm. When he arrived a few days later, Richard Hedd's *Asian Communism and the Oriental Mode of Destruction* was the paperback he carried.

The book was for me, while the General received a bottle of Jack Daniel's—a gift I would have preferred if given the choice. Nevertheless, I took care to peruse the book's cover, crowded with blurbs so breathless they might have been lifted from the transcript of a teenage girls' fan club, except that the excited giggling came from a pair of secretaries of defense, a senator who had visited our country for two weeks to find facts, and a renowned television anchor who modeled his enunciation on Moses, as played by Charlton Heston. The reason for their excitement was found in the significant type of the subtitle, *On Understanding and Defeating the Marxist Threat to Asia*. When Claude said everyone was reading this how-to manual, I said I would read it as well. The General, who had cracked open the bottle, was in no mood to discuss books or chitchat, not with eighteen enemy divisions encircling the capital. He wanted to discuss the plane, and Claude, rolling his glass of whiskey between his palms, said the best he could do was a black flight, off the books, on a C-130. It could hold ninety-two paratroopers and their gear, as the General well knew, having served in the Airborne before being called on by the president himself to lead the National Police. The problem, as he explained to Claude, was that his extended family alone amounted to fifty-eight. While he did not like some of them, and in fact despised a few, Madame would never forgive him if he did not rescue all of her relations.

And my staff, Claude? The General spoke in his precise, formal English. What of them? Both the General and Claude glanced at me. I tried to look brave. I was not the senior officer on the staff, but as the aide-de-camp and the officer most fluent in American culture, I attended all the General's meetings with Americans. Some of my countrymen spoke English as well as I, although most had a tinge of an accent. But almost none could discuss, like I, baseball standings, the awfulness of Jane Fonda, or the merits of the Rolling Stones versus the Beatles. If an

American closed his eyes to hear me speak, he would think I was one of his kind. Indeed, on the phone, I was easily mistaken for an American. On meeting in person, my interlocutor was invariably astonished at my appearance and would almost always inquire as to how I had learned to speak English so well. In this jackfruit republic that served as a franchise of the United States, Americans expected me to be like those millions who spoke no English, pidgin English, or accented English. I resented their expectation. That was why I was always eager to demonstrate, in both spoken and written word, my mastery of their language. My vocabulary was broader, my grammar more precise than the average educated American. I could hit the high notes as well as the low, and thus had no difficulty in understanding Claude's characterization of the ambassador as a "putz," a "jerkoff" with "his head up his ass" who was in denial about the city's imminent fall. Officially, there's no evacuation, said Claude, because we're not pulling out any time soon.

The General, who hardly ever raised his voice, now did. Unofficially, you are abandoning us, he shouted. All day and night planes depart from the airport. Everyone who works with Americans wants an exit visa. They go to your embassy for these visas. You have evacuated your own women. You have evacuated babies and orphans. Why is it that the only people who do not know the Americans are pulling out are the Americans? Claude had the decency to look embarrassed as he explained how the city would erupt in riots if an evacuation was declared, and perhaps

then turn against the Americans who remained. This
had happened in Da Nang and Nha Trang, where the
Americans had fled for their lives and left the residents
to turn on one another. But despite this precedent, the
atmosphere was strangely quiet in Saigon, most of the
Saigonese citizenry behaving like people in a scuppered
marriage, willing to cling gamely to each other and
drown so long as nobody declared the adulterous truth.
The truth, in this case, was that at least a million people
were working or had worked for the Americans in one
capacity or another, from shining their shoes to running
the army designed by the Americans in their own image
to performing fellatio on them for the price, in Peoria or
Poughkeepsie, of a hamburger. A good portion of these
people believed that if the communists won—which they
refused to believe would happen—what awaited them was
prison or a garrote, and, for the virgins, forced marriage
with the barbarians. Why wouldn't they? These were the
rumors the CIA was propagating.

So— the General began, only to have Claude interrupt
him. You have one plane and you should consider yourself
lucky, sir. The General was not one to beg. He finished his
whiskey, as did Claude, then shook Claude's hand and bid
him good-bye, never once letting his gaze fall away from
Claude's own. Americans liked seeing people eye to eye, the
General had once told me, especially as they screwed them
from behind. This was not how Claude saw the situation.
Other generals were only getting seats for their immediate
families, Claude said to us in parting. Even God and Noah

couldn't save everyone. Or wouldn't, anyway.

Could they not? What would my father say? He had been a Catholic priest, but I could not remember this poor man of the cloth ever sermonizing about Noah, although admittedly I went to Mass only to daydream. But regardless of what God or Noah could do, there was little doubt that every man on the General's staff, if given the chance, would rescue a hundred blood relatives as well as any paper ones who could afford the bribe. Vietnamese families were complicated, delicate affairs, and while sometimes I longed for one, being the only son of an ostracized mother, now was not one of those times.

Later that day, the president resigned. I had expected the president to abandon the country weeks ago in the manner befitting a dictator, and I spared him barely a thought as I worked on the list of evacuees. The General was fastidious and detail oriented, habituated to making quick, hard decisions, but this was one task that he deferred to me. He was preoccupied with the matters of his office: reading the morning's interrogation reports, attending meetings at the Joint General Staff compound, phoning his confidants as they discussed how to hold the city and yet be ready to abandon it at the same time, a maneuver as tricky as playing musical chairs to the tune of one's most beloved song. Music was on my mind, for as I worked on the list in the nocturnal hours, I listened to American Radio Service on a Sony in my room at the villa. The songs of the Temptations and Janis Joplin and Marvin Gaye usually always made bad things bearable and good things wonderful, but not in times like these. Every stroke of my pen through a name felt like a death sentence. All of our names, from the lowest officer to the General, had been found on a list being crammed into its owner's mouth as we broke down her door three years ago. The warning I had sent to Man had not gotten to her in time. As the policemen wrestled her to the ground, I had no choice but to reach into this communist agent's mouth and pull from it that saliva-soaked list. Its papier-mâché existence proved that members of the Special Branch, accustomed to watching, were ourselves watched. Even had I a moment alone with her, I could not have risked my cover by telling her that I was on her side. I knew what fate awaited her. Everyone talked in the Special Branch's interrogation cells, and she would have told my secret despite herself. She was younger than me, but she was wise enough to know what awaited her, too. For just a moment I saw the truth in her eyes, and the truth was that she hated me for what she thought I was, the agent of an oppressive regime. Then, like me, she remembered the role she had to play. Please, sirs! she cried. I'm innocent! I swear!

Three years later, this communist agent was still in a cell. I kept her folder on my desk, a reminder of my failure to save her. It was my fault, too, Man had said. When the day of liberation comes, I'll be the one unlocking her cell. She was twenty-two when arrested, and in the folder was a picture of her at her capture, and another one of her from a few months ago, her eyes faded and her hair thinning. Our prison cells were time machines, the inmates aging much faster than they normally would. Looking at her faces, then and now, helped me with the task of selecting a few men for salvation and condemning many more, including some I liked. For several days I worked and reworked the list while the defenders of Xuan Loc were annihilated and, across our border, Phnom Penh fell to the Khmer Rouge. A few nights later, our ex-president secretly fled for Taiwan. Claude, who drove him to the airport, noticed how the president's inordinately heavy suitcases clanked with something metallic, presumably a hefty share of our nation's gold. He told me this the next morning, when he called to say that our plane was leaving in two days. I finished my list early that evening, telling the General that I had decided to be democratic and representative, choosing the highest-ranking officer, the officer everyone thought the most honest, the one whose company I liked the most, and so on. He accepted my reasoning and its inevitable consequence, that a good number of the senior officers with the most knowledge and culpability in the work of the Special Branch would be left behind. I wound up with a colonel, a major, another captain, and two lieutenants. As for myself, I reserved one seat and three more for Bon, his wife, and his child, my godson.

When the General visited me that night to commiserate, bearing the now half-empty bottle of whiskey, I asked for the favor of taking Bon with us. Although not my real brother, he was one of my two blood brothers since our school days. Man was the other, the three of us having sworn undying loyalty to one another by slicing our adolescent palms and mingling our blood in ritual handshakes. In my wallet was a black-and-white photograph of Bon and his family. Bon had the appearance of a good-looking man beaten to a pulp, except that was simply his God-given face. Not even his paratrooper's beret and crisply ironed tiger stripe fatigues could distract from his parachute-like ears, his chin perpetually tucked into the folds of his neck, and his flat nose bent hard right, the same as his politics. As for his wife, Linh, a poet might compare her face to the harvest moon, insinuating not only its fullness and roundness but also how it was mottled and cratered, dappled with acne scars. How those two concocted a child as cute as Duc was a mystery, or perhaps simply as logical as how two negatives when multiplied together yield a positive. The General handed me the photo and said, It's the least I could do. He's Airborne. If our army was just Airborne men, we'd have won this war.

If . . . but there was no if, only the incontrovertible fact of the General sitting on the edge of my chair while I stood by the window, sipping my whiskey. In the courtyard, the General's orderly fed fistfuls of secrets into a fire blazing in a fifty-five-gallon drum, making the hot night hotter. The General got up and paced my small chamber, glass in hand, clad only in his boxer shorts and a sleeveless undershirt, a midnight shadow of stubble across his chin. Only his housekeepers, his family, and myself ever saw him like this. At any hour of the day when visitors came to the villa, he would pomade his hair and don his starched khakis, the breast festooned with more ribbons than could be found in a beauty queen's hair. But this evening, with the villa's hush punctuated only by occasional shouts of gunfire, he allowed himself to be querulous about how the Americans had promised us salvation from communism if we only did as we were told. They started this war, and now that they're tired of it, they've sold us out, he said, pouring me another drink. But who is there to blame but ourselves? We were foolish enough to think they would keep their word. Now there's nowhere to go but America. There are worse places, I said. Perhaps, he said. At least we'll live to fight again. But for now, we are well and truly fucked. What kind of toast is right for that?

The words came to me after a moment.

Here's blood in your eye, I said.

Damn right.

I forget from whom I learned this toast, or even what it meant, except that I had acquired it sometime during my years in America. The General had been to America, too, if only for a few months as a junior officer, training with a platoon of his fellows at Fort Benning in '58, where the Green Berets inoculated him permanently against communism. In my case, the inoculation did not take. I was already undercover, part scholarship student, part spy-in-training, the lone representative of our people at a sylvan little college called Occidental, its motto *Occidens Proximus Orienti*. There I passed six idyllic years in the dreamy, sun-besotted world of Southern California during the sixties. Not for me the study of highways, sewage systems, or other such useful enterprises. Instead, the mission assigned to me by Man, my fellow conspirator, was to learn American ways of thinking. My war was psychological. To that end, I read American

history and literature, perfected my grammar and absorbed
the slang, smoked pot and lost my virginity. In short, I earned
not only my bachelor's but my master's degree, becoming
expert in all manner of American studies. Even now I can see
quite clearly where I first read the words of that greatest of
American philosophers, Emerson, on a lawn by an iridescent
grove of jacaranda trees. My attention was divided between
the exotic, tawny co-eds in halter tops and shorts, sunning
themselves on beds of June grass, and the words so stark and
black on a bare white page—"consistency is the hobgoblin
of little minds." Nothing Emerson wrote was ever truer of
America, but that was not the only reason I underlined his
words once, twice, thrice. What had smitten me then, and
strikes me now, was that the same thing could be said of
our motherland, where we are nothing if not inconsistent.

On our last morning, I drove the General to his office at the
National Police compound. My office was down the hallway
from the General's, and from there I summoned the five
chosen officers for a private meeting, one by one. We leave
tonight? asked the very nervous colonel, his eyes big and wet.
Yes. My parents? The parents of my wife? asked the major, a
crapulent devotee of the Chinese restaurants in Cholon. No.
Brothers, sisters, nieces and nephews? No. Housekeepers
and nannies? No. Suitcases, wardrobes, collections of
china? No. The captain, who hobbled a bit because of venereal disease, threatened to commit suicide unless I found
more seats. I offered him my revolver and he skulked off. In

contrast, the young lieutenants were grateful. Having earned their precious positions via parental connections, they bore themselves with the herky-jerky nervousness of marionettes.

I closed the door on the last of them. When distant booms rattled the windows, I saw fire and smoke boiling from the east. Enemy artillery had ignited the Long Binh ammunition depot. Feeling a need both to mourn and to celebrate, I turned to my drawer, where I kept a fifth of Jim Beam with several ounces remaining. If my poor mother were alive, she would say, Don't drink so much, son. It can't be good for you. But can't it, Mama? When one finds oneself in as difficult a situation as I did, a mole in the General's staff, one looked for comfort wherever one could find it. I finished the whiskey, then drove the General home through a storm, the amniotic water bursting over the city a hint of the forthcoming season. Some hoped the monsoon might slow down the advancing northern divisions, but I thought that unlikely. I skipped dinner and packed my rucksack with my toiletries, a pair of chinos and a madras shirt bought at a J. C. Penney in Los Angeles, loafers, three changes of underwear, an electric toothbrush from the thieves' market, a framed photograph of my mother, envelopes of photographs from here and America, my Kodak camera, and *Asian Communism and the Oriental Mode of Destruction*.

The rucksack was a gift from Claude, given in honor of my college graduation. It was the handsomest thing I owned, capable of being worn on my back or, with a tuck of a strap here and there, converted to a hand-carried valise. Fabricated of supple brown leather by an esteemed New

England manufacturer, the rucksack smelled richly, mysteriously of autumn leaves, grilled lobster, and the sweat and sperm of boys' boarding schools. A monogram of my initials was branded on the side, but the most special feature was the false bottom. Every man should have a false bottom in his luggage, Claude had said. You never know when you'll need it. Unbeknownst to him, I used it to hide my Minox mini-camera. The cost of the Minox, a present from Man, was a few times my annual salary. It was this I had used to photograph certain classified documents to which I had access, and I thought perhaps it would be useful again. Lastly, I sorted through the rest of my books and my records, most purchased in the States and all bearing the fingerprints of memory. I had no room for Elvis or Dylan, Faulkner or Twain, and while I could replace them, my spirit was still heavy when I wrote Man's name on the box of books and records. They were too much to bear, as was my guitar, displaying its full, reproachful hips on my bed as I left.

I finished packing and borrowed the Citroën to retrieve Bon. The military police at the checkpoints waved me by when they saw the General's stars on the automobile. My destination was across the river, a wretched waterway lined with the shanties of refugees from the countryside, their homes and farms obliterated by pyromaniacal soldiers and clean-cut arsonists who had found their true calling as bombardiers. Past this haphazard expanse of hovels, deep in District Four, Bon and Man waited at a beer garden where the three of us had passed more drunken hours than I could recall. Soldiers and marines crowded the tables, rifles under their stools, hair cropped close by sadistic military barbers intent on revealing the contours of their skulls for some nefarious phrenological purpose. Bon poured me a glass of beer as soon as I sat down, but would not allow me to drink until he offered a toast. Here's to reunion, he said, lifting his own glass. We'll meet again in the Philippines! I said it was actually Guam, for the dictator Marcos was fed up with refugees and no longer accepting any more. Groaning, Bon rubbed his glass against his forehead. I didn't think it could get any worse, he said. But now we've got Filipinos looking down on us? Forget the Philippines, Man said. Let's drink to Guam instead. They say it's where America's day begins. And our day ends, Bon muttered.

Unlike Man and I, Bon was a genuine patriot, a republican who had volunteered to fight, having hated the communists ever since the local cadre encouraged his father, the village chief, to kneel in the village square and make his confession before forcefully inserting a bullet behind his ear. Left to his own devices, Bon was sure to go Japanese and fight to the end or even put a gun to his own head, so Man and I had persuaded him to think of his wife and child. Leaving for America was not desertion, we claimed. This was strategic retreat. We had told Bon that Man would also flee with his family tomorrow, whereas the truth was that Man would stay to witness the liberation of the south by the northern communists Bon so despised. Now Man squeezed him on the shoulder with fingers long and delicate and said, We're blood brothers, us three. We'll be blood brothers even if we lose this war, even if we lose our country. He looked at me and his eyes were damp. For us there is no end.

You're right, Bon said, shaking his head vigorously to disguise the tears in his eyes. So enough sadness and gloom. Let's drink to hope. We'll return to take our country back. Right? He, too, looked at me. I was not ashamed of the tears in my own eyes. These men were better than any real brothers I could have had, for we had chosen each other. I raised my beer glass. Here's to coming back, I said. And to a brotherhood that never ends. We drained our glasses, shouted for another round, threw our arms around one another's shoulders, and settled into an hour of brotherly love and song, the music provided by a duo at the other end of the garden. The guitarist was a long-haired draft dodger, sickly pale from having lived for the last ten years in between the walls of the bar owner's house during the day, emerging only at night. His singing partner was an equally long-haired woman of dulcet voice, her slim figure outlined by a silk ao dai the same shade as a virgin's blush. She was singing the lyrics of Trinh Cong Son, the folk singer beloved even by the paratroopers. *Tomorrow I'm going, dear . . .* Her voice rose above the chatter and rain. *Remember to call me home . . .* My heart trembled. We were not a people who charged into war at the beck and call of bugle or trumpet. No, we fought to the tunes of love songs, for we were the Italians of Asia.

Tomorrow I'm going, dear. The city's nights are no longer beautiful . . . If Bon knew this was the last time he would see Man for years, perhaps ever, he would never step on the airplane. Ever since our lycée days, we had fancied ourselves the Three Musketeers, all for one and one for all. Man had introduced us to Dumas: first, because he was a great novel-ist, and second, because he was a quadroon. Hence he was a model for us, colonized by the same French who despised him for his ancestry. An avid reader and storyteller, Man would have likely become a teacher of literature at our lycée if we had lived in a time of peace. Besides translating three of the Perry Mason mysteries of Erle Stanley Gardner into our native tongue, he had also written a forgettable Zolaesque novel under a pen name. He had studied America but never been there himself, as was the case with Bon, who called for another round and asked if America had beer gardens. They have bars and supermarkets where you can always get a beer, I said. But are there beautiful women who sing songs like these? he asked. I refilled his glass and said, They have beautiful women but they do not sing songs like these.

Then the guitarist began strumming the chords of another song. They do sing songs like this, Man said. It was *Yesterday* by the Beatles. As the three of us joined in singing, my eyes grow moist. What was it like to live in a time when one's fate was not war, when one was not led by the craven and the corrupt, when one's country was not a basket case kept alive only through the intravenous drip of American aid? I knew none of these young soldiers around me except for my blood brothers and yet I confess that I felt for them all, lost in their sense that within days they would be dead, or wounded, or imprisoned, or humiliated, or abandoned, or forgotten. They were my enemies, and yet they were also brothers-in-arms. Their beloved city was about to fall, but mine was soon to be liberated. It was the end of their world, but only a shifting of worlds for me. So it was that for two minutes we sang with all our hearts, feeling only for the past and turning our gaze from the future, swimmers doing the backstroke toward a waterfall.

The rain finally ceased by the time we left. We were smoking a final cigarette at the mouth of the dank, dripping alley that was the beer garden's exit when a trio of hydrocephalic marines stumbled out of the vaginal darkness. *Beautiful Saigon!* they sang. *Oh, Saigon! Oh, Saigon!* Although it was only six, they were inebriated, fatigues stained with beer. Each had an M16 hanging from a shoulder strap, and each showed off a spare pair of testicles. These, on closer inspection, turned out to be two grenades clamped to either side of their belt buckles. Although their uniforms, weapons, and helmets were all of American manufacture, as were ours, it was impossible to mistake them for Americans, the dented helmets being the giveaway, steel pots sized for American heads that were too big for any of us. The first marine's head swung this way and that before he bumped into me and cursed, the brim of his helmet falling all the way to his nose. When he pushed up the brim, I saw bleary eyes trying to focus. Hello! he said, breath reeking, his southern accent so thick I had some trouble understanding him. What's this? A policeman? What're you doing with the real soldiers?

Man flicked ashes at him. This policeman's a captain. Salute your superior, Lieutenant.

The second marine, also a lieutenant, said, If you say

so, Major, to which the third marine, a lieutenant as well, said, The hell with majors and colonels and generals. The president's run off. The generals—*poof!* Like smoke. Gone. Saving their own asses like they always do. Guess what? That leaves us to cover the retreat. Like we always do. What retreat? the second marine said. There's nowhere to go. The third agreed: We're dead. As good as dead, the first said. Our job is to be dead.

I tossed away my cigarette. You're not dead yet. You should get back to your posts.

The first marine focused once more on my face, taking a step closer until his nose nearly touched mine. What *are* you?

You are out of line, Lieutenant! Bon shouted.

I'll tell you what you are. The marine poked his finger in my chest.

Don't say it, I said.

A bastard! he cried. The two other marines laughed and chimed in. A bastard!

I drew my revolver and placed the muzzle between the marine's eyes. Behind him, his friends fingered their rifles nervously but did no more. They were impaired, but not enough to think they could be faster on the draw than my more sober friends.

You're drunk, aren't you, Lieutenant? Despite myself, my voice trembled.

Yes, the marine said. Sir.

Then I won't shoot you.

It was then, to my great relief, that we heard the first of the bombs. Everybody's head swiveled in the direction of the explosion, which was followed by another and another, to the northwest. It's the airport, Bon said. Five-hundred-pound bombs. He would turn out to be correct in both cases. From our vantage point, we could see nothing except, after a few moments, billowing plumes of black smoke. Then it seemed as if every gun in the city went off from downtown to the airport, light weaponry going *clack-clack-clack* and heavy weaponry going *chug-chug-chug*, flurries of orange tracers swirling into the sky. The racket drew all the residents of the pitiful street to their windows and into the doorways, and I holstered my revolver. Likewise sobered by the presence of witnesses, the marine lieutenants clambered into their jeep without another word and drove off, weaving through the handful of motorbikes on the street until they reached the intersection. Then the jeep braked to a halt and the marines stumbled out with M16s in hand, even as the explosions continued and civilians thronged the sidewalks. My pulse quickened when the marines glared at us from under the jaundiced light of a streetlamp, but all they did was aim skyward, howling and screaming as they fired their weapons until the magazines were empty. My heart was beating fast and the sweat was trickling down my back, but I smiled for the sake of my friends and lit another cigarette.

Idiots! Bon shouted as the civilians crouched in doorways. The marines called us a few choice names before they got back into the jeep, turned the corner, and vanished. Bon and I said good-bye to Man, and after he left in his own jeep I tossed Bon the keys. The bombing and the gunfire had ceased, and as he drove the Citroën to his apartment he swore bloody murder at the Marine Corps the entire way. I kept my silence. One did not depend on marines for good table manners. One depended on them to have the right instincts when it came to matters of life and death. As for the name they had called me, it upset me less than my reaction to it. I should have been used to that misbegotten name by now, but somehow I was not. My mother was native, my father was foreign, and strangers and acquaintances had enjoyed reminding me of this ever since my childhood, spitting on me and calling me bastard, although sometimes, for variety, they called me bastard before they spit on me.

CHAPTER 2

Even now, the baby-faced guard who comes to check on me every day calls me a bastard when he feels like it. This hardly surprises me, although I had hoped for better from your men, my dear Commandant. I confess that the name still hurts. Perhaps, for variety, he could call me mongrel or half-breed, as some have in the past? How about métis, which is what the French called me when not calling me Eurasian? The latter word lent me a romantic varnish with Americans but got me nowhere with the French themselves. I still encountered them periodically in Saigon, nostalgic colonizers who stubbornly insisted on staying in this country even after their empire's foreclosure. Le Cercle Sportif was where they congregated, sipping Pernod while chewing on the steak tartare of memories that had happened on Saigonese streets they called by their old French names: Boulevard Norodom, Rue Chasseloup-Laubat, Quai de l'Argonne. They bossed the native help with nouveau riche arrogance and, when I came around, regarded me with the suspicious eyes of border guards checking passports.

It was not they who invented the Eurasian, however. That claim belongs to the English in India, who also found it impossible not to nibble on dark chocolate. Like those pith-helmeted Anglos, the American Expeditionary Forces in the Pacific could not resist the temptations of the locals. They, too, fabricated a portmanteau word to describe my kind, the Amerasian. Although a misnomer when applied to me, I could hardly blame Americans for mistaking me as one of their own, since a small nation could be founded from the tropical off-spring of the American GI. This stood for Government Issue, which is also what the Amerasians are. Our countrymen pre-ferred euphemisms to acronyms, calling people like me the dust of life. More technically, the Oxford English Dictionary I consulted at Occidental revealed that I could be called a "natural child," while the law in all countries I know of hails me as its illegitimate son. My mother called me her love child, but I do not like to dwell on that. In the end, my father had it right. He called me nothing at all.

No wonder, then, that I was drawn to the General, who, like my friends Man and Bon, never sneered about my mud-dled heritage. Upon selecting me for his staff, the General said, The only thing I'm interested in is how good you are at what you do, even if the things I ask you to do may not be so good. I proved my competence more than once; the evacuation was merely the latest demonstration of my abil-ity to finesse the fine line between the legal and the illegal. The men had been picked, the buses arranged, and, most important, the bribes for safe passage bestowed. I had paid the bribes from a satchel of $10,000 requisitioned from the

General, who had submitted the request to Madame. It's an extraordinary sum, she said to me over a cup of oolong in her salon. It's an extraordinary time, I said. But it's a wholesale bargain for ninety-two evacuees. She could not disagree, as anyone who placed their ears to the railroad tracks of gossip in the city could report. The rumble was that the price of visas, passports, and seats on evacuation airplanes ran to many thousands of dollars, depending on the package one chose and the level of one's hysteria. But before one could even pay a bribe, one needed to have access to willing conspirators. In our case, my solution was a louche major whom I had befriended at the Pink Nightclub on Nguyen Hue. Shouting to be heard over the psychedelic thunder of CBC or the pop beats of the Uptight, I learned that he was the airport's duty officer. For a relatively modest fee of a thousand dollars, he informed me who the guards at the airport would be for our departure, and where I might find their lieutenant.

All this arranged, and myself and Bon having retrieved his wife and child, we assembled for our departure at seven o'clock. Two blue buses waited outside the villa's gates, windows encased in wire grilles off which terrorist grenades would theoretically bounce, unless they were rocket-propelled, in which case one relied on the armor of prayers. The anxious families waited in the villa's courtyard while Madame stood on the villa's steps with the household staff. Her somber children sat in the Citroën's backseat, a blank, diplomatic mien on their faces as they observed Claude and the General smoking in front of the car's headlights.

Passenger manifest in hand, I called the men and their families forward, checking off their names and directing them to their buses. As instructed, each adult and teenager carried no more than a small suitcase or valise, with some of the children clutching thin blankets or alabaster dolls, their Western faces plastered with fanatical grins. Bon was last, steering Linh by her elbow, she in turn holding Duc's hand. He was just old enough to walk confidently, his other hand balled around a yellow yo-yo I had given him as a souvenir from the States. I saluted the boy, and he, frowning in concentration, stopped to detach his hand from his mother's and saluted me in return. Everyone's here, I said to the General. Then it's time to go, he said, grinding his cigarette under his heel.

The General's last duty was bidding farewell to the butler, the cook, the housekeeper, and a trio of pubescent nannies. Some of them had made entreaties to be taken along, but Madame was firm in saying no, already convinced of her excessive generosity in paying for the General's officers. She was correct, of course. I knew of at least one general who, having been offered seats for his staff, sold them to the highest bidder. Now Madame and all the help were weeping, except for the geriatric butler, a purple ascot tied around his goitered neck. He had begun his days with the General as an orderly when the General was only a lieutenant, both of them serving under the French during their season of hell at Dien Bien Phu. Standing at the bottom of the steps, the General could not meet the old man's eyes. I'm sorry, he said, head bowed and bared, cap in hand. It was the only time I had heard him apologize to anyone besides Madame. You've served us well, and we're not serving you well. But none of you will come to harm. Take what you want from the villa and then leave. If anyone asks, deny that you know me or that you ever worked for me. But as for me, I swear to you now, I will not give up fighting for our country! When the General began weeping, I handed him my handkerchief. In the ensuing silence, the butler said, I ask for one thing, sir. What is that, my friend? Your pistol, so I can shoot myself! The General shook his head and wiped his eyes with my handkerchief. You will do no such thing. Go home and wait for me to return. Then I will give you a pistol. When the butler tried to salute, the General offered him his hand instead. Whatever people say about the General today, I can only testify that he was a sincere man who believed in everything he said, even if it was a lie, which makes him not so different from most.

Madame distributed to each of the staff an envelope of dollars, its thickness appropriate to his or her rank. The General returned my handkerchief and escorted Madame to the Citroën. For this last drive, the General would take the leather-wrapped steering wheel himself and lead the two buses to the airport. I've got the second bus, Claude said. You take the first one and make sure that driver doesn't get lost. Before boarding, I paused at the gates for one last look at the villa, conjured into being for the Corsican owners of a rubber plantation. An epic tamarind tree towered over the eaves, the long, knuckled pods of its sour fruit dangling like the fingers of dead men. The constant staff still stood at the proscenium atop the stairs. When I waved good-bye to them, they dutifully waved back, holding in their other hands those white envelopes that had become, in the moonlight, tickets to nowhere.

The route from villa to airport was as uncomplicated as anything could be in Saigon, which is to say not uncomplicated at all. One made a right out of the gates down Thi Xuan, left on Le Van Quyet, right on Hong Thap Tu in the direction of the embassies, left on Pasteur, another left on Nguyen Dinh Chieu, right on Cong Ly, then straight to the airport. But instead of taking a left on Le Van Quyet, the General turned right. He's going in the wrong direction, my driver said. He had fingers stained yellow with nicotine and dangerously sharp toenails. Just follow, I said. I stood in the entry well, doors swung open to let in the cool night air. On the first bench behind me were Bon and Linh, Duc leaning forward on his mother's lap to peer over my shoulder. The streets were empty; according to the radio, a twenty-four-hour curfew had been declared because of the strike on the airport. Nearly as vacant were the sidewalks, haunted only by the occasional set of uniforms shed by deserters. In some cases, the gear was in such a neat little heap, with helmet on top of blouse and boots beneath trousers, that a ray gun appeared to have vaporized the owner. In a city where nothing went to waste, no one touched these uniforms.

My bus carried at least a few soldiers in civilian disguise, although the rest of the General's in-laws and cousins were mostly women and children. These passengers murmured

among themselves, complaining of this or that, which I
ignored. Even if they found themselves in Heaven, our
countrymen would find occasion to remark that it was not
as warm as Hell. Why's he taking this route? the driver said.
The curfew! We're all going to get shot, or at least arrested.
Bon sighed and shook his head. He's the General, he said,
as if that explained everything, which it did. Nevertheless,
the driver continued to complain as we passed the central market and turned onto Le Loi, not ceasing until the
General finally stopped at Lam Son Square. Before us was
the Grecian facade of the National Assembly, formerly the
city's opera house. From here our politicians managed the
shabby comic operetta of our country, an off-key travesty
starring plump divas in white suits and mustachioed prima
donnas in custom-tailored military uniforms. Leaning out
and looking up, I saw the glowing windows of the Caravelle
Hotel's rooftop bar, where I had often escorted the General
for aperitifs and interviews with journalists. The balconies
provided an unparalleled view of Saigon and its environs,
and from them a faint laughter drifted. It must have been the
foreign newsmen, ready to take the city's temperature in its
death rattle, as well as the attachés of nonaligned nations,
watching the Long Binh ammunition dump glow over the
horizon while tracers sputtered in the night.

An urge seized me to fire a round in the direction of the
laughter, just to enliven their evening. When the General
got out of the car, I thought he was following the same
impulse, but he turned in the other direction, away from
the National Assembly and toward the hideous monument

on Le Loi's grassy median. I regretted keeping my Kodak in my rucksack rather than my pocket, for I would have liked a photograph of the General saluting the two massive marines charging forward, the hero in the rear taking a rather close interest in his comrade's posterior. As Bon saluted the memorial, along with the other men on the bus, all I could ponder was whether these marines were protecting the people who strolled beneath their gaze on a sunny day, or, just as likely, were attacking the National Assembly at which their machine guns aimed. But as one of the men on the bus sobbed, and as I, too, saluted, it struck me that the meaning was not so ambiguous. Our air force had bombed the presidential palace, our army had shot and stabbed to death our first president and his brother, and our bickering generals had fomented more coups d'état than I could count. After the tenth putsch, I accepted the absurd state of our state with a mix of despair and anger, along with a dash of humor, a cocktail under whose influence I renewed my revolutionary vows.

Satisfied, the General climbed back into the Citroën and the convoy proceeded once more, crossing the intersection of one-way Tu Do as it entered and exited the square. I had a last glimpse of the Givral Café, where I had enjoyed French vanilla ice cream on my dates with proper Saigonese girls and their mummified chaperone aunts. Past the Givral was Brodard Café, where I cultivated my taste for savory crepes while doing my best to ignore the parade of paupers hopping and hobbling by. Those with hands cupped them for alms, those lacking in hands clenched the bill of a baseball cap in their teeth. Military amputees flapped empty sleeves like flightless birds, mute elderly beggars fixed cobra eyes on you, street urchins told tales taller than themselves about their pitiable conditions, young widows rocked colicky babies whom they might have rented, and assorted cripples displayed every imaginable, unappetizing illness known to man. Farther north on Tu Do was the nightclub where I had spent many evenings doing the cha-cha with young ladies in miniskirts and the latest in arch-breaking heels. This was the street where the imperious French once stabled their gilded mistresses, followed by the more déclassé Americans whooping it up in lurid bars like the San Francisco, the New York, and the Tennessee, their names inscribed in neon, their jukeboxes loaded with country music. Those who felt guilty at a debauched evening's end could totter north to the brick basilica at the end of Tu Do, which was where the General led us by way of Hai Ba Trung. In front of the basilica stood the white statue of Our Lady, her hands open in peace and forgiveness, her gaze downcast. While she and her son Jesus Christ were ready to welcome all the sinners of Tu Do, their prim penitents and priests—my father among them—spurned me more often than not. So it was always at the basilica that I asked Man to meet me for our clandestine business, both of us savoring the farce of being counted among the faithful. We genuflected, but in actuality we were atheists who had chosen communism over God.

We met on Wednesday afternoons, the basilica empty except for a handful of austere dowagers, heads shrouded in lace mantillas or black scarves as they chanted, *Our Father, who art in Heaven, hallowed be Thy name . . .* I no longer prayed, but my tongue could not help wagging along with these old women. They were as tough as foot soldiers, sitting impassively through crowded weekend Masses where the infirm and the elderly sometimes swooned from the heat. We were too poor for air-conditioning, but heat stroke was simply another way of expressing religious fortitude. It would be hard to find more pious Catholics than those in Saigon, most of whom, like my mother and myself, had already run once from the communists in '54 (my nine-year-old self having no say in the matter). To rendezvous in the church amused Man, a former Catholic like me. While we pretended to be devout officers for whom Mass once a week did not suffice, I would confess my political and personal failures to him. He, in turn, would play my confessor, whispering to me absolutions in the shape of assignments rather than prayers.

America? I said.

America, he confirmed.

I had told him of the General's evacuation plan as soon as I learned of it, and that past Wednesday in the basilica I was informed of my new task. This mission was given to me by his superiors, but who they were, I did not know. It was safer that way. This had been our system since our lycée days, when we secretly pursued one road via a study group while Bon openly continued on a more conventional path. The study group had been Man's idea, a three-man cell consisting of himself, me, and another classmate. Man was the leader, guiding us in the reading of revolutionary classics and teaching us the tenets of Party ideology. At the time, I knew that Man was part of another cell where he was the junior member, although the identities of the others were a mystery to me. Both secrecy and hierarchy were key to revolution, Man told me. That was why there was another committee above him for the more committed, and above that another committee for the even more committed, and on and on until we presumably reached Uncle Ho himself, at least when he was alive, the most committed man ever, the one who had asserted that "Nothing is more precious than independence and freedom." These were words we were willing to die for. This language, as well as the discourse of study groups, committees, and parties, came easily to Man. He had inherited the revolutionary gene from a great-uncle, dragooned by the French to serve in Europe during World War I. He was a gravedigger, and nothing will do more to bestir a colonized subject than seeing white men naked and dead, the great-uncle said, or so Man told me. This great-uncle had stuck his hands in their slimy pink viscera, examined at leisure their funny, flaccid willies, and retched on seeing the putrefying scrambled eggs of their brains. He buried them by the thousands, brave young men enmeshed in the cobwebbed eulogies spun by spidery politicians, and the understanding that France had kept its best for its own soil slowly seeped into the capillaries of his consciousness. The mediocrities had been dispatched to Indochina, allowing France to staff its colonial bureaucracies with the schoolyard bully, the chess club misfit, the natural-born accountant, and the diffident wallflower, whom the great-uncle now spotted in their original habitat as the outcasts and losers they were. And these castoffs, he fumed, were the people who taught us to think of them as white demigods? His radical anticolonialism was enhanced when he fell in love with a French nurse, a Trotskyist who persuaded him to enlist with the French communists, the only ones offering a suitable answer to the Indochina Question. For her, he swallowed the black tea of exile. Eventually he and the nurse had a daughter, and handing me a slip of paper, Man whispered that she was still there, his aunt. On the slip of paper was her name and address in the thirteenth arrondissement of Paris, this fellow traveler who had never joined the Communist Party, and thus was unlikely to be surveilled. I doubt you'll be able to send letters home, so she'll be the go-between. She's a seamstress with three Siamese cats, no children, and no suspicious credentials. That's where you'll send the letters.

Fingering that slip of paper, I recalled the cinematic scenario I had prepared, the one where I refused to board Claude's plane while the General pleaded hopelessly with me to leave with him. I want to stay, I said. It's almost over. Behind clasped hands, Man sighed. Is it almost over? *Thy kingdom come, Thy will be done.* Your general isn't the only one planning to keep on fighting. Old soldiers don't fade away. The war's been going on too long for them to simply stop. We need someone to keep an eye on them and make sure they're not going to get into too much trouble. What happens if I don't go? I asked. Man raised his eyes to the bruised, greenish Christ with his European features, suspended on a crucifix high above the altar, the lie of a loincloth draped around his groin when in all likelihood he died naked. The grin on Man's face revealed startlingly white teeth. You'll do more good there than you will here, this dentist's son said. And if you won't do it for yourself, do it for Bon. He won't go if he thinks we're staying. But in any case, you want to go. Admit it!

Dare I admit it? Dare I confess? America, land of supermarkets and superhighways, of supersonic jets and Superman, of supercarriers and the Super Bowl! America, a country not content simply to give itself a name on its bloody birth, but one that insisted for the first time in history on a mysterious acronym, USA, a trifecta of letters outdone later only by the quartet of the USSR. Although every country thought itself superior in its own way, was there ever a country that coined so many "super" terms from the federal bank of its narcissism, was not only superconfident but also truly superpowerful, that would not be satisfied until it locked every nation of the world into a full nelson and made it cry Uncle Sam?

All right, I admit it! I said. I confess.

He chuckled and said, Consider yourself lucky. I've never left our wonderful homeland.

Lucky, am I? At least you feel at home here.

Home is overrated, he said.

Easy for him to say when his father and mother got along reasonably well, while his siblings looked the other way when it came to his revolutionary sympathies. This was common enough when many a family was divided against itself, some fighting for the north and some for the south, some fighting for communism and some for nationalism. Still, no matter how divided, all saw themselves as patriots fighting for a country to which they belonged. When I reminded him that I did not belong here, he said, You don't belong in America, either. Perhaps, I said. But I wasn't born there. I was born here.

Outside the basilica, we said good-bye, our real farewell, not the one staged later for Bon. I'm leaving you my records and my books, I said. I know you've always wanted them. Thanks, he said, squeezing my hand hard. And good luck. When do I get to come home? I asked. Giving me a look of great sympathy, he said, My friend, I'm a subversive, not a seer. The timetable for your return will depend on what your General plans. And as the General drove by the basilica, I could not say what his plans were besides escaping the country. I only assumed that he had more in mind than the futile words emblazoned on the banners flanking the boulevard leading to the presidential palace, which a dissident pilot had strafed earlier in the month. NO LAND TO THE COMMUNISTS! NO COMMUNISTS IN THE SOUTH! NO COALITION GOVERNMENT! NO NEGOTIATION! I could see an impassive guardsman standing impaled at attention under his roofed post, but before we reached the palace the General finally, mercifully set a course for the airport by turning right on Pasteur. Somewhere far away, a heavy machine gun fired in uneven, staccato bursts. When a dull mortar grunted, Duc whimpered in his mother's arms. Hush, darling, she said.

We're only going on a trip. Bon stroked his son's wispy hair and said, Will we ever see these streets again? I said, We have to believe we'll see them again, don't we?

Bon draped his arm over my shoulders and we squeezed together in the stairwell, hanging our heads out the door and holding hands as the glum apartments rolled by, lights and eyes peeking from behind curtains and shutters. Noses to the wind, we inhaled a farrago of scents: charcoal and jasmine, rotting fruit and eucalyptus, gasoline and ammonia, a swirling belch from the city's poorly irrigated gut. As we approached the airport, the shadowy cross of an airplane roared overhead, all lights extinguished. At the gates, prickly rolls of barbed wire sagged with middle-aged disappointment. Behind the wire waited a squad of sullen military policemen and their young lieutenant, rifles in hand and truncheons swinging from belts. My chest thumped as the lieutenant approached the General's Citroën, leaned down by the driver's window to exchange a few words, then glanced in my direction where I stood leaning out the door of the bus. I had tracked him down on the louche major's information, to the canal-side slum he lived in with his wife, three children, parents, and in-laws, all of whom were dependent on a salary that was not enough to feed half of them. This was the typical lot of the young officer, but my task on the afternoon I visited last week was to discover what kind of man had been molded from this poor clay. In his skivvies, sitting on the edge of the wooden bed he shared with his wife and children, the half-naked lieutenant had the cornered look of a political prisoner freshly dropped into a tiger cage, wary and a bit frightened but not yet physically broken. You want me to stab my country in the back, he said tonelessly, the unlit cigarette I had given him in his hand. You want to pay me to let cowards and traitors escape. You want me to encourage my men to do the same.

I'm not going to insult your intelligence by pretending otherwise, I said. I spoke mostly for the benefit of the jury—his wife, parents, and in-laws, who sat, squatted, or stood in the tight confines of the sweltering, tin-roofed shack. Hunger had lent them emaciated cheekbones, the kind I knew from my own mother, who had suffered so much for me. I admire you, Lieutenant, I said, and I did. You're an honest man, and it's hard to find honest men when men have families to feed. The least I can do to reward you is to offer you three thousand dollars. This was a month's salary for his entire platoon. His wife did her duty and demanded ten. Eventually we agreed on five, half paid then, half due at the airport. As my bus rolled by, he snatched from my hand the envelope with the cash, and in his eyes I saw the same look the communist agent had given me when I had pulled that list of names from her mouth. Although he could have shot me or turned us back, he did what I gambled every honorable man forced to take a bribe would do. He let us all pass, holding up his end of the bargain as the last fig leaf of his dignity. I averted my eyes from his humiliation. If—let me indulge in the conditional for a moment—if the southern army comprised only men like him, it would have won. I confess that I admired him, even though he was my enemy. It is always better to admire the best among our foes rather than the worst among our friends. Wouldn't you agree, Commandant?

It was nearly nine as we drove through the metropolis that was the airport complex, on well-paved streets past Quonset huts, gabled barracks, nondescript offices, and tubular warehouses, deep into a miniature city in Saigon yet outside of it. This semiautonomous territory was once one of the world's busiest airports, a hub for all kinds of lethal and nonlethal sorties and missions, including those flown by Air America, the CIA's airline. Our generals stashed their families here, while American generals crafted their stratagems in offices stocked with imported steel furniture. Our destination was the compound of the Defense Attaché Office. With typical cheekiness, the Americans had nicknamed it Dodge City, the town where six-shooters ruled and where saloon girls danced the cancan, as was much the case here in Saigon. But while sheriffs kept the peace in the real Dodge City, American marines guarded this evacuation center. I had not seen so many since '73, when they were a ragged, defeated lot departing from this airfield. But these young marines had never seen combat and had been in this country only a few weeks. Bright-eyed and clean-shaven, with not a hint of a needle track in the crooks of their arms or a whiff of marijuana in their pressed, jungle-free fatigues, they watched impassively as our passengers disembarked into a parking lot already crowded with hundreds of other nervous evacuees. I joined the General and Claude by the Citroën, where the General was handing over his keys. I'll return them in the States, sir, Claude said. No, leave them in the ignition, the General said. I would not want anyone to damage the car while they steal it, since it will be stolen anyway. Enjoy her while you can, Claude.

When the General wandered off to find Madame and the children, I said, What's going on here? It's a mess. Claude sighed. Situation normal, all fucked up. Everybody's trying to get their relatives and cooks and girlfriends out of here. Just consider yourself lucky. I know, I said. See you in the States? He clapped me on the shoulder with affection. Just like when the communists took over in '54, he said. Who would have thought we'd be here again? But I got you out of the north then, and I'm getting you out of the south now. You'll be all right.

After Claude left, I returned to the evacuees. A marine on the bullhorn mumbled at them to form into lines, but queuing was unnatural for our countrymen. Our proper mode in situations where demand was high and supply low was to elbow, jostle, crowd, and hustle, and, if all that failed, to bribe, flatter, exaggerate, and lie. I was uncertain whether these traits were genetic, deeply cultural, or simply a rapid evolutionary development. We had been forced to adapt to ten years of living in a bubble economy pumped up purely by American imports; three decades of on-again, off-again war, including the sawing in half of the country in '54 by foreign magicians and the brief Japanese interregnum of World War II; and the previous century of avuncular French molestation. The marines, however, cared not a whit for such excuses, and their intimidating presence eventually coerced the refugees into lines. When the marines checked us for weapons, we officers dutifully, sadly turned over our guns. Mine was just a snub-nosed .38 revolver, good for covert activities, Russian roulette, and suicide, whereas Bon wielded the manly .45 Colt semiautomatic. The gun was designed to knock down Moro warriors in the Philippines with a single shot, I said to Duc. I had learned this from Claude; it was the kind of arcana he knew.

Papers! said the embassy bureaucrat at the desk after the weapons check, a young man with nineteenth-century sideburns, decked out in a beige safari suit and rose-tinted glasses. Each of the family heads had the laissez-passer documents from the Ministry of the Interior I had bought at a hefty discount, as well as the presidential parole delivered by Claude, stamped by the relevant embassy clerk. The parole assured us, even as we stood obediently in line, of the important thing: that we had cut to the head of the immigration queue in front of the huddled, hopeful millions from all over the world yearning to breathe free. We carried that small solace with us to the staging ground of the tennis courts, where earlier evacuees already occupied all the bleacher seats. We joined the tardier souls attempting a numb slumber on the green concrete of the courts. Red blackout lamps cast an eerie glow over the crowds, among which was a scattering of Americans. All of them appeared to be husbands of Vietnamese women, given how a Vietnamese family besieged each of them, or how a Vietnamese woman had practically handcuffed herself to his arm. I settled down with Bon, Linh, and Duc on an unoccupied plot. On one side was a covey of call girls, vacuum-packed into micro-miniskirts and fishnet stockings. On the other was an American, his wife, and their children, a boy and a girl of perhaps five and six. The husband sprawled on his back with his beefy forearm over his eyes, the only parts of his face visible the two furry limbs of his walrus mustache, his pink lips, and his slightly crooked teeth. His wife sat with her children's heads in her lap, stroking their brown hair. How long have you been here? Linh asked, cradling a drowsy Duc in her arms. The whole day, the woman said. It's been awful, so hot. There's nothing to eat or drink. They keep calling out the numbers of planes but not ours. Linh made sympathetic noises while Bon and I settled down to the waiting part of hurry up and wait, the tedious custom of militaries the world over.

We lit cigarettes and turned our attention to the dark sky, every now and again illuminated by a parachute flare sputtering into spermatic existence, its bright head of light trailing a long, wiggling tail of smoke as it drifted downward. Ready for a confession? Bon said. He used words the way he used bullets, in short, controlled bursts. I knew today was coming. Just never said so aloud. That's denial, right? I nodded and said, You're only guilty of the same thing that everyone else in Saigon is. We all knew and we couldn't do a thing about it, or so we thought, anyway. But anything can always happen. That's what hope is all about. He shrugged, contemplating the end of his burning cigarette. Hope's thin, he said. Despair's thick. Like blood. He pointed to the scar in the palm of the hand holding the cigarette, carved to follow the lifeline's arc. Remember?

I held up the palm of my right hand with its matching scar, the same one carried by Man. We saw this mark whenever we opened our hands for a bottle, a cigarette, a gun, or a woman. Like warriors of legend, we had sworn to die for one another, snared by the romance of schoolboy friendship, united by the eternal things we saw in each other: fidelity, honesty, conviction, the willingness to stand by friends and uphold beliefs. But what did we believe in at fourteen? Our friendship and our brotherhood, our country and our independence. We believed we could, if called upon, sacrifice ourselves for our blood brothers and our nation, but we did not know exactly how we would be called upon and what we would become. I could not predict that Bon would one day join the Phoenix Program to avenge his murdered father, his task to assassinate the people whom Man and I considered comrades. And good-hearted, sincere Bon did not know that Man and I would secretly come to believe that the only way to rescue our country was to become revolutionaries. All three of us followed our political beliefs, but only because of the reasons that led us to swear blood brotherhood in the first place. If ever circumstances forced us into a situation where death was the price of our brotherhood, I had no doubt that Man and I would pay. Our commitment was written on our hands, and under the wavering light cast by a distant magnesium flare, I held up my palm with its scar and traced the line with my finger. Your blood is mine and mine is yours, I said, which was the adolescent oath we had sworn to one another. You know what else? Bon said. Despair may be thick, but friendship's thicker. After that, nothing more needed to be said, our camaraderie enough as we heeded the call of the Katyusha rockets, hissing in the distance like librarians demanding silence.

CHAPTER 3

THANK YOU, DEAR COMMANDANT, for the notes that you and the commissar have given me on my confession. You have asked me what I mean when I say "we" or "us," as in those moments when I identify with the southern soldiers and evacuees on whom I was sent to spy. Should I not refer to those people, my enemies, as "them"? I confess that after having spent almost my whole life in their company I cannot help but sympathize with them, as I do with many others. My weakness for sympathizing with others has much to do with my status as a bastard, which is not to say that being a bastard naturally predisposes one to sympathy. Many bastards behave like bastards, and I credit my gentle mother with teaching me the idea that blurring the lines between us and them can be a worthy behavior. After all, if she had not blurred the lines between maid and priest, or allowed them to be blurred, I would not exist.

Having been thus produced outside of marriage, I confess to feeling very uncomfortable at the thought of being married myself. Bachelorhood is one of the unexpected benefits of being a bastard, as I was not considered much of a catch to most families. Not even families with a daughter of mixed ancestry welcomed me, for the daughter was herself usually frantic to squeeze into the elevator of social mobility through marriage to someone of a pure pedigree. While friends and strangers sigh over my bachelorhood as part of the tragedy of being a bastard, I find that bachelorhood not only means freedom but also suits my subterranean life as a mole, who burrows better alone. Being a bachelor also meant I could chat without consequence with the call girls, brazenly displaying their shapely shanks among the evacuees while using yesterday's tabloid paper to fan the sweaty ravines of their cleavage, artificially enhanced by atomic age bras. The girls called themselves Mimi, Phi Phi, and Ti Ti, common enough names in the demimonde, but as a triumvirate powerful enough to inject joy into my heart. Perhaps they invented those names on the spot, names changed as easily as customers. If so, their playacting was simply a professional reflex acquired through years of diligent study and dedicated practice. I had an abiding respect for the professionalism of career prostitutes, who wore their dishonesty more openly than lawyers, both of whom bill by the hour. But to speak only of the financial side misses the point. The proper way to approach a prostitute is to adapt the attitude of a theatergoer, sitting back and suspending disbelief for the duration of the show. The improper way is to doltishly insist that the play is just a bunch of people putting on charades because you have paid the price of the ticket, or, conversely, to believe utterly in what you are watching and hence succumb to a mirage. For example, grown men who sneer at the idea of unicorns will tearfully testify to the existence of an even rarer, more mythical species. Found only in remote ports of call and the darkest, deepest reaches of the most insalubrious taverns, this is the prostitute in whose chest beats the proverbial heart of gold. Let me assure you, if there is one part of a prostitute that is made of gold, it is not her heart. That some believe otherwise is a tribute to the conscientious performer.

By this degree, the three call girls were troupers, which could not be said of 70 or 80 percent of the prostitutes in the capital and outlying cities, of whom sober studies, anecdotal evidence, and random sampling indicate the existence of tens and perhaps hundreds of thousands. Most were poor, illiterate country girls with no means of making a living except to live as ticks on the fur of the nineteen-year-old American GI. His pants bulging with an inflationary roll of dollars and his adolescent brain swollen with the yellow fever that afflicts so many Western men who come to an Asian country, this American GI discovered to his surprise and delight that in this green-breasted world he was no longer Clark Kent but Superman, at least in regards to women. Aided (or was it invaded?) by Superman, our fecund little country no longer produced significant amounts of rice, rubber, and tin, cultivating instead an annual bumper crop of prostitutes, girls who had never so much as danced to a rock song before the pimps we called cowboys slapped pasties on their quivering country breasts and prodded them onto the catwalk of a Tu Do bar. Now am I daring to accuse American

strategic planners of deliberately eradicating peasant villages in order to smoke out the girls who would have little
choice but to sexually service the same boys who bombed,
shelled, strafed, torched, pillaged, or merely forcibly evacuated
said villages? I am merely noting that the creation of native
prostitutes to service foreign privates is an inevitable outcome
of a war of occupation, one of those nasty little side effects
of defending freedom that all the wives, sisters, girlfriends,
mothers, pastors, and politicians in Smallville, USA, pretend
to ignore behind waxed and buffed walls of teeth as they welcome their soldiers home, ready to treat any unmentionable
afflictions with the penicillin of American goodness.

This trio of talented stars promised another kind of goodness altogether, the bad kind. They flirted shamelessly with
me and teased Bon and the American husband with the walrus mustache, now awake. Both merely grimaced and made
themselves as still and small as they could, quite aware of
the grim silence of their wives. I, on the other hand, flirted
happily in return, perfectly mindful that each of these demi-
mondaines had a backstory capable of breaking my heart
and, most likely, my bank account. Did I not have one of
these same backstories? But performers perform at least partially to forget their sadness, a trait I am well acquainted
with. In these situations it is better to flirt and play, allowing everyone the opportunity to pretend to be happy for
so long that they might actually feel such happiness. And
it was a pleasure just to look at them! Mimi was tall, with
long straight hair and pink nail polish on all twenty digits,
their tips as glossy as jelly beans. Her throaty voice with its

mysterious Hue dialect compelled all my blood vessels to constrict, making me a touch light-headed. Ti Ti was fragile and petite, a fabulous beehive hairdo adding height. Her pale skin evoked eggshells, her eyelashes trembled with a hint of dew. I wanted to wrap her in my arms and brush my eyelashes against hers in butterfly kisses. Phi Phi was the leader, her body's curves reminding me of the dunes of Phan Thiet, where my mother had taken me for the one vacation of her life. While Mama covered herself from head to toe so she would not get any darker, I grubbed in the sunbaked sand ecstatically. That blissful memory of a ten-year-old's warmth and happiness was aroused by Phi Phi's fragrance, the same, nearly, or so I imagined, as from the one tiny vial of honey-colored perfume my mother owned, a present from my father with which she anointed herself once a year. So I fell in love with Phi Phi, a harmless enough emotion. I was wont to fall in love two or three times a year and was now well past due.

As to how they had managed to infiltrate this airbase, when evacuations were meant for the rich, the powerful, and/or the connected, it was all because of Sarge. I imagined a slab of beefcake on two legs with a white marine's cap perched on top. Sarge guards the embassy and just loves us girls, Phi Phi said. He's a sweetheart, a doll, he didn't forget us at all, just like he said he would never forget us. The other two nodded vigorously, Mimi cracking her gum and Ti Ti cracking her knuckles. Sarge got a bus and drove up and down Tu Do, rescuing as many of us girls as were around who wanted to leave. Then he got us on the airbase by telling the cops he was bringing us for a party with the poor boys here. The hard peach of my heart ripened and softened as I thought of their Sarge, this swell American who actually kept his promises, first name Ed and last name something none of the girls could pronounce. I asked them why they wanted to leave, and Mimi said because the communists were sure to imprison them as collaborators. They call us whores, she said. And they call Saigon the whore city, don't they? Honey, I can connect the dots. Plus, Ti Ti said, even if we're not tossed in jail, we couldn't do our work. You can't buy or sell anything in a communist country, right? Not for a profit, anyway, and darling, I'm not letting anyone eat this mango for free, communism or no communism. At this all three hooted and clapped. They were as ribald as Russian sailors on shore leave, but they also had a firm grasp of the theory of exchange value. What indeed would happen to girls like them once the revolution was victorious? To this matter I confess that I had not devoted much thought.

Their spirited élan made the time fly by as quickly as the C-130s flashing overhead, but even they and I got tired as the hours progressed and our numbers were not called. The marine with the bullhorn would mumble like a throat cancer victim with a mechanical larynx, and an exhausted company of evacuees would gather their pitiful belongings and stumble for the buses that would deliver them to the tarmac. Ten o'clock passed, then eleven. I lay down and could not sleep, even though I was in what soldiers, with their usual wit, called a thousand-star hotel. All I need do was look up to the galaxy to remind myself of my good luck. I squatted and smoked another cigarette with Bon. I lay down and again could not sleep, bothered by the heat. At midnight, I took a walk around the compound and poked my head in the toilets. This was a bad idea. They had been meant to handle only the normal flow of a few dozen office workers and rear-echelon military types, not the hot waste of thousands of evacuees. The scene at the swimming pool was no better. For all the years of its existence, the swimming pool was an American-only area, with passes for the whites of other countries and for the Indonesians, Iranians, Hungarians, and Poles of the International Committee of Control and Supervision. Our country was overrun by acronyms, with the ICCS otherwise known as "I Can't Control Shit," its role to oversee the cease-fire between north and south after the American armed forces strategically relocated. It was a smashingly successful cease-fire, for in the last two years only 150,000 soldiers had died, in addition to the requisite number of civilians. Imagine how many would have died without a truce! Perhaps the evacuees resented the exclusion of locals from this pool, but more likely they were just desperate when they turned it into a urinal. I joined the tinkling line standing at the pool's edge, then returned to the tennis courts. Bon and Linh dozed with their hands cupping their chins, Duc the only one getting any sleep at all in his mother's lap. I squatted, I lay down, I smoked a cigarette, and so on until, at nearly four in the morning, our number was at last called and I bid farewell to the girls, who pouted and promised we would see each other again on Guam.

We marched forth from the tennis court toward the

parking lot, where a pair of buses waited to take on more than our group of ninety-two evacuees. The crowd was around two hundred, and when the General asked me who these other people were, I asked the nearest marine. He shrugged. Y'all ain't too big, so we puttin' two of you on for every one of us. Part of me was irritated as I boarded the bus after my unhappy General, while part of me reasoned that we were used to such treatment. After all, we treated each other in the same way, cramming our motorbikes, buses, trucks, elevators, and helicopters with suicidal loads of human cargo, disregarding all regulations and manu-facturer recommendations. Was it any surprise that other people thought we were happy with conditions to which we were merely resigned? They wouldn't treat an American general this way, the General complained, pressed against me in the tight confines. No, sir, they wouldn't, I said, and it was most likely true. Our bus was immediately fetid and hot from the passengers who had been simmering outdoors all day and night, but it was only a short way to our parked C-130 Hercules. The plane was a garbage truck with wings attached, and like a garbage truck deposits were made from the rear, where its big flat cargo ramp dropped down to receive us. This maw led into a generous alimentary canal, its membrane illuminated by a ghostly green blackout light. Disembarked from the bus, the General stood to one side of the ramp and I joined him to watch as his family, his staff, their dependents, and a hundred people we did not know climbed aboard, waved on by a loadmaster standing on the ramp. Come on, don't be shy, he said to Madame, his head encased in a helmet the size and shape of a basketball. Nut to butt, lady. Nut to butt.

Madame was too puzzled to be shocked. Her forehead wrinkled as she passed with her children, attempting to translate the loadmaster's mindless refrain. Then I spotted a man coming to the ramp doing his best to avoid eye contact, a blue Pan Am travel bag clutched to his incurvate chest. I had seen him a few days prior, at his house in District Three. A mid-ranking apparatchik in the Ministry of the Interior, he was neither too tall nor too short, too thin nor too wide, too pale nor too dark, too smart nor too dumb. Some species of sub-undersecretary, he probably had neither dreams nor nightmares, his own interior as hollow as his office. I had thought of the sub-undersecretary a few times in the days since our meeting and could not recall his elusive face, but I recognized him now as he ascended the ramp. When I clapped my hand on his shoulder, he twitched and finally turned his Chihuahua eyes toward me, pretending not to have seen me. What a coincidence! I said. I didn't expect to see you on this flight. General, our seats would not have been possible without the help of this kind gentleman. The General nodded stiffly, baring his teeth just enough to indicate that he should never be expected to reciprocate. My pleasure, the sub-undersecretary whispered, slight frame quivering and wife tugging at his arm. If looks could emasculate, she would have walked off with my sac in her purse. After the crowd pushed them by, the General glanced at me and said, Was it a pleasure? Of a sort, I said.

When all the passengers had boarded, the General

motioned for me to go before him. He was the last to walk
up the ramp into a cargo hold with no seats. Adults squatted on the floor or sat on bags, children perched on their
knees. Lucky passengers had a bulkhead berth where they
could cling to a cargo strap. The contours of skin and flesh
separating one individual from another merged, everyone
forced into the mandatory intimacy required of those less
human than the ones leaving the country in reserved seat-
ing. Bon, Linh, and Duc were somewhere in the middle, as
were Madame and her children. The ramp slowly rose and
clamped shut, sealing us worms into our can. Along with the
loadmaster, the General and I leaned against the ramp, our
knees in the noses of the passengers before us. The quartet
of turboprop engines turned over with a deafening racket,
the vibrations rattling the ramp. As the plane grumbled its
way along the tarmac, the whole population rocked back
and forth with every motion, a congregation swaying to
inaudible prayers. The acceleration pressed me backward
while the woman in front of me braced her arm against my
knees, her jaw pressed to the rucksack on my lap. As the
heat in the plane climbed over forty degrees Celsius, so did
the intensity of our odor. We exuded the stink of sweat, of
unwashed clothing, and of anxiety, with the only succor
being the breeze through the open door where a crewman
stood in a rock guitarist's wide-legged pose. Instead of a six-
string electric guitar slung low across his hips, he carried an
M16 with a twenty-round magazine. As we taxied along the
runway, I caught glimpses of concrete revetments, giant cans
sliced in half lengthwise, and a desolate row of incinerated

warbirds, demolished jets blown up in a strafing run earlier this evening, wings plucked and scattered like those of
abused flies. A hush blanketed the passengers, hypnotized by
trepidation and anticipation. They were, no doubt, thinking
what I was. Good-bye, Vietnam. Au revoir, Saigon—

The explosion was deafening, the force of it launching the
crewman onto the passengers, the last thing I saw for several
moments as the flash of light through the open door washed
the sight from my eyes. The General tumbled into me and
I fell onto the bulkhead, then onto screaming bodies, hysterical civilians spraying my face with sour saliva. The tires
of the plane squealed on the runway as it spun to the right,
and when my sight returned a blaze of fire shone through the
door. I feared nothing more than burning to death, nothing
more than being pureed by a propeller, nothing more than
being quartered by a Katyusha, which even sounded like the
name of a demented Siberian scientist who had lost a few toes
and a nose to frostbite. I had seen roasted remains before,
in a desolate field outside of Hue, carbonized corpses fused
into the metal of a downed Chinook, the fuel tanks having
incinerated the three dozen occupants, their teeth exposed
in a permanent, simian rictus; the flesh of their lips and faces
burned off; the skin a finely charred obsidian, smooth and
alien, all the hair converted to ash, no longer recognizable
as my countrymen or as human beings. I did not want to die
that way; I did not want to die in any way, least of all in a
long-range bombardment from the artillery of my communist comrades, launched from the suburbs they had captured
outside Saigon. A hand squeezed my chest and reminded

me I was still alive. Another clawed my ear as the howling people beneath me struggled to heave me off. Pushing back to try to right myself, I found my hand on someone's oily head and myself pressed against the General. Another explosion somewhere on the runway heightened the frenzy. Men, women, and children caterwauled at an even higher pitch. All of a sudden the plane halted its gyrations at such an angle where the eye of the door did not look out onto fire but only onto the darkness, and a man screamed, We're all going to die! The loadmaster, cursing inventively, began the lowering of the ramp, and when the refugees surged forward against the opening, they bore me backward with them. The only way to survive being trampled to death was to cover my head with my rucksack and roll down the ramp, knocking people down as I did so. Another rocket exploded on the runway a few hundred meters behind us, lighting up an acre of tarmac and revealing the nearest shelter to be a battered concrete divider fifty meters from the runway. Even after the explosion faded, the disturbed night was no longer dark. The plane's starboard engines were aflame, two blazing torches spewing gusts of spark and smoke.

I was on my hands and knees when Bon seized me by the elbow, dragging me with one hand and Linh with the other. She in turn carried a wailing Duc, her arm wrapped around his chest. A meteorite shower of rockets and artillery shells was falling on the runways, an apocalyptic light show that revealed the evacuees dashing for the concrete divider, stumbling and tripping along the way, suitcases forgotten, the thundering prop wash from the two remaining engines blowing little children off their feet and staggering adults. Those who had reached the divider kept their whimpering heads below the concrete, and when something whizzed overhead—a fragment or a bullet—I fell to the earth and began crawling. Bon did likewise with Linh, her face tense but determined. By the time we fumbled our way to an unoccupied space at the divider, the crew had turned off the engines. The relief from the noise only made audible that someone was shooting at us. Bullets zipped overhead or ricocheted off the concrete, the gunners zeroing in on the bonfire of the burning plane. Our guys, Bon said, knees drawn up to his chest and one arm thrown around Duc, huddled between him and Linh. They're pissed. They want a seat out of here. No way, I said, that's NVA, they've taken the perimeter, even though I thought there was a fairly good chance it was our own men venting their frustrations. Then the plane's gas tanks blew, the fireball illuminating a vast stretch of the airfield, and when I turned my face away from the bonfire I found that I was next to the sub-undersecretary, civil servant unextraordinaire, his face nearly pressed against my back and the message in his Chihuahua eyes as clear as the title on a cinema marquee. Like the communist agent and the lieutenant at the gate, he would have been happy to see me dead.

I deserved his hatred. After all, I had denied him a considerable fortune as a result of my unannounced visit to his house, the address procured for me by the louche major. It is true I have some visas, the sub-undersecretary had said as we sat in his living room. I and some colleagues are making them available in the interests of justice. Isn't it unjust that only the most privileged or fortunate have the opportunity to escape? I made some sympathetic noises. If there was true justice, he went on, everyone would leave who needed to. That is clearly not the case. But this puts someone like me in rather difficult circumstances. Why should I be the judge of who gets to leave and who does not? I am, after all, merely a glorified secretary. If you were in my situation, Captain, what would you do?

I can appreciate the situation you find yourself in, sir. My dimples hurt from smiling, and I was impatient to arrive at the inevitable end game, but the middle had to be played, to provide me with the same moth-eaten moral covers he had already pulled up to his chin. You are clearly a respectable man of taste and values. Here I nodded to the left and right, gesturing at the tidy house that had to be paid for. Plastered walls were dotted with a few geckos and some decorative objects: clock, calendar, Chinese scroll, and colorized photograph of Ngo Dinh Diem in better days, when he had not yet been assassinated for believing he was a president and not an American puppet. Now the little man in a white suit was a saint to his fellow Vietnamese Catholics, having suffered an appropriately martyred death with hands hogtied, face masked in blood, a Rorschach blot of his cerebral tissue decorating the interior of an American armored personnel carrier, his humiliation captured in a photograph circulated worldwide. Its subtext was as subtle as Al Capone: *Do not fuck with the United States of America.*

The real injustice, I said, beginning to get heated, is that an honest man must live a penurious life in our country. Therefore, please allow me to extend to you a small token of the appreciation of my patron for the favor that he is requesting. You do have enough visas on hand for ninety-two people, do you not? I was not certain he would, in which case my plan was to put down a deposit and promise to return with the remainder. But when the sub-undersecretary replied affirmatively, I produced the envelope of remaining cash, $4,000, enough for two visas if he was feeling generous. The sub-undersecretary unsealed the envelope and ran his thumb, callused by experience, over the sheaf of bills. He knew immediately how much money was in the envelope—not enough! He slapped the cheek of the coffee table with the white glove of the envelope, and as if that were an insufficient expression of his outrage he slapped the cheek again. How dare you attempt to bribe me, sir!

I motioned to him to sit down. Like him, I, too, was a man trapped by difficult circumstances, forced to do what I must do. Is it just for you to sell these visas when they cost you nothing and were not yours to begin with? I asked him. And would it not be just for me to call the local police commander and have him arrest us both? And would it not be just for him to appropriate your visas and engage in some just redistribution of his own? So the most just solution is simply for us to return to the situation where I offer you four thousand dollars for ninety-two visas, since you should not even have ninety-two visas or four thousand dollars to begin with. After all, you can return to your desk tomorrow and procure another ninety-two visas easily enough. They're only paper, aren't they?

But to a bureaucrat paper was never just paper. Paper was life! He hated me then for taking his paper and he hated me now, but I was bothered not in the least. What bothered me as I huddled at the concrete divider was yet another miserable wait, only this time one with no clear resolution. The glimmer of a rising sun brought a measure of comfort, but the soothing bluish light showed the tarmac to be in an awful state, chipped and pitted by rocket and artillery explosions. In the middle of it all was the smoldering slag heap of the C-130, exuding the pungent stink of burning fuel. Between us and the embers of the plane were little dark heaps that gradually took shape, becoming suitcases and valises abandoned in the mad rush, some of them burst open and spilling their entrails hither and thither. The sun continued rising notch by notch on its rack, the light becoming harsher and brighter until it achieved the retina-numbing quality generated by an interrogator's lamp, stripping away every vestige of shade. Pinned down on the east side of the divider, people began to wilt and shrivel, beginning with the elderly and the children. Water, Mama, Duc said. All Linh could say was, No, darling, we don't have any water, but we'll get some soon.

On cue, another Hercules appeared in the sky, approaching so fast and steep a kamikaze pilot might have been at the controls. The C-130 landed with a screech of tires on a distant runway and a murmur rose from the evacuees. Only when the Hercules turned in our direction to approach haphazardly across intervening runways did that murmur turn into a cheer. Then I heard something else. When I poked my head over the divider cautiously, I saw them, darting out of the shadows of hangars and between revetments where they must have been hiding, dozens, maybe hundreds of marines and soldiers and military cops and air force pilots and crewmen and mechanics, the air base's staff and rear guard, refusing to be heroes or sacrificial goats. Spotting this competition, the evacuees stampeded toward the C-130, which had pivoted on the runway fifty meters away and lowered its ramp in a not-so-coy gesture of invitation. The General and his family ran ahead of me, Bon and his family ran behind me, and together we brought up the rear of the fleeing masses.

The first of the evacuees was running up the ramp when I heard the hiss of the Katyushas, followed a second later by an explosion as the first of the rockets detonated on a far runway. Bullets whizzed overhead, and this time we heard the distinct bark of the AK-47 along with the M16. They're at the perimeter! Bon shouted. It was clear to the evacuees that this Hercules would be the last plane out of the airport, if it could even take off with communist units closing in, and they once more began screaming with fear. As they rushed up the ramp as fast as they could, a slick little airplane on the far side of the divider shrieked into the air, a needle-nosed Tiger fighter, followed by a Huey helicopter thumping by with its doors flung wide open, revealing more than a dozen soldiers squeezed inside. What remained of the armed forces at the airport was evacuating itself with whatever air mobile vehicle was at hand. As the General pushed on the backs of the evacuees in front of him to propel them toward the ramp, and as I pushed the General, a dual-hulled Shadow gunship soared from the tarmac to my left. I watched it out of the corner of my eye. The Shadow was a funny-looking plane, the fat fuselage suspended between two hulls, but there was nothing funny about the smoke trail of the heat-seeking missile scribbling its way across the sky until its flaming tip kissed the Shadow at less than a thousand feet. When the two halves of the airplane and the bits and pieces of its crew fell to the earth like the shattered fragments of a clay pigeon, the evacuees groaned and shoved even harder to make the final climb up the ramp.

As the General set foot on the ramp, I paused to let Linh and Duc pass by. When they did not appear, I turned and saw that they were no longer behind me. Get on the plane, our loadmaster shouted beside me, his mouth open so wide I swear I saw his tonsils vibrating. Your friends are gone, man! Twenty meters away, Bon was kneeling on the tarmac, clutching Linh to his breast. A red heart slowly expanded on her white blouse. A puff of concrete dust rose when a bullet pinged off the runway between us, and every last drop of moisture in my mouth evaporated. I tossed my rucksack at the loadmaster and ran straight and fast toward them, hurdling abandoned suitcases. I slid the last two meters, feet first and shaving the skin off my left hand and elbow. Bon was making sounds I had never heard from him before, deep guttural bellows of pain. Between him and Linh was Duc, his eyes rolled back in his head, and when I pried husband and wife apart I saw the wet bloody mess of Duc's chest where something had torn through it and through his mother. The General and the loadmaster were yelling something I could not understand over the increasing whine of the propellers. Let's go, I shouted. They're leaving! I pulled at his sleeve but Bon would not move, rooted by grief. I had no choice but to punch him in the jaw, just hard enough to shut him up and loosen his grip. Then with one tug I pried Linh from his arms, and when I did so Duc tumbled onto the tarmac, his head limp. Bon screamed something inarticulate as I ran for the airplane, Linh thrown over my shoulder and making no noise as her body bumped against me, her blood hot and wet on my shoulder and neck.

The General and the loadmaster stood on the ramp beckoning me as the plane taxied away, aiming for any clear stretch of runway as the Katyushas kept arriving, singly and in salvos. I was running as fast as I could, my lungs in a knot, and when I reached the ramp I threw Linh at the General, who caught her by the arms. Then Bon was at my side running with me, extending Duc with both hands to the loadmaster, who took him as gently as he could even though it did not matter, not with the way Duc's head flopped from side to side. With his son handed off, Bon began to slow down, head bowed in agony and still sobbing. I grabbed him by the crook of his elbow and with one last push I shoved him face forward onto the ramp, where the loadmaster seized him by the collar and pulled him up the rest of the way. I leaped for the ramp, arms extended, landing on it with the side of my face and all of my rib cage, the grit of dirt and dust against my cheek while my legs flailed in open air. With the plane barreling down the runway, the General pulled me to my knees and dragged me into the hold, the ramp rising behind me. I was squeezed against the General on one side and the prostrate bodies of Duc and Linh on the other, a wall of evacuees pushing against us from the front. As the airplane ascended steeply, a terrible noise rose with it, audible not only through the straining metal but through the clamor from the open side door, where the crewman stood with his M16, firing three-round bursts from the hip. Through that open door, the patchy landscape of fields and tenements tilted and wheeled as the pilot took us into a corkscrew, and I realized that the terrible noise was not only coming from the engines but from Bon, too, pounding his head against the ramp and howling, not as if the world had ended, but as if someone had gouged out his eyes.

CHAPTER 4

Shortly after we landed on Guam, a green ambulance arrived to take the bodies. I lowered Duc onto a stretcher. His little body had grown heavier in my arms with each passing minute, but I could not lay him down on the grubby tarmac. After the medics draped him with a white sheet, they eased Linh from Bon's arms and likewise covered her before loading mother and son into the ambulance. I wept, but I was no match for Bon, who had a lifetime's worth of unused tears to spend. We continued to weep as we were trucked to Camp Asan, where, thanks to the General, we were given barracks that were luxurious compared to the tents waiting for the other late arrivals. Catatonic on his bunk, Bon would remember nothing of the evacuation playing on television that afternoon and through the next day. Nor would he remember how, in the barracks and tents of our temporary city, thousands of refugees wailed as if attending a funeral, the burial of their nation, dead too soon, as so many were, at a tender twenty-one years of age.

Along with the General's family and a hundred others in the barracks, I watched inglorious images of helicopters landing on Saigon's roofs, evacuating refugees to the decks of airplane carriers. The next day, after communist tanks crashed through the gates of the presidential palace, communist troops raised the flag of the National Liberation Front from the palace roof. As the debacle unfolded, the calcium and lime deposits of memory from the last days of the damned republic encrusted themselves in the pipes of my brain. Just a little more would be added late that night, after a dinner of baked chicken and green beans many of the refugees found exotically inedible, the children the only ones in the cafeteria with any appetite. Joining a line to turn in our trays to the dishwashers was the coup de grâce, pronouncing us no longer adult citizens of a sovereign country but stateless refugees, protected, for the moment, by the American military. After scraping his untouched green beans into the garbage, the General looked at me and said, Captain, our people need me. I'm going to walk among them and boost their morale. Let's go. Yes, sir, I said, not optimistic about his chances but also not thinking of possible complications. While it was easy enough to spread the manure of encouragement among soldiers drilled into accepting all kinds of abuse, we had forgotten that most of the refugees were civilians.

In retrospect, I was fortunate not to be wearing my uniform, stained with Linh's blood. I had shed it in favor of the madras shirt and chinos in my rucksack, but the General, having lost his luggage at the airport, still wore his stars on his collar. Outside our barracks and in the tent city, few knew

who he was by face. What they saw was his uniform and
rank, and when he said hello to the civilians and asked how
they were faring, they met him with sullen silence. The slight
crinkle between his eyes and his hesitant chuckling told me
he was confused. My sense of unease increased with every
step down the dirt lane between the tents, civilian eyes on us
and the silence unbroken. We had barely walked a hundred
meters into the tent city when the first assault came, a dainty
slipper sailing from our flank and striking the General on
his temple. He froze. I froze. An old woman's voice croaked
out, Look at the hero! We swiveled to the left and saw the
one thing charging us that could not be defended against, an
enraged elderly citizen we could neither beat down nor back
away from. Where's my husband? she screamed, barefoot,
her other slipper in her hand. Why are you here when he's
not? Aren't you supposed to be defending our country with
your life like he is?

She smacked the General across the chin with her slipper, and from behind her, from the other side, from behind
us, the women, young and old, firm and infirm, came with
their shoes and slippers, their umbrellas and canes, their
sun hats and conical hats. Where's my son? Where's my
father? Where's my brother? The General ducked and flung
his arms over his head as the furies beat him, tearing at his
uniform and his flesh. I was hardly unscathed, suffering
several blows from flying footwear and intercepting several
strokes from canes and umbrellas. The ladies pressed around
me to get at the General, who had sunk to his knees under
their onslaught. They could hardly be blamed for their ill

temper, since our vaunted premier had gone on the radio the day before to ask all soldiers and citizens to fight to the last man. It was pointless to point out that the premier, who was also the air marshal and who should not be confused with the president except in his venality and vanity, had himself left on a helicopter shortly after broadcasting his heroic message. Nor would it have helped to explain that this general was not in charge of soldiers but the secret police, which would hardly have endeared him to civilians. In any case, the ladies were not listening, preferring to scream and curse. I pushed my way through the women who had come between the General and myself, shielding him with my body and absorbing many more whacks and globs of spit until I could drag him free. Go! I shouted in his ear, propelling him in the correct direction. For the second straight day we ran for our lives, but at least the rest of the people in the tent city left us alone, touching us with nothing except contemptuous gazes and catcalls. Good for nothings! Villains! Cowards! Bastards!

While I was used to such slings and arrows, the General was not. When we finally stopped outside our barracks, the expression on his face was one of horror. He was disheveled, the stars torn from his collar, his sleeves ripped, half his buttons gone, and bleeding from scratches on his cheek and neck. I can't go in there like this, he whispered. Wait in the showers, sir, I said. I'll find you some new clothes. I requisitioned a spare shirt and pants from officers in the barracks, explaining my own bruised and tattered condition as being the result of a run-in with our ill-humored competitors in the Military Security Service. When I went to the showers, the General was standing at a sink, his face rinsed clean of everything except the shame.

General—

Shut up! The only person he was looking at was himself in the mirror. We will never speak of this again.

And we never did.

The next day we buried Linh and Duc. Their cold bodies had lain in a naval morgue overnight, cause of death now official: a single slug, type unknown. The bullet would forever spin in Bon's mind on a perpetual axis, taunting and haunting him with the even chance of coming from friend or foe. He wore a white scarf of mourning around his head, ripped from his bedsheet. After we had lowered Duc's small coffin on top of his mother's, both to share the one home for eternity, Bon threw himself into their open grave. Why? he howled, cheek against the wooden crate. Why them? Why not me? Why, God? Weeping myself, I climbed in the grave to calm him down. After I helped him out, we heaped the earth onto the coffins while the General, the Madame, and the exhausted priest watched silently. They were innocents, these two, especially my godson, who was probably the closest I would get to having a real son. With every strike of the iron shovel against the small mound of loamy earth, waiting to be poured back into the cavity from which it had been extracted, I tried believing that those two bodies were not truly dead but simply rags, shed by emigrants journeying to a land beyond human cartography where angels dwelled. Thus my sacerdotal father believed; but thus I could not.

Over the next few days, we wept and we waited. Sometimes, for variety, we waited and we wept. Just when the self-flagellation was beginning to wear me down, we were picked up and shuttled on to Camp Pendleton in San Diego, California, this time via an airliner where I sat in a real seat with a real window. Awaiting us was another refugee camp, its higher grade of amenities evidence that we were already profiting from the upward mobility of the American Dream. Whereas on Guam most of the refugees had lived under tents hastily erected by the marines, in Camp Pendleton we all had barracks, a boot camp to gird us for the rigors of learning Americana. It was here, during the summer of '75, that I wrote the first of my letters to Man's aunt in Paris. Of course, as I composed my letters, I was writing to Man. If I started a letter with a few tropes we had agreed on—the weather, my health, the aunt's health, French politics—then he would know that written in between the lines was another message in invisible ink. If such a trope was absent, then what he saw was all there was to see. But that first year in America, there was not much need for steganography, the exiled soldiers hardly in any condition to foment a counterstrike. This was useful intelligence, but not one needing secrecy.

Dear Aunt, I wrote, pretending she was mine, *I regret having to tell you something horrible as my first words to you in so long.* Bon was not in a good state. At night, as I lay sleepless in my bunk, he tossed and turned in the rack above, his memories grilling him alive. I could see what flickered on the interior of his skull, the face of Man, our blood brother whom he was convinced we had abandoned, and the faces of Linh and Duc, their blood on his hands and mine, literally. Bon would have starved to death if I had not dragged him from his bunk to the mess hall, where we ate tasteless chow at communal tables. Along with thousands of others that summer, we also bathed in showers that lacked stalls and lived with strangers in barracks. The General was not exempted from these experiences, and I passed a great deal of time with him in the quarters he shared with Madame and their four children, along with three other families. Junior officers and brats, he muttered to me on one visit. This is what I've been reduced to! Sheets strung up on clotheslines divided the barracks into family quarters, but they did little to shield the delicate ears of Madame and the children. These animals are having sex day and night, he growled as he sat with me on the cement stoop. Each of us was smoking a cigarette and sipping from a mug of tea, which was what we had instead of even the cheapest liquor. They have no shame! In front of their own children and mine. You know what my eldest asked me the other day? Daddy, what's a prostitute? She saw some woman selling herself down by the latrines!

Across the lane from us, in another barracks, a spat between a husband and wife that had started with the usual name-calling suddenly erupted into a full-blown fight. We saw none of it but heard the unmistakable sound of flesh being slapped, followed by the woman screaming. A small crowd of people soon gathered outside the doorway of the barracks. The General sighed. Animals! But among all this, some good news. He extracted a newspaper clipping from his pocket and handed it to me. Remember him? Shot himself. That's good news? I asked, fingering the article. He was a hero, the General said, or so I wrote my aunt. It was an old article, published a few days after the fall of Saigon and mailed to the General by a friend in another refugee holding pen in Arkansas. The centerpiece was a photograph of the dead man, flat on his back at the base of the memorial the General had saluted. He could have been resting on a hot day, looking up at a sky as blue as a jazz singer, except the caption said he had committed suicide. While we were flying to Guam, with tanks entering the city, the lieutenant colonel had come to the memorial, drawn his service pistol, and drilled a hole in his balding head.

A real hero, I said. He had a wife and a number of children, how many I could not recall. I had neither liked him nor disliked him, and while I had considered his name for evacuation, I had passed him over. A feather of guilt tickled the back of my neck. I didn't know he was capable of doing that, I said. If I had known . . .

If any one of us could have known. But who could have? Don't blame yourself. I've had many men die under my watch. I've felt bad for each one, but death is a part of our business. It may very well be our turn one day. Let's just remember him as the martyr he is.

We toasted with tea to the lieutenant colonel's memory. Except for this one act, he was not a hero, so far as I knew.

Perhaps the General also sensed this, for the next thing he said was, We could certainly have used him alive.

For what?

Keeping an eye on what the communists are doing. Just as they're probably keeping an eye on what we're doing. Have you done any thinking about that?

About how they're keeping an eye on us?

Exactly. Sympathizers. Spies in our ranks. Sleeper agents.

It's possible, I said, palms damp. They're devious and smart enough to do it.

So who's a likely candidate? The General looked at me intently, or perhaps he was staring at me in suspicion. He had his mug in hand and I kept it in my peripheral vision as I met his gaze. If he tried to crack me over the head with it, I'd have half a second to react. The Viet Cong had agents everywhere, he continued. It just makes sense there would be one of them with us.

You really think one of our own men could be a spy? By now the only part of me not sweating were my eyeballs. What about military intelligence? Or the general staff?

You can't think of anybody? His eyes never left my own cool ones, while his hand still gripped the mug. I had a sip of cold tea left in mine and I took it now. An X-ray of my skull would have shown a hamster running furiously in an exercise wheel, trying to generate ideas. If I said I did not suspect anyone, when he clearly did, it would look bad for me. In a paranoid imagination, only spies denied the existence of spies. So I had to name a suspect, someone who would sidetrack him but who would not be an actual spy. The first person who came to mind was the crapulent major, whose name had the desired effect.

Him? The General frowned and at last stopped looking at me. He studied his knuckles instead, distracted by my unlikely suggestion. He's so fat he needs a mirror to see his own belly button. I think your instincts are off for once, Captain.

Perhaps they are, I said, pretending to be embarrassed. I gave him my pack of cigarettes to divert him and returned to my barracks to report the gist of our conversation to my aunt, minus the uninteresting parts about my fear, trembling, sweating, etc. Fortunately, we were not much longer for the camp, where little existed to alleviate the General's rage. Shortly after arriving in San Diego, I had written to my former professor, Avery Wright Hammer, seeking his help in leaving the camp. He was Claude's college roommate and the person Claude had told about a promising young Vietnamese student who needed a scholarship to come study in America. Not only did Professor Hammer find that scholarship for me, he also became my most important teacher after Claude and Man. It was the professor who had guided my American studies and who had agreed to venture out of his field to supervise my senior thesis, "Myth and Symbol in the Literature of Graham Greene." Now that good man leaped to action once again on my behalf, volunteering to be my sponsor and, by the middle of the summer, arranging a clerical position for me in the Department of Oriental Studies. He even took up a collection on my behalf among my former teachers, a grand gesture that moved me deeply.

That sum, I wrote to my aunt at summer's end, paid for my bus ticket to Los Angeles, a few nights in a motel, the deposit on an apartment near Chinatown, and a used '64 Ford. Once situated, I canvassed my neighborhood churches for anyone who would sponsor Bon, religious and charitable organizations having proven sympathetic to the refugee plight. I came across the Everlasting Church of Prophets, which, despite its impressive name, plied its spiritual wares out of a humble storefront flanked by a bottom-feeding auto body shop and a vacant blacktop lot inhabited by heroin zealots. With minimal persuasion and a modest cash donation, the rotund Reverend Ramon, or R-r-r-r-amon as he introduced himself, agreed to be Bon's sponsor and nominal employer. By September and just in time for the academic year, Bon and I were reunited in genteel poverty in our apartment. Then, with what remained of my sponsor's money, I went to a downtown pawnshop and bought the last of life's necessities, a radio and a television.

As for the General and Madame, they, too, ended up in Los Angeles, sponsored by the sister-in-law of an American colonel who had once been the General's adviser. Instead of a villa, they rented a bungalow in a slightly less tony part of Los Angeles, the city's flabby midriff, Hollywood adjacent. Every time I dropped by for the next several months, as I wrote to my aunt, I found him still mired in a profound funk. He was unemployed and no longer a general, although his former officers all hailed him as such. During our visits, he consumed an embarrassingly varied assortment of cheap beer and wine, vacillating between fury and melancholy as one might imagine Richard Nixon to be doing not far away. Sometimes he choked on his emotions so badly I feared I would have to perform the Heimlich maneuver on him. It was not that there was nothing for him to do with his time. It was that Madame was the one who found schools for the children, wrote the rent check, shopped for groceries, cooked the meals, washed the dishes, cleaned the bathrooms, found a church—in short, undertook all the menial tasks of household drudgery that, for her entire cocooned existence, someone else had managed. She attended to these tasks with a grim grace, in short order becoming the house's resident dictator, the General merely a figurehead who occasionally bellowed at his children like one of those dusty lions in the zoo undergoing a midlife crisis. They lived in this fashion for most of the year before the credit line of her patience finally reached its limit. I was not privy to the conversations they must have had, but one day at the beginning of April I received an invitation to the grand opening of his new business on Hollywood Boulevard, a liquor store whose existence in the Cyclopean eye of the IRS meant that the General had finally conceded to a basic tenet of the American Dream. Not only must he make a living, he must also pay for it, as I myself was already doing as the dour face of the Department of Oriental Studies.

My job was to serve as the first line of defense against students who sought audiences with the secretary or the Department Chair, some addressing me by name though we had never met. I was a moderate celebrity on campus because of the feature the student newspaper had run on me, a graduate of the college, member of the dean's list and honor roll, sole Vietnamese student in the history of my alma mater, and now rescued refugee. The article also mentioned my soldiering experience, although it was not quite accurate. What did you do? the budding journalist had asked. He was a skittish sophomore with braces on his teeth and teeth marks on his yellow no. 2 pencil. I was a quartermaster, I said. A boring job. Tracking supplies and rations, making sure the troops had uniforms and boots. So you never killed anyone? Never. And that, indeed, was the truth, even if the rest of my interview was not. A college campus was a bad place to acknowledge my service record. First, I was an infantry officer in the Army of the Republic of Vietnam, where I had begun serving the General when he was a colonel. Then, when he became a general and took charge of the National Police, which was in need of some military discipline, I, too, moved with him. To say that one saw combat, much less was involved with the Special Branch, was a delicate topic on most college campuses even now. The campus had not been exempt from the antiwar fervor that had blazed like a religious revival through collegiate life when I was a student. On many college campuses including my own, *Ho Ho Ho* was not the signature call of Santa Claus, but was instead the beginning of a popular chant that went *Ho Ho Ho Chi Minh, the NLF is gonna win!* I envied the students their naked political passion, for I had to submerge my own in order to play the role of a good citizen from the Republic of Vietnam. By the time I returned to campus, however, the students were of a new breed, not interested in politics or the world like the previous generation. Their tender eyes were no longer exposed daily to stories and pictures of atrocity and terror for which they might have felt responsible, given that they were citizens of a democracy destroying another country in order to save it. Most important, their lives were no longer at stake because of the draft. The campus had, as a result, returned to its peaceful and quiet nature, its optimistic disposition marred only by the occasional spring shower thrumming on my office window. My hodgepodge of tasks, for which I was paid minimum wage, involved answering the phone, typing professorial manuscripts, filing documents, and fetching books, as well as helping the secretary, Ms. Sofia Mori of the rhinestoned, horn-rimmed glasses. These things, perfectly suitable for a student, amounted to death by a thousand paper cuts for me. To compound matters, Ms. Mori did not seem to like me.

It's nice to know you never killed anybody, she said not long after we met. Her sympathies were obvious, a peace symbol dangling from her key chain. Not for the first time, I longed to tell someone that I was one of them, a sympathizer with the Left, a revolutionary fighting for peace, equality, democracy, freedom, and independence, all the noble things my people had died for and I had hid for. But if you had killed someone, she said, you wouldn't tell anybody, would you?

Would you, Ms. Mori?

I don't know. She swiveled her chair with a twist of her womanly hips, turning her back to me. My small desk was tucked into a corner, and from here I shuffled papers and notes in a pretense of labor, the tasks not enough to fill my eight-hour days. As expected, I had smiled dutifully at my desk when the student journalist photographed me, aware I would be on the front page, yellow teeth appearing white in the black-and-white photograph. I was doing my best imitation of a Third World child on one of those milk cartons passed around elementary schools for American children to deposit their pennies and dimes in order to help poor Alejandro, Abdullah, or Ah Sing have a hot lunch and an immunization. And I was thankful, truly! But I was also one of those unfortunate cases who could not help but wonder whether my need for American charity was due to my having first been the recipient of American aid. Fearful of being seen as an ingrate, I focused on making enough subtle noise to please but not distract Ms. Mori of the avocado-green polyester slacks, my pseudo-work interrupted periodically by the need to run errands or to come to the adjoining office of the Department Chair.

As no one on the faculty possessed any knowledge of our country, the Chair enjoyed engaging me in long discussions of our culture and language. Hovering somewhere between seventy and eighty years old, the Chair nestled in an office feathered with the books, papers, notes, and tchotchkes accumulated over a lifetime career devoted to the study of the Orient. He had hung an elaborate Oriental rug on his wall, in lieu, I suppose, of an actual Oriental. On his desk facing anyone who entered was a gilt-framed picture of his family, a brown-haired cherub and an Asian wife somewhere between one-half and two-thirds his age. She was not exactly beautiful but could hardly help but look beautiful next to the bow-tied Chair, the tight neck of her scarlet cheongsam squeezing the bubble of a smile to her frosted lips.

Her name is Ling Ling, he said, seeing my gaze rest on the picture. Decades of hunching over a desk had bent the great Orientalist's back into the shape of a horseshoe, thrusting his head forward in the inquisitorial fashion of a dragon. I met my wife in Taiwan where her family had fled from Mao. Our son is considerably bigger now than in that picture. As you can see, his mother's genes are more resilient, which is not to be unexpected. Blond hair fades when mixed with black. He said all this during our fifth or sixth conversation, when we had achieved a certain degree of intimacy. As usual, he reclined in an overstuffed leather club chair that enfolded him like the generous lap of a black mammy. I was equally enveloped in the chair's twin, sucked backward by the slope and softness of the leather, my arms on the rests like Lincoln on his memorial throne. A metaphor to explain the situation is available in our own Californian landscape, he continued, where foreign weeds choke to death much of our native foliage. Mixing native flora with a foreign plant oftentimes has tragic consequences, as your own experience may have taught you.

Yes, it has, I said, reminding myself that I needed my minimum wage.

Ah, the Amerasian, forever caught between worlds and never knowing where he belongs! Imagine if you did not suffer from the confusion you must constantly experience, feeling the constant tug-of-war inside you and over you, between Orient and Occident. "East is East and West is West, and never the twain shall meet," as Kipling so accurately diagnosed. This was one of his favorite themes, and he had even concluded one of our meetings by giving me a homework assignment to test Kipling's point. I was to take a sheet of paper and fold it in half vertically. On the top, I was to write *Orient* on the left and *Occident* on the right. Then I was to write down my Oriental and Occidental qualities. Imagine this exercise as an indexing of yourself, the Chair had said. My students of Oriental ancestry inevitably find this beneficial.

At first I thought he was playing a joke on me, since the day he gave me the task was the first of April, the occasion for that funny Western custom called April Fools' Day. But he was looking at me quite seriously and I remembered that he did not have a sense of humor. So I went home and after some thought came up with this:

ORIENT	OCCIDENT
self-effacing	occasionally opinionated
respectful of authority	sometimes independent
worried about others' opinions	now and then carefree
usually quiet	talkative (with a drink or two)
always trying to please	once or twice have not given a damn
teacup is half empty	glass is half full
say yes when I mean no	say what I mean, do what I say
almost always look to the past	once in a while look to the future
prefer to follow	yet yearn to lead
comfortable in a crowd	but ready to take the stage

deferential to elders	value my youth
self-sacrificial	live to fight another day
follow my ancestors	forget my ancestors!
straight black hair	limpid brown eyes
short (for an Occidental)	tall (for an Oriental)
somewhat yellowish white	somewhat palish yellow

When I shared this exercise with him the next day, he said, Splendid! A fine beginning. You are a good student, as all Orientals are. Despite myself, I felt a small surge of pride. Like all good students, I yearned for nothing but approval, even from fools. But there is a drawback, he continued. See how so many of the Oriental qualities diametrically oppose the Occidental? In the West, many Oriental qualities unfortunately take on a negative cast. This leads to the severe problems of identity suffered by Americans of Oriental ancestry, at least those born or raised here. They feel themselves out of place. They are not so different from yourself, also split down the middle. What, then, is the cure? Is the Oriental in the West to feel forever homeless, a stranger, a foreigner, no matter how many generations lived on the soil of Judeo-Christian culture, never able to do away with the Confucian residue of his ancient, noble heritage? This is where you, as the Amerasian, offer hope.

I knew he meant to be kind, so I did my best to keep a straight face. Me?

Yes, you! You embody the symbiosis of Orient and Occident, the possibility that out of two can come one. We can no more separate the physical Oriental from you than we can separate the physical Occidental. Likewise with your psychic components. But while you are out of place today, in the future you will be the average! Look at my Amerasian child. A hundred years ago, he would have been seen as a monstrosity, whether in China or in America. Today, the Chinese would still see him as anomalous, but here we have made steady progress forward, not as fast as you or I would like, yet enough to hope that when he reaches your age no opportunity will be denied him. Born on this soil, he could even be president! There are more of you and he than you can probably imagine, but most are ashamed and seek to disappear in the foliage of American life. But your numbers are growing, and democracy gives you the best chance of finding your voice. Here you can learn how not to be torn apart by your opposing sides, but rather to balance them and benefit from both. Reconcile your divided allegiances and you will be the ideal translator between two sides, a goodwill ambassador to bring opposing nations to peace!

Me?

Yes, you! You must assiduously cultivate those reflexes that Americans have learned innately, in order to counter-weigh your Oriental instincts.

I couldn't help myself any longer. Like yin and yang?

Exactly!

I cleared my throat of a sour taste, the gastric reflux of my confused Oriental and Occidental insides. Professor?

Hmm?

Would it make any difference if I told you I was actually Eurasian, not Amerasian?

The Chair regarded me kindly and took out his pipe. No, dear boy, absolutely not.

On the way home, I stopped off at the grocery store and bought white bread, salami, a plastic liter of vodka, corn-starch, and iodine. I would have preferred rice starch for sentiment's sake, but cornstarch was easier to obtain. Once home, I put away the groceries and stuck the paper with my divided self to the refrigerator. Even poor people in America had refrigerators, not to mention running water, flush toilets, and twenty-four-hour electricity, amenities that even some of the middle class did not have back home. Why, then, did I feel poor? Perhaps it had something to do with my living situation. Home was a dismal one-bedroom, first-floor apart-ment whose most characteristic feature was the pervasive odor of belly lint, or so I wrote to my aunt. On that day as on every day previously, I found Bon listless with grief on the long tongue of our red velour sofa. The only time he left was to tend to his part-time night job as janitor for the Reverend R-r-r-r-amon's church, which aimed to save money while saving souls. To that end, and proving that one could serve God and Mammon at the same time, the church paid Bon his wages in untaxable cash. With no reportable income, Bon was eligible for welfare, which he received with only a marginal degree of shame and a considerable sense of entitlement. Having served his country for a pittance, fight-ing an American-determined war, he sensibly concluded that welfare was a better reward than a medal. He had no choice but to accept his lot, for no one had a need for a man who could jump out of airplanes, hump thirty miles with eighty pounds of kit, nail a bull's-eye with pistol and rifle, and absorb more punishment than one of those masked and oiled professional wrestlers on television.

On days when Bon collected the government handout, days like today, he spent the cash on a case of beer and the food stamps on a week's supply of frozen meals. I opened the refrigerator to collect my beer ration and joined Bon in the living room, where he had already machine-gunned himself with a half-dozen cans, the empty shells scattered on the carpet. He was on his back on the couch, holding another cold can to his forehead. I dropped into the nicest piece of furniture we had, a patched but serviceable La-Z-Boy recliner, and switched on the television. The beer had the color and taste of baby's pee, but we followed our usual routine and drank with joyless discipline until we both passed out. I woke up in the perineum of time between the very late hours of the evening and the very early hours of the morning, grotty sponge in my mouth, frightened by the severed head of a gigantic insect gaping its jaws at me until I realized it was only the wood-paneled television, its twin antennae drooping. The national anthem blared as the Stars and Stripes waved and blended with sweeping shots of majestic purple mountains and soaring fighter jets. When the curtain of static and snow finally fell on the screen, I dragged myself to the mossy, toothless mouth of the toilet, then to the lower rack of the bunk beds in the narrow bedroom. Bon had already found his way to the upper rack. I lay down and imagined we slumbered like soldiers even though the only place near Chinatown where one could buy bunk beds was the children's section of gaudy furniture stores, overseen by Mexicans or people who looked like Mexicans. I could not tell anyone from the Southern Hemisphere apart but assumed they would take no offense, given that they themselves called me Chino to my face.

An hour passed but I was unable to return to sleep. I went to the kitchen and ate a salami sandwich while I reread the letter from my aunt that had arrived yesterday. *Dear nephew,* she wrote, *thanks so much for your last letter. The weather has been terrible recently, very chilly and windy.* The letter detailed her struggles with her roses, the customers at her shop, the positive outcome of her doctor's visit, but nothing was as important as the signal about the weather, telling me that between the lines was a message from Man in an invisible ink concocted from rice starch. Tomorrow, when Bon was gone for his few hours to clean the reverend's church, I would make a solution of iodine in water that I would brush onto the letter to reveal a series of numbers in purple ink. They referred to page, line, and word of Richard Hedd's *Asian Communism and the Oriental Mode of Destruction,* the cipher Man had so artfully chosen and now the most important book in my life. From Man's invisible messages, I had learned that the spirits of the people were high, that the rebuilding of the country was progressing slowly but surely, and that his superiors were pleased with my reporting. Why would they not be? Nothing was happening among the exiles except tearing of hair and gnashing of teeth. I hardly needed to write that in the invisible ink I would make from cornstarch and water.

Somewhat hungover and somewhat sentimental, this month being the first anniversary of Saigon's fall, or liberation, or both, I wrote my aunt a letter to commemorate a year's worth of tribulation. Although I left as much by choice as by circumstance, I confess that I could not help but feel pity for my sorry countrymen, their germs of loss passed back and forth until I, too, walked around light-headed in the fog bank of memory. *My dear aunt, so much has happened.* The letter was a rambling history of the exiles since their departure from camp, told from their teary-eyed point of view, the telling of which stirred tears in me as well. I wrote about how none of us was released without the helping hand of a sponsor, whose job it was to guarantee that we would not become dependent on the welfare state. Those among us without immediate benefactors wrote pleading letters to companies that once employed us, to soldiers who once advised us, to lovers who once slept with us, to churches that might take pity, even to the merest of acquaintances, hoping for sponsorship. Some of us left alone, some of us left as families, some of our families were divvied up and parceled out, some of us got to stay in warm western climes that reminded us of home, but most were dispatched far away to states whose names we could not wrap our tongues around: Alabama, Arkansas, Georgia, Kentucky, Missouri, Montana, South Carolina, and so on. We spoke of our new geography in our own version of English, each syllable stressed, Chicago becoming *Chick-ah-go*, New York pronounced closer to *New-ark*, Texas broken down to *Tex-ass*, California now *Ca-li*. Before leaving camp, we exchanged the phone numbers and addresses of our new destinations, knowing we would need the refugee telegraph system to discover which city had the best jobs, which state had the lowest taxes, where the best welfare benefits were, where the least racism was, where the most people who looked like us and ate like us lived.

If allowed to stay together, I told my aunt, we could have incorporated ourselves into a respectably sized, self-sufficient colony, a pimple on the buttocks of the American body politic, with ready-made politicians, police officers, and soldiers, with our own bankers, salesmen, and engineers, with doctors, lawyers, and accountants, with cooks, cleaners, and maids, with factory owners, mechanics, and clerks, with thieves, prostitutes, and murderers, with writers, singers, and actors, with geniuses, teachers, and the insane, with priests, nuns, and monks, with Buddhists, Catholics, and the Cao Dai, with people from the north, the center, and the south, with the talented, the mediocre, and the stupid, with patriots, traitors, and neutralists, with the honest, the corrupt, and the indifferent, sufficiently collective to elect our own representative to the Congress and have a voice in our America, a Little Saigon as delightful, delirious, and dysfunctional as the original, which was exactly why we were not allowed to stay together but were instead dispersed by bureaucratic fiat to all the longitudes and latitudes of our new world. Wherever we found ourselves, we found each other, small clans gathering in basements, in churches, in

backyards on the weekends, at beaches where we brought
our own food and drink in grocery bags rather than buying from the more expensive concessions. We did our best
to conjure up the culinary staples of our culture, but since
we were dependent on Chinese markets our food had an
unacceptably Chinese tinge, another blow in the gauntlet
of our humiliation that left us with the sweet-and-sour taste
of unreliable memories, just correct enough to evoke the
past, just wrong enough to remind us that the past was forever gone, missing along with the proper variety, subtlety,
and complexity of our universal solvent, fish sauce. Oh, fish
sauce! How we missed it, dear Aunt, how nothing tasted
right without it, how we longed for the grand cru of Phu
Quoc Island and its vats brimming with the finest vintage
of pressed anchovies! This pungent liquid condiment of the
darkest sepia hue was much denigrated by foreigners for its
supposedly horrendous reek, lending new meaning to the
phrase "there's something fishy around here," for we were
the fishy ones. We used fish sauce the way Transylvanian
villagers wore cloves of garlic to ward off vampires, in our
case to establish a perimeter with those Westerners who
could never understand that what was truly fishy was the
nauseating stench of cheese. What was fermented fish compared to curdled milk?

But out of deference to our hosts we kept our feelings
to ourselves, sitting close to one another on prickly sofas
and scratchy carpets, our knees touching under crowded
kitchen tables on which sat crenellated ashtrays measur-
ing time's passage with the accumulation of ashes, chewing

on dried squid and the cud of remembrance until our jaws ached, trading stories heard second- and thirdhand about our scattered countrymen. This was the way we learned of the clan turned into slave labor by a farmer in Modesto, and the naive girl who flew to Spokane to marry her GI sweetheart and was sold to a brothel, and the widower with nine children who went out into a Minnesotan winter and lay down in the snow on his back with mouth open until he was buried and frozen, and the ex-Ranger who bought a gun and dispatched his wife and two children before killing himself in Cleveland, and the regretful refugees on Guam who petitioned to go back to our homeland, never to be heard from again, and the spoiled girl seduced by heroin who disappeared into the Baltimore streets, and the politician's wife demoted to cleaning bedpans in a nursing home who one day snapped, attacked her husband with a kitchen knife, then was committed to a mental ward, and the quartet of teenagers who arrived without families and fell in together in Queens, robbing two liquor stores and killing a clerk before being imprisoned for twenty years to life, and the devout Buddhist who spanked his young son and was arrested for child abuse in Houston, and the proprietor who accepted food stamps for chopsticks and was fined for breaking the law in San Jose, and the husband who slapped his wife and was jailed for domestic violence in Raleigh, and the men who had escaped but left wives behind in the chaos, and the women who had escaped but left husbands behind, and the children who had escaped without parents and grandparents, and the families missing one, two, three, or more children, and the half dozen who went to sleep in a crowded, freezing room in Terre Haute with a charcoal brazier for heat and never woke up, borne to permanent darkness on an invisible cloud of carbon monoxide. Sifting through the dirt, we panned for gold, the story of the baby orphan adopted by a Kansas billionaire, or the mechanic who bought a lottery ticket in Arlington and became a multimillionaire, or the girl elected president of her high school class in Baton Rouge, or the boy accepted by Harvard from Fond du Lac, the soil of Camp Pendleton still in the tracks of his sneakers, or the movie star you love so much, dear Aunt, who circled the world from airport to airport, no country letting her in after the fall of Saigon, none of her American movie star friends returning her desperate phone calls until with her last dime she snagged Tippi Hedren, who flew her to Hollywood. So it was that we soaped ourselves in sadness and we rinsed ourselves with hope, and for all that we believed almost every rumor we heard, almost all of us refused to believe that our nation was dead.

CHAPTER 5

Having read many confessions myself, and bearing in mind your notes on what I have confessed thus far, I suspect, my dear Commandant, that this confession is not what you are most likely used to reading. I cannot blame you for the unusual qualities of my confession—only me. I am guilty of honesty, which was rarely the case in my adult life. Why begin now, in these circumstances, a solitary chamber of three by five meters? Perhaps because I do not understand why I am here. At least when I was a sleeper agent, I understood why I had to live my life in code. But not now. If I am to be condemned—if I am already condemned, as I suspect—then I will do no less than explain myself, in a style of my own choosing, regardless of how you might consider my actions.

I should get credit, I think, for the real dangers and petty bothers that I endured. I lived like a bonded servant, a refugee whose only job perk was the opportunity to receive welfare. I barely even had the opportunity to sleep, since a sleeper agent is almost constantly afflicted with insomnia.

Perhaps James Bond could slumber peacefully on the bed of nails that was a spy's life, but I could not. Ironically, it was my most spy-like task to date that could always put me to sleep, the decoding of Man's messages and the encoding of my own in invisible ink. As each dispatch was painstakingly coded word by word, it behooved sender and receiver to keep messages as brief as possible, and the one that I decoded the next evening from Man said simply: *Good work*, *Deflect attention from yourself*, and *All subversives now detained.*

I saved encoding my response until after the grand opening of the General's liquor store, which, the General said, Claude would be attending. We had spoken a few times by phone but I had not seen Claude since Saigon. There was another reason the General wanted to see me in person, however, or so Bon reported a few days later on returning from the store. He had just been hired as the store's clerk, a job he could manage while also cleaning the reverend's church part-time. I had urged the General to hire Bon, and was glad that he would now spend more hours on his feet than on his back. What does he want to see me for? I said. Bon opened the refrigerator's arthritic jaw and extracted the most beautiful decorative object in our possession, a gleaming silver cylinder of Schlitz. There's an informer in the ranks. Beer?

I'll take two.

The grand opening would be at the end of April, timed to coincide with the anniversary of the fall, or liberation, or both, of Saigon. It fell on a Friday, and I had to ask Ms. Mori, she of the sensible shoes, if I could leave work early.

Although I would not have asked for this favor in September, by April our relationship had taken an unexpected turn. In the months after I started working with her, we had gradually surveilled each other on smoking breaks, on the chats that naturally occur between office mates, and then after work at cocktail hours far from campus. Ms. Mori was not as hostile to me as I had supposed. In fact, we had become rather friendly, if that was the word to describe the sweaty, condomless intercourse we engaged in once or twice per week at her apartment in the Crenshaw neighborhood, the furtive fornication committed once or twice per week in the Department Chair's office, and the nocturnal relations staged on the squeaky backseat of my Ford.

As she explained after our first romantic interlude, it was my reasonable, kind, good-hearted manner that had eventually persuaded her to invite me for a drink "whenever." I had taken up the invitation a few days later at a tiki bar in Silver Lake, frequented by heavyset men in Hawaiian shirts and women whose denim skirts barely harnessed their generous rumps. Flaming tiki torches flanked the entrance, while inside, ominous masks of some unknown Pacific Island origin were pinned to the planked wall, their lips seeming to say, *Ooga booga*. Table lamps in the shape of bare-breasted, brown-skinned hula girls in grass skirts cast an ambient glow. The waitress likewise wore a grass skirt whose faded straw color matched her hair, her bikini top fashioned from polished coconuts. Sometime after our third round, Ms. Mori cupped her chin with her right hand, elbow on the bar, and allowed me to light her cigarette, which, in my opinion,

was one of the most erotic acts of foreplay a man can perform
for a woman. She drank and smoked like a movie starlet
from a screwball comedy, one of those dames with padded
bras and shoulder pads who spoke in a second language of
innuendo and double entendre. Looking me in the eye, she
said, I have a confession. I smiled and hoped my dimples
impressed her. I like confessions, I said. There's something
mysterious about you, she said. Don't get me wrong, it's not
that you're tall, dark, and handsome. You're just dark and
sort of cute. At first, hearing about you and meeting you the
first time, I thought, *Great, here's an Uncle Tom-a-san, a real
sellout, a total whitewash. He's not a cracker, but he's close. He's
a rice cracker.* The way you get along with the gaijin! White
people love you, don't they? They only *like* me. They think
I'm a dainty little china doll with bound feet, a geisha who's
ready to please. But I don't talk enough for them to love me,
or at least I don't talk the right way. I can't put on the whole
sukiyaki-and-sayonara show they love, the chopsticks in the
hair kind of mumbo jumbo, all that Suzie Wong bullshit,
like every white man who comes along is William Holden
or Marlon Brando, even if he looks like Mickey Rooney. You,
though. You can talk, and that counts for a lot. But it's not
just that. You're a great listener. You've mastered the inscru-
table Oriental smile, sitting there nodding and wrinkling
your brow sympathetically and letting people go on, thinking you're perfectly in agreement with everything they say,
all without saying a word yourself. What do you say to that?

Ms. Mori, I said, I am shocked by what I am hearing. I'll
bet, she said. Call me Sofia, for Chrissakes. I'm not your

girlfriend's over-the-hill mother. Get me another drink and light me another cigarette. I'm forty-six years old and I don't care who knows it, but what I will tell you is that when a woman is forty-six and has lived her life the way she's wanted to live it, she knows everything there is to know about what to do in the sack. It's got nothing to do with the *Kama Sutra* or *The Carnal Prayer Mat* or any of that Oriental hocus-pocus of our beloved Department Chair. You've worked for him for six years, I said. And don't I know it, she said. Is it just my imagination, or does every time he opens the door to his office a gong goes off somewhere? And does he smoke tobacco in his office, or is that incense in his bowl? I can't help but feel he's a little disappointed in me because I don't bow whenever I see him. When he interviewed me, he wanted to know whether I spoke any Japanese. I explained that I was born in Gardena. He said, Oh, you nisei, as if knowing that one word means he knows something about me. You've forgotten your culture, Ms. Mori, even though you're only second generation. Your issei parents, they hung on to their culture. Don't you want to learn Japanese? Don't you want to visit Nippon? For a long time I felt bad. I wondered why I didn't want to learn Japanese, why I didn't already speak Japanese, why I would rather go to Paris or Istanbul or Barcelona rather than Tokyo. But then I thought, *Who cares?* Did anyone ask John F. Kennedy if he spoke Gaelic and visited Dublin or if he ate potatoes every night or if he collected paintings of leprechauns? So why are *we* supposed to not forget *our* culture? Isn't my culture right here since I was born here? Of course I didn't ask him those questions.

I just smiled and said, You're so right, sir. She sighed. It's a job. But I'll tell you something else. Ever since I got it straight in my head that I haven't forgotten a damn thing, that I damn well know my culture, which is American, and my language, which is English, I've felt like a spy in that man's office. On the surface, I'm just plain old Ms. Mori, poor little thing who's lost her roots, but underneath, I'm Sofia and you better not fuck with me.

I cleared my throat. Ms. Mori?

Hmm?

I think I'm falling in love with you.

It's Sofia, she said. And let's get one thing straight, playboy. If we get involved, and that's a big if, there are no strings attached. You do not fall in love with me and I do not fall in love with you. She exhaled twin plumes of smoke. Just so you know, I do not believe in marriage but I do believe in free love.

What a coincidence, I said. So do I.

According to Benjamin Franklin, as Professor Hammer taught me a decade ago, an older mistress was a wonderful thing, or so the Founding Father advised a younger man. I can't recall the entire substance of the American Sage's letter, only two points. The first: older mistresses were "so grateful!!" Perhaps true of many, but not of Ms. Mori. If anything, she expected me to be grateful, and I was. I had been resigned to the consolation of man's best friend, i.e., self-pleasure, and certainly did not possess the wherewithal to consort with prostitutes. Now I had free love, its existence an affront not only to a capitalism corseted, or perhaps chastity-locked, by its ethnic Protestant justifications, but also alien to a communism with Confucian character. This is one of the drawbacks to communism that I hope will eventually pass, the belief that every comrade is supposed to behave like a noble peasant whose hard hoe is devoted only to farming. Under Asian communism, everything but sex is free, since the sexual revolution has not yet happened in the East. The reasoning is that if one has enough sex to produce six or eight or a dozen offspring, as is generally the case for families in Asian countries (according to Richard Hedd), one hardly needs a revolution for more sex. Meanwhile, Americans, vaccinated against one revolution and thus resistant to another, are interested only in free love's tropical sizzle, not its political fuse. Under Ms. Mori's patient tutelage, however, I began to realize that true revolution also involved sexual liberation.

This insight was not so far off from Mr. Franklin's. That sly old sybarite was well aware of the importance of the erotic to the political, wooing the ladies as much as the politicians in his bid for French assistance to the American Revolution. Therefore the gist of the First American's letter to his young friend was correct: we should all have older mistresses. This is not as sexist as it sounds, for the implication was that older women should also bed younger studs. And if subtlety was not always present in the Old Goat's missive, the randy truth was. Thus our fine man's second point, namely that the gravity of age worked its way from the top downward with the years. This commenced with the facial features, then crept south to the neck, the breasts, the tummy, etc., so that an older mistress was plump and juicy where it counted long after her visage was dry and haggard, in which case one could simply put a basket on her head.

But there was no such need in Ms. Mori's case, as her features were pleasantly ageless. The only thing that could have made me happier was a companion for Bon, who, so far as I knew, was also practicing his solo stroke. Always a shy one, he swallowed his pill of Catholicism seriously. He was more embarrassed and discreet about sex than about things I thought more difficult, like killing people, which pretty much defined the history of Catholicism, where sex of the homo, hetero, or pederastic variety supposedly never happened, hidden underneath the Vatican's cassocks. Popes, cardinals, bishops, priests, and monks carrying on with women, girls, boys, and each other? Hardly ever discussed! Not that there was anything wrong with carrying on—it's hypocrisy that stinks, not sex. But the Church torturing, murdering, crusading against, or infecting with disease millions of people in the name of our Lord the Savior, from Arabia to the Americas? Acknowledged with useless, pious regret, if even that.

As for me, it was the reverse. Ever since my fevered adolescence I had enjoyed myself with athletic diligence, using the same hand with which I crossed myself in mock prayer. This seed of sexual rebellion one day matured into my political revolution, disregarding all my father's sermons about how onanism inevitably led to blindness, hairy palms, and impotence (he forgot to mention subversion). If I was going to Hell, so be it! Having made my peace with sinning against myself, sometimes on an hourly basis, it was only due time before I sinned with others. So it was that I committed my first unnatural act at thirteen with a gutted squid purloined from my mother's kitchen, where it awaited its proper fate along with its companions. Oh, you poor, innocent, mute squid! You were the length of my hand, and when stripped of head, tentacles, and guts possessed the comely shape of a condom, not that I knew what that was then. Inside, you had the smooth, viscous consistency of what I imagined to be a vagina, not that I had ever seen such a marvelous thing besides those exhibited by the toddlers and infants wandering around totally naked or naked from the waist down in my town's lanes and yards. This sight scandalized our French overlords, who saw this childhood nudity as evidence of our barbarism, which then justified their raping, pillaging, and looting, all sanctioned in the holy name of getting our children to wear some clothes so they would not be so tempting to decent Christians whose spirit and flesh were both in question. But I digress! Back to you, soon-to-be-ravished squid: when I poked my index and then middle finger inside your tight orifice, just out of curiosity, the suction was such that my restless imagination could not help but make the connection with the verboten female body part that had obsessed me for the past few months. Without bidding, and utterly beyond my control, my maniacal manhood leaped to attention, luring me forward to you, inviting, bewitching, come-hither squid! Although my mother would return soon from her errand, and while at any moment a neighbor might have walked by the lean-to of our kitchen and caught me with my cephalopodic bride, I nevertheless dropped my trousers. Hypnotized by my squid's call and my erection's response, I inserted the latter into the former, which was, unfortunately, a perfect fit. Unfortunate because from then onward no squid was safe from me, not to say that this diluted form of bestiality—after all, hapless squid, you were dead, though I now see how that raises other moral questions—not to say this transgression occurred often, since squid was a rare treat in our landlocked town. My father had given my mother the squid as a gift, as he himself ate well. Priests always had much attention lavished on them by their starstruck fans, those devout housewives and wealthy congregants who treated them as if they were guardians of the velvet rope blocking entrance into that ever so exclusive nightclub, Heaven. These fans invited them to dinner, cleaned their chambers, cooked their food, and bribed them with gifts of various kinds, including delectable, expensive seafood not meant for the likes of a poor woman like my mother. While I felt no shame at all for my shuddering ejaculation, an enormous burden of guilt fell on me as soon as my senses returned, not because of any moral violation, but because I could hardly bear depriving my mother of even a morsel of squid. We had only a half dozen, and she would notice one missing. What to do? What to do? A plan instantly came to my devious mind as I stood with the befuddled, deflowered squid in hand, my blasphemy leaking from its molested vulva. First, rinse the evidence of crime from the inert, abused squid. Second, cut shallow scars onto the skin to identify the victim squid. Then wait for dinner. My innocent mother returned to our miserable hut, stuffed the squid with ground pork, bean thread noodle, diced mushroom, and chopped ginger, then fried and served them with a ginger-lime dipping sauce. There on the plate reclined my beloved, forlorn odalisque, marked by my hand, and when my mother said to help myself I seized it instantly with my chopsticks to forestall any chance of my mother doing so. I paused, my mother's expectant, loving eyes upon me, and then I dipped the squid into the ginger-lime sauce and took the first bite. Well? she said. De-de-delicious, I stammered. Good, but you should chew it rather than swallow it whole, son. Take your time. It will taste better that way. Yes, Mama, I said. And, bravely smiling, this obedient son slowly chewed and savored the rest of his defiled squid, its salty flavor mixed with his mother's sweet love.

Some will undoubtedly find this episode obscene. Not I! Massacre is obscene. Torture is obscene. Three million dead is obscene. Masturbation, even with an admittedly nonconsensual squid? Not so much. I, for one, am a person who believes that the world would be a better place if the word "murder" made us mumble as much as the word "masturbation." Still, while I was more lover than fighter, my political choices and police service eventually did force me to cultivate a side of myself I had used only once in my childhood, the violent side. Even as a secret policeman, however, I never used violence insomuch as I allowed others to use it in front of me. Only when unfavorable conditions squeezed me into situations from which my cleverness could not extract me did I permit this violence to happen. These situations were so unpleasant that the memories of those whom I had seen interrogated continued to hijack me with fanatic persistence: the wiry Montagnard with a wire twisted around his neck and a twisted grimace on his face; the stubborn terrorist in his white room and with his purple face, impervious to everything except the one thing; the communist agent with the papier-mâché evidence of her espionage crammed into her mouth, our sour names literally on the tip of her tongue. These captured subversives had only one destination, but there were many unpleasant side roads to get there. When I arrived at the liquor store for the grand opening, I shared with these prisoners the dread certainty that snickered beneath the card tables of retirement homes. Someone was going to die. Perhaps me.

The liquor store was on the eastern end of Hollywood Boulevard, far from the camera-popping glamour of the Egyptian and Chinese theaters where the latest movies premiered. This particularly unfashionable neighborhood was a shady one despite the absence of trees, and Bon's other function, besides clerking, was to intimidate any would-be robbers and shoplifters. He nodded at me impassively from the cash register, standing before a wall with shelves displaying primo brands, theft-worthy pint bottles, and, in a discreet corner, men's magazines with airbrushed Lolitas on their covers. Claude's in the storeroom with the General, Bon said. The storeroom was in the back, abuzz with overhead fluorescent lights, smelling of disinfectant and old cardboard. Claude rose from his vinyl chair and we embraced.

He was heavier by a few pounds but otherwise unchanged, even wearing a rumpled sport jacket he used on occasion in Saigon.

Have a seat, the General said from behind his desk. The vinyl chairs squeaked obscenely when we moved. Cartons and crates hemmed us in on three sides. The General's desk was cluttered with a rotary-dial phone heavy enough for self-defense, a stamp pad bleeding red ink, a receipt book with a blue sheet of carbon paper tucked between the pages, and a desk lamp with a broken neck, its head refusing to stay raised. When the General opened his desk drawer, my heart choked. Here it was! The moment when the rat would get a hammer to the head, a knife to the neck, a bullet in the temple, or possibly all of the above just for the fun of it. At least it would be quick, relatively speaking. Back in the European Dark Ages, according to the interrogation course that Claude had taught to the secret policemen in Saigon, I would have been drawn and quartered by horses, my head stuck on a pole for all to see. One royal humorist flayed his enemy alive and then stuffed the skin with straw, mounted it on a horse, and paraded it around town. What a laugh! I stopped breathing and waited for the General to pull out the pistol with which he was going to remove my brains in an unsurgical fashion, but all he extracted was a bottle of scotch and a pack of cigarettes.

Well, said Claude, I wish we were reuniting in better circumstances, gentlemen. I heard you had a hell of a time getting out of Dodge. That, the General said, is putting it mildly. And yourself? I said. I bet you got out on the last helicopter.

Let's not be too dramatic, Claude said. He accepted the General's offer of a cigarette and a tumbler of scotch. I got out a few hours earlier on the ambassador's helicopter. He sighed. I'm never going to forget that day. We waited too damn long to get our act together. You were the last ones out on airplanes. The marines flew in on helicopters to get the rest of the people from the airport and the embassy. Air America was flying rescue choppers, too, but the problem was that everyone in town knew about our supposedly secret helipads. Turns out that we'd enlisted little Vietnamese ladies to paint those helipad numbers on the roofs. Smart, huh? Come the moment of truth, all those buildings were surrounded. The ones who were supposed to get to the helicopters couldn't get to them. Same story at the airport, no way in. The docks, totally impassable. Even the buses going to the embassy couldn't get in, since the embassy was mobbed by thousands. They were waving all kinds of paper. Marriage certificates, employment contracts, letters, even US passports. They were screaming. I know So-and-So, So-and-So can vouch for me, I'm married to a US citizen. None of that counted. The marines were on the wall and pounding anybody who tried to come up. You had to get close enough to give a marine a thousand dollars before he'd haul you up. We'd go up to the wall or to the gate every now and then and look for the people who worked for us and we'd point them out. If they got close, the marines yanked them up or opened the gates a bit to let just that person in. But sometimes we'd see people we knew in the middle of the crowd or on the fringes, and we'd wave at them to get to the wall, but they couldn't. All those Vietnamese in front weren't letting any Vietnamese in back get ahead. So we'd look and wave, and they'd look and wave, and then after a while we just looked away and left. Thank God I couldn't hear them screaming, not over all that ruckus. I'd go back inside and have a drink, but it wasn't any better. You should have heard the radio chatter. Help me, I'm a translator, we have seventy translators at this address, get us out. Help me, we have five hundred people at this compound, get us out. Help me, we have two hundred at logistics, get us out. Help me, we have a hundred at the CIA hotel, get us out. Guess what? None of those people got out. We'd told them to go to those places and wait for us. We had guys at those places and we called them and said, No one's coming. Get yourselves out now and get to the embassy. Leave those people behind. Then there were the people outside the city. Agents all over the countryside were calling in. Help, I'm in Can Tho, the VC are closing in. Help, you left me in the U Minh Forest, what am I going to do, what about my family? Help me, get me out of here. They had no chance in hell. Even some of those in the embassy had no chance. We evacuated thousands, but when the last helicopter took off, there were still four hundred people waiting in the courtyard, all neatly arranged and waiting for helicopters we told them were still coming. None of them got out.

Christ, I need another drink even to talk about this. Thank you, General. He rubbed his eyes. All I can say is, it was personal. After I left you at the airport, I went back to my villa to get some sleep. I'd told Kim to meet me at dawn. She was going to get her family. Six comes along, six fifteen, six thirty, seven. The chief calls me up and wants to know where I am. I put him off. Seven fifteen, seven thirty, eight. The chief calls me back and says, Get your ass down to the embassy now, every man on deck. The hell with the chief, that Hungarian bastard. I grab my guns and drive across town to find Kim. Forget the daytime curfew, everyone was out and running around, trying to find a way out. The suburbs were quieter, though. Life was normal. I even saw Kim's neighbors breaking out the commie flag. The previous week those same people were flying your flag. I asked them where she was. They said they didn't know where the Yankee whore was. I wanted to shoot them then and there, but everybody on the street had turned out to look at me. I sure couldn't wait for the local Viet Cong to come kidnap me. I drove back to the villa. Ten o'clock. She wasn't there. I couldn't wait any longer. I sat in the car and I cried. I haven't cried over a girl in thirty years, but hell, there you have it. Then I drove to the embassy and saw there was no way in. Like I said, thousands of people. I left the keys in the ignition just like you did, General, and I hope some communist son of a bitch is enjoying himself with my Bel Air. Then I fought my way through the crowd. Those Vietnamese who wouldn't let their own fellow Vietnamese through, they made way for me. Sure, I pushed and shoved and screamed, and plenty of them pushed and shoved and screamed right back, but I got closer, even though the closer I got, the tougher it was. I had made eye contact with the marines on the wall, and I knew if I could just get close enough I'd be saved. I was sweating like a pig, my shirt was torn, and all those bodies were packed against me. The people in front of me couldn't see I was an American and no one was turning around just because I was tapping them on the shoulder, so I yanked them by the hair, or pulled them by the ear, or grabbed them by the shirt collar to haul them out of my way. I've never done anything like that in my life. I was too proud to scream at first, but it didn't take long before I was screaming, too. Let me through, I'm an American, goddammit. I finally got myself to that wall, and when those marines reached down and grabbed my hand and pulled me up, I damn near cried again. Claude finished the last of his drink and banged the glass on the desk. I was never so ashamed in my life, but I was also never so goddamn glad to be an American, either.

We sat in silence while the General poured us each another double.

Here's to you, Claude, I said, raising my glass to him. Congratulations.

For what? he said, raising his own.

Now you know what it feels like to be one of us.

His laugh was short and bitter.

I was thinking the exact same thing.

The cue for the evacuation's final phase was "White Christmas," played on American Radio Service, but even this did not go according to plan. First, since the song was top secret information, meant only for the Americans and their allies, everyone in the city also knew what to listen for. Then what do you think happens? Claude said. The deejay can't find the song. The Bing Crosby one. He's tossing his booth looking for that tape, and of course it's not there. Then what? said the General. He finds a version by Tennessee Ernie Ford and plays that. Who's he? I said. How do I know? At least the melody and lyrics were the same. So, I said, situation normal. Claude nodded. All fucked up. Let's just hope history forgets the snafus.

This was the prayer many a general and politician said before they went to bed, but some snafus were more justifiable than others. Take the operation's name, Frequent Wind, a snafu foreshadowing a snafu. I had brooded on it for a year, wondering if I could sue the US government for malpractice, or at least a criminal failure of the literary imagination. Who was the military mastermind who squeezed out Frequent Wind from between his tightly clenched buttocks? Didn't it occur to anyone that Frequent Wind might bring to mind the Divine Wind that inspired the kamikaze, or, more likely for the ahistorical, juvenile set, the phenomenon of passing gas, which, as is well known, can lead to a chain reaction, hence the frequency? Or was I not giving the military mastermind enough credit for being a deadpan ironist, he having also possibly chosen "White Christmas" as a poke in the eye to all my countrymen who neither celebrated Christmas nor had ever seen a white one? Could not this unknown ironist foresee that all the bad air whipped up by American helicopters was the equivalent of a massive blast of gas in the faces of those left behind? Weighing stupidity and irony, I picked the latter, irony lending the Americans a last shred of dignity. It was the only thing salvageable from the tragedy that had befallen us, or that we had brought on ourselves, depending on one's point of view. The problem with this tragedy is that it had not ended neatly, unlike a comedy. It still preoccupied us, the General most of all, who now turned to business.

I am glad you are here, Claude. Your timing could not be more perfect.

Claude shrugged. Timing's one thing I've always been good at, General.

We have a problem, as you warned me before we left.

Which problem? There was more than one, as I recall.

We have an informer. A spy.

Both looked at me, as if for confirmation. I kept my face impassive even as my stomach began to rotate counterclockwise. When the General named a name, it was the crapulent major's. My stomach began to rotate in the opposite direction. I don't know that guy, Claude said.

He is not a man to be known. He is not a remarkable officer. It is our young friend here who chose to bring the major with us.

If you remember, sir, the major—

It hardly matters. What matters is that I was tired and I made a mistake by giving you that job. I do not blame you. I blame myself. Now it is time to correct a mistake.

Why do you think it's this guy?

Number one, he is Chinese. Number two, my contacts

in Saigon say his family is doing very, very well. Number three, he is fat. I do not like fat men.

Just because he's Chinese doesn't mean he's a spy, General.

I am not a racist, Claude. I treat all my men the same, no matter their origins, like our young friend here. But this major, the fact that his family is doing well in Saigon is suspicious. Why are they doing well? Who allows them to prosper? The communists know all our officers and their families. No officer's family is doing well at home. Why his?

Circumstantial evidence, General.

That never stopped you before, Claude.

Things are different here. You have to play by new rules.

But I can bend the rules, can I not?

You can even break them, if you know how.

I tabulated things learned. First, I had scored a coup, much to my chagrin and purely by accident, throwing the blame onto a blameless man. Second, the General had contacts in Saigon, meaning some kind of resistance existed. Third, the General could contact his people, though no direct communication was available. Fourth, the General was fully his old self again, a perennial plotter with at least one scheme in each pocket and another in his sock. Waving his arms to indicate our surroundings, he said, Do I look like a small-business owner to you gentlemen? Do I look like I enjoy selling liquor to drunks and blacks and Mexicans and the homeless and addicts? Let me tell you something. I am just biding my time. This war is not over. Those communist bastards . . . all right, they hurt us badly, we must admit that.

But I know my people. I know my soldiers, my men. They haven't given up. They're willing to fight and die, if they get the chance. That's all we need, Claude. A chance.

Bravo, General, said Claude. I knew you wouldn't stay down for long.

I am with you, sir, I said. To the end.

Good. Because you picked the major. Do you agree that you must correct your mistake? I thought you would. You do not have to do it alone. I have already discussed the problem of the major with Bon. You two will take care of this problem together. I leave it up to your endless imagination and skill to figure out the solution. You have never disappointed me before, except in picking the major. Now you can redeem yourself. Understood? Good. Now leave us. Claude and I have business to discuss.

The store was empty except for Bon, watching the phosphorescent, hypnotic signal of a baseball game on a tiny black-and-white television by the cash register. I cashed the check in my pocket, my tax refund from the IRS. It was not a large sum and yet symbolically significant, for never in my country would the midget-minded government give back to its frustrated citizens anything it had seized in the first place. The whole idea was absurd. Our society had been a kleptocracy of the highest order, the government doing its best to steal from the Americans, the average man doing his best to steal from the government, the worst of us doing our best to steal from each other. Now, despite my sense of fellow feeling for my exiled countrymen, I could not also help but feel that our country was being born again, the accretions of foreign corruption cleansed by revolutionary flames. Instead of tax refunds, the revolution would redistribute ill-gotten wealth, following the philosophy of more to the poor. What the poor did with their socialist succor was up to them. As for me, I used my capitalist refund to buy enough booze to keep Bon and me uneasily steeped in amnesia until next week, which if not foresightful was nevertheless my choice, choice being my sacred American right.

The major? I said as Bon bagged the bottles. You really think he's a spy?

What do I know about it? I'm just a grunt.

You do as you're told.

So do you, smart guy. Since you're so smart, you plan this. You know your way around here better than me. But the dirty stuff you leave to me. Now come and take a look. Behind the counter was a sawed-off, double-barreled shotgun on a rack beneath the cash register. Like it?

How did you get that?

Easier to get a gun here than to vote or drive. You don't even need to know any English. Funny thing is, the major got us the connection. He speaks Chinese. The Chinese gangs are all over Chinatown.

It's going to be messy with a shotgun.

We're not using a shotgun, genius. He opened a cigar box resting on a shelf beneath the counter. Inside was a .38 Special, a revolver with a snub nose, identical to the one that I carried as my service pistol. Delicate enough for you?

Once again I was trapped by circumstances, and once again I would soon see another man trapped by circumstances. The only compensation for my sadness was the expression on Bon's face. It was the first time he had looked happy in a year.

CHAPTER 6

The grand opening began later that afternoon, the General shaking hands with well-wishers while chatting easily and smiling incessantly. Like a shark who must keep swimming to live, a politician—which was what the General had become—had to keep his lips constantly moving. The constituents, in this case, were old colleagues, followers, soldiers, and friends, a platoon of thirty or so middle-aged men whom I had rarely encountered without their uniforms until our time in the refugee camps on Guam. Seeing them again in mufti, a year later, confirmed the verdict of defeat and showed these men now to be guilty of numerous sartorial misdemeanors. They squeaked around the store in bargain-basement penny loafers and creased budget khakis, or in ill-fitting suits advertised by wholesalers for the price of buy-one-get-one-free. Ties, handkerchiefs, and socks were thrown in, though what was really needed was cologne, even of the gigolo kind, anything to mask the olfactory evidence of their having been gleefully skunked by history. As for me, even though I was of lesser rank than most of these men, I was better dressed, thanks to Professor Hammer's hand-me-downs. With just a bit of tailoring, his blue blazer with gold buttons and his gray flannel slacks fit me perfectly.

Thus smartly dressed, I made my way through the men, all of whom I knew in my capacity as the General's aide. Many once commanded artillery batteries and infantry battalions, but now they possessed nothing more dangerous than their pride, their halitosis, and their car keys, if they even owned cars. I had reported all the gossip about these vanquished soldiers to Paris, and knew what they did (or, in many cases, did not do) for a living. Most successful was a general infamous for using his crack troops to harvest cinnamon, whose circulation he monopolized; now this spice merchant lorded over a pizza parlor. One colonel, an asthmatic quartermaster who became unreasonably excited discussing dehydrated rations, was a janitor. A dashing major who flew gunships, now a mechanic. A grizzled captain with a talent for hunting guerrillas: short-order cook. An affectless lieutenant, sole survivor of an ambushed company: deliveryman. So the list went, a fair percentage collecting both welfare and dust, moldering in the stale air of subsidized apartments as their testes shriveled day by day, consumed by the metastasizing cancer called assimilation and susceptible to the hypochondria of exile. In this psychosomatic condition, normal social or familial ills were diagnosed as symptoms of something fatal, with their vulnerable women and children cast as the carriers of Western contamination. Their afflicted kids were talking back, not in their native language but in a foreign tongue they were mastering faster than their fathers. As for the wives, most had been forced to find jobs, and in doing so had been transformed from the winsome lotuses the men remembered them to be. As the crapulent major said, A man doesn't need balls in this country, Captain. The women all have their own.

True, I concurred, though I suspected nostalgia had brainwashed the major and the others. Their memories had been laundered so thoroughly as to be colored differently from mine, for never had they talked so fondly about their wives in Vietnam. Have you ever thought about moving, Major? Maybe you and your wife could get a fresh start and rekindle your romance. Get away from all reminders of your past.

But what would I do for food? he said in all seriousness. The Chinese food is best where we live. I reached forth to straighten his crooked tie, which matched his crooked teeth. All right, Major. Then let me take you out. You can show me where the good Chinese food is.

My pleasure! The crapulent major beamed. He was a bon vivant who loved food and friendship, someone without an enemy in this new world, except for the General. Why had I mentioned the crapulent major's name to him? Why hadn't I given the name of someone whose sins outweighed his flesh, rather than this man whose flesh outweighed his sins? Leaving the major behind, I made my way through the crowd to the General. I was ready for some political boosterism, even of the most calculated kind. He was standing by Madame next to the chardonnay and cabernet, being interviewed by a man waving a microphone between the two of them as if it were a Geiger counter. I caught her eye, and when she amplified the wattage of her smile, the man turned around, a camera hanging around his neck and a retractable pen with four colors of ink peeking from his shirt pocket.

It took a moment for the recognition to register. I had last seen Son Do, or Sonny as he was nicknamed, in 1969, my final year in America. He was likewise a scholarship student at a college in Orange County, an hour away by car. It was the birthplace of the war criminal Richard Nixon, as well as the home of John Wayne, a place so ferociously patriotic I thought Agent Orange might have been manufactured there or at least named in its honor. Sonny's subject of study was journalism, which would have been useful for our country if Sonny's particular brand were not so subversive. He carried a baseball bat of integrity on his shoulder, ready to clobber the fat softballs of his opponents' inconsistencies. Back then, he had been self-confident, or arrogant, depending on your point of view, a legacy of his aristocratic heritage. His grandfather was a mandarin, as he never ceased reminding you. This grandfather inveighed against the French with such volume and acidity that they shipped him on a one-way berth to Tahiti, where, after supposedly befriending a syphilitic Gauguin, he succumbed to either dengue fever or an incurable strain of virulent homesickness. Sonny inherited the utter sense of conviction that motivated his honorable grandfather, who I am sure was insufferable, as most men of utter conviction are. Like a hard-core conservative, Sonny was right about everything, or thought himself so, the key

difference being that he was a naked leftist. He led the antiwar faction of Vietnamese foreign students, a handful of
whom assembled monthly at a sterile room in the student
union or in someone's apartment, passions running hot and
food getting cold. I attended these parties as well as the ones
thrown by the equally compact pro-war gang, differing in
political tone but otherwise totally interchangeable in terms
of food eaten, songs sung, jokes traded, and topics discussed.
Regardless of political clique, these students gulped from
the same overflowing cup of loneliness, drawing together
for comfort like these ex-officers in the liquor store, hoping
for the body heat of fellow sufferers in an exile so chilly even
the California sun could not warm their cold feet.

I heard you were here, too, Sonny said, gripping my hand
and unwrapping a genuine smile. The confidence I remembered so well radiated from his eyes, rendering his ascetic
face with its antiseptic lips attractive. It's great to see you
again, old friend. Old friend? That was not how I recalled
it. Son, Madame interjected, was interviewing us for his
newspaper. I'm the editor, he said, offering me his business
card. The interview will be in our first issue. The General,
flush with good cheer, plucked a chardonnay from the shelf.
Here's a token of appreciation for all your efforts in reviving
the fine art of the fourth estate in our new land, my young
friend. This could not help but prompt my memory of the
journalists to whom we had given the gift of free room and
board, albeit in a jail, for speaking a little too much truth
to power. Perhaps Sonny was thinking the same thing, for
he tried to decline the bottle, conceding only after much

insistence from the General. I commemorated the occasion
with Sonny's hulking Nikon, General and Madame flanking
him while he cupped the bottle that the General grasped by
the neck. Slap that on your front page, the General said by
way of farewell.

Left alone, Sonny and I traded brief synopses of our recent
lives. He had decided to stay after graduation, knowing if he
returned he would likely receive a complimentary airplane
ticket to the tranquil beaches and exclusive, invitation-only
prisons of Poulo Condore, built by the French with characteristic gusto. Before we refugees had arrived last year,
Sonny had been reporting for an Orange County newspaper,
making his home in a town I had never visited, Westminster,
or, as our countrymen pronounced it, *Wet-min-ter*. Moved
by our refugee plight, he started up the first newspaper in
our native tongue, an effort to tie us together with the news
that binds. But more later, my friend, he said, grasping me by
the shoulder. I have another appointment. Shall we meet for
coffee? It does my heart good to see you again. Bemused, I
agreed, giving him my number before he departed through
the thinning crowd. I looked for the crapulent major but he
had disappeared. Except for him, most of our fellow exiles
had been shrunken by their experience, either absolutely
through the aforementioned maladies of migration, or relatively, surrounded by Americans so tall they neither looked
through nor looked down on these newcomers. They simply
looked over them. For Sonny, it was the opposite. He could
not be ignored, but for different reasons from those in the
past, in our college days. I could not remember him being

as gentle or generous then, when he pounded on tables and ranted the way the Vietnamese foreign students in Paris in the twenties and thirties must have done, the original crop of communists to lead our revolution. I, too, differed in behavior now, although how so was subject to the vagaries of my memory. The historical record had been expunged, for while I kept journals as a student, I had burned them all before returning, fearing to bring with me any incriminating traces of what I really thought.

I breakfasted with the crapulent major a week later. It was an earthy, quotidian scene, the kind Walt Whitman would have loved to write about, a sketch of the new America featuring hot rice porridge and fried crullers at a Monterey Park noodle shop crammed full of unrepentantly unassimilated Chinese and a few other assorted Asians. Grease glazed the orange Formica tabletop, while chrysanthemum tea stood ready to be poured from a tin pot into chipped teacups the color and texture of the enamel on human teeth. I supped in a measured fashion while the major gorged with the undisciplined enthusiasm of a man enamored with food, mouth open and talking simultaneously, the occasional fleck of spit or rice landing on my cheek, my eyelash, or my own bowl, eating with such relish I could not help but love and pity the man in his innocence.

This, an informant? Hard to believe, but then he might be such a sly character as to be the perfect plant. The more logical conclusion was that the General had bolstered the

Vietnamese tendency for conspiracy with the American trait of paranoia, admittedly with my help. Never had the crapulent major exhibited any particular skill at deceit, covert maneuvering, or politicking. Back in Saigon, his function in the Special Branch had been to analyze Chinese-language communication and to keep track of the subterranean subterfuges of Cholon, where the National Liberation Front had constructed an underground network for political agitation, terrorist organizing, and black market smuggling. More important, he was my source for the best Chinese food in Cholon, from majestic palaces with spectacular wedding banquets, to rattling carts roaming the unpaved streets, to elusive ladies who carried their bouncing wares on a yoke across their shoulders and set up shop on the sidewalks. Likewise in California, he had promised me the best rice porridge in Greater Los Angeles, and it was over a silky smooth white pottage that I commiserated with the crapulent major. He was now a gas station attendant in Monterey Park, paid in cash so he could qualify for welfare benefits. His wife, sewing in a sweatshop, was already reduced to nearsightedness from staring so intently at the puzzle of cheap stitching. My God, she can talk, he moaned, hunched over his empty bowl with the reproachful countenance of an unfed dog, eyeing my uneaten cruller. She blames me for everything. Why didn't we stay at home? What are we doing here where we're poorer than before? Why did we have kids we can't afford to feed? I forgot to tell you, Captain, my wife got pregnant in camp. Twins! Can you believe it?

Heart overcast but voice bright, I congratulated him. He appreciated the offer of my untouched cruller. At least they're American citizens, he said, chewing on his doughy treat. Spinach and Broccoli. Those are their American names. To tell you the truth, we hadn't even thought about giving them American names until the nurse asked. I panicked. Of course they needed American names. The first thing that comes to mind is Spinach. I used to laugh at those cartoons where Popeye ate his spinach and became superpowerful all at once. No one will mess with a kid named Spinach. As for Broccoli, it just came logically. A lady on television said, Always eat your broccoli, and I remembered that. A healthy food, not like what I eat. Strong and healthy, that's what these twins will be. They'll need to be. This country isn't for the weak or the fat. I need to go on a diet. No, I do! You're too kind. I am quite aware I'm fat. The only good thing about being fat, besides the eating, is that everyone loves a fat man. Yes? Yes! People love to laugh at fat men and pity them, too. When I applied at that gas station, I was sweating even though I had walked just a couple of blocks. People look at a fat man sweating and they feel sorry for him, even if they feel a little contempt, too. Then I smiled and shook my belly and laughed as I told my story about how I needed a job, and the owner gave it to me on the spot. All he needed was a reason to hire me. Making people laugh and feel sorry always does the trick. See? You're smiling right now and feeling sorry for me. Don't feel too sorry, I have a good shift, in at ten in the morning and out by eight, seven days a week, and I can walk to work from home. I don't do a thing except punch buttons on the cash register. It's great. Come by and I'll give you some free gallons. I insist! It's the least I can do for you helping us escape. I never did properly thank you. Besides, this is a tough country. We Vietnamese have to stick together.

Oh, poor crapulent major! That night, at home, I watched Bon clean and oil the .38 Special on the coffee table, then load it with six copper bullets and lay it on a little throw pillow that came with our sofa, a tawdry, stained red velour cushion on which the pistol rested like a gift to deposed royalty. I'll shoot him through the pillow, Bon said, cracking open a beer. Reduced noise. Great, I said. Richard Hedd was being interviewed on television about the situation in Cambodia, his English accent a stark contrast to the interviewer's Bostonian one. After a minute of watching this, I said, What if he's not a spy? We'll be killing the wrong man. Then it would be murder. Bon sipped his beer. First, he said, the General knows stuff we don't. Second, we're not killing. This is an assassination. Your guys did this all the time. Third, this is war. Innocent people get killed. It's only murder if you know they're innocent. Even so, that's a tragedy, not a crime.

You were happy when the General asked you to do this, weren't you?

Is that bad? he said. He put the beer down and picked up the .38. As some men were born to handle a paintbrush or a pen, he was born to wield a gun. It looked natural in his hand, a tool of which a man could be proud, like a wrench. A man needs a purpose, he said, contemplating the gun.

Before I met Linh, I had purpose. I wanted revenge for my father. Then I fell in love, and Linh became more important than my father or revenge. I hadn't cried since he died, but after my marriage I cried at his grave because I had betrayed him where it mattered the most, in my heart. I didn't get over that until Duc was born. At first he was just this strange, ugly little thing. I wondered what was wrong with me, why I didn't love my own son. But slowly he grew and grew, and one night I noticed how his fingers and toes, his hands and feet, were perfectly made, miniature versions of mine. For the first time in my life I knew what it was to be struck by wonder. Even falling in love was not like that feeling, and I knew that this was how my father must have looked at me. He had created me, and I had created Duc. It was nature, the universe, God, flowing through us. That was when I fell in love with my son, when I understood how insignificant I was, and how marvelous he was, and how one day he'd feel the exact same thing. And it was then I knew I hadn't betrayed my father. I cried again, holding my boy, because I'd finally become a man. What I'm saying, why I'm telling you all this, is that my life once had meaning. It had a purpose. Now it has none. I was a son and a husband and a father and a soldier, and now I'm none of that. I'm not a man, and when a man isn't a man he's nobody. And the only way not to be nobody is to do something. So I can either kill myself or kill someone else. Get it?

I not only got it, I was astonished. It was the longest speech I had ever heard from him, his sorrow and rage and despair not only cracking open his heart but loosening his vocal cords. Those words even succeeded in making him less ugly than he objectively was, if not handsome, emotion softening the harsh features of his face. He was the only man I had ever met who seemed moved, deeply, not only by love but also by the prospect of killing. While he was an expert by necessity, I was a novice by choice, despite having had my opportunities. In our country, killing a man—or a woman, or a child—was as easy as turning a page of the morning paper. One only needed an excuse and an instrument, and too many on all sides possessed both. What I did not have was the desire or the various uniforms of justification a man dons as camouflage—the need to defend God, country, honor, ideology, or comrades—even if, in the last instance, all he really is protecting is that most tender part of himself, the hidden, wrinkled purse carried by every man. These off-the-rack excuses fit some people well, but not me.

I wanted to persuade the General that the crapulent major was no spy, but it would hardly do to disinfect him of the idea with which I had infected him in the first place. More than this, I knew I had to prove to the General that I could correct my ostensible mistake, and that I could be a man of action. Not doing something was not an option, as the General's demeanor made clear to me at our next meeting the following week. He deserves it, the General said, disagreeably obsessed with the indelible stain of guilt he saw stamped on the major's forehead, that tiny handprint of the major's doomed mortality left there by me. But take your time. I'm in no rush. Operations should be performed patiently and painstakingly. He affirmed this in a storeroom that channeled the dispassionate atmosphere of a war room, the walls newly decorated with maps showing our sinuous, narrow-waisted homeland in all its splendor or its parts, each suffocating behind plastic sheeting, red markers dangling on strings next to them. Better to do it well and slowly than quickly and poorly, he said. Yes, sir, I said. What I had in mind was—

No need to bore me with details. Just let me know when it's done.

So the major's demise was written. Nothing was left me but to create a believable story where his death was neither my fault nor the General's. I did not have to think very hard before the most obvious story came to me. What we had here was your usual American tragedy, only this time starring a hapless refugee.

Professor Hammer invited me to dinner the next Saturday night at his house, the occasion being Claude's imminent return to Washington. The only other guest was the professor's boyfriend, Stan, a doctoral student my own age at UCLA, writing his dissertation on the American literary expatriates of Paris. He had the white teeth and blond hair of a model in a toothpaste ad, where his role would be the young father of toothsome cherubs. The professor's homosexuality had been mentioned to me by Claude before I matriculated at the college in '63, because, Claude said, I just didn't want you to be surprised. Never having known a homosexual, I had been curious to see how one behaved in his natural environment, which is to say the West, as the East apparently had no homosexuals. Much to my disappointment, Professor Hammer seemed no different from anyone else, aside from his acute intelligence and impeccable taste in all things, extending to Stan and the culinary arts.

The three-course meal was prepared by the professor himself, a salad of mixed greens, duck confit with rosemary potatoes, and a flaky tarte Tatin, preceded by martinis, accompanied by pinot noir, and finished off with single malt scotch. All was served in the meticulously restored dining room of the professor's Craftsman bungalow in Pasadena, everything from the double-hung windows, to the art deco chandelier, to the brass hardware of the built-in cabinetry either an original from the early twentieth century or a faithful reproduction. Every now and then the professor rose from the dining table and replaced the record on the turntable, choosing a new selection from his extensive jazz collection. Over dinner, we talked about bebop, the nineteenth-century novel, the Dodgers, and America's upcoming bicentennial. Then we repaired with our scotch to the living room with its massive fireplace of river rock and its stately Mission furniture of angular wooden frames and leather cushions. Books of all heights, widths, and colors lined the walls in a democratic parade of individualism, arranged as haphazardly as they were on the walls of the professor's campus office. Ensconced thus by letters, words, sentences, paragraphs, pages, chapters, and tomes, the evening was a pleasant one, memorable for the exchange that took place after we assumed our seats. His nostalgia stimulated, perhaps, by the literature around him, the professor said, I still remember your thesis on *The Quiet American*. That was one of the best undergraduate theses I've ever read. I smiled demurely and said thanks while Claude, sitting beside me on the sofa, snorted. I didn't care too much for that book. The Vietnamese girl, all she does is prepare opium, read picture books, and twitter like a bird. Have you ever met a Vietnamese girl like her? If so, please introduce me. All the ones I meet can't keep their mouths shut in or out of bed.

Oh, Claude, the professor said.

Oh, Claude, nothing. No offense, Avery, but our American friend in that book also happens to look suspiciously like a latent homosexual.

It takes one to smell one, Stan said.

Who wrote that one for you? Noël Coward? His name is Pyle, for God's sake. How many jokes can you make with that name? It's also a pro-communist book. Or at least anti-American. Same thing, anyway. Claude waved his hand at the books, the furniture, the living room, presumably the whole well-appointed home. Hard to believe he was once a communist, isn't it?

Stan? I said.

No, not Stan. Were you, Stan? I thought not.

That left the professor, who shrugged his shoulders when I looked at him. I was your age, he said, putting his arm around Stan's shoulders. I was impressionable, I was passionate, I wanted to change the world. Communism seduced me like so many others.

Now he's the one doing the seducing, Stan said, squeezing the professor's hand, a sight that made me squirm just a little. For me, the professor was a walking mind, and to see him as a body, or having a body, was still discomfiting.

Do you ever regret being a communist, Professor?

No, I do not. Only by making that mistake could I be what I am today.

What is that, sir?

He smiled. I suppose you could call me a born-again American. An irony, but if the bloody history of the past few decades has taught me anything, it's that the defense of freedom demands the muscularity only America can provide. Even what we do at the college has its purpose. We teach you the best of what was thought and said not only to explain America to the world, as I have always encouraged you to do, but to defend it.

I sipped my scotch. It was smoky and smooth, tasting of peat and aged oak, underscored by licorice and the intangible essence of Scottish masculinity. I liked my scotch undiluted, like I liked my truth. Unfortunately, undiluted truth was as affordable as eighteen-year-old single malt scotch. What about those who have not learned the best of what was thought and said? I asked the professor. If we can't teach them, or if they won't be taught?

The professor contemplated the copper depths of his drink. I suppose you and Claude have seen more than your fair share of those types in your line of work. There's no easy answer, except to say it has always been thus. Ever since the first caveman discovered fire and decided that the ones

still living in darkness were benighted, it's been civilization against barbarism . . . with every age having its own
barbarians.

Nothing was more clear-cut than civilization versus barbarism, but what was the killing of the crapulent major? A
simple act of barbarism or a complex one that advanced revolutionary civilization? It had to be the latter, a contradictory
act that suited our age. We Marxists believe that capitalism
generates contradictions and will fall apart from them, but
only if men take action. But it was not just capitalism that
was contradictory. As Hegel said, tragedy was not the conflict between right and wrong but right and right, a dilemma
none of us who wanted to participate in history could escape.
The major had the right to live, but I was right to kill him.
Wasn't I? When Claude and I left near midnight, I came as
close as I could to broaching the subject of my conscience
with him. As we smoked farewell cigarettes on the sidewalk,
I asked the question that I imagined my mother asking of
me: What if he's innocent?

He blew a smoke ring, just to show he could. No one's
innocent. Especially in this business. You don't think he
might have some blood on his hands? He identified Viet
Cong sympathizers. He might have gotten the wrong man.
It's happened before. Or if he himself is a sympathizer, then
he definitely identified the wrong people. On purpose.

I don't know any of that for sure.

Innocence and guilt. These are cosmic issues. We're all
innocent on one level and guilty on another. Isn't that what
Original Sin is all about?

True enough, I said. I let him go with a handshake. The airing of moral doubts was as tiresome as the airing of domestic squabbles, no one really interested except for the ones directly involved. In this situation, I was clearly the only one involved, except for the crapulent major, and no one cared to hear his opinion. Claude, meanwhile, had offered me absolution, or at least an excuse, but I did not have the heart to tell him I could not use it. Original Sin was simply too unoriginal for someone like me, born from a father who spoke of it at every Mass.

The next evening I began reconnoitering the major. On that Sunday and the following five, from May until the end of June, I parked my car half a block from the gas station, waiting for eight o'clock when the crapulent major would leave, walking slowly home, lunch box in hand. When I saw him turn the corner, I started the car and drove it to the corner, where I waited and watched him walk down the first block. He lived three blocks away, a distance a thin, healthy man could walk briskly in five minutes. It took the crapulent major approximately eleven, with myself always at least a block behind. During six Sundays, he never varied his routine, faithful as a migratory mallard, his route taking him through a neighborhood of apartments that all seemed to be dying of boredom. The major's own diminutive quadriplex was fronted by a carport with four slots, one vacant and three occupied by cars with the dented, drooping posteriors of elderly bus drivers. An overhanging second floor, its two sets of windows looking onto the street, shaded the cars. At 8:11 in the evening or so, the morose eyes of those bedroom windows were open but curtained, only one of them lit. On the first two Sundays, I parked at the corner and watched as he turned into the carport and vanished. On the third and fourth Sundays, I did not follow him from the gas station but waited for him half a block past his apartment. From there, I watched in my mirror as he entered the carport's shadowed margin, a lane leading to the bottom apartments. As soon as he disappeared those first four Sundays, I went home, but on the fifth and sixth Sundays I waited. Not until ten o'clock did the car that parked in the vacant spot appear, as aged and dinged as the others, the driver a tired-looking Chinese man wearing a smeared chef's smock and carrying a greasy paper bag.

On the Saturday before our appointment with the crapulent major, Bon and I drove to Chinatown. In an alley off Broadway lined with vendors selling wares from folding tables, we bought UCLA sweatshirts and baseball caps at prices that guaranteed they were not official merchandise. After a lunch of barbecued pork and noodles, we browsed one of the curio shops where all manner of Orientalia was sold, primarily to the non-Oriental. Chinese chess sets, wooden chopsticks, paper lanterns, soapstone Buddhas, miniature water fountains, elephant tusks with elaborate carvings of pastoral scenes, reproductions of Ming vases, coasters with images of the Forbidden City, rubber nunchaku bundled with posters of Bruce Lee, scrolls with watercolor paintings of cloud-draped mountain forests, tins of tea and ginseng, and, neither last nor least, red firecrackers. I bought two packets and, before we returned home, a mesh sack of oranges from a local market, their navels protruding indecently.

Later that evening, after dark, Bon and I ventured out one more time, each of us with a screwdriver. We toured the neighborhood until we reached an apartment with a carport like the crapulent major's, the cars not visible from any neighboring windows. It took less than thirty seconds for Bon to remove the front license plate from one car, and myself the plate from the rear. Then we went home and watched television until bedtime. Bon fell asleep immediately, but I could not. Our visit to Chinatown reminded me of an incident that had taken place in Cholon years before with the crapulent major and myself. The occasion was the arrest of a Viet Cong suspect who had graduated from the top of our gray list to the bottom of our blacklist. Enough people had fingered this person as a Viet Cong for us to neutralize him, or so the major said, showing me the thick dossier he had compiled. Official occupation: rice wine merchant. Black market occupation: casino operator. Hobby: Viet Cong tax collector. We cordoned off the ward with roadblocks on all streets and foot patrols in the alleys. While the secondary units did ID checks in the neighborhood, fishing for draft dodgers, the major's men entered the rice wine merchant's shop, pushed past his wife to reach the storeroom, and found the lever that opened a secret door. Gamblers were shooting craps and playing cards, their rice wine and hot soup served for free by waitresses in outrageous outfits. On seeing our policemen charging through the door, all the players and employees promptly dashed for the rear exit, only to find another squad of heavies waiting outside. The usual high jinks and hilarity ensued, involving much screaming, shrieking, billy clubs, and handcuffs, until, at last, it was only the crapulent major, myself, and our suspect, whom I was surprised to see. I had tipped off Man about the raid and fully expected the tax collector to be absent.

VC? the man cried, waving his hands in the air. No way! I'm a businessman!

A very good one, too, the major said, hefting a garbage bag filled with the casino's cash.

So you got me there, the man said, miserable. He had an overbite and three long, lucky hairs sprouting from a mole the size of a marble on his cheek. Okay, take the money, it's yours. I'm happy to contribute to the cause of the police.

That's offensive, the major said, poking the man's gut with his billy club. This is going to the government to pay your fines and back taxes, not to us. Right, Captain?

Right, I said, the straight man in this routine.

But as to future taxes, that's a different matter. Right, Captain?

Right. There was nothing I could do for the tax collector. He spent a week in the interrogation center being beaten black and blue, as well as red and yellow. By the end, our men were convinced that he was not a VC operative. The proof was incontrovertible, arriving in the form of a sizable bribe the man's wife brought to the crapulent major. I guess I was mistaken, he said cheerfully, handing me an envelope with my share. It was equivalent to a year's salary, which, to put it into perspective, was actually not enough to live on for a year. Refusing the money would have aroused suspicion, so I took it. I was tempted to use it for charitable activity, namely the support of beautiful young women hampered by poverty, but I remembered what my father said, rather than what he did, as well as Ho Chi Minh's adages. Both Jesus and Uncle Ho were clear that money was corrupting, from the moneylenders desecrating the temple to the capitalists exploiting the colony, not to mention Judas and his thirty pieces of silver. So I paid for the major's sin by donating the money to the revolution, handing it to Man at the basilica. See what we're fighting against? he said. *Holy Mary, mother of God, pray for us sinners,* droned the dowagers. This is why we'll win, Man said. Our enemies are corrupt. We are not. The point of writing this is that the crapulent major was as sinful as Claude estimated. Perhaps he had even done worse than simply extort money, although if he did it did not make him above average in corruption. It just made him average.

The next evening we were parked down the street from the gas station by seven thirty, wearing the UCLA sweatshirts and caps. If anyone noticed us, they would see, hopefully, UCLA students. My car had the stolen license plates affixed to it, my legitimate ones in the glove compartment. Every little bit of distraction helped, but most important of all were the distractions we did not control but which I had antici- pated. With my window rolled down, we could hear distant explosions from the city's fireworks show, as well as the *pop-pop* of occasional small arms fire as an individual celebrated independence. Smaller fireworks exploded closer, illegally detonated somewhere in this neighborhood as people lit cherry bombs, launched the occasional streaker into the low sky, or burned through ammo belts of Chinese firecrackers. Bon was tense as we waited for the major, his jaw clenched tight and shoulders hunched, refusing to let me turn on the radio. Bad memories? I said. Yeah. For a while he said nothing more, both of us watching the gas station. Two cars pulled in and gassed up, then left. This one time outside Sa Dec, the point man stepped on a Bouncing Betty. A little pop when it bounces. Then a big bang. I was two guys behind him, didn't get a scratch. But it blew his balls off. Worst part of all, the poor son of a bitch lived.

I mumbled regretfully and shook my head, but otherwise had nothing more to offer, castration being something that was unspeakable. We watched two more cars gas up. There was only one favor I could perform for the crapulent major. I don't want him to feel anything, I said.

He's not even going to see it coming.

At eight, the crapulent major left the station. I waited until he turned the corner, then started the car. We drove to his apartment using a different route so he would not see us passing him. The fourth parking slot was open, and I parked the car there. I checked my watch. Three minutes, eight more until the major came. Bon took out the gun from the glove compartment and popped the cylinder open one more time to inspect the bullets. Then he clicked the cylinder into place and laid the gun on the red velour pillow in his lap. I looked at the gun and the pillow and said, What if some of the stuffing gets blown onto him? And pieces of the cover? The police will see it and wonder what it is.

He shrugged. So no pillow. That means there'll be noise.

Somewhere down the street, someone set off another string of Chinese firecrackers, the same kind I had enjoyed so much as a little boy during New Year's. My mother would light up the long red string, and I would plug my ears and screech along with my mother in the patch of garden next to our hut while the serpent leaped this way and that, consuming itself from tail to head, or perhaps it was head to tail, ecstatically ablaze.

It's just one shot, I said after the firecrackers ceased. No one's coming out to see what happened, not with all this noise.

He looked at his watch. All right, then.

He slipped on a pair of latex gloves and kicked off his sneakers. I opened my door, got out, closed it softly, and took my position at the other end of the carport, next to the path leading from the sidewalk to the apartment's mailboxes. The path continued past the mailboxes to the two ground-floor apartments, the entrance to the first one ten feet down. Poking my head around the corner, I could see the lights of the apartment through the curtains of the living room window, pulled shut. A tall wooden fence lined the other side of the path, and above it rose the wall of an identical apartment complex. Half of its windows were bathroom windows, and the other half were bedroom windows. Anyone at the windows on the second floor could see the path leading to the apartment but would not be able to see into the carport.

Bon walked on socked feet to his position, in between the two cars nearest to the path, where he knelt down and kept his head below the windows. I looked at my watch: 8:07. I held a plastic bag with a yellow happy face and the words THANK YOU! on it. Inside were the firecrackers and the oranges. Are you sure you want to do this, son? my mother said. It's too late, Mama. I can't figure a way out.

I was halfway finished with a cigarette when the major appeared at the carport for the last time. Hey. His face broke into a puzzled smile. He carried his lunch box in his hand. What are you doing here? I forced myself to smile in return. Lifting the plastic bag, I said, I was in the neighborhood and thought I'd drop this off.

What is it? He was halfway to me.

A gift for the Fourth of July. Bon emerged from behind the car by which the major was walking, but I kept my gaze on the major. He was within three feet when he said, Do they give gifts on the Fourth of July?

The expression on his face was still puzzled. When I offered him the bag with both hands, he leaned forward to peer at its contents. Behind him Bon walked up, noiseless on his socked feet and gun in hand. You didn't have to, said the major. When he put his hands on the bag, it was the moment for Bon to shoot. But instead of pulling the trigger, Bon said, Hey, Major.

The major turned around, gift in one hand, lunch box in the other. I stepped to one side and heard him start to say a word when he saw Bon, and then Bon shot him. The report echoed in the carport, hurting my ears. The major's skull cracked when his head hit the pavement, and if the bullet had not already killed him, perhaps the fall did. He lay flat on his back, the bullet hole in his forehead a third eye, weeping blood. Move, Bon hissed, tucking the gun into the waistband of his pants. As he knelt down and rolled the major onto his side, I leaned over the body and picked up the plastic bag, its yellow happy face freckled with blood. The major's open mouth was wrapped around the shape of his last word. Bon tugged the wallet out of the major's hip pocket, stood up, and pushed me toward the car. I looked at my watch: 8:13.

I pulled out of the carport. A numbness descended on me, beginning from my brain and my eyeballs and extending to my toes and fingers. I thought he wasn't going to see it coming, I said. I just couldn't shoot him in the back, he said. Don't worry. He didn't feel a thing. I was not worried about whether the crapulent major felt a thing. I was worried about whether I felt a thing. We said nothing more, and before we reached our apartment, I pulled into an alley where we replaced the license plates. Then we went home, and when I took my sneakers off I saw spots of blood on the white toes. I took the shoes into the kitchen and wiped them off with a wet paper towel before I dialed the General's number from the phone hanging by the refrigerator, its door decorated with the twin columns of my divided self. He answered on the second ring. Hello? he said. It's done. There was a pause. Good. I hung up the phone, and when I returned to the living room with two glasses and a bottle of rye, I found that Bon had emptied the contents of the major's wallet onto the coffee table. What do we do with this? Bon asked. There was his Social Security card, his state ID (but no driver's license, as he did not have a car), a wad of receipts, twenty-two dollars, a handful of change, and some photos. A black-and-white one showed him and his wife on their wedding day, very young and dressed in Western garb. He had been fat back then, too. There was also a color photo of his twins at a few weeks of age, genderless and wrinkled. Burn them, I said. The wallet I would dispose of tomorrow, along with the license plates, the plastic bag, and the ashes.

When I handed him a glass of rye, I saw the red scar on his hand. Here's to the major, Bon said. The medicinal taste of the rye was so awful we had a second drink to wash it away, then a third, and so forth, all while watching television specials celebrating the nation's birthday. It was not just any birthday, but the bicentennial of a great, brawny nation, a little punch-drunk from recent foreign excursions but now on its feet again and ready to swing, or so proclaimed the chatterati. Then we ate three of the oranges and went to bed. I lay down on my bunk, closed my eyes, knocked my knees against the rearranged furniture of my thoughts, and shuddered at what I saw. I opened my eyes but it made no difference. No matter whether my eyes were open or shut, I could still see it, the crapulent major's third eye, weeping because of what it could see about me.

CHAPTER 7

I confess that the major's death troubled me greatly, Commandant, even if it does not trouble you. He was a relatively innocent man, which was the best one could hope for in this world. In Saigon, I could have depended on my weekly visits to the basilica with Man to discuss my misgivings, but here I was alone with myself, my deeds, and my beliefs. I knew what Man would say to me, but I just needed him to say it to me again, as he had on other occasions, such as the time I passed to him a cartridge of film recording the heliborne assault plans of a Ranger battalion. Innocent men would die as a result of my actions, wouldn't they? Of course men will die, Man said, masking his words behind his folded hands as we knelt in a pew. But they aren't innocent. Neither are we, my friend. We're revolutionaries, and revolutionaries can never be innocent. We know too much and have done too much.

I shivered in the humid climate of the basilica while the dowagers droned. *As it was in the beginning, is now, and ever shall be, world without end. Amen.* Contrary to some perceptions, revolutionary ideology, even in a tropical country, is not hot. It is cold, man-made. Little surprise, then, that revolutionaries needed natural heat sometimes. Thus, when I received an invitation to a wedding not long after the crapulent major's demise, I accepted with enthusiasm. Sofia Mori was my curious guest to this reception for a couple whose names I had to check on the invitation before greeting them. The bride's father was a legendary marine colonel whose battalion fought off an NVA regiment during the Battle of Hue with no American assistance, while the groom's father was the vice president of the Saigon branch of Bank of America. His family had fled Saigon on a jet chartered by Bank of America, thus avoiding the indignity of the refugee camps. The most distinctive thing about the vice president, besides his air of effortless distinction, was the Clark Gable mustache playing dead on his upper lip, an adornment favored by southern men who fancied themselves debonair playboys. I had received an invitation since I had met the man several times in Saigon as the General's aide. My status was indicated by how far I sat from the stage, which is to say very far. We were positioned near the restrooms, buffered from the scent of disinfectant only by the tables for the children and the band. Our companions were a couple of former junior officers, two mid-tier bank executives who had found lower-tier jobs with Bank of America branches, an in-law who looked inbred, and their wives. In dire times I would not merit a seat, but now we were more than a year into our American exile, and flush times had returned for some. The Chinese restaurant was in Westminster, where the man with the Clark Gable mustache had settled his family in a

ranch-style suburban home, a demotion from his villa in
Saigon but many rungs above almost all the evening's attendees. Westminster was Sonny's town, and I spotted him at a
table several rings closer to the center of power, Clark Gable's
attempt to ensure positive press coverage.

Despite the noise and activity in the restaurant, where
Chinese waiters tucked into red jackets scurried through
the maze of banquet tables, a touch of melancholy per-
vaded the huge dining room. The bride's father was notably
absent, captured along with the remnants of his battalion
as they defended the western approach to Saigon on the last
day. The General praised him at the beginning of the banquet in a speech that stirred emotions, tears, and drinks.
All the veterans toasted the hero with voluble bursts of
bravado that helped to obscure their own uncomfortable
lack of heroism. One simply must grin and drink unless
one wants to sink to one's neck in the quicksands of contradiction, or so said the sad crapulent major, his severed
head serving as the table's centerpiece. So I grinned and
poured cognac down my throat. Then I mixed a libation
of Rémy Martin and soda for Ms. Mori while explaining
the exotic customs, habits, hairstyles, and fashion of our
fun-loving people. I yelled my explanations, struggling to
be heard over the loud cover band that was fronted by a
petite dude in a sequined blazer. He sported a glam rocker's
perm modeled on a Louis XIV wig, minus the powder, and
strutted on gold platform shoes while fondling his mike,
pressing the ball of it to his lips suggestively as he sang.
The heterosexually certified bankers and military men

absolutely loved him, roaring approval at every flagrant pelvic gesture of flirtation from the singer's extraordinarily tight satin pants. When the singer invited manly men to the stage for a dance, it was the General who immediately offered himself. He grinned as he sashayed with the singer to "Black Is Black," the theme song of riotous Saigonese decadence, the audience cheering and clapping in appreciation, the singer winking over his shoulder à la Mae West. This was the General's element, among men and women who appreciated him or who knew better than to voice any disagreements or discomfort with him. The execution— no, the *neutralization*—of the poor crapulent major had pumped life back into him, enough so that he had masterfully eulogized at the funeral. There he praised the major as a quietly self-sacrificial and humble man who always performed his duties to country and family without complaint, only to be tragically cut down in a senseless robbery. I had taken photographs of the funeral with my Kodak, the images later dispatched to my aunt in Paris, while Sonny sat in the front row of mourners, taking notes for an obituary. After the funeral, the General slipped the widow an envelope of cash from the operational funds provided by Claude, then stooped to peer into the bassinet where Spinach and Broccoli slept. As for myself, I could only mumble something generically appropriate to the widow, whose veil cloaked a waterfall of tears. How was it? Bon asked when I came home. How do you think? I said, heading for the refrigerator, its ribs lined as always with beer. Besides my conscience, my liver was the most abused part of my body.

Weddings often exacerbated the abuse, aggravated by the sight of a happy, innocent bride and groom. Their marriage might lead to alienation, adultery, misery, and divorce, but it might also lead to affection, loyalty, children, and contentment. While I had no desire to be married, weddings reminded me of what had been denied to me through no choice of my own. Thus, if I began every wedding as a pulp movie tough guy, mixing laughs with the occasional cynical comment, I ended each wedding as a watered-down cocktail, one-third singing, one-third sentimental, and one-third sorrowful. It was in this state that I took Ms. Mori to the dance floor after the wedding cake was cut, and it was then, near the stage, that I recognized one of the two female singers taking turns at the microphone with our gay blade. She was the General's oldest daughter, safely ensconced in the Bay Area as a student while the country collapsed. Lana was nearly unrecognizable from the schoolgirl I had seen at the General's villa during her lycée years and on summer vacations. In those days, her name was still Lan and she wore the most modest of clothing, the schoolgirl's white ao dai that had sent many a Western writer into near-pederastic fantasies about the nubile bodies whose every curve was revealed without displaying an inch of flesh except above the neck and below the cuffs. This the writers apparently took as an implicit metaphor for our country as a whole, wanton and yet withdrawn, hinting at everything and giving away nothing in a dazzling display of demureness, a paradoxical incitement to temptation, a breathtakingly lewd exhibition of modesty. Hardly any male travel writer, journalist, or casual observer of our country's life could restrain himself from writing about the young girls who rode their bicycles to and from school in those fluttering white ao dai, butterflies that every Western man dreamed of pinning to his collection.

In reality, Lan was a tomboy who had to be straitjacketed into her ao dai every morning by Madame or a nanny. Her ultimate form of rebellion was to be a superb student who, like me, earned a scholarship to the States. In her case, the scholarship was from the University of California at Berkeley, which the General and Madame regarded as a communist colony of radical professors and revolutionary students out to beguile and bed innocents. They wanted to send her to a girls' college where the only danger was lesbian seduction, but Lan had applied to none of them, insisting on Berkeley. When they forbade her from going, Lan threatened suicide. Neither the General nor Madame took her seriously until Lan swallowed a fistful of sleeping pills. Thankfully she had a small fist. After nursing her back to health, the General was willing to concede, but Madame was not. Lan then threw herself into the Saigon River one afternoon, albeit at a time when the quay was well stocked with pedestrians, two of whom jumped in to save her as she floated in her white ao dai. At last Madame, too, conceded, and Lan flew off to Berkeley to study art history in the fall of '72, a major her parents felt would enhance her feminine sensibilities and keep her suitable for marriage.

During her returns home in the summers of '73 and '74, she reappeared as a foreigner in bell-bottomed jeans and feathered hair, blouses stretched tight as a trampoline over the swell of her bosom, clogs adding several inches to her modest height. Madame would sit her down in her salon and, according to the nannies, lecture her on the importance of maintaining her virginity and of cultivating the "Three Submissions and Four Virtues"—a phrase that calls to mind the title of a highbrow erotic novel. The mere mention of her endangered or putatively lost virginity provided ample wood for the cookstove of my imagination, a fire I stoked in the privacy of my room, down the hall from the one she shared with a little sister. Lan had visited the General and Madame a few times since our arrival in California, but I had not been invited to the home on such occasions. Nor had I been invited to go with the General and Madame to her graduation cum laude a few months before. The most I heard of Lan was when the General muttered something about his unfilial daughter, who was now going by the name of Lana and who had not returned home after graduation but instead chosen to live on her own. Although I tried to draw out the General on what Lana was doing postgraduation, he had been uncharacteristically incommunicative.

Now I knew, and now I knew why. This Lana onstage bore no relationship to the Lan that I remembered. In the band's arrangement, the other female singer was the angel of tradition, clad in a chartreuse ao dai, hair long and straight, makeup tasteful, her songs of choice estrogen-soaked ballads about lovelorn women hailing distant soldier lovers or lost Saigon itself. No such sadness or loss tinted Lana's songs, no looking backward over the shoulder for this temptress of modernity. Even I was shocked by the black leather miniskirt that threatened to reveal a glimpse of that secret I had so often fantasized about. Above the miniskirt, her gold silk halter top shimmered with every gyration of her torso as she flexed her lungs, her specialty being the rock-'em, sock-'em numbers that the blues and rock bands of our homeland had mastered in order to entertain American troops and Americanized youth. I had heard her sing "Proud Mary" earlier in the evening without realizing it was she, and now I had to remind myself not to stare at her as she let loose a throaty version of "Twist and Shout" that called nearly everyone under the age of forty to the dance floor. Besides the simple yet elegant cha-cha, the twist was the favorite dance of the southern people, requiring as it did no coordination. Even Madame usually did the twist, innocent enough that she allowed her children to flock to the floor and dance, too. But glancing at the General's table, which occupied a place of honor on the dance floor's edge, I saw both the General and the Madame remaining seated, looking as if they were sucking on the sour fruit of the tamarind tree that had shaded their lost villa. And no wonder! For no one was twisting more than Lana herself, every rotation of her hips working an invisible ratchet that pulled the heads of the men on the dance floor forward and then pushed back. I might have participated if I was not so aware of Ms. Mori dancing with me, twisting with such childlike glee that I had to smile. She was looking remarkably feminine compared with her usual style. A lily nestled in her marcelled hair, and she wore a chiffon dress that actually exposed her knees. I had flattered her more than once on her appearance, and I took the occasion of seeing her knees during the twist to compliment her on her dancing as well. I haven't danced like that in a long time, she said when the song was over. Neither have I, Ms. Mori, I said, kissing her on the cheek. Sofia, she said.

Before I could respond, Clark Gable took to the stage and announced a surprise visitor, a congressman who served in our country as a Green Beret from '62 to '64 and who was the representative for this district we found ourselves in. The Congressman had achieved a significant degree of renown in Southern California as an up-and-coming young politician, his martial credentials serving him well in Orange County. Here, his nicknames of Napalm Ned or Knock-'em-Dead Ned or Nuke-'em-All Ned, used depending on one's mood and the geopolitical crisis, were affectionate rather than derogatory. He was so anti-red in his politics he might as well have been green, one reason he was one of the few politicians in Southern California to greet the refugees with open arms. The majority of Americans regarded us with ambivalence if not outright distaste, we being living reminders of their stinging defeat. We threatened the sanctity and symmetry of a white and black America whose yin and yang racial politics left no room for any other color, particularly that of pathetic little yellow-skinned people pickpocketing the American purse. We were strange aliens rumored to have a predilection for *Fido Americanus*, the domestic canine on whom was lavished more per capita than the annual income of a starving Bangladeshi family. (The true horror of this situation was actually beyond the ken of the average American. While some of us indeed had been known to sup on the brethren of Rin Tin Tin and Lassie, we did not do so in the Neanderthalesque way imagined by the average American, with a club, a roast, and some salt, but with a gourmand's depth of ingenuity and creativity, our chefs able to cook canids seven different virility-enhancing ways, from extracting the marrow to grilling and boiling, as well as sausage making, stewing, and a few varieties of frying and steaming—yum!) The Congressman, however, had written editorials defending us and welcoming the émigrés to his Orange County district.

Good God, look at you, he said, with microphone in hand, Clark Gable by his side, flanked by angel and temptress. He was in his forties, a crossbreed between lawyer and politician, exhibiting the former's aggressiveness and the latter's smoothness, typified by his head. Shiny, polished, and pointed as the tip of a fountain pen, words flowed from it as easily as the finest India ink. This head was the difference in height between him and the shorter Clark Gable, and in every dimension was the Congressman so much more expansive that two Vietnamese men of average height and size could have squeezed themselves into the confines of his body. Look at yourselves, ladies and gentlemen, look at yourselves the way I wish my fellow Americans would look at you, which is as fellow Americans. I am truly thankful for the chance to be here tonight and to share in the joy of this occasion, this marriage of two lovely young Vietnamese people in a Chinese restaurant on California soil under an American moon and in a Christian universe. Let me tell you something, ladies and gentlemen, for two years I lived among your people in the Highlands and fought with your

soldiers and shared your fears and faced your enemy, and I
thought then and I think now how I could do nothing finer
with my life than sacrifice it in the cause of your hopes,
dreams, and aspirations for a better life. While I believed
as surely as you that those hopes, dreams, and aspirations
would be fulfilled in your homeland, we have been dealt
another hand by history and the mysterious and unquestion-
able grace of God. I am here to tell you, ladies and gentlemen,
that this is a hand of temporary bad luck, for your soldiers
fought well and bravely, and would have prevailed if only
Congress had remained as steadfast in their support of you
as the president promised. This was a promise shared by
many, many Americans. But not all. You know who I mean.
The Democrats. The media. The antiwar movement. The
hippies. The college students. The radicals. America was
weakened by its own internal divisions, by the defeatists
and communists and traitors infesting our universities,
our newsrooms, and our Congress. You, sad to say, merely
remind them of their cowardice and their treachery. I am
here to tell you that what you remind me of is America's
great promise! The promise of the immigrant! The promise
of the American Dream! The promise that the people of this
country used to hold dear and will one day soon hold dear
again, that America is a land of freedom and independence,
a land of patriots who have always stood up for the little man
no matter where he is in the world, a land of heroes who will
never relent in the cause of helping our friends and smiting
our enemies, a land that welcomes people like you, who have
sacrificed so much in our common cause of democracy and

liberty! One day, my friends, America will stand tall again, and it will be because of people like you. And one day, my friends, the land you have lost will be yours again! Because nothing can stop the inevitable movement of freedom and the will of the people! Now, affirm with me in your beautiful language what we all believe—

The entire audience had been cheering and applauding wildly throughout the speech, and if he had rolled out a communist in a cage, the spectators would have gladly called for him to rip out the red's beating heart with his massive fists. There was no way he could possibly get them even more excited, but he did. Raising his arms to form a V, presumably for Victory, or for Vietnam, or for Vote for me, or for something even more subliminally suggestive, he shouted into the microphone, in the most perfect Vietnamese, *Vietnam Muon Nam! Vietnam Muon Nam! Vietnam Muon Nam!* Everyone sitting leaped to his or her feet, and everyone standing stood a little taller, and everyone roared after the Congressman the refrain of *Vietnam Forever!* Then Clark Gable made a motion to the band, and it swung into the rhythms of our national anthem, which the angel and the temptress and Clark Gable and the Congressman all sang with zeal, as did everyone in the audience, myself included, except for the stoic Chinese waiters, who could finally take a rest.

When the anthem finished, the Congressman was mobbed by well-wishers onstage while the rest of the audience members sunk into their seats with postcoital smugness. I turned to find Sonny, notepad and pen in hand, standing by Ms. Mori. Funny, he said, pink from a glass or two of cognac.

It's the same slogan the Communist Party uses. Ms. Mori shrugged. A slogan is just an empty suit, she said. Anyone can wear it. I like that, Sonny said. Mind if I use it? I introduced the two of them and asked him if he was going to get up close for a photograph. He grinned. The newspaper's been doing well enough for me to hire a photographer. As for me, I already interviewed the good Congressman. I should have worn a flak jacket. He was practically shooting bullets at me.

Typical white man behavior, Ms. Mori said. Have you ever noticed how a white man can learn a few words of some Asian language and we just eat it up? He could ask for a glass of water and we'd treat him like Einstein. Sonny smiled and wrote that down, too. You've been here longer than we have, Ms. Mori, he said with some admiration. Have you noticed that when we Asians speak English, it better be nearly perfect or someone's going to make fun of our accent? It doesn't matter how long you've been here, Ms. Mori said. White people will always think we're foreigners. But isn't there another side to that? I said, my words a little slurred from the cognac in my bloodstream. If we speak perfect English, then Americans trust us. It makes it easier for them to think we're one of them.

You're that kind of person, right? Sonny's eyes were as opaque as the tinted windows of a car. I was mistaken about him having changed that much. In the few times we had seen each other since our initial reunion, he had shown that he had merely turned down the volume on his personality. So what do you think of our Congressman?

Are you going to quote me?

You'll be an anonymous source.

He's the best thing that could have happened to us, I said. And that was no lie. It was, instead, the best kind of truth, the one that meant at least two things.

The next weekend provided further opportunity to refine my understanding of the Congressman's potential. On a bright Sunday morning, I chauffeured the General and Madame from Hollywood to Huntington Beach, where the Congressman lived and where he had invited them for lunch. My title of chauffeur was more impressive than the vehicle, a Chevrolet Nova whose best feature was its relative newness. But the fact remained that the General and the Madame, nestled in the backseat, had a chauffeur. My function was to be a trapping of their past and possibly future life. Their conversation for the hour-long drive revolved mostly around the Congressman until I asked about Lana, who, I said, struck me as having become all grown up. In the rearview mirror, I saw Madame's face darken with barely repressed fury.

She's completely insane, Madame declared. We've been trying to keep her insanity within the family, but now that she's strutting in public as a *singer*—Madame said the word as if it were *communist*—there's nothing we can do. Someone persuaded her that she had talent as a *singer*, and she took the compliment seriously. She is rather talented, I said. Don't start! Don't encourage her! Look at her. She looks like a *slut*. Is this what I raised her to be? What decent man would want to marry *that*? Would you, Captain? Our eyes met in the rearview mirror. No, Madame, I said, I wouldn't want to marry that, also the two-faced truth, for marriage was not the first thing on my mind when I saw her onstage. Of course not, she fumed. The worst thing about living in America is the *corruption*. At home, we could contain it in the bars and nightclubs and bases. But here, we will not be able to protect our children from the *lewdness* and the *shallowness* and the *tawdriness* Americans love so much. They're too permissive. No one even thinks twice of what they call *dating*. We all know that "date" is a euphemism. What parent not only allows their daughter to copulate in her teenage years, but willingly encourages it? It's shocking! It's an abnegation of moral responsibility. Ugh.

Somehow, at lunch, the conversation turned exactly in this direction, allowing Madame to repeat her points to the Congressman and his wife, Rita, a refugee from Castro's revolution. She bore a passing resemblance to Rita Hayworth, with ten or fifteen years and pounds added to the movie star at her most glamorous period, circa *Gilda*. *Castro*, she said, in the way Madame said *singer*, is the devil. The only good thing about living with the *devil*, General and Madame, is that one knows evil and can recognize it. That is why I am happy you are here today, because we Cubans and Vietnamese are cousins in our shared cause against communism. These words sealed the bond between the Congressman and Rita and the General and Madame, who was comfortable enough that she eventually mentioned Lana to them while the mute housekeeper policed the empty dishes. Rita immediately sympathized. She was the domestic equivalent of her husband, an anticommunist warrior housewife to whom nothing was just an isolated incident but was almost always a symptom by which the disease of communism could be linked to poverty, depravity, atheism, and decay of many kinds. I won't allow rock music in this house, she said, gripping Madame's hand to console her for the loss of her daughter's virtue. None of my children will be allowed to date until eighteen and, so long as they live in this house, will have a curfew by ten. It's our weak spot, this freedom we allow people to behave any way they please, what with their drugs and their sex, as if those things aren't infectious.

Every system has its excesses that must be checked internally, the Congressman said. We let the hippies steal the meaning of the words "love" and "freedom," and we've only just begun to fight back. That fight begins and ends in the home. Unlike his public persona, the Congressman in private was soft-spoken and measured in his tones, baronially assured as he sat at the head of the table, the General and Madame to either side. We control what our children read and listen to and watch, but it's a tough fight when they can just turn on the television or radio any time they want. We need the government to make sure Hollywood and the record labels don't go too far.

Aren't you the government? the General said.

Exactly! Which is why one of my priorities is legislation that regulates movies and music. This is not censorship, only advice with teeth. But you can bet the Hollywood and music types don't like me at all, until they meet me, that is, and see I'm not some kind of ogre out to feast on their creations. I'm just trying to help them refine their product. Now one thing that happened as a consequence of my work on the subcommittee is that I became friendly with some of the Hollywood people. I'll admit I had my prejudices about them, but some of them are actually smart and passionate guys, too. Smart and passionate—that's what I care about. The rest, we negotiate. Anyway, one of them is making a movie about the war and wanted my advice. I'm going to give him some notes on his script about what he got right and wrong. But the reason I mention it to you, General, is because the story's about the Phoenix Program, and I know you're an expert on that. Me, I left before that even got started. Maybe you can give some feedback. Otherwise who knows what kind of Hollywood story they're going to make.

This is why I have my captain, the General said, nodding toward me. He is, in effect, my cultural attaché. He would be more than happy to read the screenplay and offer his insight. When I asked the Congressman for the title, I was taken aback. *Hamlet*?

No, *The Hamlet*. The director's also the writer. Never served a day in the armed forces, just got fed John Wayne and Audie Murphy movies as a kid. The main character's a Green Beret who has to save a hamlet. I did serve two years on an A-Team in a number of hamlets, but nothing like this fantasyland he's cooked up.

I'll see what I can do, I said. I had lived in a northern hamlet only a few years as a young boy, before our flight south in '54, but lack of experience had never stopped me from trying anything. This was my mind-set when I approached Lana after her commanding performance, my intent to congratulate her on her new career. We stood in the restaurant's foyer, by an imposing photograph of the newlyweds displayed on an easel, and it was here that she studied me with the objective, unsentimental eye of an art appraiser. She smiled and said, I was wondering why you were keeping your distance from me, Captain. When I protested that I simply had not recognized her, she asked me if I liked what I saw. I don't look like the girl you knew, do I, Captain?

Some men preferred those innocent schoolgirls in their white ao dai, but not me. They belonged to some pastoral, pure vision of our culture from which I was excluded, as distant to me as the snowcapped peaks of my father's homeland. No, I was impure, and impurity was all I wanted and all I deserved. You don't look like the girl I knew, I said. But you look exactly like the woman I imagined you would one day become. No one had ever said anything like this to her, and the unexpected nature of my remark made her falter for a moment before she recovered. I see I'm not the only person who's changed since coming here, Captain. You're so much more . . . direct than you were when you lived with us.

I don't live with you any longer, I said. If Madame had not appeared at that moment, who knew where the conversation would have taken us then? Without a word to me, she seized Lana by the elbow and pulled her toward the ladies' room with a force that would not be denied. Although that was the last I saw of her for quite a while, she returned in my fantasies many times over the subsequent weeks. Regardless of what I wanted or deserved, she inevitably appeared in a white ao dai, her long black hair sometimes framing her face and sometimes obscuring it. In the nameless dream city where I encountered her, my shadow self wavered. Even in my somnambulent state I knew that white was not only the color of purity and innocence. It was also the sign of mourning and death.

CHAPTER 8

We own the day, but CHARLIE owns the night. Never forget that. These are the words that blond twenty-one-year-old Sergeant JAY BELLAMY hears on his first day in the torrid tropics of 'Nam from his new commanding officer, Captain WILL SHAMUS. Shamus was baptized in the blood of his own comrades on the beaches of Normandy, survived another near-death experience under a Chinese human-wave attack in Korea, then hauled himself up the ranks on a pulley oiled with Jack Daniel's. He knows he will not ascend any higher, not with his Bronx manners and his big, knobby knuckles over which no velvet gloves fit. This is a political war, he informs his acolyte, the words emanating from behind the smoke screen produced by a Cuban cigar. But all I know is a killing war. His task: save the prelapsarian Montagnards of a bucolic hamlet perched on the border of wild Laos. What's threatening them is the Viet Cong, and not just any Viet Cong. This is the baddest of the bad—King Cong. King Cong will die for his country, which is more than can be said for most Americans. More important, King Cong will kill for his country, and nothing makes King Cong lick his lips like the ferric scent of the white man's blood. King Cong has stocked the dense jungle around the hamlet with veteran guerrillas, battle-wizened men (and women) who have slaughtered Frenchmen from the Highlands to the Street Without Joy. What's more, King Cong has infiltrated the hamlet with subversives and sympathizers, friendly faces only masks for calculating wills. Standing against them are the hamlet's Popular Forces, a ragtag bunch of farmers and teenagers, Vietnam's own minutemen trained by the dozen Green Berets of the US Army Special Forces A-Team. *This is enough*, Sergeant Bellamy thinks, alone in his watchtower at midnight. He's dropped out of Harvard and run far from his St. Louis home, his millionaire daddy, and his fur-cloaked mother. *This is enough, this stunningly beautiful jungle and these humble, simple people. This is where I, Jay Bellamy, make my first and maybe my last stand—at* THE HAMLET.

This, at any rate, was my interpretation of the screenplay mailed to me by the director's personal assistant, the thick-ish manila envelope arriving with my name misspelled in a beautifully cursive hand. That was the first whiff of trouble, the second being how the personal assistant, Violet, did not even bother to say hello or good-bye when she called for my mailing information and to arrange a meeting with the director in his Hollywood Hills home. When Violet opened the door, she continued with her bewildering manner of discourse in person. Glad to see you could make it, heard a lot about you, loved your notes on *The Hamlet*. And that's precisely how she spoke, trimming pronouns and periods, as if punctuation and grammar were wasted on me. Then, without deigning to make eye contact, she inclined her head in a gesture of condescension and disdain, signaling me to enter.

Perhaps her abruptness was merely part of her personality, for she had the appearance of the worst kind of bureaucrat, the aspiring one, from blunt, square haircut to blunt, clean fingernails to blunt, efficient pumps. But perhaps it was me, still morally disoriented from the crapulent major's death, as well as the apparition of his severed head at the wedding banquet. The emotional residue of that night was like a drop of arsenic falling into the still waters of my soul, nothing having changed from the taste of it but everything now tainted. So perhaps that was why when I crossed over the threshold into the marble foyer, I instantly suspected that the cause of her behavior was my race. What she saw when she looked at me must have been my yellowness, my slightly smaller eyes, and the shadow cast by the ill fame of the Oriental's genitals, those supposedly minuscule privates disparaged on many a public restroom wall by semiliterates. I might have been just half an Asian, but in America it was all or nothing when it came to race. You were either white or you weren't. Funnily enough, I had never felt inferior because of my race during my foreign student days. I was foreign by definition and therefore was treated as a guest. But now, even though I was a card-carrying American with a driver's license, Social Security card, and resident alien permit, Violet still considered me as foreign, and this misrecognition punctured the smooth skin of my self-confidence. Was I just being paranoid, that all-American characteristic? Maybe Violet was

stricken with colorblindness, the willful inability to distin-
guish between white and any other color, the only infirmity
Americans wished for themselves. But as she advanced along
the polished bamboo floors, steering clear of the dusky maid
vacuuming a Turkish rug, I just knew it could not be so. The
flawlessness of my English did not matter. Even if she could
hear me, she still saw right through me, or perhaps saw someone else instead of me, her retinas burned with the images of
all the castrati dreamed up by Hollywood to steal the place
of real Asian men. Here I speak of those cartoons named
Fu Manchu, Charlie Chan, Number One Son, Hop Sing—
Hop Sing!—and the bucktoothed, bespectacled Jap not so
much played as mocked by Mickey Rooney in *Breakfast at
Tiffany's*. The performance was so insulting it even deflated
my fetish for Audrey Hepburn, understanding as I did her
implicit endorsement of such loathsomeness.

By the time I sat down opposite the director in his
office, I was seething from the memory of all these previous wounds, although I did not show it. On the one hand,
I was sitting for a meeting with the famed Auteur, when
once I was just another lovelorn movie fan passing Saturday
afternoons in the cinematic bliss of matinee screenings from
which I emerged, blinking and slightly shocked, into sunlight as bright as the fluorescent bulbs of a hospital birthing
room. On the other hand, I was flummoxed by having read
a screenplay whose greatest special effect was neither the
blowing up of various things nor the evisceration of various
bodies, but the achievement of narrating a movie about our
country where not a single one of our countrymen had an

intelligible word to say. Violet had scraped my already chafed ethnic sensitivity even further, but since it would not do to make my irritation evident, I forced myself to smile and do what I did best, remaining as unreadable as a paper package wrapped up with string.

The Auteur studied me, this extra who had crept into the middle of his perfect mise-en-scène. A golden Oscar statuette exhibited itself to the side of his telephone, serving as either a kingly scepter or a mace for braining impertinent screenwriters. A hirsute show of manliness ruffled along his forearms and from the collar of his shirt, reminding me of my own relative hairlessness, my chest (and stomach and buttocks) as streamlined and glabrous as a Ken doll. He was the hottest writer-director in town after the triumph of his last two films, beginning with *Hard Knock*, a critically lauded movie about the travails of Greek American youth in the inflamed streets of Detroit. It was loosely autobiographical, the Auteur having been born with an olive-tinged Greek surname he had bleached in typical Hollywood fashion. His most recent film declared that he had had enough with off-white ethnicity, exploring cocaine-white ethnicity instead. *Venice Beach* was about the failure of the American Dream, featuring a dipsomaniac reporter and his depressive wife writing competing versions of the Great American Novel. As the foolscap mounted endlessly, their money and their lives slowly drained away, leaving the audience with a last image of the couple's dilapidated cottage strangled by bougainvillea while beautifully lit by the sun setting beyond the Pacific. It was Didion crossed with Chandler as prophesied by Faulkner and shot by Welles. It was very good. He had talent, no matter how much it might have pained me to say so.

Great to meet you, the Auteur began. Loved your notes. How about something to drink. Coffee, tea, water, soda, scotch. Never too early for scotch. Violet, some scotch. Ice. I said ice. No ice, then. Me too. Always neat for me. Look at my view. No, not at the gardener. José! José! Got to pound on the glass to get his attention. He's half deaf. José! Move! You're blocking the view. Good. See the view. I'm talking about the Hollywood sign right there. Never get tired of it. Like the Word of God just dropped down, plunked on the hills, and the Word was Hollywood. Didn't God say let there be light first. What's a movie but light. Can't have a movie without light. And then words. Seeing that sign reminds me to write every morning. What. All right, so it doesn't say Hollywood. You got me. Good eye. Thing's falling to pieces. One O's half fallen and the other O's fallen altogether. The word's gone to shit. So what. You still get the meaning. Thanks, Violet. Cheers. How do they say it in your country. I said how do they say it. Yo, yo, yo, is it. I like that. Easy to remember. Yo, yo, yo, then. And here's to the Congressman for sending you my way. You're the first Vietnamese I've ever met. Not too many of you in Hollywood. Hell, none of you in Hollywood. And authenticity's important. Not that authenticity beats imagination. The story still comes first. The universality of the story has to be there. But it doesn't hurt to get the details right. I had a Green Beret who actually fought with the Montagnards vet the script. He found me. He had a screenplay. Everyone has a screenplay. Can't write but he's a real American hero. Two tours of duty, killed VC with his bare hands. A Silver Star and a Purple Heart with oak leaf clusters. You should have seen the Polaroids he showed me. Made my stomach turn. Gave me some ideas, though, for how to shoot the movie. Hardly had any corrections to make. What do you think of that.

It took me a moment to realize he was asking me a question. I was disoriented, as if I were an English as a second language speaker listening to an equally foreign speaker from another country. That's great, I said.

You bet it's great. You, on the other hand. You wrote me another screenplay in the margins. You ever even read a screenplay before.

It took me another moment to realize there was another question. Like Violet, he had a problem with conventional punctuation. No—

I didn't think so. So why do you think—

But you didn't get the details right.

I didn't get the details right. Violet, hear that. I researched your country, my friend. I read Joseph Buttinger and Frances FitzGerald. Have you read Joseph Buttinger and Frances FitzGerald. He's the foremost historian on your little part of the world. And she won the Pulitzer Prize. She dissected your psychology. I think I know something about you people.

His aggressiveness flustered me, and my flustering, which I was not accustomed to, only flustered me further, which was my only explanation for my forthcoming behavior. You didn't even get the screams right, I said.

Excuse me.

I waited for an interjection until I realized he was just interrupting me with a question. All right, I said, my string starting to unravel. If I remember correctly, pages 26, 42, 58, 77, 91, 103, and 118, basically all the places in the script where one of my people has a speaking part, he or she screams. No words, just screams. So you should at least get the screams right.

Screams are universal. Am I right, Violet.

You're right, she said from where she sat next to me. Screams are not universal, I said. If I took this telephone cord and wrapped it around your neck and pulled it tight until your eyes bugged out and your tongue turned black, Violet's scream would sound very different from the scream you would be trying to make. Those are two very different kinds of terror coming from a man and a woman. The man knows he is dying. The woman fears she is likely to die soon. Their situations and their bodies produce a qualitatively different timbre to their voices. One must listen to them carefully to understand that while pain is universal, it is also utterly private. We cannot know whether our pain is like anybody else's pain until we talk about it. Once we do that, we speak and think in ways cultural and individual. In this country, for example, someone fleeing for his life will think he should call for the police. This is a reasonable way to cope with the threat of pain. But in my country, no one calls for the police, since it is often the police who inflict the pain. Am I right, Violet?

Violet mutely nodded her head.

So let me just point out that in your script, you have my people scream the following way: *AIIIEEEEE!!!* For example, when VILLAGER #3 is impaled by a Viet Cong punji trap, this is how he screams. Or when the LITTLE GIRL sacrifices her life to alert the Green Berets to the Viet Cong sneaking into the village, this is how she screams before her throat is cut. But having heard many of my countrymen screaming in pain, I can assure you this is not how they scream. Would you like to hear how they scream?

His Adam's apple bobbed as he swallowed. Okay.

I stood up and leaned on the desk to look right into his eyes. But I didn't see him. What I saw was the face of the wiry Montagnard, an elder of the Bru minority who lived in an actual hamlet not far from the setting of this fiction. Rumor had it he served as a liaison agent for the Viet Cong. I was on my first assignment as a lieutenant and could not figure out a way to save the man from my captain wrapping a strand of rusted barbed wire around his throat, the necklace tight enough so that each time he swallowed, the wire tickled his Adam's apple. That was not what made the old man scream, however. It was just the appetizer. In my mind, though, as I watched the scene, I screamed for him.

Here's what it sounds like, I said, reaching across the desk to pick up the Auteur's Montblanc fountain pen. I wrote onomatopoeically across the cover page of the screenplay in big black letters: *AIEYAAHHH!!!* Then I capped his pen, put it back on his leather writing pad, and said, That's how we scream in my country.

* * *

After I descended from the Auteur's home to the General's, thirty blocks distant and down the hills to the Hollywood flatlands, I reported my first experience with the motion picture industry to the General and Madame, both of whom were infuriated on my behalf. My meeting with the Auteur and Violet had gone on for a while longer, mostly in a more subdued fashion, with me pointing out that the lack of speaking parts for Vietnamese people in a movie set in Vietnam might be interpreted as cultural insensitivity. True, Violet interjected, but what it boils down to is who pays for the tickets and goes to the movies. Frankly, Vietnamese audiences aren't going to watch this movie, are they? I contained my outrage. Even so, I said, do you not think it would be a little more believable, a little more realistic, a little more authentic, for a movie set in a certain country for the people in that country to have something to say, instead of having your screenplay direct, as it does now, *Cut to villagers speaking in their own language*? Do you think it might not be decent to let them actually say something instead of simply acknowledging that there is some kind of sound coming from their mouths? Could you not even just have them speak a heavily accented English—you know what I mean, ching-chong English—just to pretend they are speaking in an Asian language that somehow American audiences can strangely understand? And don't you think it would be more compelling if your Green Beret had a love interest? Do these men only love and die for each other? That is the implication without a woman in the midst.

The Auteur grimaced and said, Very interesting. Great stuff. Loved it, but I had a question. What was it. Oh, yes.

How many movies have you made. None. Isn't that right. None, zero, zilch, nada, nothing, and however you say it in your language. So thank you for telling me how to do my job. Now get the hell out of my house and come back after you've made a movie or two. Maybe then I'll listen to one or two of your cheap ideas.

Why was he so rude? Madame said. Didn't he ask you to give him some comments?

He was looking for a yes man. He thought I'd give him a rubber stamp of approval.

He thought you were going to fawn over him.

When I didn't do it, he was hurt. He's an artist, he's got thin skin.

So much for your career in Hollywood, the General said.

I don't want a career in Hollywood, I said, which was true only to the extent that Hollywood did not want me. I confess to being angry with the Auteur, but was I wrong in being angry? This was especially the case when he acknowledged he did not even know that Montagnard was simply a French catchall term for the dozens of Highland minorities. What if, I said to him, I wrote a screenplay about the American West and simply called all the natives Indians? You'd want to know whether the cavalry was fighting the Navajo or Apache or Comanche, right? Likewise, I would want to know, when you say these people are Montagnards, whether we speak of the Bru or the Nung or the Tay.

Let me tell you a secret, the Auteur said. You ready. Here it is. No one gives a shit.

He was amused by my wordlessness. To see me without

words is like seeing one of those Egyptian felines without hair, a rare and not necessarily desirable occasion. Only later, driving away from his house, could I laugh bitterly about how he had bludgeoned me into silence with my own weapon of choice. How could I be so dense? How could I be so deluded? Ever the industrious student, I had read the screenplay in a few hours and then reread and written notes for several more hours, all under the misguided idea my work mattered. I naively believed that I could divert the Hollywood organism from its goal, the simultaneous lobotomization and pickpocketing of the world's audiences. The ancillary benefit was strip-mining history, leaving the real history in the tunnels along with the dead, doling out tiny sparkling diamonds for audiences to gasp over. Hollywood did not just make horror movie monsters, it was its own horror movie monster, smashing me under its foot. I had failed and the Auteur would make *The Hamlet* as he intended, with my countrymen serving merely as raw material for an epic about white men saving good yellow people from bad yellow people. I pitied the French for their naïveté in believing they had to visit a country in order to exploit it. Hollywood was much more efficient, imagining the countries it wanted to exploit. I was maddened by my helplessness before the Auteur's imagination and machinations. His arrogance marked something new in the world, for this was the first war where the losers would write history instead of the victors, courtesy of the most efficient propaganda machine ever created (with all due respect to Joseph Goebbels and the Nazis, who never achieved global domination). Hollywood's high priests understood innately the observation of Milton's Satan, that it was better to rule in Hell than serve in Heaven, better to be a villain, loser, or antihero than virtuous extra, so long as one commanded the bright lights of center stage. In this forthcoming Hollywood trompe l'oeil, all the Vietnamese of any side would come out poorly, herded into the roles of the poor, the innocent, the evil, or the corrupt. Our fate was not to be merely mute; we were to be struck dumb.

Have some pho, Madame said. It will make you feel better.

She had been cooking and the house smelled of sentiment, a rich aroma of beef broth and star anise I can only describe as the bouquet of love and tenderness, all the more striking because Madame had never cooked before coming to this country. For women of Madame's rarefied class, cooking was one of those functions contracted out to other women, along with cleaning, nursing, teaching, sewing, and so on, everything except for the bare biological necessities, which I could not imagine Madame performing, except, perhaps, for breathing. But the exigencies of exile had made it necessary for Madame to cook, as no one else in the household was capable of anything more than boiling water. In the General's case, even that was beyond him. He could fieldstrip and reassemble an M16 blindfolded, but a gas stove was as perplexing as a calculus equation, or at least he pretended so. Like most of us Vietnamese men, he simply did not want to be even brushed with domesticity. The only domestic things he did were sleep and eat, both of which he was better at than me. He finished his pho a good five minutes before I did, although my slow speed of consumption was not due to lack of will but because Madame's pho had dissolved me and transported me back in time to my mother's household, where she concocted the broth from the gray beef bones given by my father from his leftovers. Usually we ate the pho without the thin slices of beef that were its protein, we being too poor to afford the meat itself, except for those rare occasions when my suffering mother scraped together enough wherewithal. But poor as she was, my mother brewed the most wonderfully aromatic soup, and I helped her by charring the ginger and onion that would be plunked into the iron pot for flavor. It was also my task to skim the scum that boiled to the top of the broth as the bones simmered, leaving the broth clear and rich. As the bones continued to simmer for hours, I tortured myself by doing my homework by the pot, the aroma taunting and tantalizing. Madame's pho harkened back to the warmth of my mother's kitchen, which was probably not as warm as it was in my memories, but never mind—I had to stop periodically to savor not only my soup but the marrow of my memories.

Delicious, I said. I haven't had this in years.

Isn't it amazing? I never suspected she had this talent.

You should open a restaurant, I said.

The way you talk! She was clearly pleased.

Have you seen this? The General pulled a newspaper from the stack on the kitchen countertop, the latest edition of Sonny's biweekly paper. I had not seen it yet. What disturbed the General was Sonny's article on the major's funeral, now a few weeks past, and the coverage of the wedding. On the major's demise, Sonny wrote that "the police call this a robbery-homicide, but are we sure an officer of the secret police was without enemies who might want him dead?" And in regards to the wedding, Sonny summarized the speeches and concluded by observing that "perhaps it is time for the talk of war to cease. Isn't the war over?"

He's doing what he's supposed to be doing, I said, even though I knew that he had gone too far. But I agree he may be a little naive.

Is it naïveté? That's a generous reading. He's supposed to be a reporter. That means to report the facts, not to make things up or interpret them or put ideas in people's heads.

He isn't wrong about the major, is he?

Whose side are you on? Madame said, completely shedding the role of cook. Reporters need editors and editors need beatings. That's the best newspaper policy. The problem with Son is that he is his own editor and he goes unchecked.

You're absolutely right, Madame. The Auteur's punch had unnerved me, knocked me out of character. Too much freedom of the press is unhealthy for a democracy, I declared. While I did not believe this, my character, the good captain, did, and as the actor playing this role I had to sympathize with this man. But most actors spent more time with their masks off than on, whereas in my case it was the reverse. No surprise, then, that sometimes I dreamed of trying to pull a mask off my face, only to realize that the mask was my face. Now, with the face of the captain readjusted for a proper fit,

I said, The citizenry can't sift out what is useful and good if there's too much opinion circulating.

No more than two opinions or ideas on any one issue should be out there, the General said. Look at the voting system. Same concept. We had multiple parties and candidates and look at the mess we had. Here you choose the left hand or the right and that's more than enough. Two choices and look at all the drama with every presidential election. Even two choices may be one too many. One choice is enough, and no choice may be even better. Less is more, isn't it? You know the man, Captain. He'll listen to you. Remind him of how we did things back home. Even though we're here, we still need to remember the ways we did things.

In the good old days, Sonny would already be sweating in a holding cell. Out loud, I said, Speaking of the old days, sir, are we making any progress on winning them back again?

Progress is being made, the General said, leaning back in his chair. We have friends and allies in Claude and the Congressman, and they tell me they are not alone. But it's a difficult time for getting support publicly, since the American people don't want to fight another war. So we have to assemble ourselves slowly.

We need a network here and there, I suggested.

I have a list of the officers for our first meeting. I've talked to all of them in person and they are dying for the chance to fight. There's nothing for them here. The only chance for them to regain their honor and be men again is to reclaim our country.

We'll need more than a vanguard.

Vanguard? Madame said. That's communist talk.

Maybe so. But the communists won, Madame. They weren't just lucky. Perhaps we should learn from some of their strategies. A vanguard can lead the rest of the people toward where it is they don't even know they want to go but should go.

He's right, the General said.

The vanguard works clandestinely but sometimes shows the public a different face. Voluntary organizations and the like become the fronts for the vanguard.

Exactly, the General said. Look at Son. We need to make his newspaper one of those front organizations. And we need a youth group, a women's group, even an intellectuals' group.

We also need cells. Parts of the organization need to be secluded from one another so that if one cell is lost, others can survive. This is one cell right here. Then there are the cells Claude and the Congressman are involved in, which I know nothing about.

In due time, Captain. One step at a time. The Congressman is working on certain contacts to clear the way for us to send men to Thailand.

That will be the staging area.

Exactly. A return by sea is too difficult. We have to go overland back into the country. Meanwhile, Claude is finding us money. Money can get us the rest of what we need. We can get the men, but they will need weapons, training, a place to train. They'll need transport to Thailand. We must think like communists, as you say. We must plan far ahead for decades. We must live and work underground, as they did.

At least we're already acquainted with darkness.

We are, aren't we? We had no choice. We have never had a choice, not really, not when it matters. Communism forced us to do everything we have done to oppose it. History has moved us. We have no choice but to fight, to resist evil and to resist being forgotten. This is why—and here the General picked up Sonny's newspaper—even talking about the war being over is dangerous. We must not allow our people to grow complacent.

And neither must we let them forget their resentment, I added. That's where newspapers can play a role, on the culture front.

But only if the journalists do their work as they should. The General tossed the newspaper back on the table. "Resentment." That's a good word. Always resent, never relent. Perhaps that should be our motto.

There's a ring to it, I said.

CHAPTER 9

Much to my surprise, Violet called me the next week. I don't believe we have anything to talk about, I said. He reconsidered your advice, she said. I noticed that she actually used complete sentences with me this time. He's tempestuous and doesn't take criticism well, as he's the first to admit. But after he cooled down, he thought there were some usable ideas in your notes. More than that, he respects you for standing up to him. Not too many people are willing to do that, which makes you an ideal candidate for what I'm proposing. We need a consultant who can get things right when it comes to Vietnamese matters. We've already researched the history, the costumes, the weapons, the customs, anything we could find in a book. But we'll need that human touch you can provide. There are refugees from Vietnam in the Philippines who we'll be using as extras, and we need someone to work with them.

From far away floated the susurrus of my mother's voice: Remember, you're not half of anything, you're twice of everything! Despite all the disadvantages of my poor, muddled heritage, my mother's endless encouragement and fierce belief in me meant that I never backed down from challenge or opportunity. Their offer was four months of paid vacation in a tropical paradise, six months if the shoot went over schedule, and perhaps not so much a paradise if the local rebels got a little too overconfident, and perhaps not so much of a vacation as a working jaunt, and perhaps not so much paid as underpaid, but the upshot was that I needed a respite from my American refuge. Remorse over the crapulent major's death was ringing me up a few times a day, tenacious as a debt collector. Also always there at the crowded back of my mind, front and center in the Catholic chorus of my guilt, stood the major's widow. I had given her only fifty dollars at the funeral, which was all I could afford. Even underpaid, I would be able to save money, given how my room and board would be included, and from this provide some support for the major's wife and children.

They were innocents to whom wrong had been done, as I had once been an innocent child to whom wrong was done. And not by strangers, but by my own family, my aunts who had not wanted me to play with my cousins at family gatherings and who shooed me away from the kitchen when there were treats. I associated my blood aunts with the scars they inflicted on me during the New Year, the time all other children remember with such fondness. What was the first New Year I could remember? Perhaps the one when I was five or six. I huddled with the other children, solemn and nervous, facing the prospect of approaching each adult and making a little speech wishing him or her health and happiness. But although I forgot not a word, and did not stumble like most of my cousins, and radiated sincerity and charm, Aunt Two did not grace me with a red envelope. The entire maternal family tree was watching me, on its gnarled branches my mother's parents, her nine siblings, my three dozen cousins. I do not have enough, this wicked witch said, towering above me. I am one short. I stood immobilized, my arms still folded respectfully across my chest, waiting for a magical envelope or an apology to appear, but nothing more was forthcoming until, after what seemed to be several minutes, my mother laid her hand on my shoulder and said, Thank your aunt for her kindness in teaching you a lesson.

Only later, at home, on the wooden bed we shared, did Mama weep. It did not matter that my other aunts and uncles gave me red envelopes, although when I compared mine with my cousins', I discovered that my sums of lucky money were but half theirs. That's because you're half-blooded, said one calculating cousin. You're a bastard. When I asked Mama what a bastard was, her face inflamed. If I could, she said, I'd strangle him with my bare hands. Never in my life has there been a day when I learned so much about myself, the world, and its inhabitants. One must be grateful for one's education no matter how it arrives. So I was grateful, in a way, for my aunt and my cousin, whose lessons I remember much more than many nobler things that passed before me in school. Oh, they'll see! my mother wept, squeezing me with such force I was nearly breathless, my face pressed against one comforting breast while my hand squeezed its plush other. Radiating through thin cotton fabric was the hot, rich muskiness of a young woman's body after a humid day spent mostly on feet or haunches, preparing food and serving. They'll see! You'll work harder than all of them, you'll study more than all of them, you'll know more than all of them, you'll be better than all of them. Promise your mother you will! And I promised.

I have shared this story with only two people, Man and Bon, censoring just the part about my mother's breasts. This was at the lycée, at separate moments of intimacy in our early adolescence. When Bon heard it, we were fishing in the river, and he flung down his rod in fury. If I ever meet this cousin, he said, I'll beat him until half his blood is coming out of his head. Man was more measured. Even at that age, he was calm, analytical, and precociously dialectical-materialist in his attitude. He had treated me to sugarcane juice after school, and we were sitting on a curb, little plastic sacks in hand, sipping through straws. The red envelope is a symbol, he said, of all that's wrong. It's the color of blood, and they singled you out for your blood. It's the color of fortune and luck. Those are primitive beliefs. We don't succeed or fail because of fortune or luck. We succeed because we understand the way the world works and what we have to do. We fail because others understand this better than we do. They take advantage of things, like your cousins, and they don't question things. As long as things work for them, then they support those things. But you see the lie beneath those things because you never got to take part. You see a different shade of red than them. Red is not good luck. Red is not fortune. Red is revolution.

All of a sudden I, too, saw red, and in that throbbing vision the world began to make sense to me, how so many degrees of meaning existed in a single color, the tone so potent it must be applied sparingly. If one ever sees something written in red, one knows trouble and change lie ahead.

My letters to my aunt, then, were not written in such an alarming shade, even if the cipher I used to code my sub rosa reports disturbed me. Here was one representative example of Richard Hedd's highly esteemed *Asian Communism and the Oriental Mode of Destruction*:

> The Vietnamese peasant will not object to the use of airpower, for he is apolitical, interested only in feeding himself and his family. Bombing his village will of course upset him, but the cost is outweighed ultimately by how airpower will persuade him that he is on the wrong side if he chooses communism, which cannot protect him. (p. 126)

From these kinds of insights, I reported on my decision to take the Auteur's offer, a job I characterized as *undermining the enemy's propaganda*. I also coded the names of the officers in the General's vanguard. Just in case my letter would be read by any eyes other than those of Man's aunt, I kept my tone upbeat about life in Los Angeles. Perhaps unknown censors were reading refugee mail, looking for dejected, angry refugees who could not or would not dream the American Dream. I was careful, then, to present myself as just another immigrant, glad to be in the land where the pursuit of happiness was guaranteed in writing, which, when one comes to think about it, is not such a great deal. Now a guarantee of happiness—that's a great deal. But a guarantee to be allowed to pursue the jackpot of happiness? Merely an opportunity to buy a lottery ticket. Someone would surely win millions, but millions would surely pay for it.

It was in the name of happiness, I told my aunt, that I helped the General toward the next step in his plan, the creation of a nonprofit charitable organization that could receive tax-deductible donations, the Benevolent Fraternity of Former Soldiers of the Army of the Republic of Vietnam. In one reality, the Fraternity served the needs of thousands of veterans who were now men without an army, a country, and an identity. It existed, in short, to increase their meager measure of happiness. In another reality, this Fraternity was a front that allowed the General to receive funds for the Movement from whoever wished to donate, which was not primarily the Vietnamese community. Its refugee members were hobbled by their structural function in the American Dream, which was to be so unhappy as to make other Americans grateful for their happiness. Instead of these refugees, broke and broken, the main donors were to be magnanimous individuals and charitable foundations interested in boosting America's old friends. The Congressman had mentioned his charitable foundation to the General and me at a meeting at his district office, where we presented him the idea for the Fraternity and asked if Congress might help our organization in some way. His district office was a modest outpost in a Huntington Beach strip mall, a two-story arrangement of shops on a major intersection. Drenched in café au lait stucco, the mall was bordered by an example of America's most unique architectural contribution to the world, a parking lot. Some bemoan the brutalism of socialist architecture, but was the blandness of capitalist architecture any better? One could drive for miles along a boulevard and see nothing but parking lots and the kudzu of strip malls catering to every need, from pet shops to water dispensaries to ethnic restaurants and every other imaginable category of mom-and-pop small business, each one an advertisement for the pursuit of happiness. As a sign of his humility and closeness to the people, the Congressman had chosen such a strip mall for his headquarters, and in the windows were plastered white campaign signs with CONGRESSMAN in red and his name in blue, as well as his last campaign slogan: *ALWAYS TRUE.*

An American flag decorated one wall of the Congressman's office. On another wall hung photos of him posing with various tuxedoed luminaries of his Republican Party: Ronald Reagan, Gerald Ford, Richard Nixon, John Wayne, Bob Hope, and even Richard Hedd, whom I recognized immediately from his author photograph. The Congressman offered us cigarettes and we partook for a while, canceling the side effects of the smoke by simultaneously inhaling good cheer, the healthy air of pleasantries concerning wives, children, and favorite sports teams. We also spent some time discussing my forthcoming adventure in the Philippines, which the Madame and General had both approved. What was that line from Marx?

the General said, stroking his chin thoughtfully as he prepared to quote my notes about Marx. Oh, yes. "They cannot represent themselves; they must be represented." Isn't that what's happening here? Marx refers to peasants but he may as well refer to us. We cannot represent ourselves. Hollywood represents us. So we must do what we can to ensure that we are represented well.

I see where this is going, the Congressman said with a grin. He rubbed out his cigarette, leaned his elbows on his desk, and said: So what can this representative do for you? After the General explained the Fraternity and its functions, the Congressman said, Great idea, but Congress isn't touching that. No one even wants to say the name of your country right now.

Understood, Congressman, the General said. We do not need the official support of the American people, and we understand why they would not be enthused.

But their unofficial support is another matter altogether, I said.

Go on.

Even if Congress will not send money our way, there's no preventing civically minded people or organizations, for example charitable foundations, from helping the cause of our traumatized and needy veterans. They've defended freedom and stood shoulder-to-shoulder with the American soldier, sometimes giving blood and sometimes giving limbs.

You've been talking to Claude.

It's true Claude planted certain ideas in my head. During our Saigon days, he mentioned that it was routine for the

CIA to fund various activities. Not in its name, as that might be illegal or at least quite questionable, but through front organizations controlled by its agents and sympathizers, oftentimes respectable people of varied careers.

And the lucky recipients of such money were themselves often front organizations.

Indeed, with all these front organizations professing to help the poor, or feed the hungry, or spread democracy, or aid downtrodden women, or train artists, it can sometimes be difficult to know who does what and for whom.

Let me play devil's advocate. There are many good causes to which I, for example, might donate. But to be frank, there is only so much money that I, for example, might have. Inevitably, self-interest comes into play.

Self-interest is good. It's an instinct that keeps us alive. It's also very patriotic.

Absolutely. So: What is my self-interest in this organization of yours?

I looked at the General. It was on his lips, one of two magical words. If we possessed the things these words named, we would propel ourselves to the front rank of American citizens, able to access all the glittering treasures of American society. Unfortunately, we had only a tentative grasp on one. The word that identified what we did not possess was "money," of which the General might have enough for his own use, but certainly not for a counterrevolution. The other word was "votes," so that together "money votes" was "open sesame" to the deep caverns of the American political system. But even when just one-half of that magical combination floated from my aspiring Ali Baba's lips, the Congressman's eyebrows rippled ever so faintly. Think of our community as an investment, Congressman. A long-term investment. Think of us as a small, sleeping child who has not yet awaken and grown. It is true this child cannot vote. This child is not a citizen. But one day this child will be a citizen. One day this child's children will be born as citizens, and they must vote for somebody. That somebody might as well be you.

As you can see when I attended the wedding, General, I already value your community.

With words, I said. With all due respect, Congressman, words are free. Money is not. Isn't it funny that in a society that values freedom above all things, things that are free are not valued? So please permit me to be blunt. Our community appreciates your words, but in the process of becoming American it has learned the expression "money talks." And if voting is our best way of participating in American politics, we must vote for those who deliver the money. This would hopefully be you, but of course the beauty of American politics is that we have a choice, do we not?

But even if I, for example, give your organization money, the irony is that I myself need money in order to run for election and to pay my staff. In other words, money talks both ways.

That is indeed a tricky situation. But what you are speaking of is official money that must be accounted for to the government. What we are speaking of is unofficial money that circulates to us, which returns to you in all officialness as votes delivered by the General.

That is correct, the General said. If my country has prepared me for one thing, it's dealing with what my young friend describes so imaginatively as unofficial money.

Our performance entertained the Congressman, we the two little ingenious monkeys and he the organ-grinder, watching us hop and beg to a score not our own. We were well trained in this show from our previous exposure to Americans in our homeland, where the plays were all about unofficial money, i.e., corruption. Corruption was like the elephant in Indian lore, myself one of the blind wise men who could feel and describe only one part of it. It is not what one sees or feels that is confusing, it is what one does not see and does not feel, such as that part of the scheme we had just laid before the Congressman that was out of our control. This was the part where he found ways to funnel unofficial money to us via official channels, that is to say, foundations that had on their boards of trustees the Congressman, or his friends, or the friends of Claude. These foundations were, in short, fronts themselves for the CIA and perhaps even other, more enigmatic governmental or nongovernmental organizations I did not know of, just as the Fraternity was a front for the Movement. This the Congressman knew full well when he said, I just hope this organization of yours doesn't engage in anything illegal when it comes to its patriotic activities. Of course he meant that we should engage in illegal activities, so long as he did not know about them. The unseen is almost always underlined with the unsaid.

* * *

Three months later I was en route to the Philippines, my rucksack in the overhead luggage bin, in my lap a copy of *Fodor's Southeast Asia*, a tome as thick as *War and Peace*. It said this about traveling to Asia:

> Why go east? The East has always woven a spell to enchant the West. Asia is vast and teeming and infinitely complex, an inexhaustible source of riches and wonder . . . Asia still holds, for the mind of the West, the lure, the challenge, the spell, and the rewards that have drawn generation after generation of Westerners from their snug, familiar lives into a world utterly different from everything they have known, thought, and believed. For Asia is half the world, the other half . . . The East may well be strange, but it doesn't have to be frustrating. Once you have actually been there you may still find it mysterious, but that's what will make it *really* interesting.

Everything my guidebook said was true and also meaningless. Yes, the East was vast, teeming, and infinitely complex, but wasn't the West also? Pointing out that the East was an inexhaustible source of riches and wonder only implied that it was peculiarly the case, and not so for the West. The Westerner, of course, took his riches and wonder for granted, just as I had never noticed the enchantment of the East or its mystery. If anything, it was the West that was often mysterious, frustrating, and *really* interesting, a world utterly different from everything I had known before I began my education. As with the Westerner, the Easterner was never so bored as he was when on his own shores.

Flipping the pages to the countries that concerned me, I was not surprised to see our country described as "the most devastated land." I, too, would not recommend going there for the casual tourist, as the book proscribed, but I was rather insulted to read the description of our neighboring Cambodians as "easy-going, sensuous, friendly, and emotional . . . Cambodia is not only one of the most charming countries in Asia, it is one of the most fascinating." Surely that could also be said about my homeland, or most homelands with spa-like atmospheric conditions. But what did I know? I had only lived there, and people who live in a given place may have difficulty seeing its charms as well as its faults, both of which are easily available to the tourist's freshly peeled eyes. One could choose between innocence and experience, but one could not have both. At least in the Philippines I would be a tourist, and since the Philippines was east of our homeland, perhaps I would find it infinitely complex. The book's description of the archipelago only made my mind salivate further, for it was "old and new, East and West. It's changing by the day, but traditions persist," a description that might have been written to describe me.

Indeed, I felt at home the instant I stepped from the air-conditioned chamber of the airplane into the humidity-clogged Jetway. The spectacle of the constabulary in the terminal with automatic weapons slung on their shoulders also made me homesick, confirming I was again in a country with its malnourished neck under a dictator's loafer. Further evidence was found in the local newspaper, which had a few inches buried in the middle about the recent unsolved murders of political dissidents, their bullet-riddled bodies dumped in the streets. In a puzzling situation such as this, all riddles lead to one riddler, the dictator. This state of martial law was underwritten once more by Uncle Sam, who was supporting the tyrant Marcos in his efforts to stamp out not only a communist insurgency but also a Muslim one. That support included genuine made-in-the-USA planes, tanks, helicopters, artillery, armored personnel carriers, guns, ammunition, and kit, just as was the case for our homeland, although on a much smaller scale. Toss in a heap of jungle flora and fauna and some teeming masses and all in all the Philippines made a nice substitute for Vietnam itself, which is why the Auteur had chosen it.

The base camp was in a provincial city of the northern Luzon Cordillera, which played the role of the mountainous Annamese Cordillera that separated Vietnam and Laos. My hotel room's amenities included a stream of water that did not so much run as jog, a flush toilet that gave a depressive sigh every time I pulled its chain, a wheezy air conditioner, and an on-call prostitute, or so said the bellboy on first showing me my room. I declined, conscious of myself as a privileged semi-Westerner in an impoverished country. After tipping him, I laid down on the slightly damp sheets, which also reminded me of home, where the humidity soaked into everything. The workmates I met later that night in the hotel bar were less thrilled about the weather, none of them having ever been mugged by the full-force humidity of a tropical climate. It's like getting licked from throat to balls by my dog every time I go outside, the unhappy production designer groaned. He was from Minnesota. His name was Harry. He was hairy.

While the Auteur and Violet would not yet arrive for another week, Harry and his all-male production crew had already been sweating in the Philippines for months, building the sets, preparing the wardrobe, sampling the massage parlors, and being waylaid by various illnesses of gut and crotch. Harry showed me the main set the next morning, a complete reproduction of a Central Highlands hamlet down to the outhouse mounted on a platform above a fishpond. A stack of banana leaves and some old newsprint constituted the toilet paper. Peering through the round porthole of the toilet seat, we could see directly into the deceptively calm waters of the fishpond, which, Harry proudly pointed out, was stocked with a variety of whiskered catfish closely related to the ones of the Mekong Delta. Really ingenious, he said. He had a Minnesotan's admiration for resourcefulness in the face of hardship, bred by generations of people one very bad winter away from starvation and cannibalism. I hear there's a real feeding frenzy when someone's taking a poop.

I had sat on exactly such a splintery toilet seat throughout my childhood, and remembered very well the catfish jockeying for the best seat at the dining table when I assumed the position. The sight of an authentic outhouse stirred neither any sentimental feelings in me nor any admiration for my people's environmental consciousness. I preferred a flush toilet with a smooth porcelain seat and a newspaper on my lap as reading matter, not between my legs. The paper with which the West wiped itself was softer than the paper with which the rest of the world blew its nose, although this was only a metaphorical comparison. The rest of the world would have been stunned at the luxurious idea of even using paper to blow one's nose. Paper was for writing things like this confession, not for mopping up excretions. But those strange, mysterious Westerners had exotic ways and wonders, symbolized in Kleenex and double-ply toilet paper. If longing for these riches made me an Occidentalist, I confess to it. I had no desire for the authenticity of my village life with my spiteful cousins and my ungracious aunts, or the rustic realities of being bit on one's behind by a malarial mosquito when visiting the loo, which might be the case for some of the Vietnamese extras. Harry was planning to make them use this toilet in order to nourish the catfish, while the crew would bask in a battery of chemical toilets on dry land. So far as I was concerned, I was one of the crew, and when Harry invited me to be the first to bless the latrine, I regretfully declined, softening my rejection with a joke.

You know how we can tell that catfish sold in the markets come from ponds like this?

How so? said Harry, ready to take mental notes.

They're cross-eyed from looking up at assholes all the time.

Good one! Harry laughed and slapped my arm. Come on, let me show you the temple. It's really beautiful. I'm going to hate it when the special effects guys blow it up.

Harry may have loved the temple the most, but for me the pièce de résistance was the cemetery. I saw it for the first time that night and returned to it several nights later, after a field trip to the refugee camp at Bataan, where I recruited a hundred Vietnamese extras. The trip had left me dispirited, encountering as I did thousands of ragged fellow countrymen who had fled from our homeland. I had seen refugees before, Commandant, the war having rendered millions of the southern people homeless within their own country, but this mess of humanity was a new kind of species. It was so unique the Western media had given it a new name, the *boat people*, an epithet one might think referred to a newly discovered tribe of the Amazon River or a mysterious, extinguished prehistoric population whose only surviving trace was their watercraft. Depending on one's point of view, these boat people were either runaways from home or orphaned by their country. In either case, they looked bad and smelled a little worse: hair mangy, skin crusty, lips chapped, various glands swollen, collectively reeking like a fishing trawler manned by landlubbers with unsteady digestive tracts. They were too hungry to turn up their noses at the wages I was mandated to offer, a dollar a day, their desperation measured by the fact that not one—let me repeat, *not one*—haggled for a better wage. I had never imagined the day when one of my countrymen would not haggle, but these boat people clearly understood that the law of supply and demand was not on their side. What truly brought my spirits down, however, was when I asked one of the extras, a lawyer of aristocratic appearance, if the conditions in our homeland were as bad as rumored. Let's put it this way, she said. Before the communists won, foreigners were victimizing and terrorizing and humiliating us. Now it's our own people victimizing and terrorizing and humiliating us. I suppose that's improvement.

I trembled at hearing her words. For a few days my conscience had been purring smoothly, the crapulent major's death seemingly behind me in the rear view of my memory, a smear on the blacktop of my past, but now it was hiccuping again. What was happening at home, and what was I doing here? I had to remind myself of Ms. Mori's parting words. When I told her I was taking the job, she had cooked me a farewell dinner where I almost gave in to the sneaky suspicion that perhaps I really did love her, even if I did have feelings for Lana, too. But as if anticipating such weakness on my part, Ms. Mori preemptively reminded me of our commitment to free love. Don't feel obligated to me, she said over the orange sorbet. You can do whatever you want. Of course, I said, a little saddened. I could not have it both ways, free love and bourgeois love, no matter if I wanted to. Or could I? Society of any kind was well stocked with satin bilinguals who said and did one thing in public while saying and doing another in private. But Ms. Mori was not one of those people, and in the darkness of her bedroom, clinging to each other in the aftermath of our exercise in free love, she said, You have it in you to do something wonderful with this movie. I have confidence in you that you can make it better than it could be. You can help shape how Asians look in the movies. That's no small thing.

Thank you, Ms. Mori.

Sofia, goddammit.

Could I really make any difference? What would Man or Ms. Mori think, knowing that I was little more, perhaps, than a collaborator, helping to exploit my fellow countrymen and refugees? The sight of their sad, confused faces had undermined my confidence, reminding me of the ligaments of sentimentality and sympathy that twined my tougher, more revolutionary parts together. I even came down with the hot fever of homesickness, and so it was that when I returned to the base camp, I sought comfort in the hamlet that Harry had created. The dusty lanes, the thatched roofs, the earthen floors of the cottages and their simple bamboo furniture, the piggeries with real pigs already snorting softly in the night, the warble of the innocent chickens, the soupy air, the bite of the mosquitoes, the plop of my unsuspecting foot into a mushy cake of buffalo dung—all of it left me dizzy with the vertigo of sadness and longing. Only one thing was missing from the hamlet and that was the people, the most important of which was my mother. She had died during my junior year in college, when she was just thirty-four. For the first and only time, my father wrote me a letter, brief and to the point: *Your mother has passed away of tuberculosis, poor thing. She is buried in the cemetery under a real headstone.* A real headstone! He had noted it to say in his own way that he had paid for it, since my mother did not have the savings to afford any such thing. I read his letter twice in numb disbelief before the pain struck, the hot lead of sorrow pouring into the mold of my body. She had been sick, but not this sick, unless she had been hiding the real state of her condition from me. We had seen so little of each other over the past few years, what with me hundreds of miles away at the lycée in Saigon and then thousands of miles abroad. The last time I saw her was the month before I left for the States, when I returned to say good-bye for four years. I would have no money to return for Tet, or for the summer, or at all until I finished my degree, my scholarship paying for only one round-trip ticket. She smiled bravely and called me her *petit écolier*, after the chocolate-covered biscuits I loved so much as a child and which my father blessed me with once per year on Christmas. Her parting gifts to me were a box of those imported biscuits—a fortune for a woman who had only nibbled on the corner of one once and saved the rest for me each Christmas—as well as a notebook and a pen. She was barely literate and read out loud, and she wrote with a cramped, shy hand. By the time I was ten, I wrote everything for her. To my mother, a notebook and a pen symbolized everything she could not achieve and everything I, through the grace of God or the accidental combination of my genes, seemed destined for. I ate the biscuits on the airplane and wrote all over the notebook as a college diary. Now it was nothing but ashes. As for the pen, it had run out of ink and I had lost it at some point.

What I would give to have those useless things with me now, kneeling by my mother's tomb and resting my forehead against its rough surface. Not the tomb in the hamlet where she had died, but here, in Luzon, in the cemetery built by Harry just for authenticity's sake. When I had seen his field of stones, I had asked to have the biggest tomb for my own use. On the tombstone I had pasted a reproduction of my mother's black-and-white picture that I carried in my wallet, the only extant image of her besides the rapidly fading ones in my mind, which had taken on the quality of a poorly preserved silent movie, its frames cracked by hairline fractures. On the gray face of the tombstone I painted her name and her dates in red, the mathematics of her life absurdly short for anyone but a grade-schooler to whom thirty-four years seemed an eternity. Tombstone and tomb were cast from adobe rather than carved from marble, but I took comfort in knowing no one would be able to tell on film. At least in this cinematic life she would have a resting place fit for a mandarin's wife, an ersatz but perhaps fitting grave for a woman who was never more than an extra to anyone but me.

CHAPTER 10

When the Auteur arrived the next week, he threw himself a welcome party replete with barbecue, beer, burgers, Heinz ketchup, and a sheet cake big enough to sleep on. The prop department fashioned a fake cauldron from plywood and papier-mâché, stocked it with dry ice, and plopped in a couple of strippers with bleached blond hair from one of the bars around Subic Bay, their job to play white women boiled alive by natives. A handful of obliging young local men played the natives, wearing loincloths and shaking nasty-looking spears also concocted by the prop department. With the Vietnamese extras not due for another day, I was the lone representative of my people wandering among the more than a hundred actors and crew members, with an additional hundred or so Filipino laborers and cooks. These locals thought it was a gas to go up to the cauldron and slice carrots into the stripper soup. I could see the film shoot was going to generate tales of the movie people from Hollywood that would be passed on for decades, stretched ever taller for each succeeding generation. As for the extras, the boat people, they would be forgotten. No one remembered the extras.

Although I was neither one of the extras nor one of the boat people, the tide of sympathy pulled me toward them. The current of alienation simultaneously pushed me away from the movie people, even though I was one of them. In short, I was in a familiar place, the place of feeling unfamiliar, which I responded to in my usual fashion by arming myself with a gin and tonic, my first of the evening. I was sure to be defenseless after my fourth or fifth such drink at this party, which took place under the stars as well as under a huge thatched pavilion that served as the canteen. After trading jokes with Harry, I watched the men of the crew crowd around the few white girls on the set. Meanwhile, a blond-wigged band from Manila pounded out a perfect cover of Diana Ross's "Do You Know Where You're Going To," and I wondered if it had perhaps been one of the same Filipino bands that had played in Saigon's hotels. On the edge of the dance floor sat the Auteur, chatting with the Thespian, while Violet flirted with the Idol at the same table. The Thespian was playing Captain Will Shamus; the Idol was Sergeant Jay Bellamy. While the Thespian had started his long career off Broadway, the Idol was a singer who had flashed to fame with a bubble-gum pop hit so sweet my teeth hurt just on hearing it. *The Hamlet* was the first movie role for the young man, who had shown his commitment by shaving off the evanescent hairdo much imitated by teen-age boys into a GI haircut, then submitting himself to the military drilling required for his role with the enthusiasm of a sexually repressed fraternity initiate. Leaning back on his rattan chair, sporting a white T-shirt and khakis, his perfect ankles exposed because he wore no socks with his boat shoes, he was cool as ice cream even in the tropical weather. That was why he was an Idol, fame his natural aura. Rumor had it that he and the Thespian did not get along, the Thespian being an actor's actor's actor who not only stayed in character the entire time but kept his uniform on as well. The GI fatigues and combat boots he wore were the same set he'd donned three days before, when he arrived and became possibly the first actor in history to demand a pup tent instead of his air-conditioned trailer. Since frontline soldiers did not shower and shave, neither had he, and as a result he had begun to give off the aroma of slightly less than fresh ricotta. On his web belt was a holstered .45, and while all the other guns on the set were empty of ammunition or had blanks, his packed real bullets, or so went another rumor that I am fairly certain originated with the Thespian. He and the Auteur discussed Fellini while Violet and the Idol reminisced about a Sunset Strip nightclub. No one paid any attention to me at all, so I sidled over to the next table, where the Vietnamese actors sat.

Or, to put it more accurately, the actors playing the Vietnamese. My notes to the Auteur had actually effected some change in how we were represented, and more than simply how the screams were now all rendered as *AIEYAAHHH!!!* The most crucial change was the addition of three Vietnamese characters with actual speaking parts, an older brother, a younger sister, and a little brother whose

parents had been slaughtered by King Cong. Older brother
Binh, nicknamed Benny by the Green Berets, was filled with
hatred of King Cong. He loved his American rescuers and
served as their translator. Along with the one black Green
Beret, he would meet the grisliest of deaths at the hands of
King Cong. As for the sister, Mai, she would fall in love with
the young, handsome, idealistic Sergeant Jay Bellamy. She
would then be kidnapped and raped by King Cong, which
served as the justification for the Green Berets utterly anni-
hilating every last trace of King Cong. As for the little boy,
he would be crowned with a Yankees cap in the final scene
and airlifted into the heavens, his ultimate destination being
Jay Bellamy's family in St. Louis, where he would be given a
golden retriever and the nickname Danny Boy.

This was better than nothing, right?

In my naïveté, I had simply assumed that once roles were
created for Vietnamese people, Vietnamese actors would be
found. But no. We looked, Violet told me yesterday, when we
had found time to sip iced tea together on the hotel veranda.
Frankly, there just weren't any qualified Vietnamese actors.
Most of them were amateurs and the handful of professionals all overacted. It must be the way they were trained. You'll
see. Just withhold judgment until you see these actors act.
Unfortunately, withholding judgment was not one of my
strong suits. What Violet was telling me was that we could
not represent ourselves; we must be represented, in this case
by other Asians. The little one playing Danny Boy was the
scion of a venerable Filipino acting family, but if he looked
Vietnamese, then I could pass for the pope. He was simply

too round and well fed to be a boy living in a hamlet, the typical such stripling having been raised without the benefit of any milk except his mother's. No doubt the young actor was talented. He had won the hearts of everyone on set when, on first being introduced, he had rendered a high-pitched version of "Feelings" at the bidding of his mother, who was sitting with him now and fanning him as he nursed a soda. During his performance, the maternal affection of this Venus was so strong I was pulled into her orbit, convinced by her that one day, mark her words, he would be on Broadway. You hear how he says *feelings* and not *peelings*? she whispered. Lessons in elocution! He does not speak like a Filipino at all. Modeling himself on the Thespian, Danny Boy insisted on inhabiting his role and demanded to be called Danny Boy instead of his name, which I could not remember anyway.

The actor playing his older brother could not stand the child, mostly because Danny Boy stole the show with malicious ease whenever the two appeared next to each other. This was especially galling for James Yoon, the best-known performer on the set after the Thespian and the Idol. Yoon was the Asian Everyman, a television actor whose face most people would know but whose name they could not recall. They would say, Oh, that's the Chinese guy on that cop show, or That's the Japanese gardener in that comedy, or That's the Oriental guy, what's his name. Yoon was, in fact, a Korean American in his midthirties who could play a decade older or a decade younger and assume the mask of any Asian ethnicity, so malleable were his generically handsome features. Despite his many television roles, however, he would most likely go down in history for a highly popular recurring television commercial selling Sheen, a brand of dishwashing soap. In each commercial, a different housewife would be confronted by a different kind of sticky dishwashing challenge that could only be solved by the appearance of her chuckling, knowing houseboy, who offered her not his manhood but his ever-ready bottle of Sheen. Relieved and amazed, the housewife would inquire as to how he had come across such cleaning wisdom, whereon he would turn to the camera, wink, smile, and utter the slogan now famous across the nation: *Confucius say, Clean with Sheen!*

Not surprisingly, Yoon was an alcoholic. His face was an accurate thermometer of his condition, the mercurial redness an indicator that the liquor had worked its way up from his toes to his vision, tongue, and brain, for he was flirting with the actress playing his sister even though neither was heterosexual. Yoon had made his intentions known to me over a dozen raw oysters at the hotel bar, their moist, open ears cocked upward to eavesdrop on his attempted seduction. No offense, I said, his hand on my knee, but I've never been so inclined. Yoon shrugged and removed his hand. I always assume a man is at least a latent homosexual until proven otherwise. In any case, you can't blame a gay for trying, he said, smiling a smile utterly unlike my own. Having studied my smile and its effect on people, I knew it had the value of a second-rate global currency like the franc or the mark. But Yoon's smile was the gold standard, so bright it was the only thing you could see or look at, so utterly overpowering in person it was understandable how he had won the role of the Sheen actor. I was happy to buy him a drink to show that I was not bothered by his advances, and he in turn bought me another, and we bonded that night and almost every night that followed.

As Yoon had tried with me, I had tried with Asia Soo, the actress. Like me, she was of mixed-race descent, although of a much more refined pedigree, in her case a British fashion designer mother and a Chinese hotelier father. Her given name really was Asia, her parents foreseeing that any progeny of their unlikely union would surely be blessed with sufficient attributes to live up to the name of an entire ill-defined continent. She had three unfair advantages over any man on the set, with the exception of James Yoon: she was in her early twenties, was a high-end fashion model, and was a lesbian. Every man on the set, myself included, was convinced that he possessed the magic wand that could convert her back to heterosexuality. If that was not achievable, then he would settle for convincing her that he was the kind of liberated man so open to female homosexuality he would not be offended, not at all, in watching her have sex with another woman. Some of us confidently declared that all high-end fashion models did was have sex with each other. If we were high-end fashion models, so the reasoning went, with whom would we rather have sex, men like us or women like them? Such a question was a little deflating to the masculine ego, and it was with some trepidation that I had approached her at the hotel pool. Hi, I said. Perhaps it was my body language, or something in my eyes, for before I could go any further she laid down her copy of *Jonathan Livingston Seagull* and said, You're lovely, but just not my type. It's not your fault. You're a man. Yet again flabbergasted, all I could say was, You can't blame a guy for trying. She did not, so we, too, were friends.

These, then, were the major dramatis personae of *The Hamlet*, all recorded in the letter I sent to my aunt, along with glazed Polaroids of myself and the cast, even one with the reluctant Auteur. Also included were Polaroids of the refugee camp and its denizens, as well as newspaper clippings that the General had provided me before my departure. Drowning! Pillage! Rape! Cannibalism? So went the headlines. The General had read them to me with alternating and escalating notes of horror and triumph, about how refugees were reporting that only one in two boats was surviving the crossing from the beaches and inlets of our homeland to the nearest semifriendly shores in Hong Kong, Indonesia, Malaysia, and the Philippines, storms and pirates sinking the rest. Here it is, the General said, shaking a newspaper at me. The evidence that those communist bastards are purging the country! To Man's aunt, I wrote visibly in my letter about how sad it was to see these stories. Invisibly, I wrote, *Is this really happening? Or propaganda?* As for you, Commandant, what dream do you think compelled these refugees to escape, taking to the sea in leaky little boats that would have terrified Christopher Columbus? If our revolution served the people, why were some of these people voting by fleeing? At the time, I had no answers to these questions. Only now am I beginning to understand.

* * *

Things on set went along smoothly until Christmas, by which time the weather had cooled down considerably, although it still felt like a constant warm shower, according to the Americans. Most of the scenes shot before December were of the noncombat variety: Sergeant Bellamy arrives in Vietnam and promptly gets his camera ripped out of his hand by a motorbike-riding cowboy, a scene shot in the nearby town whose square had been remade in the likeness of downtown Saigon, complete with Renault taxis, authentic Vietnamese-lettered billboards, and haggling sidewalk vendors; Captain Shamus is called to headquarters in the same town, where a general verbally flogs him for blowing the whistle on a corrupt ARVN colonel, then punishes him by dispatching him to command the hamlet; bucolic scenes of rural life with peasants planting rice stalks in paddies, while hardworking Green Berets oversee the construction of hamlet fortifications; a disgruntled Green Beret scrawling, *I believe in God, but God believes in napalm*, on his helmet; Captain Shamus giving a motivational speech to the village militia with their rusty bolt-action rifles and shuffling, sandaled feet; Sergeant Bellamy leading the same militia in battle drills involving marksmanship, crawling under barbed wire, preparing L-shaped night ambushes; and the first skirmishes between the invisible King Cong and the hamlet's defenders, which mostly involved the militia firing their one mortar into the darkness.

My moviemaking days were consumed by ensuring that the extras knew where the wardrobe department was and when to shuffle to their scenes, that their dietary needs were met, that they were paid on a weekly basis their dollar a day, and that the roles for which they were needed were filled. The majority of the roles fell under the category of civilian (i.e., Possibly Innocent but Also Possibly Viet Cong and Therefore Possibly Going to Be Killed for Either Being Innocent or Being Viet Cong). Most of the extras were already familiar with this role, and therefore needed no motivation from me to get into the right psychology for possibly being blown up, dismembered, or just plain shot. The next largest category was the soldier of the Army of the Republic of Vietnam (i.e., the freedom fighter). All the male extras wanted to play this role, even though from the point of view of the American soldiers this was the category of Possibly Friend but Also Possibly Enemy and Therefore Possibly Going to Be Killed for Being Either a Friend or an Enemy. With a good number of ARVN veterans among the extras, I had no problem casting this role. The most troublesome category was the National Liberation Front guerrilla, pejoratively known as the Viet Cong (i.e., Possibly Freedom-Loving Nationalist but Also Possibly Hateful Red Communist but Really Who Cares so Kill Him [or Her] Anyway). Nobody wanted to be the Viet Cong (i.e., the freedom fighters), even though it meant only playing one. The freedom fighters among the refugees despised these other freedom fighters with an unsettling, if not unsurprising, vehemence.

As always, money solved the problem. After some strong persuasion on my part, Violet agreed to double the wages for those extras playing Viet Cong, an incentive that allowed these freedom fighters to forget that playing those other freedom fighters had once been so repugnant an idea. Part of what they found repugnant was that some of them would be called on to torture Binh and rape Mai. My relationship with the Auteur began to unravel around the question of Mai's rape, although he was already irritated with me for speaking up on behalf of the extras in regards to their salary. Undeterred, I sat down at his lunch table the day before the filming of her rape scene and asked him whether a rape was really necessary. It just seems a little heavy-handed, I said. A little shock treatment never hurt an audience, he said, pointing at me with his fork. Sometimes they need a kick in the ass so they can feel something after sitting down for so long. A slap on both cheeks, and I don't mean the ones on their faces. This is war, and rape happens. I have an obligation to show that, although a sellout like you obviously would disagree.

The unprovoked attack stunned me, "sellout" vibrating in my mind with the electrical colors of a Warhol painting. I am not a sellout, I finally managed to say. He snorted. Isn't a sellout what your people would call someone who helps a white man like me? Or is "loser" a better term?

On this latter point I could not disagree. The man who I presented myself as did belong to the losing side, and pointing out that the American side had lost, too, would not help matters any. All right, a loser is what I am, I said. I'm a loser for believing in all the promises your America made to people like me. You came and said we were friends, but what we didn't know was that you could never trust us, much less respect us. Only losers like us couldn't have seen what's so obvious now, how you wouldn't want anyone for your friend who actually wanted to be your friend. Deep down you suspect only fools and traitors would believe your promises.

It was not that he let me speak uninterrupted. That was not his style. Oh, that's rich! he said soon after I began. A moral runt sucks at my teats. A know-it-all who doesn't know anything, an idiot savant minus the savant. You know who else has an opinion about everything that no one pays any attention to? My senile grandmother. You think that because you went to college people should listen to what you say? Too bad you've got a bachelor of science in bullshit.

Perhaps I went too far when I invited him to perform fellatio on me, but he also went too far in threatening to kill me. He's always saying he's going to kill somebody, Violet said after I informed her of what happened. It's just a figure of speech. Promising to gouge out my eyes with a spoon and force-feeding me with them hardly sounded figurative, any more than the depiction of Mai's rape was simply figurative. No, the rape was a brutal act of the imagination, at least as evidenced by the script. As for the actual shooting of the scene, only the Auteur, a handful of select crew, the four rapists, and Asia Soo herself were present. I would have to wait for a year to see the scene myself, at a raucous movie theater in Bangkok. But I was an eyewitness to James Yoon's master scene two weeks later, for which he was stripped naked from the waist up and strapped to a plank. The plank was propped on the body of an extra playing a dead militiaman, leaving the somewhat anxious-looking James Yoon to lie with his head angled toward the earth, braced for the water cure that he was about to receive from the same four Viet Cong who had raped Mai. Standing by James Yoon, the Auteur addressed the extras through me, although he never once looked at me, the two of us no longer on speaking terms.

At this point in the script, you've just made first contact with your enemy, he said to the rapists. The Auteur had picked them because of the particular ferocity they had displayed in various scenes, as well as their distinctive physical features: the rotten banana brownness of their skin and the reptilian slits of their eyes. You ambushed a patrol and this is the sole survivor. He's an imperialist puppet, a lackey, a stooge, a traitor. There's nothing worse in your eyes than someone who sells out his country for some rice and a couple of dollars. As for you, your legendary battalion's been cut in half. Hundreds of your brothers are dead, and hundreds more will die in the battle to come. You're intent on sacrificing yourself for the fatherland but you're naturally fearful. Now comes this sniveling son of a bitch, this backstabber with yellow skin but a white soul. You hate this bastard. You're going to make him confess all his reactionary sins, then make him pay for them. But most of all, remember this: have fun, be yourselves, and just act natural!

These instructions caused some confusion among the extras. The tallest one, and the ranking noncommissioned officer, a sergeant, said, He wants us to torture this guy and look like we're enjoying ourselves, right?

The shortest extra said, But what's that got to do with acting natural?

The tall sergeant said, He tells us that every time.

But it's not natural to act like a VC, Shorty said.

What's wrong? the Auteur said.

Yes, what's wrong? James Yoon said.

Nothing wrong, the tall sergeant said. We okay. We number one. Then he switched back to Vietnamese and told the others, Look. Who cares what he says. He wants us to act natural but we got to act unnatural. We are motherfuckin' VC. Got it?

They certainly did. Here was method acting at its finest, four resentful refugees and former freedom fighters imagining the hateful psychology of the freedom fighters on the other side. With no more prodding from the Auteur once the film started rolling, this gang of four began to howl, slither, and slather over the object of their hatred. At this point in the script, James Yoon's character of Binh, a.k.a. Benny, had been caught on a probe led by the A-Team's only black soldier, Sergeant Pete Attucks. As established in an early anecdote, Attucks traced his genealogy two centuries back to Crispus Attucks, martyred by the British Redcoats in Boston and the first famous black man to sacrifice his life for the cause of white people. Once Attucks's genealogy had been explained, his fate was sealed with superglue. In due time, he stepped into a booby trap, a bear-claw clamp made of bamboo spikes that seized his left foot. While the rest of the Popular Forces squad was handily exterminated, he and Binh fired back until Attucks lost consciousness and Binh ran out of ammunition. When the Viet Cong captured them, they committed one of their infamous, heinous acts

of desecration on Attucks, castrating him and stuffing
his manhood in his mouth. This, according to Claude in
his interrogation course, was something certain Native
American tribes also inflicted on trespassing white settlers,
despite being of a different race thousands of miles away and
more than a century past. See? Claude said, showing us the
slide of an archaic black-and-white illustration depicting
such an indigenous massacre. He followed this with another
slide, a black-and-white photograph featuring the similarly
mutilated corpse of a GI captured by the Viet Cong. Who
says we don't share a common humanity? Claude said,
advancing to the next slide of an American GI urinating on
a Viet Cong corpse.

Binh's fate now rested in the hands of these Viet Cong,
who reserved their scarce water not for bathing but for torture. While James Yoon (or his stunt double, in another
set of shots) was strapped to the plank, a dirty cloth was
wrapped around his head. One of the VC then slowly poured
water from a foot above Binh's head onto the cloth, using
Attucks's own canteens. Fortunately for James Yoon, the
water torture only occurred in the shots involving the stuntman. Under the rag, the stuntman had his nostrils sealed
and a tube for breathing in his mouth, since one cannot, of
course, breathe under the cascade. The sensation suffered
by the victim was close to drowning, or so I have been told
by prisoners who have survived being put to the question,
as the Spanish inquisitors described the infliction of the
water cure. Again and again the question was asked of James
Yoon, and while the water was surging onto his face, the VC

clustered around, cursing, kicking, and punching him—
all in simulation, of course. Such thrashing! Such gurgling!
Such heaving of the breast and belly! After a while, out under
a tropical sun as sultry as Sophia Loren, it was not just James
Yoon but even the extras who started to sweat from their
efforts. This was what few people realize—it's hard work to
beat somebody. I have known many an interrogator who has
strained a back, pulled a muscle, torn a tendon or a ligament,
even broken fingers, toes, hands, and feet, not to mention
going hoarse. For while the prisoner is screaming, crying,
choking, and confessing, or attempting to confess, or simply lying, the interrogator must produce a steady stream of
epithets, insults, grunts, demands, and provocations with
all the concentration and creativity of a woman manning a
dirty-talk sex line. It takes significant mental energy to be
nonrepetitive in heaping verbal abuse, and here, at least, the
extras faltered in their performance. Blame should not be
directed at them. They were not professionals, and the script
merely said, *VC interrogators curse and berate Binh in their
own language.* Left to improvise, the extras proceeded to give
a repetitive lesson in gutter Vietnamese no one on set would
ever forget. Indeed, while most of the crew never learned
how to say "thank you" or "please" in Vietnamese, by the end
of the shoot everyone knew how to say "fuck your mother,"
or "motherfucker," depending on how one translates *du ma.*
I never cared much for the obscenity myself, but I could not
help admiring how the extras squeezed every ounce of juice
from the lime of it, spitting it out as a noun, verb, adjective,
adverb, and exclamation, lending it intonations of not only

hate and anger, but even, at some points, sympathy. *Du ma! Du ma! Du ma!*

Then, after the beating, cursing, and application of the water cure, the wet cloth would be unwrapped from Binh's face to reveal James Yoon, who knew this was his best chance for a supporting actor Oscar. He had been disposed of many times before on-screen as the evanescent Oriental, but none of those deaths possessed this agony, this nobility. Let's see, he had told me one night at our hotel's bar, I've been beaten to death with brass knuckles by Robert Mitchum, knifed in the back by Ernest Borgnine, shot in the head by Frank Sinatra, strangled by James Coburn, hanged by a character actor you don't know, thrown off a skyscraper by another one, pushed out the window of a Zeppelin, and stuffed in a bag of laundry and dropped in the Hudson River by a gang of Chinese guys. Oh, yes, I was also disemboweled by a squad of Japanese. But those were all quick deaths. All I ever got was a few seconds of screen time at most and sometimes barely that. This time, though—and here he trotted out the giddy smile of a freshly crowned beauty pageant queen—it's going to take forever to kill me.

So whenever that cloth was unwrapped, and it was unwrapped many a time during the interrogation session, James Yoon gorged on the scenery with the starved fervor of a man who knew he was not going to be upstaged for once by the perennially cute and unbeatable little boy whose mother would not allow him to watch this scene. He grimaced, he groaned, he grunted, he cried, he wept, he bawled, all with real tears hauled up by the buckets from some well deep inside his body. After this, he yelled, he screamed, he shrieked, he wriggled, he twisted, he contorted, he thrashed, and he heaved, the climax being when he vomited, a chunky regurgitated soup of his salty, vinegary breakfast of chorizo and eggs. At the conclusion of this extended first take there was only cathedral silence on the part of the crew, stunned as they regarded what was left of James Yoon, as scarified and beaten as an uppity slave on an American plantation. The Auteur himself came with a wet towel, knelt by the still strapped-down actor, and tenderly wiped the vomit from James Yoon's face. That was amazing, Jimmy, absolutely amazing.

Thank you, James Yoon gasped.

Now let's try it one more time, just to be sure.

In fact, six more takes were required before the Auteur declared himself satisfied. At noon, after the third take, the Auteur had asked James Yoon if he wanted to break for lunch, but the actor had shuddered and whispered, No, don't unstrap me. I'm being tortured, aren't I? While the rest of the cast and crew retired to the somnolent shade of the canteen, I sat by James Yoon and offered to shelter him with a parasol, but he shook his head with tortoise determination. No, dammit, I'm seeing this through. It's only an hour in the sun. People like Binh went through worse, didn't they? Much worse, I agreed. James Yoon's harrowing experience would at least be finished today, or so he hoped, whereas a real prisoner's mortification continued for days, weeks, months, years. This was true of those captured by my communist comrades, according to our intelligence reports, but it was also true of those interrogated by my colleagues in the Special Branch. Did the Special Branch interrogations take so long because the policemen were being thorough, unimaginative, or sadistic? All of the above, said Claude. And yet the lack of imagination and the sadism contradict the thoroughness. He was lecturing to a classroom of these secret policemen in the National Interrogation Center, the unblinking eyes of the windows looking out onto the Saigon dockyards. The twenty pupils of his subterranean specialty, including myself, were all veterans of the army or police, but we were still intimidated by his authority, the way he held forth with the pedigree of a professor at the Sorbonne or Harvard or Cambridge. Brute force is not the answer, gentlemen, if the question is how to extract information and cooperation. Brute force will get you bad answers, lies, misdirection, or, worse yet, will get you the answer the prisoner thinks you want to hear. He will say anything to stop the pain. All of this stuff—here Claude waved his hand at the tools of the trade assembled on his desk, much of it made in France, including a billy club, a plastic gasoline container repurposed for soapy water, pliers, a hand-cranked electrical generator for a field telephone—all of it is useless. Interrogation is not punishment. Interrogation is a science.

Myself and the other secret policemen dutifully wrote this down in our notebooks. Claude was our American adviser, and we expected state-of-the-art knowledge from him and all the other American advisers. We were not disappointed. Interrogation is about the mind first, the body second, he said. You don't even have to leave a bruise or a mark on the body. Sounds counterintuitive, doesn't it? But it's true.

We've spent millions to prove it in the lab. The principles are basic, but the application can be creative and tailored to the individual or to the imagination of the interrogator. Disorientation. Sensory deprivation. Self-punishment. These principles have been scientifically demonstrated by the best scientists in the world, American scientists. We have shown that the human mind, subject to the right conditions, will break down faster than the human body. All this stuff—again he waved his hand in contempt at what we now saw as Gallic junk, the tools of old world barbarians rather than new world scientists, of medieval torture rather than modern interrogation—it will take months to wear the subject down with these things. But put a sack on the subject's head, wrap his hands in balls of gauze, plug his ears, and drop him in a completely dark cell by himself for a week, and you no longer have a human being capable of resistance. You have a puddle of water.

Water. Water, James Yoon said. Can I get some water, please?

I fetched him some water. Despite the water cure, he had not actually had any water except what was absorbed through the wet cloth, which was just wet enough, he said, to be suffocating. As his arms were still bound, I slowly trickled the water down his throat. Thanks, he muttered, just as any prisoner would be grateful to his torturer for the drop of water, or the morsel of food, or the minute of sleep that the torturer doled out. For once I was relieved to hear the Auteur's voice, calling out, All right, let's get this done so Jimmy can get back to the pool!

By the final take two hours later, James Yoon really was lachrymose with pain, his face bathed in sweat, mucus, vomit, and tears. It was a sight that I had seen before—the communist agent. But that was real, so real I had to stop thinking about her face. I focused on the fictional state of total degradation that the Auteur wanted for the next scene, which itself required several takes. In this scene, the last one of the movie for James Yoon, the Viet Cong, frustrated because of their inability to break their victim and get him to confess to his crimes, beat his brains out with a spade. Being a bit exhausted from torturing their victim, however, the quartet first decide to take a break smoking Pete Attucks's Marlboros. Unfortunately for them, they underestimated the will of this Binh, who, like many of his southern brethren, whether they be freedom fighters or freedom fighters, was as laid-back as a California surfer regarding every matter except the question of independence from tyranny. Left alone without the towel around his head, he was free to bite off his own tongue and drown under a faucet of his own fake blood, a commercial product that cost thirty-five dollars a gallon and of which approximately two gallons were used to paint James Yoon and decorate the earth. When it came to Binh's brains, though, Harry had concocted his own homemade cerebro-matter, a secret recipe of oatmeal mixed with agar, the result being a gray, clumpy, congealed mess that he lovingly daubed on the earth around James Yoon's head. The cinematographer got especially close to capture the look in Binh's eyes, which I could not see from where I was watching, but which I assumed to be some saintly mix of ecstatic pain and painful ecstasy. Despite all the punishment inscribed on him, he had never uttered a word, or at least an intelligible one.

CHAPTER 11

The longer I worked on the Movie, the more I was convinced that I was not only a technical consultant on an artistic project, but an infiltrator into a work of propaganda. A man such as the Auteur would have denied it, seeing his Movie purely as Art, but who was fooling whom? Movies were America's way of softening up the rest of the world, Hollywood relentlessly assaulting the mental defenses of audiences with the hit, the smash, the spectacle, the blockbuster, and, yes, even the box office bomb. It mattered not what story these audiences watched. The point was that it was the American story they watched and loved, up until the day that they themselves might be bombed by the planes they had seen in American movies.

Man, not surprisingly, understood Hollywood's function as the launcher of the intercontinental ballistic missile of Americanization. I had written him a worried letter about the relevance of my work on the Movie, and he had written back his most detailed messages ever. First he addressed my concerns about the refugees: *Conditions here exaggerated there. Remember our Party's principles. Enemies of the Party must be rooted out.* His second message concerned my fear of being a collaborator with the Auteur: *Remember Mao at Yan'an.* That was all, but it dispelled the black crow of doubt sitting on my shoulder. When was the last time an American president found it worth his while to write a speech on the importance of art and literature? I cannot recall. And yet at Yan'an, Mao said that art and literature were crucial to revolution. Conversely, he warned, art and literature could also be tools of domination. Art could not be separated from politics, and politics needed art in order to reach the people where they lived, through entertaining them. By urging me to remember Mao, Man was telling me that my mission with this Movie was important. Perhaps the Movie itself was not terribly important, but what it represented, the genus of the American movie, was. An audience member might love or hate this Movie, or dismiss it as only a story, but those emotions were irrelevant. What mattered was that the audience member, having paid for the ticket, was willing to let American ideas and values seep into the vulnerable tissue of his brain and the absorbent soil of his heart.

When Man first discussed such issues with me, in our study group, I was dazed with his brilliance as well as Mao's. I was a lycée student who had never read Mao, never thought that art and literature had any relationship to politics. Man imparted that lesson by leading myself and the third member of our cell, a bespectacled youth named Ngo, in a spirited discussion of Mao's lecture. The Great

Helmsman's arguments about art thrilled us. Art could be both popular, aimed for the masses, and yet advanced, raising its own aesthetic standard as well as the taste of the masses. We discussed how this could be done in Ngo's garden with blustery teenage self-confidence, interrupted every now and again when Ngo's mother served us a snack. Poor Ngo eventually died in a provincial interrogation center, arrested for possession of antigovernment pamphlets, but back then he was a boy passionately in love with the poetry of Baudelaire. Unlike Man and Ngo, I was never much of an organizer or agitator, which was one reason, Man would say later, that the committees above decided I would be a mole.

He used the English word, which we had learned not so long ago in our English course, taught by a professor whose greatest joy was diagramming sentences. A mole? I said. The animal that digs underground?

The other kind of mole.

There's another kind?

Of course. To think of a mole as that which digs underground misunderstands the meaning of the mole as a spy. A spy's task is not to hide himself where no one can see him, since he will not be able to see anything himself. A spy's task is to hide where everyone can see him and where he can see everything. Now ask yourself: What can everyone see about you but you yourself cannot?

Enough with the riddles, I said. I give up.

There—he pointed at the middle of my face—in plain sight.

I went to the mirror to see for myself, Man peering over my shoulder. There it indeed was, such a part of myself I had long ago ceased to notice it. Keep in mind that you will be not just any mole, Man said, but the mole that is the beauty spot on the nose of power itself.

Man had the natural ability to make the role of a mole, and other potentially dangerous tasks, seem attractive. Who would not want to be a beauty spot? I kept that in mind when I consulted my English dictionary, where I discovered that a mole could also be a kind of pier or harbor, a unit of measurement in chemistry, an abnormal mass of uterine tissue, and, if pronounced differently, a highly spiced Mexican sauce of peppers and chocolate that I would one day try and very much enjoy. But what caught my eye and has stayed with me ever since was the accompanying illustration, which depicted not a beauty spot but the animal, a subterranean, worm-eating mammal with massive clawed feet, a tubular whiskered snout, and pinhole eyes. It was surely ugly to all except its own mother, and nearly blind.

Crushing victims in its path, the Movie rolled with the momentum of a Panzer division toward the climactic firefight at King Cong's lair, which would be followed by said lair's incendiary vaporization by the US Air Force. Several weeks of shooting were required for what amounted to fifteen minutes of screen time popping with helicopters, rocket fire, gun battles, and the utter and magnificent destruction of the elaborate sets that had been raised with every intention of being brought low. Enormous supplies of canned smoke ensured that bewildering mists draped the set every so often, while so many blank rounds were fired, and such significant quantities of detonation cord and explosives used, that all the birds and beasts of the locality vanished in fear and the crew walked around with wicks of cotton in their ears. Of course it was not enough to merely destroy the hamlet and the cave where King Cong hid; to satisfy the Auteur's need for realistic bloodshed, all the extras also had to be killed off. As the script called for the deaths of several hundred Viet Cong and Laotians, while there were only a hundred extras, most died more than once, many four or five times. The demand for extras was reduced only after the pièce de résistance of the firefight, an awesome napalm strike delivered by a pair of low-flying F-5s flown by the Philippine air force. Most of the enemy thus exterminated, all that was required for the shoot's last days were twenty extras, a reduced population that left the hamlet a ghost town.

It was here that the living went to sleep but the undead awoke, as for three dawns the set rang to the cry, *Dead Vietnamese, take your places!* An obedient tribe of zombies rose from the earth, a score of dismembered dead men stumbling forth from the makeup tent all bruised and bloodied, clothing ripped and torn. Some leaned on comrades and hobbled on only one leg, the other leg strapped up to their thigh. In a free hand they carried a fake limb, the white bone protruding, which they positioned somewhere close once they lay down. Others, with an arm inside a shirt and a sleeve hanging empty, carried a fake mangled arm, while a few cupped the brains falling out of their heads. Some gingerly clutched their exposed intestines, which looked for all the world like glistening strings of white, uncooked sausages because that was what they were. The use of sausages was an inspired move, for at the appropriate moment when the shooting started Harry would unleash a stray hound who would dash hungrily onto the scene and begin gnawing madly at the innards of the dead. These corpses were all that remained of the enemy in the smoldering remains of King Cong's lair, scattered about in grotesque poses where they had fallen after being shot, stabbed, beaten, or choked to death in the bitter hand-to-hand melee between the Viet Cong and the Green Berets, along with their Popular Forces. The dead included numerous unfortunate, anonymous Popular Force troops as well as the four Viet Cong who had tortured Binh and raped Mai, their end dealt to them with appropriate vengeance by Shamus and Bellamy, wielding their KA-BAR knives with Homeric frenzy until

They stood panting in a battlefield from which arose only the hiss of embers.

SHAMUS

You hear that?

BELLAMY

I don't hear anything.

SHAMUS

Exactly. It's the sound of peace.

If only! The Movie was not yet complete. An old woman dashed from the cave to fall, wailing, onto the body of her dead VC son. The astonished Green Berets recognized her as the friendly, black-toothed madame of the dismal brothel where they had so often played the venereal disease lottery.

BELLAMY

Christ, Mama San's VC.

SHAMUS

They all are, kid. They all are.

BELLAMY

What do we do with her?

SHAMUS

Nothing. Let's go home.

Shamus forgot the cardinal rule of westerns, detective stories, and war movies: never turn your back on an enemy or a wronged woman. When they did, the enraged Mama San seized her son's AK-47, blasted Shamus from hip to shoulder blades, then fell victim herself to Bellamy, who, spinning quickly, unloaded the last of his magazine. So she died in slow motion, bathed with fourteen lifelike squirts of blood from squibs rigged by Harry, who provided her with two more to bite on. This tastes awful, she said afterward, mouth and chin covered in the fake blood I was wiping off. Was I convincing? Astonishing, I said to her great satisfaction. No one dies like you.

Except, of course, for the Thespian. To ensure that no one could claim that Asia Soo or James Yoon had outacted him, he demanded that his death be filmed eighteen times. The greater acting job was required of the Idol, however, who had to embrace the dying Will Shamus in his arms, a difficult task as the Thespian had still not taken a shower after seven months of shooting. This was despite the fact that no soldier ever passed up the opportunity for a shower or bath, even if it amounted to no more than lathering himself with soap and cold water from a helmet. I mentioned this to the Thespian one night early in the shooting, and he responded with one of those looks of pity and amusement I was by now so used to getting, the kind that implied not only that my fly was undone, but that there was nothing to see even if it was. It is exactly because no soldier has done this that I am, he declared. As a result, no one could force themselves to eat at his table or stand nearer than fifteen or twenty feet, his stink so ghastly that it drew tears to the Idol's face as he leaned in close with every take, weeping and gagging, to hear Shamus whisper his last words: The whore! The whore!

With Shamus dead the stage was set for Bellamy to call for the Arc Light strike on King Cong's lair. In the heavens above, an unseen B-52 Stratofortress would squeeze out thirty thousand pounds of dumb bombs onto the lair, the purpose being not to kill the living but to cleanse the land of the dead, to do a victory dance on King Cong's corpse, to wipe the hippie smile from Mother Earth's face, and to say to the world, *We can't help it—we're Americans*. The scene was a massive industrial production that required the digging of several trenches, which were then filled with two thousand gallons of gasoline, as well as a thousand smoke bombs, several hundred sticks of phosphorous, a few dozen sticks of dynamite, and untold numbers of rockets, flares, and tracers, all deployed to simulate the explosions coming from King Cong's detonating ammunition stockpile, supplied by the Chinese and the Soviets. Everyone on the crew had been waiting for this moment, the greatest blowup ever in cinematic history. It is the moment, the Auteur proclaimed to the massed crew during the last week, when we show that making this movie was going to war itself. When your grandchildren ask you what you did during the war, you can say, I made this movie. I made a great work of art. How do you know you've made a great work of art? A great work of art is something as real as reality itself, and sometimes even more real than the real. Long after this war is forgotten, when its existence is a paragraph in a schoolbook students won't even bother to read, and everyone who survived it is dead, their bodies dust, their memories atoms, their emotions no longer in motion, this work of art will still shine so brightly it will not just be about the war but it will be the war.

And there you have the absurdity. Not that there was not some truth to what the Auteur claimed, for the absurd often has its seed in a truth. Yes, art eventually survives war, its artifacts still towering long after the diurnal rhythms of nature have ground the bodies of millions of warriors to powder, but I had no doubt that in the Auteur's egomaniacal imagination he meant that his work of art, now, was more important than the three or four or six million dead who composed the real meaning of the war. *They cannot represent themselves; they must be represented.* Marx spoke of the oppressed class that was not politically conscious enough to see itself as a class, but was anything ever more true of the dead, as well as the extras? Their fate was so inane that they drank away their dollar a day every night, an act in which I gladly joined them, feeling a small part of myself dying with them, too. For I had an encroaching sense of the meanness of my accomplishment, that I had been deluded in thinking I could effect change in how we were represented. I had altered the script here and there, and incited the creation of a few speaking parts, but to what end? I had not derailed this behemoth, or changed its direction, I had only made its path smoother as the technical consultant in charge of authenticity, the spirit haunting bad movies that aspired to be good ones. My task was to ensure that the people scuttling in the background of the film would be real Vietnamese people saying real Vietnamese things and dressed in real Vietnamese clothing, right before they died. The swing of a dialect and the trim of a costume had to be real, but the truly important things in such a movie, like emotions or ideas, could be fake. I was no more than the garment worker who made sure the stitching was correct in an outfit designed, produced, and consumed by the wealthy white people of the world. They owned the means of production, and therefore the means of representation, and the best that we could ever hope for was to get a word in edgewise before our anonymous deaths.

The Movie was just a sequel to our war and a prequel to the next one that America was destined to wage. Killing the extras was either a reenactment of what had happened to us natives or a dress rehearsal for the next such episode, with the Movie the local anesthetic applied to the American mind, preparing it for any minor irritation before or after such a deed. Ultimately, the technology used to actually obliterate natives came from the military-industrial complex of which Hollywood was a part, doing its dutiful role in the artificial obliteration of natives. I realized this, eventually, on the day the final spectacle was supposed to be shot, when, at the last minute, the Auteur decided to improvise with the plentiful quantities of leftover gasoline and explosives. The day before, unbeknownst to me, the special effects wizards had received the Auteur's instructions: rig the cemetery for destruction. This cemetery had been spared in the original script when King Cong attacked the hamlet, but now the Auteur wanted one more scene illustrating the true depravity of both sides. In this scene, a squad of suicidal guerrillas defiladed amid the tombs, whereon Shamus would call down a white phosphorous strike on the sacred realm of the hamlet's ancestors, obliterating living and dead with 155 mm shells. I learned of this new scene the morning of its shooting, when the Arc Light strike was originally scheduled. Nope, said Harry. The special effects guys finished prepping the cemetery last night.

I love that cemetery. It's the greatest thing you built.

You got thirty minutes to take a picture before boom-boom time.

It was only a fake cemetery with its fake tomb for my mother, but the eradication of this creation, in its wantonness and its whimsy, hurt me with unexpected severity. I had to pay my last respects to my mother and the cemetery, but I was alone in such sentiments. The cemetery was abandoned, the crew still having breakfast. Among the tombs now ran a maze of shallow trenches gleaming with gasoline, while bundled to the backs of the headstones were sticks of dynamite and phosphorous. Clusters of smoke bombs were staked to the ground, hidden from camera view by headstones and the knee-high grass that tickled my bare ankles and shins. With my camera slung around my neck I passed by the names of the dead that Harry had written on the tombstones, copied from the Los Angeles phonebook and attached to people presumably still alive. Among these names of the living in this little plaza of the passed, my mother's name was the only one that genuinely belonged. It was at her headstone I knelt down to say good-bye. The desecration by weather over the past seven months had eroded much of her face in the photographic reproduction, while the red paint with which her name was written had faded to the hue of dried blood on a sidewalk. Melancholy slipped her dry, papery hand into mine as she always did when I thought about my mother, whose life was so short, whose opportunities were so few, whose sacrifices were so great, and who was due to suffer one last indignity for the sake of entertainment.

Mama, I said, my forehead on her headstone. Mama, I miss you so much.

I heard the disembodied voice of the crapulent major, chuckling. Was it just my imagination, or did all the ambient noise of nature cease? In the preternatural calm of my séance with my mother, I thought I might have been successful in communing with her soul, but just when my mother might have whispered something to me, a giant clap of noise ripped the hearing from my ears. At the same time a slap in the face lifted me from my knees and hurled me through a blister of light, knocking me out of focus, one self flying while another self watched. Later, it would be claimed that it was all an accident, the result of a faulty blasting cap that triggered the first explosion, although by then I had decided that it was no accident at all. Only one man could have been responsible for what happened on the set, the man who was so meticulous about every detail that he planned the weekly menu, the Auteur. But at the time of the conflagration, my calm self believed God Himself had struck my blasphemous soul. Through these eyes of my calm self I saw my hysterical, screaming self spread his arms and flail them about like a flightless bird. A great sheet of flame shot up before him, while a wave of heat swept over him with such intensity both he and I lost any sense of feeling. An immense python of helplessness wrapped its smothering grip around us, squeezing us back together into one self with such force I nearly blacked out until my back hit the earth. The meat of my body was now salted, broiled, and tenderized, the world around me afire and stinking of the gasoline sweat emanating from the woolly beasts of black smoke lunging and lurching toward me with ever-mutating faces. Another giant clap tore away the silence clogging my ears as I stumbled to my feet. Meteoritic chunks of earth and rock whizzed by, and I flung one arm over my head and pulled my shirt over my nose and mouth. There was a narrow path through the fire and smoke, and with my eyes blinded by tears and stinging with soot, I ran, yet again, for my life. The shock wave of another explosion slapped my back, an entire tombstone sailed overhead, a smoke grenade tumbled across the path, and a gray cloud blindfolded me. I found my way by avoiding the heat, coughing and wheezing until I reached open air. Still blind, I kept running, hands waving, gasping in oxygen, feeling the sensation a coward always wants to feel and never wants to feel, that he was alive. It was a feeling possible only after surviving a round of Russian roulette with the gambler who never loses, Death. As I was about to thank the God I did not believe in, because yes, ultimately, I was a coward, a blare of trumpets deafened me. In the silence, the earth vanished— the glue of gravity dissolved—and I was propelled skyward, the wreckage of the cemetery blazing before me, receding as I was blown backward, the world passing by in a blurred haze that faded into mute darkness.

That haze . . . that haze was my life flashing before my eyes, only it unreeled so fast I could not see much of it. What I could see was myself, but what was strange was that my life unreeled in reverse, as in those film sequences where someone who has fallen out of a building and gone splat on the sidewalk suddenly leaps up into the air and flies back through the window. So it was with me, running madly backward against an impressionistic background of blotches of color. I gradually shrank in size until I was a teenager, then a child, and then, at last, a baby, crawling, until inevitably I was sucked naked and screaming through that portal every man's mother possesses, into a black hole where all light vanished. As that last glimmer faded, it occurred to me that the light at the end of the tunnel seen by people who have died and come back to life was not Heaven. Wasn't it much more plausible that what they saw was not what lay ahead of them but what lay behind? This was the universal memory of the first tunnel we all pass through, the light at its end penetrating our fetal darkness, disturbing our closed eyelids, beckoning us toward the chute that will deliver us to our inevitable appointment with death. I opened my mouth to scream and then I opened my eyes . . .

I was in a bed shielded by a white curtain, pressed beneath a white sheet. Beyond the curtain came ethereal voices; the ice cube clink of metal; the somersaulting of wheels on linoleum; the maddening squeak of rubber soles; the pitiful beeping of lonely electronic machines. I was dressed in a flimsy crepe gown, but despite the lightness of this and the sheet, a soporific heaviness pressed down on me, scratchy as an army blanket, oppressive as unwanted love. A man in a white coat stood at the foot of my bed, reading a chart on a clipboard with the intensity of a dyslexic. He had the wild, neglected hair of a graduate student in astrophysics; his protuberant belly spilled over the dam of his belt; and he was mumbling into a tape recorder. Patient admitted yesterday suffering from first-degree burns, smoke inhalation, bruises, concussion. He is— At this point he noticed me staring at him. Ah, hello, good morning, said he. Can you hear me, young man? Nod your head. Very good. Can you say something? No? Nothing's wrong with your vocal cords or your tongue.

Still in shock, I'd say. Remember your name? I nodded. Good! Know where you are? I shook my head. A hospital in Manila. The best money can buy. In this hospital, all the doctors not only have MDs. We also have PhDs. That means we are all Philippine Doctors. The MD stands for Manila Doctors. Ha, just joking, my sallow young friend. Of course the MD stands for a medical doctorate and the PhD stands for a philosophy doctorate, which means I can analyze both what I can see and what I cannot see. Everything physical about you is in relatively good shape, given your recent scare. Some damage, yes, but not bad considering you should be dead or seriously maimed. A broken arm or leg, at least. In short, you are remarkably lucky. That being said, I suspect you have a headache of Zsa Zsa Gabor's va-va-va-voom proportions. I recommend anything but psychoanalysis. What I would recommend is a nurse, but we've exported all the pretty ones to America. Any questions? I struggled to speak but nothing came out, so I only shook my head. Rest, then. Remember that the best medical treatment is a sense of relativism. No matter how badly you might feel, take comfort in knowing there's someone who feels much worse.

With that, he slipped through the curtain and I was alone. Above me the ceiling was white. My sheets, white. My hospital gown, white. I must be fine if everything was all white but I was not. I hated white rooms, and now I was alone in one with nothing to distract me. I could live without television, but not without books. Not even a magazine or a fellow patient alleviated the solitude, and as the seconds, minutes, and hours dribbled away like saliva from a mental patient's mouth, a deep unease descended on me, the claustrophobic sense that the past was beginning to emerge from these blank walls. I was saved from any such visitations by the arrival later that afternoon of the four extras who played the Viet Cong torturers. Freshly shaven and in jeans and T-shirts, they did not look like torturers or villains but harmless refugees, slightly befuddled and out of place. They bore, of all things, a cellophane-wrapped fruit basket and a bottle of Johnnie Walker. How you doing, chief? the shortest extra said. You look like hell.

All right, I croaked. Nothing serious. You shouldn't have.

The gifts aren't from us, the tall sergeant said. The director sent them.

That's nice of him.

The tall sergeant and Shorty exchanged a glance. If you say so, Shorty said.

What's that mean?

The tall sergeant sighed. I didn't want to get into it this early, Captain. Look, have a drink first. The least you can do is drink the man's booze.

I wouldn't mind some, said Shorty.

Pour everyone a drink, I said. What do you mean the least I can do?

The tall sergeant insisted I have my drink first, and that warm, sweet glow of affordable blended scotch really did help, as comforting as a homely wife who understands her man's every need. The word is that what happened yesterday was an accident, he said. But it's a hell of a coincidence, isn't it? You get in a fight with the director—yeah, everybody's heard about it—and then you of all people get blown up. I don't have any proof. It's just a hell of a coincidence.

I was silent as he poured me another. I looked at Shorty. What do you think?

I wouldn't put anything past the Americans. They weren't afraid of taking out our president, were they? What's to make you think they wouldn't go after you?

I laughed, even though inside me the little dog of my soul was sitting at attention, nose and ears turned to the wind. You guys are paranoid, I said.

Every paranoid person is right at least once, said the tall sergeant. When he dies.

Believe it or don't, said Shorty. But look, the reason we all came here wasn't just to talk about this. We all wanted to say thanks, Captain, for all the work you did during this whole shoot. You did a swell job, taking care of us, getting us extra pay, talking back to the director.

So let's drink that bastard's liquor in your honor, Captain, said the tall sergeant.

My eyes welled up with tears as they raised their glasses to me, a fellow Vietnamese who was, despite everything, like them. My need for validation and inclusion surprised me, but the trauma of the explosion must have weakened me. Man had already warned me that for the kind of subterranean work we did, there would be no medals or promotions or parades. Having resigned myself to those conditions, the praise of these refugees was unexpected. I comforted myself with the memory of their words after they left, as well as with

Johnnie Walker, forgoing my glass and drinking straight from the bottle. But after the bottle was empty sometime that night, I was finally left with nothing but myself and my thoughts, devious cabdrivers that took me where I did not want to go. Now that my room was dark, all I could see was the only other all-white room I had been in, at the National Interrogation Center back in Saigon, working my first assignment under Claude's supervision. In that instance I was not the patient. The patient, whom I should properly call the prisoner, had a face I could remember very clearly, so often had I studied him via the the cameras mounted in the corners of his room. Every inch of it had been painted white, including his bed frame, his desk, his chair, and his bucket, the only other occupants. Even the trays and the plates with his food and the cup for his water and his bar of soap were white, and he was only allowed to wear a white T-shirt and white boxer shorts. Besides the door, the only other opening was for sewage, a little dark hole in the corner.

I was there when the workmen built the room and painted it. The idea for the all-white room was Claude's, as was the use of air conditioners to keep the room at eighteen degrees Celsius, cool even by Western standards and freezing for the prisoner. This is an experiment, Claude said, to see whether a prisoner will soften up under certain conditions. These conditions included overhead fluorescents that were never turned off. They provided his only light, the timelessness matching the spacelessness induced by the overwhelming whiteness. White-painted speakers were the final touch, mounted on the wall and ready to broadcast at every minute of the day. What should we play? Claude asked. It has to be something he can't stand.

He looked at me expectantly, ready to grade me. There was little I could do for the prisoner, try as I might. Claude would eventually find the music he could not stand, and if I did not help him my reputation as a good student would lose a little of its luster. The prisoner's only real hope of escaping from his situation lay not with me, but with the liberation of the entire south. So I said, Country music. The average Vietnamese cannot bear it. That southern twang, that peculiar rhythm, those strange stories—the music drives us a little crazy.

Perfect, Claude said. So what song's it going to be?

After a little research, I procured a record from the jukebox of one of the Saigon bars popular with white soldiers. "Hey, Good Lookin'" was by the famous Hank Williams, the country music icon whose nasal voice personified the utter whiteness of the music, at least to our ears. Even someone as exposed to American culture as I shivered a little on hearing this record, somewhat scratchy from having been played so many times. Country music was the most segregated kind of music in America, where even whites played jazz and even blacks sang in the opera. Something like country music was what lynch mobs must have enjoyed while stringing up their black victims. Country music was not necessarily lynching music, but no other music could be imagined as lynching's accompaniment. Beethoven's Ninth was the opus for Nazis, concentration camp commanders, and possibly President Truman as he contemplated atomizing Hiroshima, classical music the refined score for the high-minded extermination of brutish hordes. Country music was set to the more humble beat of the red-blooded, bloodthirsty American heartland. It was for fear of being beaten to this beat that black soldiers avoided the Saigon bars where their white comrades kept the jukeboxes humming with Hank Williams and his kind, sonic signposts that said, in essence, *No Niggers*.

It was with confidence, then, that I chose this song to be played on an endless loop in the prisoner's room except for the times when I was in it. Claude had assigned me to be the chief interrogator, the task of breaking the prisoner my graduation exam from his interrogation course. We kept the prisoner in the room for a week before I even saw him, nothing interrupting the constant light and music except the opening of a slot in his door three times a day, when his meal was shoved through: a bowl of rice, one hundred grams of boiled greens, fifty grams of boiled meat, twelve ounces of water. If he behaved well, we told him, we would give him the food of his choice. I watched him on the video feed as he ate his food, as he squatted over his hole, as he washed himself from his bucket, as he paced his room, as he lay on his bed with his forearm over his eyes, as he did push-ups and sit-ups, and as he plugged his ears with his fingers. When he did so, I turned up the volume, forced to do something with Claude standing by my side. When he took his fingers out of his ears and I lowered the volume, he looked up at one of the cameras and shouted in English, Fuck you, Americans! Claude chuckled. At least he's talking. It's the ones who don't say anything you really have to worry about.

He was the leader of cell C-7 of terrorist unit Z-99. Based in the secret zone of Binh Duong Province, Z-99 was collectively responsible for hundreds of grenade attacks, minings, bombings, mortarings, and assassinations that had killed a few thousand and terrorized Saigon. Z-99's trademark was the dual bomb attack, the second designed to kill the rescuers who came to help the victims of the first. Our prisoner's specialty was the adaptation of wristwatches as triggering devices for these improvised bombs. The second and hour hands were removed from a watch, a battery wire was inserted through a hole in the crystal, and the minute hand was set to the desired delay time. When the ticking minute hand touched the wire, the bomb detonated. Bombs were built from landmines, stolen from US supplies, or bought on the black market. Other bombs were assembled from TNT that was smuggled into the city in small quantities—hidden in hollowed-out pineapples and baguettes and the like, even in women's bras, which led to endless jokes among the Special Branch. We knew Z-99 had a watchmaker, and before we had known exactly who he was we called him the Watchman, which was how I thought of him.

The Watchman regarded me with amusement the first time I entered his room, a week after we began his treatment. It was not the reaction I expected. Hey, good lookin', he said in English. I sat on his chair and he on his bed, a tiny, shivering man with a full head of coarse hair, shockingly black in the white room. I appreciate the English lesson, he said, grinning at me. Keep playing that music! I love it! Of course he didn't. There was a glint in his eye, the briefest hint of unwellness, although that might have come from being a graduate of philosophy from the University of Saigon and the eldest son of a respectable Catholic family who had disowned him for his revolutionary activities. Watchmaking of the legitimate kind—for that was indeed his profession before he became a terrorist—was simply to pay the bills, as he told me during our initial conversation. This was small talk, get-to-know-you kind of stuff, but lurking underneath the flirtation was our mutual awareness of our roles as prisoner and interrogator. My awareness was compounded by knowing that Claude was watching us on the video monitor. I was thankful for the air-conditioning. Otherwise I would have been sweating, trying to figure out how to be both enemy and friend to the Watchman.

I laid out the charges against him of subversion, conspiracy, and murder, but emphasized that he was innocent until proven guilty, which made him laugh. Your American puppet masters like to say that, but it's stupid, he said. History, humanity, religion, this war tells us exactly the reverse. We are all guilty until proven innocent, as even the Americans have shown. Why else do they believe everyone is really Viet Cong? Why else do they shoot first and ask questions later? Because to them all yellow people are guilty until proven innocent. Americans are a confused people because they can't admit this contradiction. They believe in a universe of divine justice where the human race is guilty of sin, but they also believe in a secular justice where human beings are presumed innocent. You can't have both. You know how Americans deal with it? They pretend they are eternally innocent no matter how many times they lose their innocence. The problem is that those who insist on their innocence believe anything they do is just. At least we who believe in our own guilt know what dark things we can do.

I was impressed with his understanding of American culture and psychology, but I could not show it. Instead, I said, So you would rather be presumed guilty?

If you haven't understood that your masters already believe me to be guilty and will treat me as such, then you're not as smart as you think you are. But that is hardly a surprise. You're a bastard, and like all hybrids you are defective.

In retrospect, I do not believe he meant to insult me. Like most philosophers, he simply lacked social skills. In his graceless way, he was merely stating what he and many others thought to be scientific fact. And yet, in that white room, I admit that I saw red. I could have dragged out this interrogation for years if I wanted to, asking him relentless questions that led nowhere as I tried, seemingly, to find his weakness, secretly keeping him safe. But instead all I wanted at that moment was to prove to him that I was, indeed, as smart as I thought I was, which meant smarter than him. Between the two of us, only one could be the master. The other had to be the slave.

How did I prove this to him? One night in my quarters, after my rage had cooled and hardened, it struck me that I, the bastard, understood him, the philosopher, with perfect clarity. A person's strength was always his weakness, and vice versa. The weakness was there to be seen if one could see it. In the Watchman's case, he was the revolutionary willing to walk away from the most important thing to a Vietnamese and a Catholic, his family, for whom the only acceptable sacrifice was for God. His strength was in his sacrifice, and that had to be destroyed. I sat down immediately at my desk and wrote the Watchman's confession for him. He read my scenario the next morning in disbelief, then read it again before glaring at me. You're saying that I'm saying I'm a faggot? Homosexual, I corrected. You're going to spread filth about me? he said. Lies? I have never been a faggot. I have never dreamed of being a faggot. This—this is dirty. His voice rose and his face flushed. To have me say I joined the revolution because I loved a man? To say this was why I ran away from my family? That my faggotry explains my love for philosophy? That being a faggot is the reason for my wish to destroy society? That I betrayed the revolution so I could save the man I loved, who you have captured? No one will believe this!

Then no one will care when we publish it in the newspapers along with your lover's confession and intimate photographs of the two of you.

You will never get me in such a photograph.

The CIA has remarkable talents with hypnosis and drugs. He fell silent. I continued: When the newspapers cover this, you realize it's not only your revolutionary comrades who will condemn you. The road back to your family will be closed forever, too. They might accept a reformed revolutionary, or even a victorious one, but they will never accept a homosexual no matter what happens to our country. You'll be a man who sacrificed everything for nothing. You will not even be a memory to your comrades or your family. At least if you talk to me this confession won't be published. Your reputation will stay intact until the day the war is over. I stood up. Think about it. He said nothing and did nothing except stare at his confession. I paused at the door. Still think I'm a bastard?

No, he said tonelessly. You're just an asshole.

Why had I done that? In my white room, I had nothing but time on my hands to ponder this event I had whitewashed from my mind, the event to which I am confessing now. The Watchman had infuriated me, pushing me into irrational action with his pseudoscientific judgment. But he would not have been able to do so if I had simply executed my role as the mole. Instead, I confess I took pleasure in doing what I was supposed to do and not supposed to do, interrogate him until he broke, as Claude had requested. He replayed the scene for me later in the surveillance room, where I watched myself watching the Watchman as he stared at his confession, knowing he was out of time, a character in a movie, as it were, that Claude had produced and I had directed. The Watchman could not represent himself; I had represented him.

Brilliant work, Claude said. You really fucked this guy.

I was a good student. I knew what my teacher wanted and, more than that, I enjoyed his praise at the expense of the bad student. For wasn't that what the Watchman was? He had learned what the Americans taught, but he had rejected those teachings outright. I was more sympathetic to the thinking of Americans, and I confess that I could not help but see myself in their place as I broke the Watchman. He threatened them, and thus, to some extent, me. But the satisfaction I had at his expense did not last long. In the end, he would show everyone what it was that a bad student could accomplish. He would outsmart me by proving that it was possible to sabotage the means of production that you did not own, to destroy the representation that owned you. His final move happened one morning a week after I had shown him his confession, when I got a call at the officers' quarters from the guard in the surveillance room. By the time I reached the National Interrogation Center, Claude was also there. The Watchman was curled up on his white bed, facing the white wall, clad in his white shorts and T-shirt. When we rolled him over, his face was purple and his eyes bulged. Deep in his open mouth, at the back of his throat, a white lump. I just went to the bathroom, the guard blubbered. He was eating breakfast. What was he going to do in two minutes? What the Watchman had done was choke himself to death. He had been on good behavior for the past week, and we had rewarded him with what he wanted for breakfast. I like hard-boiled eggs, he said. So he had peeled and eaten the first two before swallowing the third one whole, shell and all. *Hey, good lookin'* . . .

Turn off that goddamn music, Claude said to the guard.

Time had stopped for the Watchman. What I did not realize until I woke up in my own white room was that time had stopped for me, too. I could see that other white room with utter clarity from my own, my eye peering through a camera in the corner, watching Claude and myself standing over the Watchman. It's not your fault, said Claude. Even I didn't think about this. He patted my shoulder reassuringly but I said nothing, the smell of sulfur driving everything out of my mind except for the thought that I was not a bastard, I was not a bastard, I was not, I was not, I was not, unless, somehow, I was.

CHAPTER 12

By the time I emerged from the hospital, my services were no longer needed, and I was not invited back to the set for the mopping-up operation that took place after the shooting was completed. Instead, I found that an airplane ticket had been reserved for my instant departure from the Philippines, and I spent the entire trip brooding over the problem of representation. Not to own the means of production can lead to premature death, but not to own the means of representation is also a kind of death. For if we are represented by others, might they not, one day, hose our deaths off memory's laminated floor? Still smarting from my wounds even now, I cannot help but wonder, writing this confession, whether I own my own representation or whether you, my confessor, do.

The sight of Bon waiting for me at the Los Angeles airport made me feel a little better. He looked exactly the same, and when I opened our apartment door I was relieved to see that while it had not improved, neither had it worsened. The Frigidaire remained our decrepit diorama's main attraction, thoughtfully stocked by Bon with enough beer to cure me of my jet lag, though not enough to cure me of the unexpected sadness massaged into my pores. I was still awake when he went to sleep, leaving me with the latest letter from my Parisian aunt. Before I retired, I dutifully composed my report to her. *The Hamlet* was complete, I wrote. But, more important, the Movement had established a revenue source.

A restaurant? I had said when Bon broke the news over our first round of beer.

That's what I said. Madame's actually a good cook.

Hers was the last decent Vietnamese food I had eaten, reason enough for me to call the General the next day and congratulate him on Madame's new enterprise. As expected, he urged me to come for a welcome back meal at the restaurant, which I found on Chinatown's Broadway, bracketed by a tea shop and an herbalist. Once we had surrounded the Chinese in Cholon, the General said from behind his cash register. Now we're surrounded by them. He sighed, his hands resting on the keys of the register, ready to bash out a harsh tune on that makeshift piano. Remember when I came here with nothing? Of course I remember, I said, even though the General had not actually come here with nothing. Madame had sewn a considerable number of gold ounces into the lining of her clothes and her children's, and the General had strapped a money belt full of dollars around his waist. But amnesia was as American as apple pie, and it was much preferred by Americans over both humble pie and the fraught foods of foreign intruders. Like us, Americans were suspicious of unfamiliar food, which they identified with the strangers who brought them. We instinctively knew that in order for Americans to find refugees like us acceptable, they first had to find our food digestible (not to mention affordable and pronounceable). Because it was no easy thing to overcome this digestive skepticism or make a profit from it, a dimension of courage existed in General and Madame's enterprise, as I told him.

Courageous? I find it degrading. Did you ever foresee the day when I would own a restaurant? The General gestured at the small confines of what had previously been a chop suey house, brown measles of grease still speckling the walls. No, sir, I said. Well, neither did I. It could at least have been a nice restaurant, instead of this. He spoke with such pathetic resignation I felt a renewed sympathy for him. Nothing had been done to renovate the restaurant, the linoleum floor battered, the yellow paint dull, the overhead lighting flat and harsh. The waiters were, he pointed out, veterans. That one's Special Forces, and that one's Airborne. In trucker caps and ill-fitting dress shirts that must have been rummaged from a thrift store, or bestowed on them by a strapping sponsor, the waiters did not look like killers. They looked like the anonymous men with bad haircuts who delivered Chinese takeout, the men who waited nervously in hospital emergency rooms without insurance, who fled the scenes of car accidents because they did not have licenses or registration. They wobbled as much as the table that the General led me to, its base uneven. Madame herself brought me a bowl of the pho special and joined us, both watching me eat one of the best examples I had ever indulged in of our national soup.

It's still delicious, I said after the first sip and bite. Madame remained unmoved, as glum as her husband. You should be proud of such . . . such soup.

We should be proud of selling soup? Madame said. Or owning a hole-in-the-wall? That's what one of our customers called this place. We don't even own it, said the General. We lease it. Their moroseness was matched by their appearance. Madame's hair was pinned back in a librarian's stale bun, when before it had almost always been worn in a glamor-ous bouffant or beehive that recalled the go-go days of the early sixties. She, like the General, wore off-the-rack clothing consisting of a mannish polo shirt, shapeless khakis, and the American footwear of choice, sneakers. They wore, in short, what almost every other middle-aged American couple I had encountered at the supermarket, the post office, or the gas station wore. The sartorial impression was to make them, like many American adults, look like overgrown children, the effect enhanced when these adults were spotted, as they often were, sucking on extra-large sodas. These petit bourgeois restaurateurs were not the aristocratic patriots I had lived with for five years and for whom I felt not only some fear but also a degree of affection. Their sadness was my sadness, too, so I turned the conversation toward a topic I knew might lift their spirits.

So, I said, what's this about the restaurant funding the revolution?

A wonderful idea, isn't it? said the General, brightening. Seeing Madame's eyes turn to the ceiling, I suspected that it was, in fact, her idea. Hole-in-the-wall or not, this is the first such restaurant in this city, he said. Perhaps even in this country. As you can see, our countrymen are starving for a taste of home. Although it was only eleven thirty in the morning, every table and booth was occupied by people eating soup with chopsticks in one hand and spoon in the other. The restaurant was redolent with the fragrance of home and resonant with its sounds, the chatter of our native tongue competing with heartfelt slurping. This is a nonprofit enterprise, so to speak, said the General. All profits go to the Movement.

When I asked who knew about this, Madame said, Everyone and no one. It's a secret, but an open secret. People come here and their soup is spiced with the idea they're helping the revolution. As for the revolution, the General said, everything is almost in place, even the uniforms. Madame is in charge of those, as well as the women's auxiliary and the making of flags. What a spectacle she can create! You missed the Tet celebration she organized in Orange County. You should have seen it! I have photos to show you. How the people cried and cheered when they saw our men in camouflage and uniform, carrying our flag. We've assembled the first companies of volunteers, all veterans. They train every weekend. From this group, we're going to cull the best for the next step. He leaned over the table to whisper the rest. We're sending a reconnaissance team to Thailand. They'll link up with our forward field base and reconnoiter a path overland to Vietnam. Claude says the time is nearly right.

I poured myself a cup of tea. Is Bon a part of this team?

Of course. I hate to lose such a good worker, but he's the best we have for this kind of work. What do you think?

I was thinking that the only route overland from Thailand involved trekking through Laos or Cambodia, avoiding established roads and choosing the treacherous terrain of disease-ridden jungles, forests, and mountains where the only inhabitants would be brooding monkeys, man-eating tigers, and hostile, frightened locals unlikely to give aid. These badlands were the perfect setting for a movie, and a horrible one for a mission that was almost certainly do or die. I would not have to tell Bon this. My crazy friend had volunteered not despite the fact that his chances of returning were slim, but because of them. I looked at my hand, at the red scar engraved there. I was suddenly aware of the outline of my body, of the sensation of the chair underneath my thighs, of the fragility of the force holding together my body and my life. It would not take much to destroy that force, which most of us took for granted until the moment when we could not. What I think, I said, not allowing myself to deliberate any further, is that if Bon is going I should go, too.

The General clapped his hands together in delight and turned to Madame. What did I tell you? I knew he would volunteer. Captain, I never had any doubt. But you know as well as I that you'll do better staying here and working with me on the planning and logistics, not to mention the fund-raising and the diplomacy. I've told the Congressman the community is gathering funds to send an aid team to help the refugees in Thailand. That is, in a sense, what we're doing, but we'll need to continue persuading our supporters of that cause.

Or at least give them a reason to pretend to believe that is our cause, I said.

The General nodded with satisfaction. Exactly right! I know you're disappointed, but it's for the best. You'll be more useful here than there, and Bon can take care of himself. Now look, it's nearly noon. I think it's the right time for a beer, don't you?

Visible over Madame's shoulder was a clock, hanging on the wall between a flag and a poster. The poster was for a new brand of beer, featuring three bikini-clad young women sprouting breasts the size and shape of children's balloons; the flag was of the defeated Republic of Vietnam, three bold red horizontal stripes on a vivid field of yellow. This was the flag, as the General had noted more than once to me, of the free Vietnamese people. I had seen the flag countless times before, and posters like that one often, but I had never seen this type of clock, carved from hardwood into the shape of our homeland. For this clock that was a country, and this country that was a clock, the minute and hour hands pivoted in the south, the numbers of the dial a halo around Saigon. Some craftsman in exile had understood that this was exactly the timepiece his refugee countrymen desired. We were displaced persons, but it was time more than space that defined us. While the distance to return to our lost country was far but finite, the number of years it would take to close that distance was potentially infinite. Thus, for displaced people, the first question was always about time: When can I return?

Speaking of punctuality, I said to Madame, your clock is set to the wrong time.

No, she said, rising to fetch the beer. It's set to Saigon time.

Of course it was. How could I not have seen it? Saigon time was fourteen hours off, although if one judged time by this clock, it was we who were fourteen hours off. Refugee, exile, immigrant—whatever species of displaced human we were, we did not simply live in two cultures, as celebrants of the great American melting pot imagined. Displaced people also lived in two time zones, the here and the there, the present and the past, being as we were reluctant time travelers. But while science fiction imagined time travelers as moving forward or backward in time, this timepiece demonstrated a different chronology. The open secret of the clock, naked for all to see, was that we were only going in circles.

After lunch, I debriefed the General and Madame on my Philippine adventures, which simultaneously lightened their gloominess and heightened their sense of resentment. Resentment was an antidote to gloominess, as it was for sadness, melancholy, despair, etc. One way to forget a certain kind of pain was to feel another kind of pain, as when the doctor examining you for mandatory military service (an exam that you never fail, unless you are afflicted by wealth) slaps you on one butt cheek while injecting you in the other cheek. The one thing I did not tell the General and Madame—besides myself nearly meeting the fate of

one of those roasted ducks hung from its anus in the neighboring Chinese eatery's window—was that I had been paid
compensation for my near butchering. The morning after
the extras had come bearing gifts, I had received two other
visitors, Violet and a tall, thin white man in a powder-blue
suit, his paisley tie as fat as Elvis Presley and his shirt the
rich yellow color of urine after a meal of asparagus. How
do you feel? she asked. All white, I whispered, although I
could speak perfectly fine. She looked at me suspiciously
and said, We're all concerned about you. He wanted you to
know he would have come himself but President Marcos is
visiting the set today.

He who did not need to be named was, of course, the
Auteur. I merely nodded, sagely and sadly, and said, I understand, though the mere mention of him infuriated me. This is
the best hospital in Manila, the man in the suit said, flashing
a searchlight of a smile onto my face. We all want the best
possible care for you. How are you feeling? To tell you the
truth, I said, proceeding to lie, I feel terrible. What a shame,
he said. Let me introduce myself. He produced a pristine
white business card with edges so sharp I feared a paper
cut. I am a representative for the film studio. We want you
to know we are paying all the bills for your hospital care.

What happened?

You don't remember? Violet asked.

An explosion. A lot of explosions.

It was an accident. I have the report here, said the representative, lifting a liver-colored briefcase high enough for me
to see its gleaming gold buckles. Such efficiency! I skimmed

the report. Its details were not as significant as what its existence proved, that fast work of this type, as in our homeland, was only possible by an application of grease to the palms.

Am I lucky to be alive?

Extremely lucky, he said. You have your life, your well-being, and a check in my briefcase for the sum of five thousand dollars. According to the medical reports I've seen, you suffered smoke inhalation, some scrapes and bruises, a few mild burns, a bump on your head, and a concussion. Nothing broken, nothing ruptured, nothing permanent. But the studio wants to ensure that all your needs are met. The representative opened the briefcase and produced a stapled document of white papers and a long slip of green paper, the check. Of course, you will have to sign a receipt, as well as this document releasing the studio from any future obligations.

Was five thousand dollars the worth of my miserable life? Admittedly it was a considerable amount, more than I had ever seen at any one time. That was what they were counting on, but even in my dazed state, I knew better than to settle for the first offer. Thank you for this generous pledge, I said. It is decent of the studio to worry on my behalf, to be so concerned with me. But as you may know, or maybe you do not, I am my extended family's principal support. Five thousand dollars is wonderful if I thought only of myself, but an Asian—here I paused and allowed a faraway look to come into my eyes, the better to give them time to imagine the vast genealogical banyan tree extending above me, overshadowing me with the oppressive weight of generations come to root on the top of my head—an Asian cannot think just about himself.

So I've heard, said the representative. The family is everything. Like us Italians.

Yes, you Italians! The Asian must think of his mother, his father. His siblings, his grandparents. His cousins, his village. If word got out of my good luck . . . it would be endless. The favors. The requests for fifty dollars here, a hundred dollars there. Hands tugging at me from all directions. I could not decline. So you see the situation I find myself in. It would be better to take none of the money. I would spare myself these emotional hardships. Or the alternative. To have enough money to take care of all those favors as well as myself.

The representative waited for me to continue, but I waited for him to reply. At last he gave in and said, Not being aware of the complications of Asian families, I am also not aware of the appropriate sum that might satisfy all your familial obligations, which I understand are important to your culture, and which I respect greatly.

I waited for him to continue, but he waited for me to reply. I cannot be certain, I said. But although without certainty, I believe twenty thousand dollars would suffice. To satisfy any needs of my relatives. Anticipated and unanticipated.

Twenty thousand dollars? The representative's eyebrows performed a graceful yoga pose, arching their backs in disturbingly steep concern. Oh, if you only knew the actuarial charts as I know them! For twenty thousand dollars you must lose at least a finger or, preferably, a larger appendage.

If we are speaking of less visible matters, a vital organ or one of your five senses will do.

But in fact, ever since I had awoken from the explosion, something had been nagging at me that I could not name, an itch that was not physical. Now I knew what it was—I had forgotten something, but what that something was, I did not know. Of the three types of forgetting, this was the worst. To know what one had forgotten was common, as was the case with dates of history, mathematical formulas, and people's names. To forget without knowing one has forgotten must be even more common, or maybe less, but it is merciful: in this case one cannot realize what is lost. But to know that one has forgotten something without knowing what that something was made me shudder. I *have* lost something, I said, pain getting the better of me and making itself audible in my voice. I've lost a piece of my mind.

Violet and the representative exchanged glances. I'm afraid I don't understand, he said.

A portion of my memory, I said, completely erased, from the explosion until now.

Unfortunately, you may find that hard to prove.

How to prove to someone else that one has forgotten something, or that one has known something and now no longer knows it? Nevertheless, I persisted with the representative. Even in my bedridden state, the old instincts remained. Like rolling one's own cigarettes, or rolling one's *R*'s, lying was a skill and a habit not easily forgotten. This was true also for the representative, whose kindred tricky spirit I recognized. In negotiations, as in interrogations, a lie was not only acceptable but also expected. All sorts of situations exist where one tells lies in order to reach an acceptable truth, and our conversation continued thus until we agreed on the mutually acceptable sum of ten thousand dollars, which, if being only half what I asked for, was twice their original offer. After the representative wrote a new check, I signed the documents and we traded farewell pleasantries that were worth as little as the trading cards of unknown baseball players. At the door, Violet paused with her hand on the knob, looked over her shoulder at me—was there ever a more romantic pose, even with a woman such as her?—and said, You know we couldn't have done this movie without you.

To believe her was to believe in a femme fatale, in an elected official, in little green men from outer space, in the benevolence of the police, in holy men like my father, who not only had holes in his socks but also had a hole somewhere in his soul. But I wanted to believe, and what did it hurt to believe in her little white lie? Nothing. I was left with the beat of a trashy discotheque in my head and a green check that proved I was somebody, worth more dead than alive. All it cost me, unless they had lied, was a lump on my head and a portion of my memory, something of which I already had too much. Even so, why did I suspect that an operation had been performed on me while I was under the influence, leaving me with numbness more disturbing than pain? Why did I feel some phantom limb of memory, an absence on which I kept trying to rest my weight?

Returning to California with these questions unanswered, I cashed my check and left half in my heretofore barren bank account. The day I visited the General and Madame, the other half was in an envelope in my pocket. Later that afternoon I drove to Monterey Park, where, amid that city's suburbs, soft and bland as tofu, I had an appointment with the crapulent major's widow. I confess that my plan was to give her the money in my pocket, money that I admit could have been used for more revolutionary purposes. But what is more revolutionary than helping one's enemy and his kin? What is more radical than forgiveness? Of course he was not the one asking for forgiveness; I was, for what I had done to him. There was no sign of what I had done to him in the carport, nor did the apartment building's microclimate shimmer with the atmospheric disturbance of his ghost. Although I did not believe in God, I believed in ghosts. I knew this to be true because while I did not fear God, I feared ghosts. God would never appear to me whereas the crapulent major's ghost had, and when his door opened, I held my breath, fearing that it might be his hand on the doorknob. But it was only his widow who was there to greet me, a poor woman whom bereavement had thickened rather than starved.

Captain! It's so good to see you! She invited me to sit on her floral sofa, covered in transparent plastic that squeaked whenever I shifted my weight. Already waiting for me on the coffee table were a pot of Chinese tea and a plate of French ladyfingers. Have a ladyfinger, she urged, pressing the treats on me. I knew the brand, the exact company that manufactured the *petit écolier* biscuits of my childhood. No one could make a guilty pleasure like the French. Ladyfingers had been my mother's favorite, given to her by my father as a lure, although she used the word "gift" when she mentioned it to me in my teenage years. I had enough consciousness to realize what a priest bearing ladyfingers to a child meant, for my mother was nothing but a child at thirteen when my father came wooing. In some cultures today or in the past, thirteen was good enough for mattress, marriage, and motherhood, or perhaps just two out of three on some occasions, but not in contemporary France or our homeland. Not that I did not understand my father, who at the time he fathered me was a few years older than I was now with a ladyfinger melting in my mouth. A girl at thirteen—I admit to having thoughts on occasion about particularly mature American girls, some of whom at thirteen were more developed than college girls in our homeland. But these were thoughts, not deeds. We would all be in Hell if convicted of our thoughts.

Have another ladyfinger, the crapulent major's widow urged, picking one up and leaning forward to thrust it in my face. She would have forced that sweet digit between my lips with maternal urgency but I intercepted her hand, taking the ladyfinger for myself. They're delicious, absolutely delicious, I said. Let me just have a sip of tea first. At this, the good lady burst into tears. What's the matter? I said. Those are the exact words he'd say, she said, which made me nervous, as if the crapulent major was even now manipulating me from behind the curtain separating the theater of life from the backstage of the afterlife.

I miss him so much! she cried. I squeaked my way across the plastic expanse between us and patted her on the

shoulder as she wept. I could not help but see the crapulent
major as I last encountered him in person if not in spirit,
on his back with the third eye in his forehead, his other
eyes open and blank. If God did not exist, then neither did
divine punishment, but this meant nothing to ghosts who
did not need God. I did not need to confess to a God I did
not believe in, but I did need to appease the soul of a ghost
whose face even now gazed at me from the altar on the side
table. There in full cadet uniform was the young crapulent
major, photographed at that phase before his first chin even
dreamed of grandfathering a third chin, dark eyes staring at
me as I comforted his widow. All he had to eat in the afterlife
was a navel orange frosted with mold, a dusty can of Spam,
and a roll of Lifesavers, arrayed in front of his photograph
and illuminated by the incongruous, blinking Christmas
lights she had hung on the altar's edge. Inequality ruled even
in the afterlife, where the descendants of the rich feted them
with heaping platters of fresh fruit, bottles of champagne,
and cans of pâté. Genuinely devoted descendants burned
paper offerings that included not only the usual cutouts of
cars and homes, but also *Playboy* centerfolds. The hot body
of a pliant woman was what a man wanted in the cold, long
afterlife, and I swore to the crapulent major I would make
him an offering of the fantastic, pneumatic Miss June.

To his widow, I said, I promised your husband that if the
need ever arose I would do my utmost to take care of you
and your children. Everything else I told her was the truth,
my supposed accident in the Philippines and my reward, half
of it in the envelope I pressed on her. She resisted gracefully

but when I said, Think of the children, she gave in. There was nothing after that but to surrender to her demand that I see the children. They were in the bedroom, asleep as all children should be. They're my joy, she whispered as we gazed down on the twins. They're keeping me alive in these difficult days, Captain. Thinking about them I don't think about myself so much, or my dear, beloved husband. I said, They're beautiful, which may or may not have been a lie. They were not beautiful to me, but they were beautiful to her. I admit to not being an aficionado of children, having been one and having found my cohort and myself generally despicable. Unlike many, I was not intent on reproducing myself, deliberately or accidentally, since one of myself was more than enough for me to handle. But these children, just a year old, were still unconscious of their guilt. In their sleeping, alien faces I could see them as the naked and easily frightened new immigrants they were, so recently exiled into our world.

The only advantage I had over these twins was that I had had a father in my childhood to teach me about guilt, and they would not. My father taught classes for the children of the diocese, which my mother forced me to attend. In his schoolroom I learned my Bible and the history of my divine Father, the story of my Gallic forefathers, and the catechism of the Catholic Church. At that time, when my years could be counted on the fingers of two hands, I was naive and ignorant of the fact that this father in his black cassock, this holy man who sweated in his unnatural garb to save us from our tropical sins, was also my father. When I did know, it recast everything I learned from him, beginning with this

most basic tenet of our faith, drilled into our young platoon
of Catholics by the father as he walked before our class, reading our lips as we collectively droned the answer:

Q. What is the sin called that we inherit from our first
parents?
A. The sin that we inherit from our first parents is called
Original Sin.

For me, the truly important Question that had always preoccupied me was related to this Original Sin, for it concerned
my father's identity. I was eleven when I learned the Answer,
my knowledge triggered by an incident on the dusty grounds
of the church after Sunday school, a territory where we children reenacted on one another many a biblical atrocity. As
we watched the father's imported bulldog thrust away at
a whining female companion in the shade of a eucalyptus
tree, his tongue hanging, the pink balloon of his enormous
scrotum swinging back and forth with hypnotic rhythm,
one of my more knowledgeable classmates offered a supple-
ment to this lesson in sex education. A dog and a bitch, that's
natural, he said. But him—and here he turned scornful eyes
and finger on me—he's like what happens when a cat and a
dog do that. Everyone's attention turned to me. I stood there
as if on a boat drifting away from the shore where they all
waited, seeing myself through the eyes of others as a creature
neither dog nor cat, neither human nor animal.

A dog and a cat, this little comedian said to me. A dog
and a cat—

When I punched him in the nose, the comedian bled but was silent, shocked, his eyes momentarily crossed as he tried to see the damage. When I punched him again in the nose, the blood gushed, and this time the comedian cried out loudly. I punched him again, working my way from ears to cheeks to solar plexus and then to the hunched shoulders that he drew up around his head to protect himself when he fell to the ground and I fell on top of him. Our peers gathered around us, yelling, screaming, and laughing as I continued to pummel him until my knuckles stung. Not a single one of these witnesses offered to intervene on behalf of the comedian, who finally stopped me when his sobs began sounding like the strangled laughter of someone hearing the best joke ever told. When I stood up, the yelling, screaming, and laughing subsided, and in the adorable faces of those little monsters I could see fear, if not respect. I walked home in confusion, wondering what, exactly, I had learned, unable to put it into words. My mind had no room for anything but the obscene picture of a dog mounting a cat, her animal face replaced by that of no one else but my mother, an image so upsetting that when I arrived home and saw her I burst into tears and confessed everything that had transpired that afternoon.

My child, my child, you are not unnatural, my mother said, clutching me to her as I sobbed against the cushion of her bosom, musky with her distinct fragrance. You are God's gift to me. Nothing or no one could be more natural. Now listen to me, child. When I looked up into her eyes through the mist of my tears, I saw that she, too, was weeping. You have always wanted to know who your father is, and I told you that when you knew, you would be a man. You would have to say good-bye to your childhood. Are you sure you want to know?

When a mother asks her boy if he is ready to be a man, can he say anything else but yes? So I nodded and held her tight, my chin on her breast and my cheek on her collarbone.

You must not tell anyone what I am about to tell you. Your father is . . .

She said his name. Seeing the confusion in my eyes, she said, I was very young when I was his maid. He was always very kind to me, and I was grateful. He taught me how to read and how to count in his language, when my parents couldn't afford to send me to school. We spent a great deal of time together in the evenings, and he would tell me stories of France and his childhood. I could see he was very lonely. He was the only one of his kind in our village, and it seemed to me that I was the only one of my kind, too.

I broke away from my mother's bosom, covering my ears. I no longer wanted to hear, but I was mute, and my mother continued talking. I no longer wanted to see, but images floated before me even though I closed my eyes. He taught me the Word of God, she said, and I learned to read and to count by studying the Bible and memorizing the Ten Commandments. We read sitting at each other's side at his table, by lamplight. And one night . . . but you see, that is why you are not unnatural, child. God Himself sent you, because God would never have permitted what happened between your father and me unless He had some role for you in His Great Plan. That is what I believe and what you must, too. You have a Destiny. Remember that Jesus washed the feet of Mary Magdalene, and welcomed the lepers to his side, and stood against the Pharisees and the powerful. The meek shall inherit the earth, child, and you are one of the meek.

If my mother saw me now, standing over the crapulent major's children, would she still think me one of the meek? And as for these sleeping children, how long would they stay unawake to the guilt they already bore, to the sins and crimes they were doomed to commit? Was it not possible that each of them in his little heart, as they tussled next to each other for their mother's breasts, had already yearned, however briefly, for the disappearance of the other? But the widow was not waiting for an answer to these questions as she stood next to me, peering down at her womb's wonders. She was waiting for me to sprinkle on them the holy water of meaningless compliments, a necessary baptism that I reluctantly gave and that so delighted the widow she insisted on cooking me dinner. I needed little encouragement, given my steady diet of frozen foods, and it soon became clear why the crapulent major had grown ever fatter under her love. Her shaking beef was beyond compare, her stir-fried morning glory evoked my mother's, her winter melon soup soothed my guilty agitation. Even her white rice was fluffier than what I usually ate, the equivalent of goose down when I had slept for years on synthetic fiber. Eat! Eat! Eat! she cried, and in that command it was impossible not to hear my mother's voice urging the same no matter how meager our spread. So I ate until I could eat no more, and when I was done, she insisted there was still the unfinished plate of ladyfingers.

Afterward I drove to a nearby liquor store, an immigrant outpost operated by an impassive Sikh with an impressive handlebar mustache I could never hope to replicate. I bought a copy of *Playboy*, a carton of Marlboro cigarettes, and an achingly lovely see-through bottle of Stolichnaya vodka. That name, with its echoes of Lenin, Stalin, and Kalashnikov, made me feel better about my capitalist indulgences. Vodka was one of the three things the Soviet Union made that were suitable for export, not counting political exiles; the other two were weapons and novels. Weapons I professionally admired, but vodka and novels I loved. A nineteenth-century Russian novel and vodka accompanied each other perfectly. Reading a novel while one sipped vodka legitimized the drink, while the drink made the novel seem much shorter than it truly was. I would have returned to the store to buy such a novel, but instead of *The Brothers Karamazov* it stocked *Sgt. Rock* comics.

It was then, hesitating in the parking lot with my arms wrapped protectively around my paper bag of treasures, that I spotted a pay phone. The urge to call Sofia Mori nagged at me. I had been delaying it for some perverse reason, playing hard to get even though she had no idea I was here to be gotten. Rather than waste a dime and call her, I jumped into my car and drove across the great expanse of Los Angeles.

I felt somewhat at peace after having made my blood payment to the crapulent major's widow, and as I sped down the freeway, sparse with traffic in the postprandial hours, I heard the crapulent major's ghost chortling in my ear. I parked my car down the crowded street from Ms. Mori's apartment and took my paper bag of treasures with me, except for the *Playboy*, which I left in the rear seat for the crapulent major's ghost, opened to the centerfold of Miss June sprawled fetchingly on a stack of hay with nothing on except cowgirl boots and a neckerchief.

Ms. Mori's neighborhood was as I remembered it, beige houses with fading toupees of lawn and gray apartment buildings with the institutional charm of army barracks. The lights glowed in her apartment, the scarlet curtains pulled shut. When she opened the door, the first thing I noticed was her hair, grown down to her shoulders and no longer permed but straight, rendering her younger than I remembered, an effect compounded by her simple clothes, a black T-shirt and blue jeans. It's you! she cried, opening her arms to me. When we embraced, it all came back, her use of baby powder instead of perfume, her perfect body temperature, her small, plush breasts, usually encased in bras well padded enough to handle fragile objects, but tonight free of all such restraint. Why didn't you call? Come in. She pulled me inside the familiar, minimally decorated apartment, furnished in the spirit of revolutionary self-denial she admired in the likes of Che Guevara and Ho Chi Minh, men who traveled light. The largest piece of furniture she owned was a foldable futon in the living room on which her black cat usually sat. This cat had always kept her distance from me. This was not due to fear or respect, for whenever Ms. Mori and I made love, the cat perched on the nightstand and evaluated my performance with disdainful green eyes, occasionally spreading a paw and licking between her bared claws. The cat was present, but she was not lounging directly on the futon. Instead she lay on the lap of Sonny, who sat on the futon with legs crossed underneath himself, barefooted. He grinned apologetically, but nevertheless exuded an aura of ownership as he shooed the cat off his lap and rose. It's good to see you again, old friend, he said, extending his hand. Sofia and I talk often about you.

CHAPTER 13

What did I expect? I had been missing for seven months and had never once phoned, the extent of my communication a few scribbled postcards. As for Ms. Mori, she was dedicated to neither monogamy nor man, much less to any one man in particular. She declared her allegiances through the most prominent furnishings in her living room, bookshelves bowed as the backs of coolies with the weight of Simone de Beauvoir, Anaïs Nin, Angela Davis, and other women who had wrestled with the Woman Question. Western men from Adam to Freud had also asked that question, although they had phrased it as "What does woman want?" At least they had considered the subject. It occurred to me only then that we Vietnamese men never even bothered to ask what woman wanted. I had not even a germ of an idea about what Ms. Mori wanted. Perhaps I would have had a dim sense if I had read some of these books, but all I knew of them were the summaries found on their dust jackets. My intuition told me Sonny had actually read some of them in their entirety, and taking a seat next to him I could feel an anaphylactic reaction to his presence prickling on my skin, an eruption of hostility inflamed by his genial smile.

What do you have there? Sonny said, nodding at the paper bag on my lap. Ms. Mori had gone to fetch another wineglass. A pair already sat on the coffee table, along with an open bottle of red wine, a corkscrew with the wine-bloodied cork still skewered on it, and a photo album. Cigarettes, I said, taking out the carton. And vodka.

I had no choice but to offer Sonny the vodka, which he showed to Ms. Mori when she returned from the kitchen. You shouldn't have, she said brightly, putting it next to the bottle of wine. The beautiful, transparent Stolichnaya maintained a stoic Russian demeanor as we regarded it in silence. Every full bottle of alcohol has a message in it, a surprise that one will not discover until one drinks it. I had planned to read that bottle's message with Ms. Mori, as was obvious to her and Sonny, and we might have all simply sat there soaking in the frigid waters of embarrassment if it had not been for Ms. Mori's grace. It's very thoughtful of you, she said. Especially as we've almost run out of cigarettes. I'll have one, if you don't mind.

So, Sonny said, how was your trip to the Philippines?

I want to hear all about it, Ms. Mori said, pouring me a glass of wine and refilling theirs. I've always wanted to go ever since my uncle talked about his time there in the war. I cracked open the carton and offered her a cigarette, took one myself, and began my well-rehearsed tale. The cat yawned in regal contempt, climbed back onto Sonny's lap, stretched out, sneered at me, then fell asleep from boredom. I had the

distinct impression that Sonny and Ms. Mori were only marginally more interested as they listened to me, smoked my
cigarettes, and asked some polite questions. Dispirited, I did
not even have the heart to tell them about my near-death
experience, and my story tapered off without a climax. My
gaze fell on the photo album, which was open to a page of
black-and-white photos depicting middle-class scenes from
a few decades earlier: a father and a mother at home in their
lace-covered armchairs, their sons and daughters playing
the piano, crocheting, gathered around a dining table for a
meal, wearing the fashion and hairstyle of the thirties. Who
are they? I said. My family, said Ms. Mori. Your family? The
answer stupefied me. Of course I knew that Ms. Mori had
a family, but she rarely talked about them, and certainly
had never shown me photographs of them. All I knew was
that they lived far north of here, in one of the dusty, hot
San Joaquin valley towns. That's Betsy and that's Eleanor,
Sonny said, leaning over to point at the relevant faces. Here's
George and Abe. Poor Abe.

I looked at Ms. Mori, sipping her wine. He died in the
war?

No, she said. He refused to go to war. So he got sent to
prison instead. He's still bitter about it. Not that he shouldn't
be. God knows I'd probably be bitter if I were him. I'd just
like for him to be happier than he is. The war's thirty years
past and it still lives with him, even though he didn't go
and fight.

He fought, Sonny said. He just fought at home. Who can
blame him? The government puts his family in a camp and

then asks him to go fight for the country? I'd be mad as hell, too.

A mist of smoke now separated the three of us. The faint eddies of our thoughts took fleeting, evanescent material shape, and for a brief moment a ghostly version of myself hovered over Sonny's head. Where's Abe now? I said.

Japan. Not that he's any happier there than he was here. After the war ended and he was freed, he thought he'd go back to his people, the way that he'd been told to all his life by white people, even though he was born here. So he went and found out that the people in Japan didn't think he was one of them, either. To them he's one of us, and to us he's one of them. Neither one thing nor another.

Maybe our Department Chair can help him, I said.

God, I hope you're joking, said Ms. Mori. Of course I was joking, but as an unwilling partner in this complicated ménage à trois I was off my rhythm. I steadied myself by finishing my wine. When I looked at the wine bottle, I saw that it was empty. Would you like some of the vodka? Ms. Mori said. Her gaze was loaded with pity, which was ever only served lukewarm. Longing flooded the basement of my heart, and all I could do was nod mutely. She went to the kitchen and retrieved clean tumblers for the vodka while Sonny and I sat in awkward silence. The vodka, when served, was as pungent and wonderful as I had imagined it would be, the paint thinner I needed to strip down the stained, flaking walls of my interior.

Maybe we'll go to Japan someday, Sonny said. I'd like to meet Abe.

I'd like you to meet him, too, said Ms. Mori. He's a fighter just like you are.

Vodka was good for honesty, especially on ice, as mine was. Vodka on ice was so transparent, so clear, so powerful, it inspired its drinkers to be the same. I swallowed the rest of mine, preparing myself for the bruises sure to come. There's something I've always wondered since our college days, Sonny. You always talked then about how much you believed in the people and the revolution so much. You should have heard him, Ms. Mori. He gave very good speeches.

I would have liked to hear them, Ms. Mori said. Very much.

But if you had heard them, you would have asked yourself why he didn't go back and fight for the revolution he believed in. Or why he doesn't go back now and be a part of the people and the revolution tomorrow? Even your brother Abe went to prison and went to Japan for what he believed in.

And look where that's got him, said Ms. Mori.

I'd just like an answer to my question, Sonny. Are you still here because you're in love with Ms. Mori? Or are you still here because you're afraid?

He winced. I had hit him where it hurt, in the solar plexus of his conscience, where everyone who was an idealist was vulnerable. Disarming an idealist was easy. One only needed to ask why the idealist was not on the front line of the particular battle he had chosen. The question was one of commitment, and I knew, even if he did not, that I was one of the committed. He looked at his bare feet, ashamed, but for some reason this had no effect on Ms. Mori. She only glanced at him with understanding, but when she turned her full gaze to me it remained marked by pity and something else—regret. It was time to stop and make a graceful exit, but the vodka that could not drain fast enough through the plugged-up sinkhole in the basement of my heart compelled me to swim on. You always talked with so much admiration of the people, I said. If you want to be with the people so much, go home.

His home is here, Ms. Mori said. I had never wanted her more than she was now, smoking a cigarette and fighting back. He stayed here because the people are here, too. There's work to be done with them and for them. Can't you see that? Isn't this your home now, too?

Sonny laid his hand on her arm and said, Sofia. There was a lump in my throat but I could not swallow, watching her put her hand on his. Don't defend me. He's right. I was right? I had never heard him say this before. I should have been joyful, but it was more and more evident that there was little I could say that would persuade Ms. Mori to turn her heart, or her mind, away from Sonny. He swallowed the rest of his vodka and said, I've lived in this country for fourteen years now. In a few more years, I'll have spent as much time here as I have in our homeland. That was never my intention. I came here, like you, just to study. I remember so clearly saying farewell to my parents at the airport and promising them that I would come back and help our country. I'd have an American degree, the best education the world could offer. I'd use that knowledge and help our people liberate themselves from the Americans. Or so I hoped.

He held out his glass to Ms. Mori, and she poured him a

double. After taking a sip, he continued, looking somewhere between Ms. Mori and myself. What I learned, against my will, is that it's impossible to live among a foreign people and not become changed by them. He swirled his vodka and knocked it back in one punishing swallow. Sometimes I feel a little foreign to myself as a result, he said. I admit that I am afraid. I admit my cowardice, my hypocrisy, my weakness, and my shame. I admit that you are a better man than me. I don't agree with your politics—I despise them—but you went home when you had the choice and you fought the fight that you believed in. You stood up for the people as you see them. For that, I respect you.

I could not believe it. I had gotten him to confess to his failures and to surrender. I had won an argument with Sonny, something I had never done in our college days. So why was Ms. Mori clinging to his hand and murmuring something soothing? It's all right, she said. I know exactly how you feel. It's all right? I needed another drink. Look at me, Sonny, Ms. Mori went on. What am I? A secretary for a white man who thinks he's complimenting me when he calls me Miss Butterfly. Do I protest and tell him to go to hell? No. I smile and say nothing and continue typing. I'm no better than you, Sonny. They stared into each other's eyes as if I did not exist. I refilled all of our glasses but it was only me who took a slug. The part that was me said, I love you, Ms. Mori. No one heard that. What they heard was the part I was playing say, It's never too late to fight, is it, Ms. Mori?

Their spell was broken. Sonny turned his gaze back to me. He had performed some kind of intellectual judo and turned my blow against myself. But he exhibited none of the triumph he would have in our college days. No, it's never too late to fight, he said, sober despite the wine and vodka. You are quite right about that, my friend. Yeah, Ms. Mori said. In the way she slowly exhaled that syllable, in the way she focused on Sonny with a hungry intensity never shown toward me, in the way she chose that word over yes, I knew it was all over between us. I had won the argument, but somehow, as in our college days, he had won the audience.

The General also thought it was never too late to fight, as I reported in the next letter to my Parisian aunt. He had found an isolated stretch of terrain to carry out the training and maneuvers for his nascent army, in the sun-exposed hills far east of Los Angeles, near a remote Indian reservation. Some two hundred men had driven themselves across the freeways and past the suburbs and exurbs to this stretch of scrubby land where, in the past, the mob might have buried a few of its victims. Our gathering was not as strange a thing as it might have appeared. A xenophobe would see a company of foreigners in camouflage uniforms, carrying out military drills and calisthenics, and might imagine us to be the lead element of some nefarious Asian invasion of the American homeland, a Yellow Peril in the Golden State, a diabolical dream of Ming the Merciless sprung to life. Far from it. The General's men, by preparing themselves to invade our now communist homeland, were in fact turning themselves into new Americans. After all, nothing was more American than wielding a gun and committing oneself to die for freedom and independence, unless it was wielding that gun to take away someone else's freedom and independence.

Ten score of the best, the General had called these men in his restaurant, where he had sketched out for me the organization of his compact army on a napkin. I later pocketed that napkin and sent it to my Parisian aunt, the sketch depicting a headquarters platoon, three rifle platoons, and a heavy weapons platoon, even though there were as yet no heavy weapons. No problem, said the General. Southeast Asia is awash in heavy weaponry. We'll get them there. Here the goal is to build discipline, harden bodies, prepare minds, get these volunteers to think of themselves as an army again, get them to imagine the future. He wrote down the names of the platoon commanders and the officers of his staff, explaining to me their histories: this one formerly the executive officer from such-and-such division, this one formerly a battalion commander of such-and-such regiment, and so on. These details I transmitted to my Parisian aunt as well, this time in arduous code. I also paraphrased what the General told me, that these were all experienced men, down to the lowliest private. They've all seen action back home, he said. All volunteers. I didn't put out a general call. I organized my officers first, had them contact men they trust who would be the noncommissioned officers, then had the NCOs find the enlisted men. It's taken over a year to collect this nucleus. Now we're ready for the next phase. Physical training, drilling, maneuvers, turning them into a fighting unit. Are you with me, Captain?

Always, sir. This was how I found myself in uniform again, although my task for the day was to be documentarian rather than foot soldier. The two hundred or so men sat Indian style on the earth, legs crossed, while the General stood before them and I stood behind them, camera in hand. Like his men, the General was uniformed in battle camouflage, purchased at an army surplus store and tailored by the Madame to fit. In his uniform, the General was no longer the morose proprietor of a liquor store and a restaurant, a petty bourgeois who counted his hopes as he did the change in his register. His uniform, his red beret, his polished field boots, the stars on his collar, and the Airborne patch on his sleeve had restored to him the nobility he had once possessed in our homeland. As for my uniform, it was a suit of armor cut from cloth. Though a bullet or knife would have sliced through the uniform with ease, I felt less vulnerable than in my everyday civilian clothes. If I was not bulletproof, I was at least charmed, as all the men were.

I photographed them from several different angles, these men who had been humbled by what they had been turned into here in exile. In their working outfits as busboys, waiters, gardeners, field hands, fishermen, manual laborers, custodians, or simply the un- and underemployed, these shabby examples of the lumpen blended into the background wherever they happened to be, always seen as a mass, never noticed as individuals. But now, in uniform and with their raggedy haircuts hidden by field caps and berets, they were impossible to miss. Their renewed manhood was manifest in the way their backs were stiff and straight, rather than slouched in the refugee slump, and in the way they marched proudly across the earth, rather than shuffling as they usually did in cheap shoes with worn-down soles. They were men again, and that was how the General addressed them. Men, he called out. Men! The people need us. Even from where I was, I heard him clearly, though he seemed to exert no effort in projecting his voice. They need hope and leaders, the General said. You are those leaders. You will show the people what can happen if they have the courage to rise up, to take arms, and to sacrifice themselves. I watched the men to see if they would flinch at the idea of sacrificing themselves, but they did not. This was the occult power of the uniform, of the mass, that men who would never dream of sacrificing themselves in the course of their everyday lives waiting on tables would agree to do so while waiting under a hot sun. Men, the General said. Men! The people cry out for freedom! The communists promise freedom and independence, but deliver only poverty and enslavement. They have betrayed the Vietnamese people, and revolutions don't betray the people. Even here we remain with the people, and we will return to liberate the people who have been denied the freedom given to us. Revolutions are for the people, from the people, by the people. That is our revolution!

Nothing was so true, and yet nothing was so mysterious, for the questions of who the people were and what they might want remained unanswered. The lack of an answer mattered not; indeed, the lack of an answer was part of the power in the idea of the people that brought the men to their feet and the tears to their eyes as they shouted, *Down with communism!* Like salmon that instinctively knew when to swim upstream, we all knew who the people were and who were not the people. Anyone who had to be told who the people were probably was not part of the people, or so I soon wrote to my Parisian aunt. I also sent her photos of the cheering men in uniform, along with others showing them exercising and engaging in maneuvers the rest of that weekend. Perhaps these men looked silly or foolish, doing push-ups while the grizzled captain yelled at them, or crouching behind trees aiming vintage rifles under the command of the affectless lieutenant, or conducting a mock patrol with Bon amid the brush where Indians once hunted. But don't be fooled, I warned Man in my coded notes. Revolutions begin this way, with men willing to fight no matter what the odds, volunteering to give up everything because they had nothing. This was an apt description of the grizzled captain, the former guerrilla hunter who was now a short-order cook, and the affectless lieutenant, sole survivor of an ambushed company who made his living as a deliveryman. Like Bon, they were certifiably insane men who had volunteered for the reconnaissance mission to Thailand. They had decided that death was just as good as life, which was fine for them but was worrisome for me if I was to go along with them.

What about your wives and kids? I said. The four of us sat under an oak tree, sleeves rolled up past our elbows, eating a midday meal of army surplus C rations, which looked almost exactly the same entering the human body as they did exiting it. The grizzled captain rattled his spoon in his can and said, We got separated during the whole mess at Da Nang. They didn't make it out. Last I heard the VC sent them to clear swampland for the crime of being related to me. Guess I can either wait for them to get out or I can go get them myself. He had the habit of speaking with his teeth clenched, gnawing at his words like bones. As for the affectless lieutenant, his emotional strings had been cut. He had the semblance of a human being, but while his body moved, his face and voice moved not at all. Thus, when he said, They're dead, the toneless announcement was more forbidding than if he had wailed or cursed. I was afraid to ask him what had happened. Instead I said, You guys don't plan on coming back, do you? The affectless lieutenant rotated the turret of his head a few degrees and aimed his eyes at me. Come back to what? The grizzled captain chuckled. Don't be shocked, kid. I've ordered more than a few men to certain death. Now maybe it's my turn. Not that I want to sound all emotional. Don't feel sorry for me. I'm looking forward to it. War may be hell, but you know what? Hell's better than this shithole. With that, the affectless lieutenant and the grizzled captain departed to take a piss.

I didn't need to write in my letter to Paris that these men were not fools, at least not yet. The minutemen were not fools in believing they could defeat the British Redcoats, any more than the first armed propaganda platoon of our revolution was foolish as it drilled with a motley assembly of primitive weapons. From that militia eventually arose an army of a million men. Who was to say the same fate did not await this company? *Dear Aunt,* I wrote in visible ink, *These men are not to be underestimated. Napoleon said men will die for bits of ribbon pinned to their chests, but the General understands that even more men will die for a man who remembered their names, as he does theirs. When he inspects them, he walks among them, eats with them, calls them by their names and asks about wives, children, girlfriends, hometowns. All anyone ever wants is to be recognized and remembered. Neither is possible without the other. This desire drives these busboys, waiters, janitors, gardeners, mechanics, night guards, and welfare beneficiaries to save enough money to buy themselves uniforms, boots, and guns, to want to be men again. They want their country back, dear Aunt, but they also yearn for recognition and remembrance from that country that no longer exists, from wives and children, from future descendants, from the men they used to be. If they fail, call them fools. But if they do not fail, they are heroes and visionaries, whether alive or dead. Perhaps I shall return with them to our country, regardless of what the General has to say.*

Even as I was planning for the possibility of returning, I also did my best to dissuade Bon of doing the same. We were smoking a final cigarette under the oak tree, our last gesture before embarking on a ten-mile hike. We watched as the men commanded by the grizzled captain and the affectless lieutenant rose and stretched, scratching at various parts of their lumpy bodies. Those guys have death wishes, I said. Don't you get it? They've got no intention of coming back. They know it's a suicide mission.

Life's a suicide mission.

That's very philosophical of you, I said. It doesn't change the fact that you're crazy.

He laughed with genuine humor, such a rare occasion ever since Saigon I was taken aback. For only the second time since I had known him, he embarked on a speech that was, for him, an epic. What's crazy is living when there's no reason to live, he said. What am I living for? A life in our apartment? That's not a home. It's a jail cell without bars. All of us—we're all in jail cells without bars. We're not men anymore. Not after the Americans fucked us twice and made our wives and kids watch. First the Americans said we'll save your yellow skins. Just do what we say. Fight our way, take our money, give us your women, then you'll be free. Things didn't work out that way, did they? Then, after fucking us, they rescued us. They just didn't tell us they'd cut off our balls and cut out our tongues along the way. But you know what? If we were real men, we wouldn't have let them do that.

Usually Bon used words like a sniper, but this was a spray of machine-gun fire that silenced me for several moments. Then I said, You don't give these guys enough credit for what they did, for what they faced. Though they were my enemies, I understood their soldiers' hearts, beating with the belief that they had fought bravely. You're being too hard on them.

He laughed again, this time without humor. I'm hard on myself. Don't call me a man or a soldier, either. Call the guys who stayed behind men and soldiers. The men in my company. Man. All dead or in prison, but at least they know they're men. They're so dangerous it takes other men with guns to keep them locked up. Here, no one's frightened of us. The only people we scare are our wives and kids. And ourselves. I know these guys. I sell them liquor. I hear their stories. They come home from work, yell at their wives and kids, beat them once in a while just to show that they're men. Only they're not. A man protects his wife and children. A man isn't afraid to die for them, his country, his buddies. He doesn't live to see them all die before him. But that's what I've done.

You retreated, that's all, I said, putting my hand on his shoulder. He shrugged it off. I had never seen him speak about his pain so bluntly before. I wanted to comfort him and it hurt me that he would not let me. You had to save your family. That doesn't make you less of a man or a soldier. You are a soldier, so think like one. Is it better to go on this suicide mission and not come back, or is it better to go with the next wave that's actually got a chance?

He spat and ground out his cigarette against the heel of his boot, then buried it under a mound of dirt. That's what most of these guys are saying. They're losers and losers always have excuses. They dress up, talk tough, play soldier. But how many are really going back home to fight? The General asked for volunteers. He got three. The rest of them hide behind their wives and kids, the same wives and kids they beat because they can't stand hiding behind them. Give a coward a second chance, he'll just run again. So it is with most of these guys. They're bluffing.

You cynical bastard, I cried. What are you dying for then?

What am I dying for? he cried back. I'm dying because this world I'm living in isn't worth dying for! If something is worth dying for, then you've got a reason to live.

And to this, I had nothing to say. It was true, even for this small detachment of heroes or perhaps fools. Whatever they were, they now had something to live for if not die for. They had eagerly shed the funereal clothes of their mediocre civilian lives, understanding the allure of tailored tiger stripe fatigues with dashing scarves of yellow, white, or red around their necks, a military splendor akin to the costumes of superheroes. But, like superheroes, they would not want to keep themselves a secret for long. How could you be a superhero if no one knew you existed?

Rumors had already spread about them. Even before the desert assembly, during that night when Sonny had admitted his failure and yet still won, he had asked me about these mysterious men. The wheels of our conversation had stopped spinning, the black cat was gloating over my defeat, and in the vodka-infused silence Sonny raised the reports of a secret army preparing for a secret invasion. I replied that I had not heard of any such thing, to which he said, Don't play the innocent. You're the General's man.

If I were his man, I said, more reason not to tell a communist.

Who said I'm a communist?

I pretended to be surprised. You're not a communist?

If I were, would I tell you?

That was the subversive's dilemma. Rather than flaunt ourselves in the sexually dubious costumes of superheroes, we hid beneath cloaks of invisibility, here just as in Saigon. There, when I attended clandestine meetings with other subversives, conducted in the fusty cellars of safe houses, sitting on crates of black market hand grenades manufactured in the USA, I donned a clammy cotton hood that revealed only my eyes. Lit by candlelight or oil lamp, we knew one another only by the peculiarity of our aliases, by the shape of our bodies, by the sound of our voices, by the whites of our eyes. Now, watching Ms. Mori recline under Sonny's arm, I was sure my ever-absorbent eyes were no longer white but bloodshot from the wine, vodka, and tobacco. Our lungs had achieved smoky equilibrium with the stale air, while on the coffee table the ashtray silently suffered its usual indignity, mouth crammed full of butts and bitter ash. I dropped what remained of my cigarette into the well of the wine bottle, where it drowned in the remaining liquid with a faint, reproachful hiss. The war's over, Ms. Mori said. Don't they know that? I wanted to say something profound as I stood up to say good night. I wanted to impress Ms. Mori with the intellect she could never have again. Wars never die, I said. They just go to sleep.

Is that true for old soldiers, too? she asked, not looking impressed. Of course it's true, Sonny said. If they didn't go to sleep, how else would they dream? I almost answered before I realized it was a rhetorical question.

Ms. Mori offered me her cheek to kiss and Sonny offered me his hand to shake. He showed me the door and I slid home through the cool sheets of night and into my own bed, Bon asleep and hovering above me in his rack. I closed my eyes and, after a spell of darkness, floated on my mattress across a black river to the foreign country that needed no passport to visit. Of its many gnomic features and shady denizens I now recall only one, my mind wiped clean except for this fatal fingerprint, an ancient kapok tree that was my final resting place and on whose arthritic bark I laid my cheek. I was almost asleep within my sleep when I gradually understood that the knot of gnarled wood on which my ear rested was actually an ear itself, curled and stiff, the wax of its auditory history encrusted in the green moss of its twisted canal. Half of the kapok tree towered above me, half was invisible below me in the rooted earth, and when I looked up I saw not just one ear but many ears swelling from the bark of its thick trunk, hundreds of ears listening and having listened to things I could not hear, the sight of those ears so horrible it hurled me back into the black river. I woke drenched and gasping, clutching the sides of my head. Only after I kicked off the damp sheets and looked under the pillow could I lie down again, trembling. My heart still beat with the force of a savage drummer, but at least my bed was not littered with amputated ears.

CHAPTER 14

Sometimes the work of a subversive is purposeful, but sometimes, I confess, it is accidental. In retrospect, perhaps my questioning of Sonny's courage pushed him to write the headline that I saw two weeks after the field maneuvers, "Move On, War Over." I saw it on the General's desk in his war room at the liquor store, fixed squarely on the writing pad and weighed down by a stapler. The sentiments of the headline might be hailed by some, but certainly not by the General. Beneath that headline was a photograph of a rally staged by the Fraternity at a Westminster park, with ranks and files of grim veterans in paramilitary uniforms of brown shirts and red berets. In another photo, civilians in the cast-off couture of refugees waved signs and clutched banners with the telegraphic messages of political protests. HO CHI MINH = HITLER! FREEDOM FOR OUR PEOPLE! THANK YOU, AMERICA! To the degree that the article might sow doubt in the hearts of exiles about continuing the war, and create divisions among exile factions, I knew that my provocation of Sonny had had an unintentional, but desirable, effect.

I photographed the article with the Minox mini-camera that was finally finding some use. For the last few weeks, I had been photographing the General's files, all of which I had access to as his aide-de-camp. Ever since my return from the Philippines, I had been unemployed except for this considerable pro bono work done for the General, the Fraternity, and the Movement. Even secret armies and political fronts needed clerks. Memos must be written; documents filed; meetings called; flyers designed, printed, and distributed; photos taken; interviews scheduled; donors found; and, most important for my purposes, correspondence taken and mailed, then received and read before it was handed over to the General. I had photographed the General's complete order of battle, from the company here to the battalion in Thailand, from the Fraternity's public parades to the Movement's private maneuvers, as well as the communiqués between the General and his officers in the Thai refugee camps, led by a landlocked admiral. Not least, I photographed the statements of the bank accounts where the General stashed the modest funds for the Movement, raised in small donations from the refugee community, the revenues of Madame's restaurant, and a handful of respectable charitable organizations that had donated to the Fraternity for the relief of sad refugees and sadder veterans.

All this information had been packaged into a parcel dispatched to my Parisian aunt. The parcel's contents were a letter and a chintzy souvenir, an automatically rotating snowball featuring the Hollywood sign. This gift required nine-volt batteries, which I included and which I had

hollowed out. Into each I inserted a cartridge of Minox film,
a more sophisticated method than how my courier in Saigon
traded information with me. When Man first told me of my
courier, I had immediately conjured up one of those supple
beauty queens for which our country was deservedly famous,
white as refined sugar on the outside, scarlet as sunrise on
the inside, a Cochin-Chinese Mata Hari. What showed up
at my door every morning was an aging auntie, the lines on
her face promising more secrets than the lines on her palms,
hawking gobs of betel juice as well as her specialty, sticky rice
wrapped in banana leaves. I bought a packet for breakfast
every morning, and in it there might or might not be a message, rolled and wrapped in plastic. Likewise, in the small
wad of folded piastres I paid her with, there might or might
not be a cartridge of film or a message of my own, written
invisibly with rice water on cement paper. The only flaw in
this method was that auntie was a terrible cook, her sticky
rice a ball of glue that I had to swallow, lest the maid find it
in my garbage and wonder why I was buying what I would
not eat. I complained to auntie once, but she cursed me at
such length and with such inventiveness I had to check both
my watch and my dictionary. Even the cyclo drivers hanging around the General's villa for fares were impressed. You
better marry that one, Captain, a driver missing a left arm
called out. She won't be single for long!

I winced at the memory and poured myself a drink from
the bottle of fifteen-year-old scotch the General kept in his
drawer. Given that I was not being paid, the General kept
me happy, and admittedly dependent, with generous gifts of

fine and not-so-fine liquor from his ample supply. I needed it. Written invisibly in the letter were the dates and details of Bon's itinerary and those of the grizzled captain and affectless lieutenant, from their airplane tickets to the location of the training camp. The information was no different in substance from what I had dispatched through auntie, the classified logistics of operations that would inevitably lead to devastating ambushes. Newspaper articles would report the number of American or republican soldiers dead or wounded, but they were as abstract as the faceless dead in history books. I could write these dispatches with ease, but the one about Bon had taken me all night, not because of the amount of words, but because he was my friend. *I'm coming back, too,* I wrote, even though I had not yet figured out how I would do that. *The better to report on the movement of the enemy,* I wrote, even though what I really intended was to save Bon's life. This feat I also had no idea how to accomplish, but ignorance had never stopped me from taking action before.

With no idea how I would manage to betray Bon and save him at the same time, I searched for inspiration in the bottom of a bottle. I was sipping from my second tumbler of scotch when the General entered. It was a little past three, the routine time of his return from Madame's restaurant after its midday rush. He was, as usual, irritated from his hours manning the cash register. Former soldiers would salute him, a sign of respect that nevertheless reminded him of the stars he was not wearing, while the occasional snide civilian, always a woman, would say, Weren't you that general? If she was very snide, she would leave him the tip, the typically grand sum of one dollar, our nod to what we considered a ludicrous American practice. Thus the General would arrive in the afternoons at the liquor store, as he did today, throw a handful of crumpled dollar bills on his desk, and wait for me to pour him a double. Reclining in his chair, he would sip the scotch with closed eyes and sigh dramatically. But today, instead of reclining, he leaned forward at his desk, tapped the newspaper, and said, Did you read this?

Not wanting to deprive the General of the opportunity to fulminate, I said I had not. He nodded grimly and began to read excerpts out loud. "Rumors abound about this Fraternity and what its true purpose is," the General said, face blank and voice even. "The overthrow of the communist regime is clearly its objective, but how far is it willing to go? While the Fraternity asks for donations to help refugees, these funds may possibly be going toward a Movement of armed refugees in Thailand. Rumors are that the Fraternity has invested in certain businesses whose profits it reaps. The most disappointing aspect of the Fraternity is the false hope it peddles to our countrymen that we can one day take our country back through force. We would be better off if we pursued reconciliation peacefully, in the hopes that one day we in exile can return to help rebuild our country." The General folded the newspaper and laid it back on his desk in the exact same position it had occupied before. Someone's been feeding this man some reliable information, Captain.

I sipped my scotch to disguise the fact that I was swallowing the saliva that had pooled in my mouth. We have leaks, sir, just like we did at home. Look at that picture. All those men know something about what's going on. All Sonny had to do was walk around with a bucket catching one drop here and another drop there. Soon enough he'd have a glass or two of information.

You're right, of course, the General said. We can keep mistresses but we can't keep secrets. This—he tapped the newspaper—sounds wonderful, doesn't it? Reconcile, return, rebuild. Who wouldn't want that? And who would benefit the most? The communists. But for us, the greater likelihood if we return is a bullet in the head or a long stay in reeducation. That's what the communists mean by reconciliation and rebuilding, getting rid of people like us. And this newsman is peddling this leftist propaganda to poor people who are desperate for any kind of hope. He's getting more troublesome, don't you think?

Of course, I said, reaching for the bottle of scotch. Like me, it was half empty and half full. Newsmen are always troublesome if they're independent.

How do we know he's just a newsman? Half of the newsmen in Saigon were communist sympathizers, and a good percentage of them were just communists. How do we know the communists didn't send him here years ago with exactly this plan in mind, to spy on any of us who made it here and undermine us? You knew him in college. Did he display these sympathies back then? If I said no and the General later heard otherwise from someone else, I would be in trouble. The only answer was yes, to which the General said, As my intelligence officer, you're not showing much intelligence,

are you, Captain? Why didn't you warn me of this when I
met him? The General shook his head in disgust. Do you
know what your problem is, Captain? I had a rather long
list of my problems, but it was better to simply say I had no
idea. You're too sympathetic, the General said. You didn't
see the danger in the major because he was fat and you took
pity on him for that. Now the evidence shows that you've
been willfully blind to the fact that Sonny is not only a left-
wing radical but potentially a communist sleeper agent. The
General's gaze was intense. My face started to itch but I did
not dare scratch. Something may need to be done, Captain.
Don't you agree?

Yes, I said, throat dry. Something may need to be done.

I had plenty of time to contemplate the General's vague
demand in the ensuing days. How could one disagree with
something needing to be done? Something always needed
doing by somebody. An ad in Sonny's newspaper announcing that Lana was singing as part of a revue called *Fantasia*
provided me the opportunity for action, although not the
kind the General likely had in mind. What I needed was
a vacation, if only for a night, from the stressful, solitary
work of being a subversive. For a mole used to darkness, a
nightclub was an ideal place to emerge. Persuading Bon to
go to *Fantasia* to hear the songs and sounds of our gone but
not forgotten country was less of a struggle than I thought it
would be, for Bon, having decided to die, was finally showing
signs of life. He even allowed me to cut his hair, which he

afterward slicked down with Brylcreem until it matched our glossy black shoes. The Brylcreem and our cologne lent my car an intoxicatingly masculine atmosphere as we listened to the Rolling Stones, the car transporting us not only west to Hollywood but back to the glory days of Saigon circa 1969, after my return from America. Then, before Bon and Man became fathers, the three of us had wasted the weekends of our youth in Saigon's bars and nightclubs, exactly as one was supposed to do. If youth was not wasted, how could it be youth?

Perhaps I could blame youth for my friendship with Bon. What drives a fourteen-year-old to swear a blood oath to a blood brother? And more important, what makes a grown man believe in that oath? Should not the things that count, like ideology and political belief, the ripe fruit of our adulthood, matter more than the unripe ideals and illusions of youth? Let me propose that truth, or some measure of it, can be found in these youthful follies that we forget, to our loss, as adults. Here was the scene of how our friendship first became established: a football pitch of the lycée, myself a new student surrounded by older, taller ones, the prancing steeds of the school. They were about to repeat a scene rehearsed by man from the dawn of time, the moment when the strong turn on the weak or the odd for sport. I was odd but I was not weak, as I had proven against the village comedian who called me unnatural. Although I had beaten him, I had also been beaten before, and I prepared myself for a losing fight. It was then that another new boy unexpectedly spoke out in my defense, stepping forward from the ring of voyeurs and saying, This isn't right. Don't single him out. He's one of us. An older boy scoffed. Who are you to say who's one of us? And why do you think you're one of us? Now get out of the way. Man did not get out of the way, and for this he received the first blow, a slap on the ear that sent him reeling. I drove my head into the older boy's ribs and knocked him down, landing astride his chest, from where I commenced to land two blows before his fellow oafs hurled themselves on me. The odds were five-to-one against me and my new friend Man, and even though I fought back with all my heart and rage, I knew we were doomed. All the other schoolboys surrounding us did, too. So why, then, did Bon jump forth from that crowd and take our side? He was a new boy who was as big as the older boys, true, but even so he could not beat them all. One he slugged, another he elbowed, a third he rammed, and then he, too, was brought down by the horde. So they kicked us, and hit us, and beat us, and left us bruised, bloody, and elated. Yes, elated! For we had passed some mysterious test, one that separated us from the bullies on the one side and the cowards on the other. That very night, we snuck out of our dormitory and made our way to a tamarind grove, and under its boughs we cut our palms. We mingled our blood once more with boys we recognized as more kin to us than any real kin, and then gave one another our word.

A pragmatist, a true materialist, would dismiss this story and my attachment to it as romanticism. But the story says everything about how we saw ourselves and one another at that age, as boys who knew instinctively that their cause was to stand up for the weaker. Bon and I had not talked about that incident in a long time, but I sensed that it was in his bloodstream as well as mine as we sang songs from our youth on the way to our destination at the Roosevelt Hotel. Once a swinging establishment on Hollywood Boulevard for celebrities in the black-and-white era, the Roosevelt was now as unfashionable as a silent film star. Worn rugs masked shabby tiles, and for some reason the lobby's furniture comprised card tables and chairs with the spindly legs of cranes, ready for games of penny poker and solitaire. I had expected some residual splash of Hollywood glamour, with paunchy porn producers in butterfly collars and powder-blue blazers, leading demi-glazed women by their bejeweled hands. But the best-dressed people in the hotel appeared to be my fellow countrymen, bedecked in sequins, polyester, and attitude as we headed to the lounge where *Fantasia* waited. The other patrons, presumably the hotel guests, wore plaid shirts, pediatric shoes, and seven o'clock shadows, the only thing in tow an oxygen tank. We always arrived late for everything, including, apparently, Hollywood's fashionable moment.

Nevertheless, the atmosphere inside the hotel's cozy lounge was buoyant. Some entrepreneur had rented out the space to stage *Fantasia*, and the result was a refuge without any sign of refugees, the men sharp in tailored suits and the women delectable in ball gowns. Our aspiring bourgeoisie had found forty-hour-a-week jobs with overtime and, having padded their wallets enough to sit more comfortably, were now on the hunt for wine and song. As Bon and I settled into a table at the back, a winsome singer in a bolero jacket serenaded the lounge with a heartache-soaked version of Pham Duy's "City of Sadness." Was there any other way to sing about a city of sadness, the portable city carried by all of us in exile? After love, was sadness not the most common noun in our lyrical repertoire? Did we salivate for sadness, or had we only learned to enjoy what we were forced to eat? These questions required either Camus or cognac, and as Camus was not available I ordered cognac.

I paid for the snifters without a twinge from my dwindling settlement cash, being of the firm belief that money did not live until it was spent, particularly in the company of friends. When I spotted the grizzled captain and the affectless lieutenant standing at the bar nursing beers, I even sent them snifters of cognac. They came over to our table and toasted our comradeship, even though I had not yet brought up the matter of my return with the General again. That was my intent, though, and I was happy to buy us all another round. Cognac made everything better, the equivalent of a mother's kiss for a grown man, and so it was that we indulged as the singers shimmied on the stage one by one. Men and women, they crooned, they wailed, they sighed, they belted, they moaned, they roared, and no matter what they sang or how, the crowd adored them. We were, all of us, even Bon, airlifted back in time by the lungs of the singers, across years and miles to nightclubs in Saigon where the taste of champagne, besides the usual flavors and hints, always carried a touch of tears. Too many tears, and one was overpowered; none, and one was not enslaved. But a drop of this elixir was all one's tongue needed before it could utter only one name: Saigon.

That word was mentioned by nearly every one of the performers and by the emcee himself. This guide to *Fantasia* was a modestly built man modestly dressed in a gray flannel suit, the only shiny thing about him being his spectacles. I could not see his eyes but I recognized his name. The Poet was a writer whose works had appeared in the literary journals and newspapers, gentle and nostalgic verses about the textures of everyday life. I remembered one in particular about the epiphany to be found in the washing of rice, and while I could not remember the Poet's epiphany, I remembered the urge in the poem to find meaning in even the meanest of chores. Sometimes, when I washed rice and sunk my hand into the wet grains, I thought of the Poet. I was proud to see that in our culture a Poet could be an emcee for a night of song and wine for the common people. We respected our poets and assumed they had something important to teach us, and this Poet did. He had written a few columns for Sonny's newspaper, explaining the vagaries of American life or the cultural miscommunications between Americans and us, and in this vein he interspersed his introductions of the singers with brief lessons in our culture or the American culture. When it came time for Lana, he began by saying, Some of you may have heard that the Americans are a people who like to dream. It's true, and although some say that America is a welfare state, in actuality it is a dream state. Here, we can dream of anything, can't we, ladies and gentlemen? I will tell you what my American Dream is, he said, holding the microphone with the care one reserved for a stick of dynamite. My American Dream is to see once more, before I die, the land where I was born, to taste once more the ripe persimmons from the tree of my family's garden in Tay Ninh. My American Dream is to return home so I can light incense at the tomb of my grandparents, to roam that beautiful country of ours when it is at last peaceful and the sound of guns cannot be heard over the shouts of joy. My American Dream is to walk from city to village to farm and to see boys and girls laughing and playing who have never heard of war, from Da Nang to Da Lat, from Ca Mau to Chau Doc, from Sa Dec to Song Cau, from Bien Hoa to Ban Me Thuot—

The train ride through our cities and towns great and small continued, but I had gotten off at Ban Me Thuot, my hometown, hill town, town of red earth, Highland country of the finest coffee beans, land of booming waterfalls, of exasperated elephants, of the half-starved Gia Rai in their loincloths, barefoot and bare breasted, land where my mother and father died, land where my umbilical cord was buried in my mother's meager plot, land where the heroic People's Army struck first in its liberation of the south during the great campaign of '75, land that was my home.

That is my American Dream, said the Poet, that no matter the clothes I wear or the food I eat or the language I speak, my heart will be unchanged. This is why we gather here tonight, ladies and gentlemen. Though we cannot be home in reality, we can return in *Fantasia*.

The audience applauded sincerely and enthusiastically for our diasporic poet laureate, but he was a wise man who knew that we were gathered here for another purpose besides hearing him. Ladies and gentlemen, he said, raising his hand to still the crowd, may I present to you another American Dream, our very own Vietnamese fantasy . . .

Now known by just one name, like John, Paul, George, Ringo, and Mary, she stepped onstage clad in a red velvet bustier, a leopard-print miniskirt, black lace gloves, and thigh-high leather boots with stiletto heels. My heart would have paused at the boots, the heels, or the flat, smooth slice of her belly, naked in between miniskirt and bustier, but the combination of all three arrested my heart altogether and beat it with the vigor of a Los Angeles police squad. Pouring cognac over my heart freed it, but thus drenched it was easily flambéed by her torch song. She turned on the heat with her first number, the unexpected "I'd Love You to Want Me," which I had heard before sung only by men. "I'd Love You to Want Me" was the theme song of the bachelors and unhappily married males of my generation, whether in the English original or the equally superb French and Vietnamese renditions. What the song expressed so perfectly from lyric to melody was unrequited love, and we men of the south loved nothing more than unrequited love, cracked hearts our primary weakness after cigarettes, coffee, and cognac.

Listening to her sing, all I wanted was to immolate myself in a night with her to remember forever and ever. Every man in the room shared my emotion as we watched her do no more than sway at the microphone, her voice enough to move the audience, or rather to still us. Nobody talked and nobody stirred except to raise a cigarette or a glass, an utter concentration not broken for her next, slightly more upbeat

number, "Bang Bang (My Baby Shot Me Down)." Nancy
Sinatra sang it first, but she was merely a platinum princess
whose only knowledge of violence and guns was derived sec-
ondhand from the mob friends of her father, Frank. Lana, in
contrast, had grown up in a city where gangsters were once
so powerful the army fought them in the streets. Saigon was
a metropolis where grenade attacks were commonplace, terror bombings not unexpected, and wholesale invasion by the
Viet Cong a communal experience. What did Nancy Sinatra
know when she sang *bang bang*? To her, those were bubble-
gum pop lyrics. *Bang bang* was the sound track of our lives.

Moreover, Nancy Sinatra was afflicted, as the overwhelming majority of Americans were, with monolingualism.
Lana's richer, more textured version of "Bang Bang" lay-
ered English with French and Vietnamese. *Bang bang, je
ne l'oublierai pas* went the last line of the French version,
which was echoed by Pham Duy's Vietnamese version, *We
will never forget*. In the pantheon of classic pop songs from
Saigon, this tricolor rendition was one of the most memorable, masterfully weaving together love and violence in
the enigmatic story of two lovers who, regardless of having
known each other since childhood, or because of knowing
each other since childhood, shoot each other down. *Bang
bang* was the sound of memory's pistol firing into our heads,
for we could not forget love, we could not forget war, we
could not forget lovers, we could not forget enemies, we
could not forget home, and we could not forget Saigon. We
could not forget the caramel flavor of iced coffee with coarse
sugar; the bowls of noodle soup eaten while squatting on

the sidewalk; the strumming of a friend's guitar while we
swayed on hammocks under coconut trees; the football
matches played barefoot and shirtless in alleys, squares,
parks, and meadows; the pearl chokers of morning mist
draped around the mountains; the labial moistness of oysters shucked on a gritty beach; the whisper of a dewy lover
saying the most seductive words in our language, *anh oi*; the
rattle of rice being threshed; the workingmen who slept in
their cyclos on the streets, kept warm only by the memories
of their families; the refugees who slept on every sidewalk
of every city; the slow burning of patient mosquito coils;
the sweetness and firmness of a mango plucked fresh from
its tree; the girls who refused to talk to us and who we only
pined for more; the men who had died or disappeared; the
streets and homes blown away by bombshells; the streams
where we swam naked and laughing; the secret grove where
we spied on the nymphs who bathed and splashed with the
innocence of the birds; the shadows cast by candlelight on
the walls of wattled huts; the atonal tinkle of cowbells on
mud roads and country paths; the barking of a hungry dog in
an abandoned village; the appetizing reek of the fresh durian
one wept to eat; the sight and sound of orphans howling by
the dead bodies of their mothers and fathers; the stickiness
of one's shirt by afternoon, the stickiness of one's lover by
the end of lovemaking, the stickiness of our situations; the
frantic squealing of pigs running for their lives as villagers
gave chase; the hills afire with sunset; the crowned head of
dawn rising from the sheets of the sea; the hot grasp of our
mother's hand; and while the list could go on and on and

on, the point was simply this: the most important thing we could never forget was that we could never forget.

When Lana was finished, the audience clapped, whistled, and stomped, but I sat silent and stunned as she bowed and gracefully withdrew, so disarmed I could not even applaud. As the Poet introduced the next performer, all I heard was *bang bang*, and when Lana returned to the table reserved for the performers, with the seat next to her left empty by the singer who had replaced her, I told Bon I would be back in ten minutes. I heard him say, Don't do it, you stupid bastard, but without further thought I began my walk across the lounge. The hardest thing to do in talking to a woman was taking the first step, but the most important thing to do was not to think. Not thinking is more difficult than it sounds, and yet, with women, one should never think. Never. It simply won't do. The first few times in approaching girls, during my lycée years, I had thought too much, hesitated, and, as a result, flailed and failed. But even so, I discovered that all the childhood bullying directed at me had toughened me, making me believe that being rejected was better than not having the chance to be rejected at all. Thus it was that I approached girls, and now women, with such Zen negation of all doubt and fear the Buddha would approve. Sitting down next to Lana and thinking of nothing, I merely followed my instincts and my first three principles in talking to a woman: do not ask permission; do not say hello; and do not let her speak first.

I had no idea you could sing like you do when I first met you, I said. She looked at me with eyes that evoked those on ancient Grecian statues, empty and yet expressive. Why would you? I was only sixteen.

And I was only twenty-five. What did I know? I leaned close to be heard over the music and to offer her a cigarette. Fourth principle: give a woman the chance to reject something else besides me. If she declined the cigarette, as any of our proper young women should, I had an excuse to take one myself, which gave me a few seconds to say something while she focused on my cigarette. But Lana unexpectedly accepted, giving me the chance to fire up her cigarette with a suggestive flame, as I had once lit up Ms. Mori. What do your mother and father think of all this?

They think it's a waste of time to sing and dance. I suppose you agree with them?

I lit my own cigarette. If I agreed with them, would I be here?

You agree with everything my father says.

I agree with only some of the things your father says. But I don't disagree with anything.

So you agree with me when it comes to music?

Music and singing keep us alive, give us hope. If we can feel, we know we can live.

And we know we can love. She blew smoke away from me, though I would have been delighted to have her blow smoke in my eyes or on any part of my body. My parents fear singing will ruin me for marriage, she said. What they want for me is to get married tomorrow to someone very respectable and very rich. You're neither of those things, are you, Captain?

Would you rather I be respectable and rich?

You'd be much less interesting if you were.

You might be the first woman in the history of the world who's ever felt that way, I said. All this time I kept my gaze fixed on hers, an enormously difficult task given the gravitational pull exerted by her cleavage. While I was critical of many things when it came to so-called Western civilization, cleavage was not one of them. The Chinese might have invented gunpowder and the noodle, but the West had invented cleavage, with profound if underappreciated implications. A man gazing on semi-exposed breasts was not only engaging in simple lasciviousness, he was also meditating, even if unawares, on the visual embodiment of the verb "to cleave," which meant both to cut apart and to put together. A woman's cleavage perfectly illustrated this double and contradictory meaning, the breasts two separate entities with one identity. The double meaning was also present in how cleavage separated a woman from a man and yet drew him to her with the irresistible force of sliding down a slippery slope. Men had no equivalent, except, perhaps, for the only kind of male cleavage most women truly cared for, the opening and closing of a well-stuffed billfold. But whereas women could look at us as much as they wanted, and we would appreciate it, we were damned if we looked and hardly less damned if we didn't. A woman with extraordinary cleavage would reasonably be insulted by a man whose eyes could resist the plunge, so, just to be polite, I cast a tasteful glance while reaching for another cigarette. In between those marvelous breasts bumped a gold crucifix on a gold chain, and for once I wished I were a true Christian so I could be nailed to that cross.

Care for another cigarette? I said, our gazes meeting once more as I offered her my pack. Neither of us acknowledged my expert appraisal of her cleavage. Instead, she silently accepted my offer, reached forth her delicate hand, plucked out a cigarette, inserted it between her candied lips, waited for it to be ignited from a flame in my hand, and then, gradually, smoked the cigarette until it dwindled to a handful of ashes, easily blown away. If a man survived the time taken to smoke the first cigarette, he had a fighting chance on the beachhead of a woman's body. That I had survived a second cigarette boosted my confidence immeasurably. Thus, when the permed chanteuse whose chair I occupied returned, it was with confidence that I stood up and said to Lana, Let's go to the bar. Principle five: statements, not questions, were less likely to lead to no. She shrugged and offered me her hand.

Over the next hour, in between the times when Lana scorched the earth and the hair on my forearms with a few more songs, I learned the following. She loved vodka martinis, of which I ordered her three. Each one was shaken with top-shelf liquor in whose clear solution floated a pair of plump green olives, the suggestive nipples of pimentos protruding from them. Her employer was an art gallery in tony Brentwood. She had had boyfriends, plural, and when a woman discussed past boyfriends, she was informing you that she was evaluating you in comparison with defective and effective partners past. Although I was too tactful to ask about politics or religion, I learned that she was socially and economically progressive. She believed in birth control, gun control, and rent control; she believed in the liberation of homosexuals and civil rights for all; she believed in Gandhi, Martin Luther King Jr., and Thich Nhat Hanh; she believed in nonviolence, world peace, and yoga; she believed in the revolutionary potential of disco and the United Nations of nightclubs; she believed in national self-determination for the Third World as well as liberal democracy and regulated capitalism, which was, she said, to believe that the invisible hand of the market should wear the kid glove of socialism. Her favorite singers were Billie Holiday, Dusty Springfield, Elvis Phuong, and Khanh Ly, and she believed Vietnamese people could also sing the blues. Of American cities, she believed New York was where she wanted to live if she could not live in Los Angeles. But of all the things I learned about her, the most important was this: whereas most Vietnamese women kept their opinions to themselves until they were married, whereon they never kept their opinions to themselves, she was not hesitant to say what she thought.

At the end of the hour I waved Bon over, desperate for another pair of ears to relieve the stress on mine. He, too, was punchy with cognac, its influence making him unusually voluble. Lana was not above socializing with a common man, and for the next hour they became partners on a walk down memory lane, reminiscing about Saigon and songs while I quietly quaffed my cognac, discreetly admiring Lana's legs. Longer than the Bible and a hell of a lot more fun, they stretched forever, like an Indian yogi or an American highway shimmering through the Great Plains or the southwestern desert. Her legs demanded to be looked at and would not take no, *non, nein, nyet*, or even maybe for an answer. I was being held captive by the sight of them when I heard Lana say, And your wife and child? The tears trickling down Bon's cheeks broke the spell she had cast on me, the sight rousing me from deafness. Somehow the conversation had taken a turn from Saigon and songs to the fall of Saigon, which was not surprising. Most of the songs the exiles listened to were soaked in melancholic, romantic loss, which could not help but remind them of the loss of their city. Every conversation among the exiles about Saigon eventually became a conversation about the fall of Saigon and the fate of those left behind. They're dead, Bon now said. I was astonished, for Bon never talked about Linh and Duc with anyone but me, a function of the fact that Bon hardly talked to anyone. This was the problem with a walk down memory lane. It was almost always foggy, and one was likely to trip and fall. But perhaps this embarrassing collapse was worth it, for Lana, to my even greater astonishment, embraced him and pressed his stubborn, ugly head against her cheek. You poor man, Lana said. You poor, poor man. I was overwhelmed by a great, aching love for my best friend and this woman whose divine figure was the symbol of infinity turned upright onto its rounded bottom. I yearned to prove the hypothesis of my desire for her by empirically examining her naked curves with my eyes, her breasts with my hands, her skin with my tongue. I knew then, as she focused all her attention on the weeping Bon, who was so insensate with grief he seemed unaware of the enchanted valley exposed to his view, that I would possess her and that she would have me.

CHAPTER 15

A great deal of what I have confessed so far may seem foreign to you, dear Commandant, and to this mysterious, faceless commissar of yours whom I have heard so much about. The American Dream, the culture of Hollywood, the practices of American democracy, and so on can altogether make America a disorienting place for those like us who hail from the Orient. Presumably my half-Occidental status has helped me, perhaps innately, in understanding the American character, culture, and customs, including those concerning romance. The most important thing to understand is that while we courted, Americans dated, a pragmatic custom whereby a male and a female set a mutually agreeable time to meet, as if to negotiate a potentially profitable business venture. Americans understood dating to be about investments and gains, short or long term, but we saw romance and courtship as being about losses. After all, the only worthwhile courtship involved persuading a woman who could not be persuaded, not a woman already predisposed to examine her calendar for her availability.

Lana was clearly a woman in need of courting. I wrote her letters in which I pleaded my case, using the perfect cursive taught to me by pterodactyl nuns; I composed villanelles, sonnets, and couplets of doubtful prosody but resolute sincerity; I seized her guitar when she let me sit on a Moroccan cushion in her living room and sang her songs by Pham Duy, Trinh Cong Son, and the newest lyrical darling of our diaspora, Duc Huy. She rewarded me with the enigmatic smiles of an alluring apsara, a reserved seat at the front row of her performances, and the favor of continuing audiences, of which I was given no more than one a week. I was both grateful and tormented, as I recounted to Bon on listless afternoons at the liquor store. His response was as unenthusiastic as you might anticipate. Tell me this, lover boy, he said one day, back to his terse self. His attention was divided between me and a pair of teenage patrons creeping, possum-like, toward an aisle, a duo whose years and IQ were measurable in the low double digits. What happens when the General finds out? I was sitting with him behind the counter, awaiting the General's afternoon arrival. Why would the General ever find out? I said. Nobody would tell him. Lana and I aren't sentimental enough to think that one day we'll get married and confess to him. Then what's all this wooing and daring despair? he asked, quoting from my narration of our courtship. I said: Must wooing and daring despair end in marriage? Can't it end in love? What does marriage have to do with love? He snorted. God made us to be married. Love has everything to do with marriage. I wondered if he was about to dissolve as he had that night at *Fantasia*, but discussing love, marriage, and death had no visible effect on him this afternoon, perhaps because he was focused on the convex mirror suspended over the rear corner. The mirror's monocular eye revealed the teenagers gazing on the chilled beer with reverence, entranced by the reflection of fluorescent light on amber glass. Marriage is slavery, I said. And when God made us human—if God exists—He didn't intend for us to be slaves to each other.

You know what makes us human? In the mirror, the shorter of the duo slipped a bottle into his pocket. With a weary sigh, Bon reached for the baseball bat beneath the cash register. What makes us human is that we're the only creatures on this planet that can fuck ourselves.

Perhaps the point could have been made more delicately, but he was never one to be interested in delicacy. He was more interested in threatening the shoplifters with severe bodily harm until they fell to their knees, surrendered the items hidden in their jackets, and kowtowed for forgiveness. Bon was merely teaching them the way we had been taught. Our teachers were firm believers in the corporal punishment that Americans had given up, which was probably one reason they could no longer win wars. For us, violence began at home and continued in school, parents and teachers beating children and students like Persian rugs to shake the dust of complacency and stupidity out of them, and in that way make them more beautiful. My father was no exception. He was simply more high-minded than most, working the xylophone of his students' knuckles with his ruler until our poor joints were bruised purple, blue, and black. Sometimes we deserved to be whacked, sometimes not, but my father never showed any regret when evidence of our innocence surfaced. Since all were guilty of Original Sin, even punishment wrongly given was in some way just.

My mother was guilty, too, but hers was such an unoriginal sin. I was the kind bothered less by sinning than by unoriginality. Even in courting Lana, I suspected any sin I committed with her would never be enough because it would not be original. Yet I believed that sinning with her might be enough, since I would never know unless I tried. Perhaps I would glimpse infinity when I lit her up with the spasmodic spark that came from striking my soul against hers. Perhaps I would finally know eternity without resorting to this:

Q. Say the Apostles' Creed.
A. I believe in God, the Father Almighty, Creator of Heaven and earth . . .

Even these two thieves had likely heard of this prayer, Christian ideas being so important to the American people that they had granted them a place on the most precious document of all, the dollar bill. IN GOD WE TRUST must even now be printed on the money in their wallets. Bon tapped the shoplifters' foreheads gently with the baseball bat as they cried, Please, forgive us! At least these cretins knew fear, one of the two great motives for belief. The question the baseball bat would not resolve was whether they knew the other motive, love, which, for some reason, was much harder to teach.

* * *

The General arrived at his usual time, and as soon as he did, we left, myself chauffeuring while he sat in the back. He was not verbose as usual, nor did he spend his time poring through papers in his briefcase. Instead, he gazed out the window, which he normally considered a waste of time, and the only command he issued was to turn off the music. In the ensuing silence I heard the muted cello of foreboding, announcing the theme I was sure preoccupied him: Sonny. The newspaper article Sonny had written on the alleged operations of the Fraternity and the Movement had circulated with the ease of the common cold through the exiled community, his microbial allegations becoming confirmed facts and his facts becoming infectious rumors. By the time the rumors reached me, the story was that the General was either broke in his efforts to fund the Movement or wallowing in ill-gotten lucre. This was either the payoff from the US government for keeping mum about its failure to help us at war's end, or the profits from not just a chain of restaurants, but also drug dealing, prostitution, and extortion of small-time business owners. The Movement, some insisted, was simply a racket, and its men in Thailand a rabble of scurvy degenerates dependent on the community's donations. Others said those men were actually a regiment of the finest Rangers, bloodthirsty and mad for revenge. According to this ever-proliferating gossip, the General was either going to send these fools to their deaths from his armchair or he was going to return, like MacArthur to the Philippines, to lead the heroic invasion himself. If I was hearing this gossip, then Madame certainly was, and therefore the General, too, all of us tuned in to the humming, crackling AM channel of hearsay. This included the crapulent major, his fat body spilling over the edges of the bucket seat next to me. I dared not turn my head to look, although from the corner of my eye I saw him facing me, all three of his eyes surely wide open. I had not drilled that hole into his head that had given him his third eye, but I had come up with the plot that led to his fate. Now it was this third eye that allowed him to continue watching me even though he was dead, a spectator and not just a specter. I can't wait to see the end of this little story, he said. But I already know how it's going to end. Don't you?

Did you say something? the General said.

No, sir.

I heard you say something.

I must have been talking to myself.

Stop talking to yourself.

Yes, sir.

The only problem with not talking to oneself was that oneself was the most fascinating conversational partner one could imagine. Nobody had more patience in listening to one than oneself, and while nobody knew one better than oneself, nobody misunderstood one more than oneself. But if talking to oneself was the ideal conversation in the cocktail party of one's imagination, the crapulent major was the annoying guest who kept butting in and ignoring the cues to scram. Plots take on a life of their own, don't they? he said. You gave birth to this plot. Now you're the only one who can kill it. So it went for the rest of the drive to the country club, the crapulent major whispering in my ear while I held my tongue for so long it hurt, swollen with the words I wanted to say to him. Mostly I wished for him what I had once desired for my father, a disappearance from my life. After I had received his letter to me in the States that conveyed the news of my mother's death, I had written to Man that if God really did exist, my mother would be alive and my father would not. *How I wish he were dead!* In fact, he died not long after I returned, but his death had not brought me the satisfaction I thought it would.

This is a country club? the General said when we arrived at our destination. I checked the address; it was the same as on the Congressman's invitation. The invitation did mention a country club, and I, too, had pictured that we would drive through winding roads bereft of vehicles and roll up a gravel driveway to a valet waiting in a black vest and bow tie, the pastel prelude to entering a hushed den carpeted with the hides of black bears. On the walls, among the picture windows, would hang the antler-crowned heads of deer, gazing with mordant wisdom through clouds of cigar smoke. Outside sprawled an expansive golfing green that demanded more water than a Third World city, where quartets of virile bankers practiced a sport whose swinging skills required both the brute, warlike force necessary to disembowel unions as well as the coup de grâce finesse of tax dodging. But instead of such a soothing haven where one could always count on an undiminished supply of dimpled golf balls and self-congratulatory bonhomie, the address we arrived at was a steak house in Anaheim with all the charm of a door-to-door vacuum salesman. It seemed an ignoble setting for a

private dinner with none other than Richard Hedd, who
was visiting on a lecture tour.

After parking the car myself in a lot populated only by
American and Teutonic vehicles of recent vintage, I followed
the General into the steak house. The maître d' possessed the
mannerisms of an ambassador from a very small country, a
careful blend of superciliousness and servitude. Hearing the
Congressman's name, he softened enough to bow his head
slightly and led us through a maze of small dining rooms
where red-blooded Americans in argyle sweater vests and
button-down oxford shirts feasted on inordinate amounts
of porterhouse steak and rack of lamb. Our destination was
a private room on the second floor, where the Congressman
was holding court with several others at a round table large
enough for a man to lie on. Each of the attendees already had
a drink in his hand, and it dawned on me that our lateness
was prearranged. As the Congressman rose, I calmed the
tremor in my gut. I was in close quarters with some representative specimens of the most dangerous creature in the
history of the world, the white man in a suit.

Gentlemen, we are delighted you can join us, the
Congressman said. Let me introduce you. There were six
others—prominent businessmen, elected officials, and
lawyers—as well as Dr. Hedd. While the Congressman
and Dr. Hedd were Very Important Persons, the others,
including the General, were Semi-Important Persons (as
for me, I was a Non-Important Person). Dr. Hedd was the
main attraction of our dinner party, and the General was
the secondary attraction. The Congressman had arranged

the dinner for the General's benefit, an opportunity to expand his network of potential advocates, supporters, and investors, with the big prize being Dr. Hedd. A good word from Dr. Hedd, the Congressman had told the General, can open doors and pocketbooks for your cause. Not by accident, then, were the seats on either side of Dr. Hedd reserved for the General and myself, and I wasted no time in presenting my copy of his book for an autograph.

I see you've read this rather closely, the doctor said, riffling through pages dogeared so exhaustively that the book swelled as if waterlogged. The young man's a student of the American character, said the Congressman. From what the General tells me, and from what I've seen, I'm afraid he might know us better than we know ourselves. The men at the table chuckled at such a thought, and I did, too. If you're a student of the American character, said Dr. Hedd, signing the title page, why are you reading this book? It's more about the Asian than it is the American. He handed the book back to me, and with the weight of it in my hand, I said, It seems to me that one way to understand a person's character is to understand what he thinks of others, especially those like oneself. Dr. Hedd regarded me intently over the tops of his rimless glasses, a species of look that always bothered me, even more so coming from a man who had written this:

> The average Viet Cong fighter does not have a dispute with the real America. He has a dispute with the paper tiger created by his overlords, for he is no more than an idealistic young man duped by communism. If he

understood the true nature of America, he would realize that America was his friend, not his enemy. (p. 213)

Dr. Hedd was not speaking of me, exactly, as I was not the
average Viet Cong fighter, and yet he was speaking of me,
in the sense that he was dealing in types. Before this meeting I had reviewed his book one more time and found two
instances where his categories addressed someone such as
myself. On the verso side of me:

The Vietnamese radical intellectual is our most dangerous foe. Likely to have read Jefferson and Montaigne,
Marx and Tolstoy, he rightly asks why the rights of
man so praised by Western civilization have not been
extended to his people. He is lost to us. Having committed his life to the radical cause, there is no going
back for him. (p. 301)

In this assessment Dr. Hedd was correct. I was the worst
kind of cause, the lost cause. But then there was this passage,
written on the recto side of myself:

The young Vietnamese who are enamored of America
hold the key to South Vietnam's freedom. They have
tasted the Coca-Cola, as it were, and discovered it to be
sweet. Cognizant of our American imperfections, they
are nevertheless hopeful about our sincerity and our
goodwill in working on those flaws. It is these young
people we must cultivate. They will eventually replace

the dictatorial generals who were, after all, trained by
the French. (p. 381)

These categories existed as pages in a book exist, but most
of us were composed of many pages, not just one. Still, I
suspected, as Dr. Hedd scrutinized me, that what he saw was
not that I was a book but that I was a sheet, easily read and
easily mastered. I was going to prove him wrong.

I wager you, gentlemen, said Dr. Hedd, returning his attention to the rest of the table, that this young man is the only one
among you to have read the entirety of my book. The table
rippled with unembarrassed laughter, and for some reason I
felt that it was I who was the butt of the joke. The entirety? said
the Congressman. Come on, Richard. I'd be amazed if anybody here even read more than the back cover and the blurbs.
Another round of laughter, but instead of being insulted Dr.
Hedd seemed amused. He was the king of this affair, but he
wore his paper crown lightly. Doubtless he was used to being
feted, given the popularity of his books, the frequency of his
appearances on the Sunday morning talk shows, and the pres-
tige of his position as a resident scholar at a Washington think
tank. Air force generals in particular loved him, employing
him as a strategic consultant and regularly dispatching him to
brief the president and his advisers on the wonders of bombing.
Senators and congressmen loved Richard Hedd, too, including
our Congressman and those like him whose districts manufactured the planes used for this bombing. So far as my book
is concerned, he said, a little less honesty and a little more
politeness in terms of saving face would seem to be needed.

Only the middle-aged man next to me did not laugh or chuckle. His suit was neutral blue, and an inoffensive striped tie was leashed around his neck. He was a personal injury lawyer, a maestro of the class-action lawsuit. Picking at his Waldorf salad, he said, It's funny you say saving face, Dr. Hedd. Things have changed, haven't they? Twenty or thirty years ago, no American would have said "saving face" with a straight face.

There were many things Americans would not have said with a straight face twenty or thirty years ago that we say today, said Dr. Hedd. "Saving face" is a useful expression, and I say this as someone who fought the Japanese in Burma.

They were tough, said the Congressman, or so my father told me. There's nothing wrong with respecting your enemies. In fact, it's noble to respect them. Look at what they've done with some help from us. You can't drive down the street today without seeing a Japanese car.

The Japanese invested big in my country, too, said the General. They sold motorbikes and tape recorders. I owned a Sanyo stereo myself.

And this was only a couple of decades after they occupied you, the Congressman said. Did you know that a million Vietnamese died of famine during the Japanese years? The comment was addressed to the other men in suits, who did not laugh or chuckle. No kidding, said the personal injury lawyer. "No kidding" was about the only thing one could say when a statistic such as this arrived after the salad and before the hanger steak and baked potato. For a moment everyone squinted at his plate or cocktail, earnest as a patient studying an eye chart. As for me, I was calculating how to repair the damage the Congressman had inadvertently inflicted. He had complicated our task of being pleasant dinner companions by mentioning famine, something that Americans had never known. The word could only conjure otherworldly landscapes of the skeletal dead, which was not the spectral image we wanted to present, for what one should never do was to require other people to imagine they were just like one of us. Spiritual teleportation unsettled most people, who, if they thought of others at all, preferred to think that others were just like them or could be just like them.

That tragedy was a long time ago, I said. To tell you the truth, most of our countrymen here are less focused on the past than they are on becoming Americans.

How are they doing that? Dr. Hedd asked, and as he stared over his lenses it seemed to me that I was being examined by four eyes, not two. They—we, that is—believe in life, liberty, and the pursuit of happiness, I said, the answer I had given to many Americans. This drew approving nods from everyone at the table except for Dr. Hedd, who I had forgotten was an English immigrant. He kept his quadriscopic vision turned on me, those dual eyes and dual lenses unsettling. So, he said, are you happy? It was an intimate question, nearly as personal as asking about my salary, acceptable in our homeland but not here. What was worse, however, was that I could not think of a satisfactory answer. If I was unhappy, it would reflect badly on me, for Americans saw unhappiness as a moral failure and thought crime. But if I was happy, it would be in bad taste to say so, or a sign of hubris, as if I was boasting or gloating.

The waiters arrived at that moment with the solemnity of Egyptian servants ready to be buried alive with their pharaoh, platters with the main courses propped on their shoulders. If I thought that having slabs of meat before us would spare me Dr. Hedd's attention, I was wrong. He repeated his question after the waiters had departed, and I said I was not unhappy. The fat balloon of my double negative hung in the air for a moment, ambiguous and vulnerable. Presumably, Dr. Hedd said, you are not unhappy because you are pursuing happiness and have not yet captured it. As we all supposedly are, correct, gentlemen? The men murmured an assent through mouthfuls of steak and red wine. Americans on the average do not trust intellectuals, but they are cowed by power and stunned by celebrity. Not only did Dr. Hedd have a measure of both, he also possessed an English accent, which affected Americans the way a dog whistle stimulated canines. I was immune to the accent, not having been colonized by the English, and I was determined to hold my own in this impromptu seminar.

What about you, Dr. Hedd? I asked. Are you happy?

The doctor was unfazed by my question, parsing his peas with his knife before deciding on a sliver of steak. As you evidently realized, he said, there is no good answer to that question.

Isn't yes the good answer? said the assistant district attorney.

No, because happiness, American style, is a zero-sum

game, sir. Dr. Hedd slowly turned his head in an arc as he spoke, making sure that he saw every man in the room. For someone to be happy, he must measure his happiness against someone else's unhappiness, a process which most certainly works in reverse. If I said I was happy, someone else must be unhappy, most likely one of you. But if I said I was unhappy, that might make some of you happier, but it would also make you uneasy, as no one is supposed to be unhappy in America. I believe our clever young man has intuited that while only the pursuit of happiness is promised to all Americans, unhappiness is guaranteed for many.

Gloom descended on the table. The unspeakable had been spoken, which people like the General and myself could never have uttered in polite white company without rendering ourselves beyond the pale. Refugees such as ourselves could never dare question the Disneyland ideology followed by most Americans, that theirs was the happiest place on earth. But Dr. Hedd was beyond reproach, for he was an *English* immigrant. His very existence as such validated the legitimacy of the former colonies, while his heritage and accent triggered the latent Anglophilia and inferiority complex found in many Americans. Dr. Hedd was clearly aware of his privilege and was amused at the discomfort he was causing his American hosts. It was in this climate that the General intervened. I'm sure the good doctor is right, he said. But if happiness is not guaranteed, freedom is, and that, gentlemen, is more important.

Hear, hear, General, said the Congressman, raising his glass. Isn't that what the immigrant has always understood?

The rest of the guests also raised their glasses, even Dr. Hedd, smiling enigmatically at the General's redirection of the conversation. Such a move was typical on the General's part. He knew how to read a crowd, a crucial skill for raising money. As I had reported to Man through my Parisian aunt, he had already achieved a degree of fund-raising success, drawing from a handful of organizations to which he had been introduced by Claude, as well as his own contacts among Americans who had visited our country or done tours of duty there. These were well-connected men of pedigree, as were those who served on the boards of trustees for these organizations. The amount of money they gifted to the Fraternity was moderate by their standards, hardly anything to draw the attention of auditors or journalists. But once the Dollar Bill was dispatched abroad to Thailand, some extraordinary hocus-pocus called the exchange rate happened. The Dollar Bill might buy a ham sandwich in America, but in a Thai refugee camp the modest green Dollar Bill transformed into colorful Baht, ready to feed a fighting man for days. For a little more Baht, our fighting man could be clothed with the latest in olive drab. Thus, in the name of helping refugees, these donations met the basic necessities of food and garb for the secret army, consisting, after all, of refugees. As for guns and ammunition, they were supplied by the Thai security forces, who in turn received their pocket money from Uncle Sam, carried out with complete transparency and full congressional approval.

It was up to the Congressman, of course, to signal the appropriate moment for us to talk about why we were really there. He did so over the baked Alaska and after several rounds of cocktails. Gentlemen, the Congressman said, there is a serious reason for our meeting today and renewing our friendship. The General has come to talk to us about the plight of our old ally the South Vietnamese soldier, without whom the world would look much worse than it does today. Indochina did fall to communism, but look what we saved: Thailand, Taiwan, Hong Kong, Singapore, Korea, and Japan. These countries are our bulwark against the communist tide.

Let us not forget your Philippines, said Dr. Hedd. Or Indonesia.

Absolutely. Marcos and Suharto had time to put their communists down because the South Vietnamese soldier was their firewall, said the Congressman. So I think we owe this soldier something besides simple gratitude, which is why I asked you to come here today. Now I turn it over to one of the finest guardians of freedom Indochina has ever known. General?

The General pushed away his empty snifter and leaned forward with his elbows on the table, his hands clasped. Thank you, Congressman. It is my humble honor to meet you all. Men like you have built the world's greatest weapon, the arsenal of democracy. We could never have fought as long as we had against overwhelming forces without your boys and your guns. You must remember, gentlemen, how arrayed against us were not only our misguided brothers, but the entire communist world. The Russians, the Chinese, the North Koreans—they were all there, just as on our side were the many Asians you had befriended. How could I ever forget the South Koreans, the Filipinos, and the Thai who fought with us, as well as the Australians and the New Zealanders? Gentlemen, we did not fight the Vietnam War. We did not fight alone. We only fought the Vietnam battle in the Cold War between liberty and tyranny—

No one is disputing that there is still trouble in Southeast Asia, said Dr. Hedd. I had ever only seen the president dare to interrupt the General, but if he was offended, which he surely was, he betrayed no sign, merely smiling just a touch to express his pleasure at Dr. Hedd's contribution. But whatever the troubled past, Dr. Hedd went on, the region is quieter now, Cambodia aside. Meanwhile there are other, immediately urgent issues to worry us. The Palestinians, the Red Brigades, the Soviets. The threats have changed and metastasized. Terrorist commandos have struck in Germany, Italy, and Israel. Afghanistan is the new Vietnam. We should be worried about that, wouldn't you say, General?

The General furrowed his brow just a bit to show his concern and understanding. As a nonwhite person, the General, like myself, knew he must be patient with white people, who were easily scared by the nonwhite. Even with liberal white people, one could go only so far, and with average white people one could barely go anywhere. The General was deeply familiar with the nature, nuances, and internal differences of white people, as was every nonwhite person who had lived here a good number of years. We ate their food, we watched their movies, we observed their lives and psyche via television and in everyday contact, we learned their language, we absorbed their subtle cues, we laughed at their jokes, even when made at our expense, we humbly accepted their condescension, we eavesdropped on their conversations in supermarkets and the dentist's office, and we protected them by not speaking our own language in their presence, which unnerved them. We were the greatest anthropologists ever of the American people, which the American people never knew because our field notes were written in our own language in letters and postcards dispatched to our countries of origin, where our relatives read our reports with hilarity, confusion, and awe. Although the Congressman was joking, we probably did know white people better than they knew themselves, and we certainly knew white people better than they ever knew us. This sometimes led to us doubting ourselves, a state of constant self-guessing, of checking our images in the mirror and wondering if that was really who we were, if that was how white people saw us. But for all we thought we knew about them, there were some things we knew we did not know even after many years of forced and voluntary intimacy, including the art of making cranberry sauce, the proper way of throwing a football, and the secret customs of secret societies, like college fraternities, which seemed to recruit only those who would have been eligible for the Hitler Youth. Not least among the unknown to us was a sanctum such as this, or so I reported to my Parisian aunt, a hidden chamber where very few of our kind had appeared before, if any. As aware of this as I, the General was on mental tiptoes, careful not to offend.

It is funny you bring up the Soviets, the General said. As you have written, Dr. Hedd, Stalin and the peoples of the Soviet Union are closer in character to Oriental than Occidental. Your argument that the Cold War is a clash of civilizations, not just a clash of countries or even ideologies, is absolutely correct. The Cold War is really a conflict of Orient and Occident, and the Soviets are really Asiatics who have never learned Western ways, unlike us. Of course it was actually I, in preparation for this meeting, or audition, who had summarized for the General these claims in Hedd's book. Now I observed Dr. Hedd closely for his reaction to my prescription, but his expression did not change. Still, I was confident that the General's comments had affected him. No author was immune from having his own ideas and words quoted back to him favorably. Authors were, at heart, no matter how much they blustered or how suavely they carried themselves, insecure creatures with sensitive egos, as delicate in the constitution as movie stars, only much poorer and less glamorous. One only needed to dig deep enough to find that white, fleshy tuber of their secret self, and the sharpest tools with which to do so were always their own words. I added my own contribution to this effort and said, It is undisputed that we should confront the Soviets, Dr. Hedd. But the reason to fight them is related to the reason you advocated for fighting their servants in our country, and why we continue to fight them now.

What reason is that? said the ever Socratic Dr. Hedd.

I'll tell you the reason, said the Congressman. And not in my words, but in the words of John Quincy Adams when he spoke of our great country. "Wherever the standard of freedom and independence has been or shall be unfurled, there will her heart, her benedictions and her prayers be . . . She"—America—"is the well-wisher to the freedom and independence of all."

Dr. Hedd smiled again and said, Very good, sir. Even an Englishman cannot argue with John Quincy Adams.

What I still don't get is how we lost, the assistant district attorney said, beckoning to the headwaiter for another cocktail. In my opinion, said the personal injury lawyer, and hopefully you gentlemen will understand, we lost because we were too cautious. We feared harming our reputation, but if we had simply accepted that any damage to it wouldn't last, we could have exerted overwhelming force and showed your people which side deserved to win.

Perhaps Stalin and Mao had the right response, the General said. After a few million have died, what's a few million more? Didn't you write something to that effect, Dr. Hedd?

You have read my book more closely than I expected, General. You are a man who has undoubtedly seen the worst of war, as have I, so you will forgive me if I speak the unpalatable truth about why the Americans lost Vietnam. Dr. Hedd pushed his glasses up the bridge of his nose until his eyes finally peered through the lenses. Your American generals fought in World War II and knew the value of your Japanese strategies, but they didn't have a free hand to run the war. Instead of waging a war of obliteration, the only kind of war the Oriental understands and respects—nota bene Tokyo,

Hiroshima, Nagasaki—they had to, or chose to, fight a war of attrition. The Oriental interprets that, quite rightly, as weakness. Am I wrong, General?

If the Orient has one inexhaustible resource, said the General, it is people.

That is right, and I will tell you something else, General. It saddens me to come to this conclusion, but I have seen the evidence for myself, not only in books and archives, but in the battlefields of Burma. It must be said. Life is plentiful, life is cheap in the Orient. And as the philosophy of the Orient expresses it—Dr. Hedd paused—life is not important. Perhaps it is insensitive to say, but the Oriental does not put the same high price on life as the Westerner.

I wrote to my Parisian aunt that a moment of silence fell on the table as we absorbed this idea and as the waiters returned with our cocktails. The Congressman stirred his drink and said, What do you think, General? The General sipped from his cognac and soda, smiled, and said, Of course Dr. Hedd is right, Congressman. The truth is so often uncomfortable. What do you think, Captain?

All the men turned their attention to me, my brimming martini glass halfway to my lips. I reluctantly eased it down. After three of these libations and two glasses of red wine, I felt full of insight, the air of truth having expanded my mind and needing to be let out. Well, I said, I beg to differ from Dr. Hedd. Life actually *is* valuable to the Oriental. The General frowned and I paused. No one else's expression changed, but I could feel the static electricity of tension accumulating. So you're saying that Dr. Hedd is wrong, said the Congressman, as affable as Dr. Mengele must have been in the right company. Oh, no, I hastened to say. I was sweating, my undershirt damp. But you see, gentlemen, while life is only *valuable* to us—I paused again, and my audience inclined toward me by a millimeter or two—life is *invaluable* to the Westerner.

The attention of the men turned to Dr. Hedd, who raised his cocktail to me and said, I could not have phrased it better myself, young man. With that, the conversation finally exhausted itself, leaving us to nuzzle our cocktails with the affection one reserved for puppies. I made eye contact with the General and he nodded approvingly. Now, our hosts satisfied with our parley, I could ask a question of my own. Perhaps this is naive, I said, but we thought we were coming to a country club.

Our hosts roared with laughter as if I had told a most excellent joke. Even Dr. Hedd seemed to be in on it, chuckling over his Manhattan. The General and I grinned, waiting for the explanation. The Congressman glanced at the headwaiter, who nodded, and said, Gentlemen, now's a good a time as any to introduce you to the country club. Don't forget your cocktails. Led by the headwaiter, we filed out of the dining room with cocktails in hand. Down the hallway was another door. Opening it, the headwaiter said, The gentlemen are here. Inside was the room I had been expecting, with wood-paneled walls on which was mounted the head of a buck, its rack of antlers sporting sufficient points for all of us to hang our jackets on. The air was smoky and the lighting was dim, the better to flatter the comely young women in slinky dresses arranged on the leather sofas.

Gentlemen, said the Congressman, welcome to the country club.

I don't get it, the General whispered.

I'll tell you later, sir, I muttered. I finished my cocktail and handed the glass to the headwaiter as the Congressman beckoned to a pair of young ladies. General, Captain, let me introduce you. Our companions stood up. Elevated by high heels, they were taller than the General and myself by two or three inches. Mine was an enormous inflated blonde whose enameled white teeth were not quite as hard and shiny as her Nordic blue eyes. In one hand was a coupe of fizzy champagne, and in the other a long-stemmed cigarette holder with a half-smoked cigarette. She was a professional who had seen the likes of me a thousand times, which I could hardly complain about, given that I had seen the likes of her a fair number of times myself. Although I cranked my cheeks and lips into the facsimile of a smile, I could not muster inside myself the usual enthusiasm as the Congressman introduced us. Perhaps it was the way she casually flicked the head of ash from her cigarette onto the carpet, but instead of being magnetized by her iron beauty I was distracted by a striation below her jaw, the hemline between the unadorned skin of her neck and the white foundation coating her face. What's your name again? she said, laughing for no good reason. I leaned forward to tell her and nearly fell into the well of her cleavage, my sudden vertigo induced by the chloroform of her thick perfume.

I like your accent, I said, pulling back. You must be from somewhere in the South.

Georgia, honey, she said, laughing again. You speak real good English for an Oriental.

I laughed, she laughed, and when I looked to the General and his redheaded companion, they, too, were laughing. Everyone in the room was laughing, and when the waiters arrived with more champagne, it was clear we were all going to have a most excellent time, including Dr. Hedd. After handing a glass to his buxom companion and another to me, he said, I hope you do not mind, young man, if I use your memorable turn of phrase in my next book. Our female companions looked at me without interest, waiting for my reply. Nothing could make me happier, I said, even though I was, for reasons unspeakable in this company, quite unhappy.

CHAPTER 16

The General delivered a surprise to me as we parked outside his unlit residence later that evening, a little past midnight. I've been thinking about your request to return to our homeland, he said from the backseat, eyes visible in my rearview mirror. I need you here, but I respect your courage. Unlike Bon and the others, however, you've never been battlefield tested. He described the grizzled captain and the affectless lieutenant as war heroes, men whom he would trust with his life in combat. But you'll need to prove you can do what they can. You'll need to do what must be done. Can you do that? Of course, sir. I hesitated, then asked the obvious question: But what is to be done? You know what needs to be done, said the General. I sat with my hands still on the steering wheel at ten o'clock and two o'clock, hoping I was wrong. I just want to make sure I do the right thing, sir, I said, looking at him in the rearview mirror. What exactly needs to be done?

The General rustled in the back, rummaging through his pockets. I brought out my lighter. Thanks, Captain. For a brief moment the flame lit the palimpsest of his face. Then the chiaroscuro died and his face was no longer legible. I never told you the story of how I came to spend two years in a communist prison camp, did I? Well, no need for graphic details. Suffice it to say the enemy had surrounded our men at Dien Bien Phu. Not just Frenchmen and Moroccans and Algerians and Germans, but ours, too, thousands of them. I volunteered to jump into Dien Bien Phu, though I knew I would also be doomed. But I could not let my fellow soldiers die while I did nothing. When Dien Bien Phu fell, I was captured along with everybody else. Even though I lost two years of my life in prison, I never regretted jumping. I became the man I am today by jumping and by surviving that camp. But no one asked me to volunteer. No one told me what needed to be done. No one discussed the consequences. All these things were understood. Do you understand, Captain?

Yes, sir, I said.

Very good, then. If what needs to be done is done, then you can return to our homeland. You are a very intelligent young man, Captain. I trust you with all the details. No need to consult me. I'll arrange your ticket. You will get it when I receive news of what has been done. The General paused, door halfway open. Country club, huh? He chuckled. I'll have to remember that. I watched him walk up the pathway to his darkened house, where Madame was likely reading in bed, staying awake for his return, as she had waited so often in the villa. She knew a general's duties extended past midnight, but was she aware what some of these duties included? That we, too, had country clubs? Sometimes, after delivering him to the villa, I stood in my socked feet in the hallway and listened for any signs of distress from their room. I never heard any, but she was too smart not to know.

As for what I knew, it was this: my Parisian aunt had replied and the invisible words that gradually became visible were succinct. *Don't come back,* Man had written. *We need you in America, not here. These are your orders.* I burned the letter in a wastebasket, as I had burned all the letters, which was until that moment only a way of getting rid of evidence. But in that moment, I confess that burning the letter was also sending it to Hell, or perhaps making an offering to a deity, not God, who could keep Bon and me safe. I did not tell Bon about the letter, of course, but I did tell him of the General's offer and sought his counsel. He was characteristically blunt. You're an idiot, he said. But I can't stop you from going. As for Sonny, nothing to feel bad about. The man's got a big mouth. This consolation was offered the only way he knew how, at a billiards hall where he bought me several drinks and several rounds of pool. Something about the fraternal atmosphere of a billiards hall reassured the soul. The isolated pool of light over a table of green felt was an indoor hydroponic zone where what grew was the prickly plant of masculine emotion, too sensitive for sunlight and fresh air. After a café, but before a nightclub or home, a billiards hall was where one was most likely to encounter the southern Vietnamese man. Here he discovered that in billiards, as in lovemaking, accurate and true aim was increasingly difficult in proportion to the amount of alcohol consumed. Thus, as the night progressed, our games gradually grew longer and longer. To Bon's credit, however, the offer he made me was given in our first game, well before the nub of the night wore away to nothing and we numbly left the pool hall in the first minutes of dawn, exiting onto a lonely street whose only sign of life was a flour-dusted baker toiling in a doughnut shop's window. I'll do it, Bon said, watching me rack the balls. Tell the General you did it, but I'll get him for you.

His offer did not surprise me at all. Even as I thanked him, I knew I could not accept it. I was venturing into a wilderness many had explored before me, crossing the threshold separating those who had killed from those who had not. The General was correct that only a man who had received this rite could be allowed to return home. What I needed was a sacrament but none existed for this matter. Why not? Who were we fooling with the belief that God, if He existed, would not want us to acknowledge the sacredness of killing? Let us return to another important question of my father's catechism:

Q. What is man?
A. Man is a creature composed of a body and soul, and made to the image and likeness of God.
Q. Is this likeness in the body or in the soul?
A. This likeness is chiefly in the soul.

I need not look in the mirror or at the faces of my fellow men to find a likeness to God. I need only look at their selves and inside my own to realize we would not be killers if God Himself was not one, too.

But of course I am talking about not only killing but its subset murder. Bon shrugged at my hesitation and leaned over the table, cue stick resting on his splayed hand. You're always wanting to learn things, he said. Well, there's no greater knowledge than in killing a man. He put some english on the cue ball, and when it struck its target it rolled backward gently, aligning itself for the next shot. What about love and creation? I said. Getting married, having children? You, of all people, should believe in that kind of knowledge. He rested his hip on the table's edge, both hands clutching the pool cue propped on his shoulder. You're testing me, right? Okay. We have all kinds of ways to talk about life and creation. But when guys like me go and kill, everyone's happy we do it and no one wants to talk about it. It would be better if every Sunday before the priest talks a warrior gets up and tells people who he's killed on their behalf. Listening is the least they could do. He shrugged. That's not ever happening. So here's some practical advice. People like to play dead. You know how to tell if someone's really dead? Press your finger on his eyeball. If he's alive, he'll move. If he's dead, he won't.

I could see myself shooting Sonny, having seen such an act so many times in the movies. But I could not see my finger wiggling the slippery fish ball of his eye. Why not just shoot him twice? I said. Because, smart guy, it makes noise. It goes bang. And who said anything about shooting him even once? Sometimes we killed VC with things other than guns. If it makes you feel any better, this isn't murder. It's not even killing. It's assassination. Ask your man Claude if you haven't already. He'd show up and say, Here's the shopping list. Go and bag some. So we'd go into the villages at night with the shopping list. VC terrorist, VC sympathizer, VC collaborator, maybe VC, probable VC, this one's got a VC in her belly. This one's thinking of being a VC. This one everybody thinks is VC. This one's father or mother is VC, therefore is VC in training. We ran out of time before we got them all. We should have wiped them out when we had the chance. Don't make the same mistake. Take out this VC before he gets too big, before he turns others into VC. That's all it is. Nothing to feel sorry about. Nothing to cry about.

If it were all so simple. The problem with killing all the Viet Cong was that there would always be more, teeming in the walls of our minds, breathing heavily under the floorboards of our souls, orgiastically reproducing out of our sight. The other problem was that Sonny was not VC, for a subversive would not, by definition, have a big mouth. But maybe I was wrong. An agent provocateur was a subversive, and his task was to shoot his mouth off, agitating others in the spin cycle of radicalization. In that case, however, the agent provocateur here would not be a communist, spurring the anticommunists to organize against him. He would be an anticommunist, encouraging like-minded people to go too far, dizzy with ideological fervor, rancid with resentment. By that definition, the most likely agent provocateur was the General. Or the Madame. Why not? Man assured me we had people in the highest ranks. You'll be surprised who gets the medals after the liberation, he said. Would I now? The joke would be on me if the General and Madame were sympathizers, too. A joke we could all laugh at when we were commemorated as Heroes of the People.

With Bon's counsel stashed away, I turned for solace to the only other person whom I could speak to, Lana. I came to her apartment the next week with a bottle of wine. At home she looked like a college student in her UC Berkeley sweatshirt, faded blue jeans, and the lightest of makeup. She cooked like one, too, but no matter. We ate dinner in the living room while watching *The Jeffersons*, a TV comedy about the unacknowledged black descendants of Thomas Jefferson, America's third president and author of the Declaration of Independence. Afterward we drank another bottle of wine, which helped to soften the heavy lumps of starch in our tummies. I pointed toward the illuminated architectural masterpieces on a hill in the distance, visible through her window, and told her that one of them belonged to the Auteur, whose opus was soon to be released. I had already recounted my misadventures in the Philippines and my suspicion, however paranoid, that the Auteur had tried to kill me. I'll admit, I told her, that I've fantasized about killing him once or twice. She shrugged and stubbed out her cigarette. We all fantasize about killing people, she said. Just a passing thought, like, oh, what if I ran over that person with a car. Or at least we fantasize what it would be like if someone were dead. My mother, for example. Not really, of course, but just what if . . . right? Don't leave me feeling like I'm crazy here. I had her guitar on my lap, and I strummed a dramatic Spanish chord. Since we're confessing, I said, I've thought about killing my father. Not really, of course, but just what if . . . Did I ever tell you he was a priest? Her eyes opened wide. A priest? My God!

Her sincere shock endeared her to me. Underneath the nightclub makeup and artificial diva gloss she was still innocent, so unsullied that all I wanted was to rub the emollient, creamy pulp of my ecstatic self onto her soft white skin. I wanted to replicate the oldest dialectic of all with her, the thesis of Adam and the antithesis of Eve that led to the synthesis of us, the rotten apple of humanity, fallen so far from God's tree. Not that we were even as pure as our first parents. If Adam and Eve had debased God's knowledge, we had in turn debased Adam and Eve, so that what I really wanted was the steamy, hot, jungle dialectic of "Me Tarzan, you Jane." Were either of these couplings any better than a Vietnamese girl and a French priest? My mother used to tell me nothing was wrong with being the love child of such a pair, I told Lana. After all, Mama said, we are a people born from the mating of a dragon and a fairy. What could be stranger than that? But people looked down on me all the same, and I blamed my father. When I was growing up, I fantasized that one day he would stand before the congregation and say, Here is my son that you may know him. Let him come before you that you should recognize him and love him as I love him. Or some such thing. I'd have been happy if he would just visit and eat with us and call me son in secret. But he never did, so I fantasized about a lightning bolt, a mad elephant, a fatal disease, an angel descending behind him at the pulpit and blowing a trumpet in his ear to call him back to his Maker.

That's not fantasizing about killing him.

Oh, but I did, with a gun.

But have you forgiven him?

Sometimes I think I have. Sometimes I think I haven't, especially when I think of my mother. That means, I suppose, that I haven't really forgiven him.

Lana leaned forward then, resting her hand on my knee. Perhaps forgiveness is overrated, she said. Her face was closer to me than ever before, and all I need do was lean forward. It was then I committed the most perverse act of my life. I declined, or rather, I reclined, putting distance between me and that beautiful face, the tempting crevice of those slightly parted lips. I should go, I said.

You should go? From the expression on her face, it was clear she had never heard those words before from a man. She would not have looked so astonished if I had asked her to commit the most heinous acts of Sodom. I stood up before I changed my mind, handing her the guitar. There's something I must do. Before I can do what needs to be done here. It was her turn to recline, amused, and strum a dramatic chord. Sounds serious, she said. But you know what? I like serious men.

If only she knew how serious I could be. I drove the hour between her apartment and Sonny's with my hands at ten and two o'clock, breathing deeply and methodically to quell my regret at leaving Lana and my nervousness at meeting him. Breathing mindfully was a lesson Claude had taught me, learned from the practices of our Buddhist monks. Everything came down to focusing on the breath. Slowly exhaling and inhaling, one cleared away life's white noise, leaving one's mind free and peaceful to be one with the object of its contemplation. When subject and object are the same, Claude said, you don't shake when you squeeze the trigger. By the time I parked my car around the corner from Sonny's apartment, my mind was a gull gliding over a beach, carried not by its own will or movement but by the breeze. I took off my blue polo shirt and slipped on a white T-shirt. I kicked off my brown loafers and removed my khakis, then pulled on a pair of blue jeans and beige canvas shoes. Last to go on was a reversible windbreaker, the plaid side exposed, and a fedora. Leaving the car, I carried with me a free tote bag I had received for subscribing to *Time* magazine, inside of which was a small backpack, the clothes I had just shed, a baseball cap, a blond wig, a pair of tinted glasses, and a black Walther P22 with a silencer. The General had given Bon an envelope of cash, and with it Bon had bought the pistol and silencer from the same Chinese gang that had supplied him with the .38. Then he had made me rehearse the plan with him until I had memorized it.

The sidewalk was barren from car to apartment. Walking the streets was not an American custom, as I had confirmed after observing the neighborhood several times. It was a little past nine o'clock when I checked my watch at the entrance to his apartment building, a gray two-story factory for manufacturing hundreds of tired replicas of the American Dream. All the inmates imagined their dreams to be unique, but they were merely tin reproductions of a lost original. I rang the intercom. *Allô?* he said. When I announced my presence, there was a slight pause before he said, I'll buzz you in. I took the stairs instead of the elevator to avoid meeting anyone. On the second floor, I peeked into the hallway to make sure no one was there. He opened the door a second after I knocked.

The apartment smelled like home, the scents of fried fish, steamed white rice, and cigarette smoke. I know why you're here, he said as I sat down on his couch. I clutched the tote bag. Why am I here? I said. Sofia, he said, as serious as I was even though his feet were in fuzzy pink slippers. He wore sweatpants and a gray cardigan. On the dining table behind him hunkered a typewriter with a lip of paper dangling from its roller, the machine abutted by haphazard mounds of documents. Under the dining table's chandelier, above an ashtray, floated a slowly dissipating cloud of smoke, the exhaust from Sonny's active brain. And on the wall above the table, through that scrim, hung the same clock as in the General and Madame's restaurant, also set to Saigon time.

We never did have the talk we should have had about her, he said. Our last conversation was uncomfortable. I apologize for that. If we had been decent about it, we would have written you a letter in the Philippines. His unexpected and seemingly genuine concern for my welfare caught me off guard. It was my fault, I said. I never wrote her in the first place myself. We both looked at each other for a moment and then he smiled and said, I'm being a bad host. I haven't even offered you a drink. How about it? Despite my protestations, he leaped up and went to the kitchen, exactly as Bon predicted. I put my hand on the Walther P22 in the tote bag but I could not find the will to stand up, follow him into the kitchen, and quickly put a bullet behind his ear as Bon had advised. It's the merciful thing to do, he said. Yes, it was, but the lump of starch in my stomach glued me to the couch, upholstered in a scratchy, stain-resistant fabric designed for motel room trysts. Stacks of books on the industrial carpet sandbagged the walls, and on top of the antique television a silver stereo muttered. Above the armchair, a blotchy, amateurish painting in the style of a demented Monet illustrated an interesting principle, that beauty is not needed to make a milieu more attractive. A very ugly object can also make an ugly room less ugly by comparison. Another affordable way to add a drop of loveliness to the world was not to change it but to change how one saw it. This was one of the purposes for the bottle of bourbon that Sonny returned with, a third full.

You hear that? he said, nodding at the stereo. The two of us cuddled the glasses of bourbon in our laps. After all the Cambodian attacks on our border towns, we just raided Cambodia. You'd think we'd had enough of war that we wouldn't want another one. I thought about how the border clash with the Khmer Rouge was an incredible stroke of good luck for the General, a distraction to keep everyone looking elsewhere than our Laotian border. The problem with winning, I said, is that everyone's so riled up they're ready to fight again. He nodded and sipped his bourbon. The good thing about losing is it keeps you from fighting another war, at least for a while. Although that's not true for your General. I was about to protest when he raised his hand and said, Forgive me. I'm talking politics again. I swear not to talk about politics tonight, my brother. You know how hard that is for someone who believes everything is political.

Even bourbon? I said. He grinned. All right, so perhaps bourbon is not political. I don't know what to talk about besides politics. It's a weakness. Most people can't tolerate it. But Sofia can. I talk to her like no one else. That's love.

So you're in love with her?

You weren't in love with her, were you? She said you weren't.

If she said so, then I guess I wasn't.

I understand. Losing her hurts even if you didn't love her. That's human nature. You want her back. You don't want to lose her to someone like me. But please, see it from my point of view. We didn't plan anything. It's just that when we started talking at the wedding, we couldn't stop. Love is being able to talk to someone else without effort, without hiding, and at the same time to feel absolutely comfortable not saying a word. At least that's one way I've figured out how to describe love. I've never been in love before. It leaves me with this strange need to find the right metaphor to describe being in love. Like I am a windmill, and she is the wind. Stupid, yes?

No, not at all, I mumbled, realizing we had broached a topic more problematic than politics. I looked down at the nearly empty glass cupped in my hand, and through the skim of bourbon at the bottom of the glass I saw the red scar. It's not her fault, he said. I gave her my number at the wedding and asked for hers, because, I said, wouldn't it be great if I could write an article about how a Japanese sees us Vietnamese? Japanese American, she corrected me. Not

Japanese. And Vietnamese American, not Vietnamese. You must claim America, she said. America will not give itself to you. If you do not claim America, if America is not in your heart, America will throw you into a concentration camp or a reservation or a plantation. And then, if you have not claimed America, where will you go? We can go anywhere, I said. You think that way because you weren't born here, she said. I was, and I have nowhere else to go. If I had children, they, too, would have nowhere else. They will be citizens. This is their country. And at that moment, with those words of hers, a desire I had never experienced came over me. I wanted to have a child with her. Me, who had never wanted marriage! Who could never imagine being a father!

Can I have another drink?

Of course! He refilled my glass. You stupid bastard, Bon's voice in my head said. You're making this worse. Get it over with. Now, Sonny continued, I realize that so far as children and fatherhood goes, it's more dream than possibility. Sofia is past her childbirthing years. But there's adoption. I think it's time to think of someone else besides me. Before I only wanted to change the world. I still want that, but it was ironic how I never wanted to change myself. Yet that's where revolutions start! And it's the only way revolutions can continue, if we keep looking inward, looking at how others might see us. That's what happened when I met Sofia. I saw myself the way she saw me.

With that, he lapsed into silence. My resolve was so weakened I could not raise my right arm to reach into the bag for the gun. Listen, I said. I have something to confess to you.

So you do love Sofia. He looked genuinely sad. I'm sorry.

I'm not here because of Ms. Mori. Can we just talk about politics instead?

As you wish.

I asked you before if you were a communist. You said you wouldn't tell me if you were. But what if I told you I was a communist? He smiled, shaking his head. I don't believe in the hypothetical, he said. What's the point of playing a game of what or who you might be? It's not a game, I said. I am a communist. I'm your ally. I have been an agent for the opposition and the revolution for years. What do you think about that?

What do I think? He hesitated in disbelief. Then his face turned bright red in fury. I don't believe it at all is what I think. I think you've come here to trick me. You want me to say I'm a communist, too, so you can kill me or expose me, don't you?

I'm trying to help you, I said.

How exactly are you trying to help me?

I had no answer to his question. I confess that I do not know what brought me to make my confession to him. Or, rather, I did not know then, but perhaps I do know now. I had worn my mask for so long, and here was my opportunity to take it off, safely. I had stumbled to this action instinctively, out of a feeling that was not unique to me. I cannot be the only one who believes that if others just saw who I really was, then I would be understood and, perhaps, loved. But what would happen if one took off the mask and the other saw one not with love but with horror, disgust, and anger? What if the self that one exposes is as unpleasing to others as the mask, or even worse?

Did the General put you up to this? he said. I can see the two of you plotting away. If I was gone, it would be good for him and for you, no doubt.

Listen to me—

You're jealous because I have Sofia, even though you don't even love her. I knew you'd be angry, but I didn't think you'd stoop this low and come bait me. How stupid do you think I am? Did you think you'd suddenly be attractive to Sofia again if you said you were a communist? You don't think she'd smell your desperation and laugh in your face? My God, I can't even imagine what she'll say when I tell her—

Although it seems impossible to miss from five feet away, it is very possible, especially after too much wine and a tumbler or two of bourbon suffused with the bitter peat of the past. The bullet punctured the radio, muffling but not silencing it. He looked at me in utter astonishment, his gaze fixed on the gun in my hand, the silencer adding a few more inches. I had stopped breathing, my heart had ceased beating. The gun jerked and he cried out, pierced in the hand that he had flung up. Suddenly awakened to his impending death, he leaped to his feet and turned to run. The third bullet struck between shoulder blade and spine, staggering but not stopping him as I jumped over the coffee table, catching up before he reached the door. Now I was in the ideal position, or so Bon told me, a foot behind my subject, in his blind spot, where one really could not miss. *Click, clack* went the gun, one bullet behind the ear, another in the skull, and Sonny fell face-first with enough graceless weight to break his nose.

I stood over his prone body, cheek down on the carpet, copious amounts of blood gushing from the holes drilled in his head. At the angle at which I stood, behind him, I could not see his eyes but I could see his upturned hand with the bloody hole in his palm, his arm bent awkwardly beside him. The lump of starch had dissolved, but now its liquid results sloshed in my guts and threatened to spill. I inhaled deeply and exhaled slowly. I thought of Ms. Mori, most likely at home, cat on her lap, reading a radical feminist treatise, waiting for Sonny to call, the call that never would come, the call that defined our relationship to God, whom we forlorn lovers were always calling. Now Sonny had crossed the greatest divide, leaving behind only his cold, darkened shade, his lamp forever extinguished. On the back of his cardigan a crimson stain spread, while around his head a bloody halo swelled. A wave of nausea and chills shook me, and my mother said, You'll be better than all of them, won't you, my son?

I inhaled deeply and exhaled slowly, once, twice, and one more time, slowing my shaking to a trembling. Remember, Bon said inside my head, you're doing what has to be done. The list of other things in need of doing returned. I took off my windbreaker and T-shirt and put my blue polo shirt back on. The jeans and canvas shoes came off, replaced by khakis and loafers. I reversed the windbreaker to expose the plain white side, swapped the fedora for the wig, its blond hair touching the base of my neck, and put on the baseball cap.

Last came the tinted glasses, my change complete after the tote bag and the gun went into the backpack. The wig, cap, and glasses were Bon's idea. He had made me try the look on in front of the bathroom mirror, foggy with a year's worth of spattered toothpaste foam. See? he said. Now you're a white man. To me I still looked like me, hidden by a disguise much too normal for a masked ball or a Halloween party. But that was the point. If someone did not know what I looked like, I did not look like I was in disguise.

I wiped the fingerprints off my glass with my handkerchief, and it was with the handkerchief wrapped around the doorknob that I thought I heard Sonny moan. I looked down at the back of his shattered head, but I could hear nothing more above the thrumming of blood in my ears. You know what you have to do, Bon said. I got on my knees, lowering my face to look Sonny in his one exposed eye. When the liquid contents of my dinner rose up against the back of my throat, I clapped my hand over my mouth. I swallowed hard and tasted vileness. Sonny's eye was lusterless and blank. He must surely be dead, but as Bon had told me, sometimes the dead did not know they were dead yet. So it was that I reached forth my index finger, slowly, closer and closer to that eye, which moved not at all. My finger hovered an inch before the eye, then a few millimeters. No movement. Then my finger touched that soft, rubbery eye, the texture of a peeled quail egg, and he blinked. I jumped back as his body shuddered, just a little, and then I fired another bullet into his temple from a foot away. Now, Bon said, he's dead.

I inhaled deeply, exhaled slowly, and almost threw up. A little more than three minutes had elapsed since the first shot. I inhaled deeply, exhaled slowly, and my liquid contents achieved precarious equilibrium. After all was still, I opened Sonny's door and walked out with presidential confidence, as Bon recommended. Breathe, Claude said. So I breathed, running down the echoing stairway, and I breathed once more as I exited into the lobby, where the front door was opening.

He was a white man, the lawn mower of middle age having blazed a broad swatch of baldness through his hair. The well-tailored, cheap-looking suit bolted to his considerable body implied he worked in one of those low-paying professions where appearances counted, where one worked on commission. His wingtips glistened with the sheen of frozen fish. I knew all this because I looked at him, which Bon said not to do. Don't make eye contact. Don't give people a reason to give you a second look. But he did not even look at me. Eyes straight ahead, he walked by as if I were invisible, a ghost or, more likely, just another unremarkable white man. I passed through his vapor trail of artificial pheromone, the dime-store cologne of the macho male, and caught the front door before it closed. Then I was on the street, breathing in the Southern Californian air, fine-grained with the particulates of smog, heady with the realization that I could go wherever I wanted. I made it as far as my car. There, kneeling by the wheel well, I vomited, heaving until nothing was left, staining the gutter with the tea leaves of my insides.

CHAPTER 17

I t's normal, Bon said the next morning. He soothed the hematoma swelling from my mind with the aid of a fine bottle of scotch, granted by the General. It just had to be done, and we're the ones who have to live with it. Now you understand. Drink up. We drank up. You know what the best cure is? I had thought the best cure was to return to Lana, which I had done after leaving Sonny's apartment, but even an unforgettable evening with her had not helped me forget what I had done to Sonny. I shook my head slowly, careful not to rattle my bruised brain. Getting back to the battlefield. You'll feel better in Thailand. If that was true, then fortunately I did not have to wait long. We were leaving tomorrow, the scheduling planned to help me avoid any possibility of entanglement with the law and to avoid my plot's obvious weakness, Ms. Mori. On hearing of Sonny's death, her first thoughts might be confused, but her subsequent thoughts would turn to me, her jilted lover. The General had trusted that I would get the deed done on the date I promised, and he had provided me with my ticket the previous week. We were in his office, the newspaper on his desk, and when I opened my mouth, he lifted his hand and said, It goes without saying, Captain. I closed my mouth. I inspected the ticket, and that evening I wrote my Parisian aunt. In code, I told Man that I accepted responsibility for disobeying his orders, but that I was returning with Bon to save his life. I did not inform Man of my plan for how to do that, because I still did not have one. But I had gotten Bon into this situation, and it was up to me to get him out of it if I could.

So, two days after the deed was done, with no one yet having noticed Sonny's absence, except, perhaps, for Ms. Mori, we left with no fanfare aside from that provided by the General and Madame at the airport gate. There were four of us departing on this unlikely trip—Bon, myself, the grizzled captain, and the affectless lieutenant—slung across the Pacific in a tubular, subsonic Boeing airliner. Good-bye, America, the grizzled captain said during our ascent, looking out the window at a landscape I could not see from my aisle seat. I've had enough of you, he said. The affectless lieutenant, sitting in the middle, agreed. Why did we ever call it the beautiful country? he said. I had no answer. I was in a daze and terribly uncomfortable, sharing my seat as I was with the crapulent major on one side and Sonny on the other. It was only my seventh time on a jet airplane. I had flown to and from America for college, then flew with Bon from Saigon to Guam and Guam to California, followed by my round trip to the Philippines, and now this. My chances of returning to America were small, and I thought with regret about all the things I would miss about America: the TV dinner;

air-conditioning; a well-regulated traffic system that people actually followed; a relatively low rate of death by gunfire, at least compared with our homeland; the modernist novel; freedom of speech, which, if not as absolute as Americans liked to believe, was still greater in degree than in our homeland; sexual liberation; and, perhaps most of all, that omnipresent American narcotic, optimism, the unending flow of which poured through the American mind continuously, whitewashing the graffiti of despair, rage, hatred, and nihilism scrawled there nightly by the black hoodlums of the unconscious. There were also many things about America with which I was less enchanted, but why be negative? I would leave the anti-American negativity and pessimism to Bon, who had never assimilated and was relieved to go. It's like I've been hiding in someone else's house, he said somewhere over the Pacific. He was sitting across the aisle from me. The Japanese stewardesses were serving tempura and tonkatsu, which tasted better than the last word the General had forced into my mouth at the departure gate. In between the walls, Bon said, listening to other people live, coming out only at night. I can breathe now. We're going back where everyone looks like us. Like you, I said. I don't look like everyone there. Bon sighed. Stop bitching and moaning, he said, filling my teacup with the whiskey the General had given him at the gate. Your problem isn't that you think too much; your problem is letting everyone know what you're thinking. So I'll just shut up then, I said. Yes, just shut up, he said. All right, then, I'll shut up, I said. Jesus Christ, he said.

After a sleepless twenty-hour trek that involved changing planes in Tokyo, we arrived in Bangkok. I was exhausted, not having been able to sleep. Every time I closed my eyes, I saw either the crapulent major's face or Sonny's, which I could not bear to look at for long. Thus it was not surprising that when I picked up my rucksack from the baggage carousel, I found it to be heavier than I remembered, loaded as it was now with guilt, dread, and anxiety. The overstuffed rucksack was my only piece of luggage, for before leaving our apartment, we had given the key to the Reverend R-r-r-r-amon and told him to sell our things and keep the money for his Church of Everlasting Prophets. All my belongings now fit in the rucksack, my copy of *Asian Communism and the Oriental Mode of Destruction* in its false bottom, the book so well worn it had nearly split in two along its cracked spine. Everything else we needed would be provided in Thailand, the General said. Matters would be handled by the admiral in charge of the base camp and by Claude, who would be there in a guise familiar to him, working for a nongovernmental organization that assisted refugees. He greeted us at the international gate dressed in a Hawaiian shirt and linen pants, looking the same as I had seen him last at Professor Hammer's house, except for being deeply tanned. It's great to see you guys, he said, shaking my hand and those of the others. Welcome to Bangkok. You guys ever been here? Didn't think so. We've got one night and we're painting the town red. My treat. He threw his arm around my shoulders and squeezed with genuine affection, leading me through the throbbing crowd and toward the exit. Perhaps it was only my state of mind, its consistency close to porridge, but every one of the natives we passed seemed to be looking at the two of us. I wondered if among them was one of Man's agents. You look good, Claude said. You ready to do this thing?

Of course, I said, all my dread and anxiety bubbling in a compartment somewhere behind my bowels. I had the vertiginous feeling one gets standing at the precipice of an unresolved plan, for I had brought Bon and myself to the brink of disaster without knowing how to save us. But was not this how all plans developed, unknown to their maker until he wove for himself a parachute, or else melted into air? I could hardly ask that question of Claude, who always seemed to be the master of his own fate, at least until the fall of Saigon. He squeezed my shoulder again. I'm proud of you, buddy. I just wanted you to know that. We both walked in silence for a moment, allowing this sentiment to circulate, and then he squeezed my shoulder again and said, I'm going to show you the best time of your life. I grinned and he grinned, the thing unsaid being that this might be the last best time of my life. His enthusiasm and concern touched me, his way of saying he loved me, or possibly his way of providing me with the equivalent of a doomed man's last meal. He led us outside the terminal and into the seasonable late December weather, the best time of the year to visit the region. We loaded ourselves into a van, and Claude said, You don't get over jet lag by going to a hotel and getting some sleep. I'm going to keep you awake until nighttime, and then tomorrow we're setting out for the camp.

The driver steered us onto a road jammed with vans, trucks, and motorbikes. We were surrounded by the honking, beeping, and roaring of an urban metropolis engorged with automotive metal, human flesh, and unspoken emotion. Remind you guys of home? said Claude. This is the closest you guys have been for years. Same-same like Saigon, the grizzled captain said. Same-same but different, said Claude. No war and no refugees. All that's on the border, where you guys are going. Claude passed out cigarettes and we all lit up. First it was the Laotians running across the border. Now we have a lot of Hmong. All very sad, but helping refugees does get us access to the countryside. The affectless lieutenant shook his head and said, Laos. Very evil communists there. Claude said, Is there any other kind? But Laos itself is the closest thing to paradise Indochina's got. I spent time there during the war and it was incredible. I love those people. They're the gentlest, most hospitable people on earth except when they want to kill you. When he exhaled smoke, the tiny fan mounted on the dashboard blew it back toward us. At some point, had Claude and other foreigners considered us to be the gentlest, most hospitable people on earth? Or had we always been a warlike, aggressive people? I suspected the latter.

As the driver exited from the freeway, Claude nudged me and said, I heard about what you did. What I did? What did I do? When Claude said nothing and kept his steady gaze on me, I remembered the one thing that I had done that must be passed over in silence. Oh, yeah, I muttered. Don't feel bad, said Claude. From what the General told me, that guy was asking for it. I can guarantee you he didn't ask for it, I said.

That's not what I meant, said Claude. It's just that I've seen plenty of his kind. Professional malcontents. Self-righteous masochists. They're so unhappy with everything that they're never going to be happy until they're trussed for execution. And you know what his kind would say when he's facing the firing squad? I told you so! The only thing different in your case is that the poor slob didn't have time to think about it. If you say so, Claude, I said. I'm not saying so, he said. It's in the book. He's the guilt-ridden character.

I could see the pages of the book that Claude was refer-ring to, the interrogation manual we had pored over in his course, the book that went under the name *KUBARK*. It had definitions of several character types the interrogator was likely to meet, and unbidden, the paragraph about the guilt-ridden character rippled before my eyes.

This kind of person has a strong, cruel, unrealistic conscience. His whole life seems devoted to reliving his feelings of guilt. Sometimes he seems determined to atone; at other times he insists that whatever went wrong is the fault of somebody else. In either event he seeks constantly some proof or external indication that the guilt of others is greater than his own. He is often caught up completely in efforts to prove that he has been treated unjustly. In fact, he may provoke unjust treatment in order to assuage his conscience through punishment. Persons with intense guilt feelings may cease resistance and cooperate if punished in some way, because of the gratification induced by punishment.

Perhaps this was, indeed, Sonny, but I would never know for sure, as I would have no more opportunities to inter-rogate him.

Here we are, said Claude. Our destination was an alley over which hung a rainbow of artificial neon light, the side-walks thronged with pale-faced primates of all ages and sizes, some with military crew cuts and some with the long hair of the hippie tribe, all inebriated or about to be inebri-ated, many howling and hooting in considerable agitation. Bars and clubs lined the entire alley, and in the doorways stood girls with bare limbs and exquisitely painted features. The van stopped at an establishment above whose door rose a gigantic vertical sign in bright yellow that spelled GOLDEN COCK. The door was held open by two girls who appeared to be twenty or so, which meant that they were mostly likely anywhere from fifteen to eighteen. They stood on six-inch heels and wore what euphemistically could be called cloth-ing—halter tops and bikini bottoms not even as substantial as their kind smiles, as loving and gentle as those of kinder-garten teachers. Oh boy, said the grizzled captain, grinning so widely I could see his decaying molars. Even the affectless lieutenant said, Nice, though he did not smile. Glad you like it, said Claude. It's all for you. The affectless lieutenant and the grizzled captain had already entered when Bon said, No. I walk. What? A walk? Claude said. You want private com-pany? You'll get it, trust me. These girls are veterans. They know how to take care of shy guys. Bon shook his head, the look in his eyes almost one of fear. It's okay, I said. I'll take a walk with you. Hell no! Claude said, grabbing Bon by the elbow. I get it. Not every guy is up for this kind of thing. But take a walk and you deny your good buddy here the night of his life. So just come on in and sit down and have some drinks. You don't have to touch. You don't even have to look if you don't want. Just sit with your eyes closed. But you're doing it for your pal, not yourself. How about it? I put my hand on Claude's arm and said, It's okay. Leave him alone. Not you, too, said Claude.

Yes, me too. Bon had apparently infected me with his morality, a disease likely to be fatal. I offered him a cigarette after Claude gave up attempting to persuade us and went inside, and together we stood there smoking, ignoring the touts tugging at our shirts but unable to ignore the passing troops of tourists who bumped and shoved us. Gawd, someone behind me said, didja see what she did with that Ping-Pong ball, mate? Ping-Pong ching-chong, someone else said. Long schlong duk dong. Bloody hell, I think the bitch pinched my wallet. Bon threw his cigarette away and said, Let's get out of here before I kill somebody. I shrugged. Where to? He pointed over my shoulder, and when I turned I saw the movie poster that had caught his eye.

We watched *The Hamlet* in a movie theater full of locals who had not yet learned that cinema was a hallowed art form, that one did not, during the performance, blow one's nose without a tissue; bring one's own snack, beverage, or picnic; beat one's child or, conversely, sing a crying baby a lullaby; call out affectionately to friends several rows away; discuss past, present, and future plot points with one's seatmate; or sprawl so widely in one's seat that one's thigh rested against a neighbor's for the entire duration. But who was to say they were wrong? How else could one tell whether a movie was faring well or badly if the audience did not respond to it? The audience seemed to enjoy themselves thoroughly, given the cheering and clapping, and God help me if I did not also find myself caught up in the story and the sheer spectacle. The scene the audience reacted to most strongly was the climactic battle, during which my own jet-lagged heart also beat faster. Perhaps it was the menacing, Beethoven-like score with its infernal repetition of notes saturated in the devil's deep pitch, *dum-dum-DA-dum-DA-dum-DA-DA-DAAAA*; perhaps it was the hissing helicopter blades, reduced to slow-motion sound; perhaps it was the crosscutting between the gazes of Bellamy and Shamus, riding their airborne steeds, with the gazes of the Viet Cong girls peering through the crosshairs of their antiaircraft cannons; perhaps it was the bombs bursting in air; perhaps it was the sight of the Viet Cong savages being given a bloodbath, the only kind of bath they were likely to take; perhaps it was all these things that made me wish for a gun in my hand so I, too, could participate in the Old Testament slaughter of the Viet Cong who looked, if not exactly like me, fairly close to me. They certainly looked exactly like my fellow spectators, who whooped and laughed as a variety of American-made weaponry vaporized, pulverized, lacerated, and splattered their not-so-distant neighbors. I twisted in my seat, fully awoken from my torpor. I wanted to close my eyes but could not, unable to do more than blink a few times rapidly since the preceding scene, the only one where the audience had fallen completely quiet.

This was also the only scene I had not seen filmed. The Auteur used no music, the agony unreeling with only Mai's screams and protests, underscored by the VC quartet's laughing, cursing, and jeering. The lack of music only made more audible the audience's sudden silence, and mothers who had not bothered to turn away their children's faces from the gutting, shooting, hacking, and decapitation now clapped their hands over the eyes of their babes. Long shots from the cave's darkened corners depicted a human octopus writhing at the cave's center, the naked Mai struggling under the backs and limbs of her half-naked rapists. While we saw glimpses of her naked body, most of it was obscured by the strategically placed legs, arms, and buttocks of the VC, with the flesh tones, the scarlet blood, and their tattered black-and-brown clothing rendered in a painterly Renaissance shading that recalled for me faint memories of an art history class. Alternating with these long shots were extreme close-ups of Mai's battered face with its howling mouth and bloody nose, one eye so swollen it had closed completely. The most extended shot of the movie was devoted to this face filling the entire screen, her open eye wheeling in its socket, blood sputtering on her lips as she screamed

Mamamamamamamamamamamamamamamamamama!
I cringed, and when finally the movie cut to the reverse shot and we saw these red-skinned demons as seen from Mai's

eye, faces flushed from home-brewed rice wine, bared teeth crusty with lichen, squinty eyes squeezed shut in ecstasy, the only possible feeling burning in one's gut was the desire for their utter extinction. This was what the Auteur provided next, in the gruesome finale of hand-to-hand combat, which could also double as a medical school training film in ana-tomical dissection.

By the movie's last shot, of innocent Danny Boy sitting in the open doorway of a Huey helicopter ascending slowly into the clear blue heavens, weeping as he gazed over his war-ravaged homeland, destined for a country where women's breasts produced not just milk but milkshakes—or so the GIs told him—I had to admit to the Auteur's talent, the way one might admire the technical genius of a master gunsmith. He had hammered into existence a thing of beauty and horror, exhilirating for some and deadly for others, a creation whose purpose was destruction. As the credits began rolling, I felt touched by shame for having contributed to this dark work, but also pride in the contributions of my extras. Faced with ungraceful roles, they had comported themselves with as much grace as possible. There were the four veterans who played VC RAPIST #1, VC RAPIST #2, VC RAPIST #3, and VC RAPIST #4, as well as the others who had made their screen debuts as DESPERATE VILLAGER, DEAD GIRL, LAME BOY, CORRUPT OFFICER, PRETTY NURSE, BLIND BEGGAR, SAD REFUGEE, ANGRY CLERK, WEEPING WIDOW, IDEALISTIC STUDENT, GENTLE WHORE, and CRAZY GUY IN WHOREHOUSE. But I did not take pride in just my own. There were also all those colleagues who dedicated themselves behind the scenes, like Harry. This artist was sure to score an Oscar nomination for his fanatically detailed sets, his valuable work unmarred even by the minor incident involving his hiring of a local fixer to furnish actual corpses from a nearby graveyard for the finale. To the gendarmes who came to arrest him, he said, with genuine contriteness, I didn't think it was illegal, officers. All was reconciled with the speedy return of the corpses to their graves and a substantial donation by the Auteur to the policemen's benevolent association, otherwise known as the local brothel. I grimaced at seeing Violet's name as assistant producer, but conceded that she had a right to come before me in the hierarchy of credits. I recalled fondly the unending sustenance supplied by the artisans of craft services, the dedicated care of the first aid team, and the efficient daily transportation provided by the drivers, although, to be frank, my services were more specialized than any of those. I do admit that perhaps my bicultural, bilingual skills were not as unique as those of the trainer who taught various tricks and commands to the adorable mutt playing the adopted native pet of the Green Berets, credited as SMITTY THE DOG, or the exotic animal handler who flew in on a DC-3 charter with a surly Bengal tiger in a cage—LILY—and who ensured the docility of the elephants, ABBOTT and COSTELLO. But while I admired the cheerful, prompt work of the laundresses—DELIA, MARYBELLE, CORAZON, and so on—did they merit appearing before me? The names of the laundresses continued their upward scroll, and it was only with the acknowledgments of the mayor, the councilmen, the head of the tourist bureau, the Philippine armed forces, and First Lady Imelda Marcos and President Ferdinand Marcos that I realized my name was never coming at all.

By the time the sound track and film stock credits had passed, my grudging acknowledgment of the Auteur had evaporated, replaced by boiling murderous rage. Failing to do away with me in real life, he had succeeded in murdering me in fiction, obliterating me utterly in a way that I was becoming more and more acquainted with. I was still steaming as we left the theater, my emotions hotter than the temperate night. What did you think? I asked Bon, silent as usual after a movie. He smoked his cigarette and waved for a taxi. Well, what did you think? He finally looked at me, his gaze a mix of pity and disappointment. You were going to make sure we came off well, he said. But we weren't even human. A rattling taxi pulled to the curb. Now you're a movie critic? I said. Just my opinion, college boy, he said, climbing inside. What do I know? If it wasn't for me, I said, slamming the door shut, there wouldn't even be any roles at all for our people. We would just be target practice. He sighed and rolled his window down. All you did was give them an excuse, he said. Now white people can say, Look, we got yellow people in here. We don't hate them. We love them. He spat out the window. You tried to play their game, okay? But they run the game. You don't run anything. That means you can't change anything. Not from the inside. When you got nothing, you got to change things from the outside.

We spoke no more for the duration of the ride, and when we got to our hotel, he fell asleep almost right away. I lay in our darkened room with an ashtray on my chest, smoking and contemplating how I had failed at the one task both Man and the General could agree on, the subversion of the Movie and all it represented, namely our misrepresentation. I tried to fall asleep but could not, kept awake by the blare of horns and the unnerving sight of Sonny and the crapulent major lying on the ceiling above me, behaving as if they always passed their time thus. The monotonous squeaking of bed springs next door did not help, the squeaking going on for such an absurdly long time that I felt sorry for what I assumed was the poor, silent woman enduring it all. When the male involved squawked his battle cry, I was relieved it was all over, although it wasn't, for when that concluded, his partner uttered his own deep, protracted, appreciative masculine mating call. The surprises just would not end, not since the General and Madame came to see us off at the airport, he in a herringbone suit and she in a lilac ao dai. He had presented us four heroes with a bottle of whiskey each, taken a picture with us, and shook each of our hands before we passed through the ticket gate, myself coming last. With me, however, he held on and said, Just a word, Captain.

I stepped aside to let the other passengers board. Yes, sir? You know Madame and I look on you as our adopted son, said the General. I didn't know that, sir. The look on his face and Madame's was grim, but that was the same look my father usually gave me. How could you, then? said Madame. I was used to dissembling and I manufactured a look of surprise. How could I what? Try to seduce our daughter, the General said. Everyone's talking about it, said Madame. Everyone? I said. The rumors, the General said. I should have seen it when you spoke with her at the wedding, but no. It never occurred to me that you would encourage my daughter in her nightclub pursuits. Not only this, Madame added, but the two of you made a spectacle out of yourselves at the nightclub. Everyone saw it. The General sighed. That you would attempt to defile her, he said, was something I could hardly believe. Not after you lived in my house and treated her as a child and a sister. A sister, Madame emphasized. I am sorely disappointed in you, said the General. I wanted you here by my side. I would never have let you go except for this.

Sir—

You should have known better, Captain. You are a soldier. Everything and everyone belongs in his proper place. How could you ever believe we would allow our daughter to be with someone of your kind?

My kind? I said. What do you mean by my kind?

Oh, Captain, said the General. You are a fine young man, but you are also, in case you have not noticed, a bastard. They waited for me to say something, but the General had stuffed the one word in my mouth that could silence me. Seeing that I had nothing to say, they shook their heads in anger, sorrow, and recrimination, leaving me at the gate with my bottle of whiskey. I wanted to crack it open then and there, for the whiskey might have helped me spit that word out. It was stuck in my throat and had the taste of a woolen sock sodden with our homeland's rich mud, the kind of meal I had forgotten was reserved for those who ranked among the meanest.

We arose before the sun to a dark morning. After a breakfast where no one uttered more than a grunt, Claude drove from Bangkok to the camp, a day's journey that ended near the border with Laos. By the time he swerved onto an unpaved side road and into a white-barked cajeput forest, dodging craters and dips, the sun was rolling on its downward slope behind us. A kilometer into the twilight forest we reached a military checkpoint consisting of a jeep and two young soldiers in olive-green battle dress, each with a protective amulet of the Buddha around his neck and an M16 in his lap. I smelled the unmistakable funk of marijuana. Without bothering either to rise from the jeep or to raise their half-lidded eyes, the soldiers waved us through. We continued on the rutted road, plunging even deeper into a forest where the skeletal hands of tall trees with their thin branches loomed over us, until we emerged into a clearing of small, square huts on stilts, the scene saved from total rusticity by the electric light illuminating the windows. Wigs of palm leaves thatched the roofs, and wooden planks led from elevated doors to the earth. Barking dogs had brought shadows to the mouths of the doorways, and by the time we clambered out a squad of those shadows was approaching. There they are, said Claude. The last men standing of the armed forces of the Republic of Vietnam.

Perhaps the pictures of them that I had seen in the General's office were taken in better times, but those stern freedom fighters bore little resemblance to these haggard irregulars. In the pictures, those clean-shaven men with red scarves cinched around their necks had been clad in jungle camouflage, combat boots, and berets, standing at attention under the forest's filtered sunlight. But instead of boots and camouflage, these men wore rubber sandals with black blouses and pants. Instead of red scarves, the Rangers' legendary emblem, they wore the checkered scarves of peasants. Instead of berets, they wore wide-brimmed bushwacker hats. Instead of clean cheeks, they were unshaven, their hair matted and untrimmed. Their eyes, once hot and bright, were dull as coal. Each carried an AK-47 with its distinctive banana clip, and the presence of this icon, combined with all the other features, led to an unusual visual effect.

Why do they look like Viet Cong? said the grizzled captain.

It was not only the guerrillas who resembled their old enemies, as we discovered when a dozen of them led us to the hut of their commander. On this hut's thin lip of a porch stood a slim man backlit by a bare electric lightbulb. Isn't that— said Bon, before stopping at asking the absurd. Everybody says so, said Claude. The admiral raised his hand in greeting and smiled a familiar, avuncular smile. His face was angular, gaunt, and almost handsome, the classic noble visage of a scholar or mandarin. The hair was gray but not white, thinning a little on top, and trimmed short. A goatee was his most distinctive feature, a neatly sculpted affair for the man of middle age, rather than the scraggle of youth or the long, flowing tuft of the elder. Welcome, men, the admiral said, and even in the gentle intonation of his voice I heard echoes of the newsreel on which Ho Chi Minh's cultivated and calm voice was recorded. You have traveled a great distance, and you must be tired. Please, come in and join me.

Like Ho Chi Minh, the admiral referred to himself as uncle. Like Ho Chi Minh, he also dressed with simplicity, his black blouse and pants matching the garb of his guerrillas. And, like Ho Chi Minh, he furnished his quarters in a sparse and scholarly fashion. We sat barefoot on reed mats in the hut's one plain room, us newcomers uneasy in the presence of this uncanny look-alike. Our apparition must have slept on the plank floor, for there was no sign of a bed. Bamboo bookshelves lined one wall, and a simple bamboo desk and chair occupied another. Over the course of dinner, as we drank the General's whiskey, the admiral quizzed us on our years in America and we quizzed him in turn on how he had come to be shipwrecked in the forest. He smiled and tapped his ashes into an ashtray made of half a coconut shell. On the last day of the war, I was in command of a transport ship full of marines, soldiers, policemen, and civilians rescued from the piers. I could have sailed to the Seventh Fleet, like many of my fellow captains. But the Americans had betrayed us before, and there was no hope of fighting again if I fled to them. The Americans were finished. Now that their white race had failed, they were leaving Asia to the yellow race. So I sailed toward Thailand. I had Thai friends and I knew the Thai would give us asylum. They had nowhere to

go, unlike the Americans. The Thai would fight communism because it was pressing up against their border with
Cambodia. Laos, too, was going to fall soon. You see, I was
not interested in being saved, unlike so many of our countrymen. He paused here and smiled once more, and none
of us needed to be reminded that we were some of those
countrymen. God had already saved me, the admiral went
on. I did not need to be saved by Americans. I swore on my
ship in front of my men that we would continue our fight for
months, years, even decades if necessary. If we looked at our
struggle from God's eyes, this was no time at all.

So, Bon said, you think we really have a chance, Uncle?
The admiral stroked his goatee before answering. My child,
he said, still stroking the goatee, remember Jesus and how
Christianity began with just him, his apostles, their faith,
and the Word of God. We are like those true believers. We
have two hundred apostles in this camp, a radio station
broadcasting the word of freedom into our enslaved homeland, and guns. We have things Jesus and his apostles never
had, but we have their faith, too, and not least—furthest
from least—God is on our side.

Bon lit another cigarette. Jesus died, he said. So did the
apostles.

So we're going to die, said the affectless lieutenant.
Despite the meaning of his words, or perhaps because of
them, his manner and pronouncement remained unemo-
tional. Not that that's a bad thing, he said.

I am not saying you will die on this mission, the admiral said. Just eventually. But if you do die on this mission,

know that those you save will be grateful to you, as those the apostles saved were grateful to them.

A lot of the people they went to save didn't want to be saved, Uncle, Bon said. That's why they ended up dead.

My son, the admiral said, no longer smiling, it does not sound like you are a believer.

If by that you mean a believer in religion or anticommunism or freedom or anything with a big word like that, no, I'm not. I used to believe, but not anymore. I don't give a damn about saving anybody, including myself. I just want to kill communists. That's why I'm the man you want.

I can live with that, the admiral said.

CHAPTER 18

We spent two weeks acclimating to the weather and our new comrades, among whom were three characters I had never expected to see again. These marine lieutenants were bearded and longer-haired than on the night Bon, Man, and I had encountered them in that Saigon alley, singing, *Beautiful Saigon! Oh, Saigon! Oh, Saigon!*, but they were still recognizably dumb. They had made their way to the docks on the day Saigon fell, and there had jumped on board the admiral's ship. We've been in Thailand ever since, said the marine who was the leader of the three. He had been steeped in the Mekong Delta his entire life, as his comrades had been, all of them branded by a life in the sun, although in different shades. He was dark, but one of the other marines was darker, and the third was the darkest of all, black as a cup of black tea. They, Bon, and I grudgingly shook hands. We're going with you across the border, said the dark marine. So we better get on each other's right sides. This was the marine on whom I had drawn my pistol, but since he chose not to mention this fact, neither did I.

Altogether there were a dozen of us on the reconnaissance team that set out early one night, led by a Lao farmer and a Hmong scout. The Lao farmer had no choice in the matter. He had been kidnapped by the admiral's men on an earlier reconnaissance, and was now being used as a guide, given his knowledge of the terrain through which we were traveling. He could not speak Vietnamese but the Hmong scout could and served as his translator. Even from a distance, one could see that the scout's eyes were a ruin, dark and shattered as the windows of an abandoned palace. He was clad in black, as we all were, but he was unique in wearing a faded green beret a size too large, the brim resting on his ears and eyebrows. Following him were two of the marines, the dark one armed with an AK-47 and the darker one with our M79 elephant gun, its stubby grenades resembling short, metallic dildos. After the marines came the affectless lieutenant and the grizzled captain, who could not bring themselves to carry the enemy's AK-47 and instead toted the M16. Behind them was the skinny RTO, grease gun in hand and PRC-25 radio on his back. Next was the philosophical medic, M3 medical kit hanging from one shoulder and M14 from the other, as no man on this reconnaissance could go unarmed. He and I had hit it off right away during an evening perfumed with jasmine and marijuana. Besides sadness and sorrow, he had asked me, what's really heavy but weighs nothing at all? When he saw that I was stumped, he said, Nihilism, which was, in fact, his philosophy. Then came the hefty machine gunner, M60 in his arms, with myself and Bon next, me with an Ak-47, Bon with the M16. Bringing up the rear was the darkest marine, his weapon the B-40 rocket launcher.

For defense, in place of bulletproof vests and helmets, each of us was given a laminated, wallet-sized picture of the Virgin Mary to wear over our hearts. The admiral had blessed us with these gifts on our departure from the camp, which was, for most of us, a relief. We had spent our days discussing tactics, preparing rations, and studying the map of our route through the southern end of Laos. This was terrain probed by the marines on earlier reconnaissance, home to the Lao farmer. Smugglers, he claimed, crossed the border all the time. Periodically we listened to Radio Free Vietnam, its crew working from a bamboo shack next to the admiral's hut. From there they broadcast the admiral's speeches, read items translated from newspapers, and aired pop songs with reactionary sentiments, James Taylor and Donna Summer being particular favorites of the season. The communists hate love songs, said the admiral. They don't believe in love or romance or entertainment. They believe the people should only love the revolution and the country. But the people love love songs, and we serve the people. The airwaves bore those love songs, laden with emotion, across Laos and into our homeland. In my pocket was a transistor radio with an earpiece so I could listen to the broadcast, and I valued it more than my weapon and the Virgin Mary. Claude, who did not believe in her or any god, gave us his secular blessing in the form of high fives as we left. Good luck, he said. Just in and out. Quick and quiet. *Easier said than done,* I thought. I kept that idea to myself, but I suspected that many of the dozen of us might have been thinking the same thing. Claude intuited my worry when he squeezed my shoulder. Take care of yourself, buddy. If anybody starts shooting, just keep your head down. Let the pros do the fighting. His estimation of my abilities was moving and most likely accurate. He wanted to keep me safe, this man who, along with Man, had taught me everything I knew about the practices of intelligence, of secrecy as a way of life. We'll be waiting for you guys to come back, said Claude. See you soon, I said. That was all.

We set off on our march under a sliver of moon, cheered by the optimism that one sometimes had at the beginning of strenuous exercise, a kind of helium that filled our lungs and carried us along. Then, after an hour, we trudged, or at least I trudged, my helium depleted and replaced with the first hints of fatigue, soaking into the body as the slow drip of water soaks into a towel. A few hours into our march we arrived at a pool of water, where the grizzled captain called for a rest. Sitting on the edge of the moonlit pool and resting my sore thighs, I could just make out the phosphorescent, disembodied hands on my wristwatch pointing to one in the morning. My hands felt as detached as the watch's hands, for what they wanted was to hold and caress one of the cigarettes in my breast pocket, the urge electrifying my nervous system. Seemingly unaffected by any similar yearning, Bon sat down next to me and silently ate a rice ball. A fetid smell of mud and decaying vegetation emanated from the pool, and on its surface bobbed a dead bird the size of a finch, floating in a corona of molting feathers. Bomb crater, Bon muttered. The bomb crater was an American footprint, a sign that we had entered Laos. We came upon more of these craters as we journeyed east, sometimes singly, sometimes in clusters, and we had to pick our way carefully past the julienned remnants of unrooted cajeputs flung this way and that. Once we came close to a village, and on the banks of the craters nearby we saw nets on poles, ready to be dipped into these pools that the farmers had stocked with fish.

Near dawn the grizzled captain halted our trek, at a spot the Lao farmer said was isolated and rarely visited by the inhabitants of this borderland. Our resting place was on the peak of a hill, and under the indifferent cajeputs we spread our ponchos and covered ourselves with hooded capes of netting into which we had woven palm fronds. I lay down with my head on my rucksack, which, besides my rations, contained *Asian Communism and the Oriental Mode of Destruction*, tucked away in my rucksack's false bottom in case I ever needed it again. Two or three of us stayed awake for shifts of three hours, and it was my misfortune to be assigned to one of the middle shifts. It seemed that I had barely managed to fall asleep with the brim of my hat on my face when the hefty machine gunner shook my shoulder and exhaled his horrendous bacterial breath all over my face, informing me that it was my turn for sentry duty. The sun was high in the sky and my throat was parched. I could see the Mekong in the far distance through my binoculars, a brown belt dividing the earth's green torso. I could see question marks and exclamation points of woodsmoke issuing from farmhouses and brick factories. I could see bare-shinned farmers wading after their water buffalos, fetlock deep in the muddy water of rice paddies. I could see countryside roads and paths trafficked by vehicles that, from a distance, moved with the tortured slowness of arthritic turtles. I could see the crumbling sandstone ruins of an ancient temple, erected long ago by some fallen race, overseen by the crowned head of some forgotten tyrant, blank eyes blinded by the waste of his empire. I could see the entire lay of the land, naked body exposed in sunlight and resembling not at all the mysterious creature of night, and suddenly a tremendous longing seized me with such force that the land itself lost focus and trembled, and I realized with equal parts amazement and dread that for all the essentials we had brought with us, none of us had brought a drop of liquor.

The second night did not proceed much as the first. It was not clear to me whether I walked that night or whether I simply hung on to a beast bucking and heaving under me. A tide of bile rose and fell in my throat, my ears swelled from my head, and I shivered as if it were wintertime. When I looked up I caught a glimpse of the stars through the branches, swirling snowflakes trapped within the glass of a snow globe. Sonny and the crapulent major laughed faintly as they watched me from outside that snow globe and shook it with their giant hands. The only solid thing anchoring me to the material world was the rifle in my hands, for my feet could not feel the ground. I gripped the AK-47 as I had Lana's arms the night after I had left Sonny's place. She had not looked surprised on opening the door, for she had always known I was coming back. I had not told the General what Lana and I had done but I should have. There was one thing he could never do and I had done it, for having just killed a man nothing was forbidden from me, not even what belonged to or issued from him. Even the scent of the forest was her scent, and when I shrugged off my rucksack and sat down between Bon and the affectless lieutenant in the midst of a bamboo grove, the dampness of the earth reminded me of her. Above us innumerable fireflies lit the branches, and I had the sense that the snouts and eyes of the forest were fixed upon us. Some animals could see in the dark, but it was only humans who deliberately sought out every possible route into the darkness of our own interiors. As a species, we have never encountered a cave, a door, or an entrance of any kind that we did not want to enter. We are never satisfied with only one way in. We will always try every possibility, even the blackest and most forbidding passages, or so I was reminded in my night with Lana. I got to pee, said the affectless lieutenant, standing up again. He disappeared into the gloom of the forest, while above him the fireflies turned off and on in unison. You know why I like you? she had asked in the aftermath. You're everything my mother would hate. I was not offended. I had been force-fed so much hate that a little more hardly mattered to my fattened liver. If my enemies ever cut out my liver and ate it, as the Cambodians were rumored to do, they would smack their lips in delight, for nothing was more delicious than the foie gras of hatred, once one had acquired the taste for it. I heard the crack of a branch in the direction taken by the lieutenant. Are you okay? Bon said. I nodded, concentrating on the fireflies, their collective signal outlining the shapes of the bamboo trees in a wilderness Christmas. The underbrush rustled and the dim shape of the lieutenant emerged from the bamboo.

Hey, he said. I—

A flash of light and sound blinded and deafened me. Earth and gravel pelted me and I flinched. My ears rang and somebody was screaming as I huddled on the ground, arms over my head. Somebody was screaming and it was not me. Somebody was cursing and it was not me. I shook off the earth that had fallen onto my face and overhead the trees had gone dark. The fireflies had stopped blinking and somebody was screaming. It was the affectless lieutenant, writhing in the ferns. The philosophical medic bumped against me as he sprinted to reach the lieutenant. Looming out of the darkness, the grizzled captain said, Take up your defensive positions, goddammit. Beside me, Bon turned his back to the mess, racked his slide—*click-clack*—and aimed his weapon into the darkness. I heard the *click-clack* all around me of weapons being primed for firing, and I did the same. Someone turned on a flashlight and even with my back turned to the scene I could see its luminescence. Leg's gone, said the philosophical medic. The lieutenant kept on

screaming. Hold the light while I tie him off. Everybody in
the valley's hearing this, said the dark marine. Is he going
to make it? said the grizzled captain. He might make it if
we get him to a hospital, said the medic. Hold him down.
We have to shut him up, said the dark marine. It must have
been a mine, said the grizzled captain. It's not an attack.
Either you do it or I do it, said the dark marine. Someone put
his hand on the lieutenant's mouth, muffling his screams.
Looking over my shoulder, I saw the dark marine's flashlight illuminating the philosophical medic as he pointlessly
tied the tourniquet on the lieutenant's stump, the molar of a
bone protruding where the leg had been blown off above the
knee. The grizzled captain had one hand clapped over the
lieutenant's mouth, his other hand squeezing shut the nostrils. The lieutenant heaved, clutching at the sleeves of the
philosophical medic and the grizzled captain, and the dark
marine switched off the flashlight. Gradually the thrashing
and strangled noises ceased, and at last he was still, dead. But
if he was really gone, why could I still hear him screaming?

We have to move, said the dark marine. No one's coming
now but they will when it's light. The grizzled captain said
nothing. Did you hear me? The grizzled captain said yes.
Then do something, said the dark marine. We've got to be as
far away from here as possible before morning. The grizzled
captain said to bury him. When the dark marine said that
was going to take too long, the grizzled captain gave the
order to carry the body with us. We divvied up the lieutenant's ammunition and gave his rucksack to the Lao farmer,
with the dark marine carrying the lieutenant's M16. The

hefty machine gunner handed his M60 to the darker marine and picked up the lieutenant's body. We were about to set off when the gunner said, Where's his leg? The dark marine turned on his flashlight. There the leg lay, served on a bed of shredded ferns, meat tattered and strips of black cloth still clinging to it, mangled white bone jutting through a jagged rip in the flesh. Where's the foot? said the dark marine. I think it was just blown away, said the philosophical medic. Bits of pink flesh and skin and tissue hung on the ferns, already crawling with ants. The dark marine grabbed the leg, and when he looked up I was the first one he saw. It's all yours, he said, thrusting the leg at me. I thought about refusing it, but someone else would have to carry it. *Remember, you're not half of anything, you're twice of everything.* If someone else had to do this, I could, too. It was only a hunk of meat and bone, its flesh sticky with blood and gritty with embedded dirt. When I took it and brushed off the ants, I found it to be a little heavier than my AK-47, the leg having been detached from a smallish man. The grizzled captain ordered us to march and I followed the hefty gunner, the lieutenant's body slung over his shoulder. The lieutenant's shirt had ridden up his back, and the exposed plank of flesh was blue in the moonlight.

I carried his leg with one hand, my other hand on the strap of the AK-47 hanging from my shoulder, and the burden of carrying a man's leg seemed far heavier than carrying a man's body. I carried his leg as far away from me as possible, its weight growing more and more, like the Bible my father made me hold in front of the classroom as punishment for some transgression, my arm outstretched with the book on the scale of my hand. I carried that memory still, along with the memory of my father in his coffin, corpse as white as the affectless lieutenant's protruding bone. The chanting of the congregation in the church hummed in my ears. I had learned of my father's death when his deacon called me at police headquarters. How did you get this phone number? I said. It was in the father's papers on his desk. I looked at the document on my own desk, a classified investigation about an unremarkable event last year, 1968, when an American platoon had pacified a mostly abandoned village near Quang Ngai. After executing the water buffalos, pigs, and dogs, and after gang-raping four girls, the soldiers had gathered them as well as fifteen elders, women, and children in the village square, where they fired on them until they were dead, according to a regretful private's testimony. The platoon leader's report certified that his men had killed nineteen Viet Cong, although they had recovered no weapons besides some spades, some hoes, a crossbow, and a musket. I don't have time, I said. It would be important for you to go, said the deacon. Why would it be important? I said. After a long pause, the deacon said, You were important to him and he was important to you. It was then I knew, without any need for words, that the deacon was aware of who my father was.

We ended our forced march after two hours, the same amount of time devoted to my father's funeral Mass. A creek gurgled in the arroyo where we stopped and where

I scratched my face against a vine of bougainvillea. I set down the leg as the marines began digging a shallow grave. My hand was gummy with blood and I knelt by the creek to wash it in the cold water. By the time the marines finished, my hand was dry and a faint stroke of pink light was on the horizon. The grizzled captain unrolled the affectless lieutenant's cape of palm leaves and the hefty machine gunner laid his body on it. I only realized then that I would have to bloody my hand again. I picked up the leg and put it in its place. In the pink light I saw his open eyes and slack mouth, and I could still hear him screaming. The grizzled captain closed the eyes and mouth and wrapped his body in the cape, but when he and the hefty machine gunner lifted the body, the leg slipped out of the cape. I was already wiping my sticky hand on my pants but there was nothing to do but pick up the leg once more. After his body was lowered into the grave, I leaned in and tucked his leg under the cape, below his knee. Glistening worms were already wriggling out of the earth as I helped scoop dirt back into the grave. It was just deep enough to cover our tracks for a day or two, until the animals dug up the corpse and ate it. What I want to know, said Sonny, squatting by me as I knelt by the grave, is whether the lieutenant will hang around here with one leg or two, or whether he'll have worms crawling out of his eyes or not. Truly, said the crapulent major, head sticking out of the grave as he talked to me, it's a mystery what shape a ghost will take. Why am I all here except for this hole in my head and not a disgusting mess of bones and meat? Tell me that, won't you, Captain?

You know everything about everything, don't you? I would have answered if I could, but it was hard to do so when I felt that I, too, had a hole in my head.

The day passed with us undiscovered, and by late in the evening, after a short march, we reached the banks of the Mekong, gleaming under the moonlight. Somewhere on the other side you were waiting for me, Commandant, as well as the faceless man who is the commissar. While I was still innocent of this knowledge, it was impossible not to sense something foreboding as we plucked off the leeches adhering to us with the stubbornness of bad memories. We had been carrying them without knowing, until the Lao farmer pulled an animated black finger from his ankle. I could not help but wish, prying away a little monster sucking my leg, that it was Lana thus attached to me. The skinny RTO radioed the base camp, and while the grizzled captain reported to the admiral, the marines again showed they were good for something by constructing a raft of bamboo trunks strapped together with lianas. Four men could row themselves across the river with makeshift paddles fashioned of bamboo, with the first team trailing a rope carried by the darker marine. That rope, tied to a tree on either side of the river, would guide the darker marine on his return with the raft. It would take four trips to transport all of us, and the first group set off before midnight: the darker marine, the Hmong scout, the hefty machine gunner, and the dark marine. The rest of us were scattered on the exposed bank, huddled under our capes of leaves, backs to the river and weapons aimed at the vast forest crouched on its haunches.

A half hour later the darker marine returned with the raft. Three more went with him, the Lao farmer, the darkest marine, and the philosophical medic, who, at the affectless lieutenant's grave, had said as a kind of benediction, All of us who are living are dying. The only ones not dying are the dead. What the hell does that mean? said the dark marine. I knew what it meant. My mother was not dying because she was dead. My father was also not dying because he was dead. But I was on this embankment, dying, because I was not yet dead. What are *we*, then? asked Sonny and the crapulent major. Dying or dead? I shivered, and gazing into the darkness of the forest, staring down the length of my weapon, I saw the shapes of other ghosts among the haunted trees. Human ghosts and beast ghosts, plant ghosts and insect ghosts, the spirits of dead tigers and bats and cycads and hobgoblins, vegetable world and animal world heaving with claims to the afterlife as well. The entire forest shimmered with the antics of death, the comedian, and life, the straight man, a duo that would never break up. To live was to be haunted by the inevitability of one's own decay, and to be dead was to be haunted by the memory of living.

Hey, hissed the grizzled captain, it's your turn. Another half hour must have passed. The raft was scraping onto the bank again, pulled along the rope by the darker marine. Bon and I rose along with Sonny and the crapulent major, ready to follow me across the river. I remember the river's white noise, the soreness of my knees, and the weight of my weapon in my arms. I remember the injustice of how my mother never came to visit me after her death no matter how many times I cried out for her, unlike Sonny and the crapulent major, whom I would carry with me forever. I remember how none of us looked human on the riverbank, shrouded by our capes of leaves, our faces painted black, clutching weapons extracted from the mineral world. I remember the grizzled captain saying, Take the paddle, as he thrust it at me, right before a whip snapped by my ear and the grizzled captain's head cracked open, spilling its yolk. A fleck of something wet and soft landed on my cheek and a thunderous racket rose on both sides of the river. Muzzle flashes rippled on the far side and the boom of grenades rent the air. The darker marine had taken one step off the raft when a rocket-propelled grenade whooshed by me and struck the raft, shattering it in a hail of fire and sparks and throwing him into the shallow water lapping against the riverbank, where he lay not quite dead, screaming.

Get down, dumbass! Bon pulled me to earth. The skinny RTO was already returning fire into our side of the forest, the sound of his submachine gun hammering my eardrums. I could feel the volume of the guns and the velocity of the bullets passing overhead. Fear inflated the balloon of my heart and I pressed my cheek into the earth. Being on the bank's downward slope saved us from the ambuscade, keeping us below the eyeline sight of the forest's vengeful ghosts. Shoot, goddammit, said Bon. Dozens of insane, murderous fireflies flickered on and off in the forest, only they were muzzle flashes. To shoot I would have to lift my head and take aim, but the guns were loud and I could feel their bullets striking the earth. Shoot, goddammit! I lifted my weapon and aimed it into the forest, and when I squeezed the trigger the gun kicked me in the shoulder. The muzzle flash was so bright in the darkness that everyone who was trying to kill us now knew exactly where I was, but the only thing to do was to keep squeezing the trigger. My shoulder was hurting from the gun kicking me, and when I paused to eject a magazine and load another, I could feel my ears aching as well, subjected to the stereophonic effects of our firefight on this side of the river and the clash of the ignorant squads on the other side. At any moment I feared that Bon would rise and order me to charge with him into the enemy's fire, and I knew that I would not be able to do it. I feared death and I loved life. I yearned to live long enough to smoke one more cigarette, drink one more drink, experience seven more seconds of obscene bliss, and then, perhaps, but most likely not, I could die.

All of a sudden they stopped shooting at us and it was just Bon and me blasting at the darkness. Only then did I notice that the skinny RTO was no longer joining in. I paused once more in my shooting and saw, under the moonlight, his head bowed over his silent gun. Bon was the only one still firing, but after discharging the last of his magazine he, too, stopped. The firefight across the river had already ceased, and from the other side a few men were shouting in a foreign language. Then, from the recesses of the gloomy forest on our side, someone called out in our language. Give up! Don't die for nothing! His accent was northern.

All was quiet on the riverbank except for the river's throaty whisper. No one was screaming for his mother, and it was then I knew that the darker marine was also dead. I turned to Bon and in the lunar light I saw the whites of his eyes as he looked at me, wet with the sheen of tears. If it wasn't for you, you stupid bastard, Bon said, I'd die here. He was crying for only the third time since I had known him, not in that apocalyptic rage as when his wife and son died, or in the sorrowful mood that he shared with Lana, but quietly, in defeat. The mission was over, he was alive, and my plot had worked, no matter how clumsily or inadvertently. I had succeeded in saving him, but only, as it turned out, from death.

CHAPTER 19

Only from death? The commandant appeared genuinely wounded, his finger resting on the last words of my confession. In his other hand was a blue pencil, the color chosen because Stalin had also used a blue pencil, or so he told me. Like Stalin, the commandant was a diligent editor, always ready to note my many errata and digressions and always urging me to delete, excise, reword, or add. Implying that life in my camp is worse than death is a little histrionic, don't you think? The commandant seemed eminently reasonable as he sat in his bamboo chair, and for a moment, sitting in my bamboo chair, I, too, felt that he was eminently reasonable. But then I remembered that only an hour earlier I had been sitting in the windowless, redbrick isolation cell where I had spent the last year since the ambush, rewriting the many versions of my confession, the latest of which the commandant now possessed. Perhaps your perspective differs from mine, Comrade Commandant, I said, trying to get used to the sound of my own voice. I had not spoken to anyone in a week. I'm a prisoner, I went on, and you're the one in charge. It may be hard for you to sympathize with me, and vice versa.

The commandant sighed and laid the final sheet of my confession on top of the 294 other pages that preceded it, stacked on a table by his chair. How many times must I tell you? You're not a prisoner! Those men are prisoners, he said, pointing out the window to the barracks that housed a thousand inmates, including my fellow survivors, the Lao farmer, the Hmong scout, the philosophical medic, the darkest marine, the dark marine, and Bon. You are a special case. He lit a cigarette. You are a guest of myself and the commissar.

Guests can leave, Comrade Commandant. I paused to observe his reaction. I wanted one of his cigarettes, which I would not get if I angered him. Today, however, he was in a rare good mood and did not frown. He had the high cheekbones and delicate features of an opera singer, and even ten years of warfare fought from a cave in Laos had not ruined his classically good looks. What rendered him unattractive at times was his moroseness, a perpetual, damp affliction he shared with everyone else in the camp, including myself. This was the sadness felt by homesick soldiers and prisoners, a sweating that never ceased, absorbed into a perpetually damp clothing that could never be dried, just as I was not dry sitting in my bamboo chair. The commandant at least had the benefit of an electric fan blowing on him, one of only two in the camp. According to my baby-faced guard, the other fan was in the commissar's quarters.

Perhaps a better term than "guest" is "patient," the commandant said, editing once more. You have traveled to strange lands and been exposed to some dangerous ideas. It wouldn't do to bring infectious ideas into a country unused to them. Think of the people, insulated for so long from foreign ideas. Exposure could lead to a real catastrophe for minds that aren't ready for them. If you saw the situation from our point of view, you would see that it was necessary to quarantine you until we could cure you, even if it hurts us to see a revolutionary like yourself kept in such conditions.

I could see his point of view, albeit with some difficulty. There were reasons to be suspicious of someone like me, who had endured suspicion all his life. But still, it was hard for me not to feel that a year in an isolation cell from which I was allowed to emerge only an hour a day for exercise, blinking and white, was unwarranted, as I had informed him at each of these weekly sessions where he criticized my confession and I, in turn, criticized myself. These reminders I had given him must also have been on his mind, because when I opened my mouth to speak again, he said, I know what you're going to say. As I told you all along, when your confession reaches a satisfactory state, based on our reading of it and on my reports of these self-criticism sessions to the commissar, you will move on to the next and, we hope, last stage of your reeducation. In short, the commissar believes you ready to be cured.

He does? I had yet to even meet the faceless man, otherwise known as the commissar. None of the prisoners had. They saw him only during his weekly lectures, sitting behind a table on the dais of the meeting hall where all the prisoners gathered for political lectures. I had not even seen him there, for these lectures, according to the commandant, amounted only to an elementary school education designed for pure reactionaries, puppets brainwashed by decades of ideological saturation. The faceless man had decreed me exempt from these simple lessons. Instead, I was privileged by having no burdens except to write and to reflect. My only glimpses of the commissar had come on those rare moments when I looked up from my exercise pen and saw him on the balcony of his bamboo quarters, atop the larger of the two hills overlooking the camp. At the base of the hills clustered the kitchen, mess hall, armory, latrines, and warehouses of the guards, along with the solitary rooms for special cases like me. Barbed-wire fencing separated this interior camp of the guards from the exterior camp where the inmates slowly eroded, the former soldiers, security officers, or bureaucrats of the defeated regime. Next to one of the gates in this fencing, on the interior side, was a pavilion for family visits. The prisoners had become emotional cacti in order to survive, but their wives and children inevitably wept at the sight of their husbands and fathers, whom they saw, at most, a couple of times a year, the trek from even the nearest city an arduous one involving train, bus, and motorbike. Beyond the pavilion, the exterior camp itself was fenced off from the wasteland of barren plains surrounding us, the fence demarcated with watchtowers where pith-helmeted guards with binoculars could observe female visitors and, according to the prisoners, entertain themselves. From the elevated height of the commandant's patio, one could see not only these voyeurs but also the cratered plains and denuded trees surrounding the camp, a forest of toothpicks over which gusts of crows and torrents of bats soared in ominous black formations. I always paused on the patio before entering his quarters, savoring for a moment the view denied to me in my isolation cell, where, if I had not yet been cured, I had certainly been baked by the tropical sun.

You have complained often about the duration of your visit, the commandant said. But your confession is the necessary prelude to the cure. It is not my fault that it took you a year to write this confession, one that is not, in my opinion, even very good. Everyone except you has confessed to being a puppet soldier, an imperialist lackey, a brainwashed stooge, a colonized comprador, or a treacherous henchman. Regardless of what you think of my intellectual capacities, I know they're just telling me what I want to hear. You, on the other hand, won't tell me what I want to hear. Does that make you very smart or very stupid?

I was still somewhat dazed, the bamboo floor wobbling under my bamboo seat. It always took me at least an hour to become readjusted to light and space after my cell's cramped darkness. Well, I said, gathering the tattered coat of my wits about me, I believe the unexamined life is not worth living. So thank you, Comrade Commandant, for giving me the opportunity to examine my life. He nodded approvingly. No one else has the luxury I have of simply writing and living the life of the mind, I said. My orphaned voice, which had detached itself in my cell and spoken to me from a cobwebbed corner, had returned. I am smart in some ways, stupid in others. For example, I am smart enough to take your criticism and editorial suggestions seriously, but I am too stupid to understand how my confession has not met your high standards, despite my many drafts.

The commandant regarded me through glasses that magnified his eyes to twice their size, his poor eyesight a condition of having lived in cavernous darkness for ten years. If your confession was even just satisfactory, the commissar would let you proceed with what he calls your oral examination, he said. But my opinion of what he calls your written examination is that it hardly seems like a genuine confession to me.

Haven't I confessed to many things, Commandant?

In content, perhaps, but not in style. Confessions are as much about style as content, as the Red Guards have shown us. All we ask for is a certain way with words. Cigarette?

I hid my relief and merely nodded casually. The commandant inserted the dart of a cigarette between my cracked lips, then lit it for me with my own lighter, which he had appropriated. I inhaled the oxygen of smoke, its infusion into the folds of my lungs calming the trembling in my hands. Even in this latest revision, you quote Uncle Ho only once. This is but one symptom, among many in your confession, that you prefer foreign intellectuals and culture over our native traditions. Why is that?

I'm contaminated by the West?

Exactly. That wasn't so hard to admit, was it? Funny, then, how you can't put it into writing. Of course, I can understand why you didn't quote *How the Steel Was Tempered* or *Tracks in the Snowy Forest*. You wouldn't have had access to them, even though everyone of my generation from the north has read them. But not to mention To Huu, our greatest revolutionary poet? And to cite, instead, the yellow music of Pham Duy and the Beatles? The commissar actually has a collection of yellow music that he keeps for what he calls research purposes. He's offered to let me listen to them, but no thanks. Why would I want to be contaminated by that decadence? Contrast the songs you discuss with To Huu's "Since Then," which I read in high school. He talks about how "The sun of truth shone on my heart," which was exactly how I felt about the revolution's effect on me. I carried a book of his with me to China for infantry training, and it helped sustain me. My hope is that the sun of truth will shine on you as well. But I also think of another poem of his about a rich child and a servant child. Closing his eyes, the commandant recited a stanza:

> A child lives in a life of plenty
> With abundant toys made in the West
> While the other child is an onlooker
> Watching silently from far away

He opened his eyes. Worth a mention, don't you think?

If you would give me that book, I'd read it, I said, not having read anything for a year besides my own words. The commandant shook his head. You won't have any time to read anything in the next phase. But implying you only needed a book in order to be better read is hardly a good defense. Not quoting Uncle Ho or revolutionary poetry is

one thing, but not even a folk saying or a proverb? Now you
may be from the south—

I was born in the north and lived nine years there, sir.

You chose the southern side. Regardless, you share a common culture with me, a northerner. Yet you will not quote
from that culture, not even this:

The good deeds of Father are as great as Mount Thai Son
The virtue of Mother is as bountiful as springwater gush-
ing from its source
Wholeheartedly is Mother to be revered and Father
respected
So that the child's way may be accomplished.

Did you not learn something as basic as this in school?

My mother did teach it to me, I said. But my confession
does show my reverence for my mother and why my father
is not to be respected.

The relations between your mother and father are indeed
unfortunate. You may think that I'm heartless, but I am not. I
look at your situation and feel great sympathy for you, given
your curse. How can a child be accomplished if his source
is tainted? Yet I can't help but feel that our own culture, and
not Western culture, tells us something about your difficult
situation. "Talent and destiny are apt to feud." Don't you
think Nguyen Du's words apply to you? Your destiny is being
a bastard, while your talent, as you say, is seeing from two
sides. You would be better off if you only saw things from
one side. The only cure for being a bastard is to take a side.

You're right, Comrade Commandant, I said, and perhaps he was. But the only thing harder than knowing the right thing to do, I went on, is to actually do the right thing.

I agree. What puzzles me is that you are perfectly reasonable in person, but on the page you are recalcitrant. The commandant poured himself a shot of unfiltered rice wine from a recycled soda bottle. Any urges? I shook my head, even though my priapic desire for a drink bumped against the back of my throat. Tea, please, I said, voice cracking. The commandant poured me a cup of lukewarm tinted water. It was quite sad watching you in those first few weeks. You were a raving lunatic. Isolation did you good. Now you're purified, at least in body.

If spirits are so bad for me, then why do you drink, Commandant?

I don't drink to excess, unlike you. I disciplined myself during the war. You rethink your entire life living in a cave. Even things like what to do with one's waste. Ever thought of that?

Once in a while.

I sense sarcasm. Still not satisfied with the camp's amenities and your chamber? This is nothing compared to what I went through in Laos. That's why I'm also puzzled by the unhappiness of some of our guests. You think I'm feigning perplexity, but no, I'm genuinely surprised. We haven't stuck them in a box underground. We haven't shackled them until their legs waste away. We haven't poured lime on their heads and beaten them bloody. Instead, we let them farm their own food, build their own homes, breathe fresh air, see sunlight, and work to transform this countryside. Compare that to how their American allies poisoned this place. No trees. Nothing grows. Unexploded mines and bombs killing and maiming innocents. This used to be beautiful countryside. Now it's just a wasteland. I try to bring these comparisons up with our guests and I can see the disbelief in their eyes even as they agree with me. You, at least, are honest with me, even though, to be honest with you, that may not be the healthiest strategy.

I've lived my life underground for the revolution, Commandant. The least the revolution can grant me is the right to live above ground and be absolutely honest about what I have done, at least before you put me below ground again.

There you go again, defiant for no reason. Don't you see we live in a sensitive time? It will take decades for the revolution to rebuild our country. Absolute honesty isn't always appreciated at moments like this. But that's why I keep this here. He pointed at the jar on the bamboo cabinet, covered with a jute cloth. He had already shown the jar to me more than once, though once was more than enough. Nevertheless, he leaned over and slipped the cloth off the jar, and there was nothing to do but turn my gaze onto the exhibit that should, if there were any justice in the world, be exhibited in the Louvre and other great museums devoted to Western accomplishments. Floating in formaldehyde was a greenish monstrosity that appeared to have originated from outer space or the deepest, weirdest depths of the ocean. A chemical defoliant invented by an American

Frankenstein had led to this naked, pickled baby with one body but two heads, four eyes shut but two mouths agape in permanent, mongoloid yawns. Two faces pointed in different directions, two hands curled up against the chest, and two legs spread to reveal the boiled peanut of the masculine sex.

Imagine what the mother felt. The commandant tapped his finger on the glass. Or the father. Imagine the shrieks. *What is that thing?* He shook his head and drank his rice wine, its color that of thin milk. I licked my lips, and while the scratching of my dessicated tongue on my brittle lips was loud in my ears, the commandant did not notice. We could have just shot all these prisoners, he said. Your friend Bon, for example. A Phoenix Program assassin deserves the firing squad. Protecting him and excusing him as you do reflects poorly on your character and judgment. But the commissar is merciful and believes anyone can be rehabilitated, even when they and their American masters killed anyone they wanted. In contrast to the Americans and their puppets, our revolution has shown generosity by giving them this chance for redemption through labor. Many of these so-called leaders never worked a day on a farm. How do you lead an agricultural society into the future with no idea of the peasant's life? Without bothering to drape the cloth over the jar again, he poured himself another drink. Lack of understanding is the only way to characterize how some prisoners think they're being poorly fed. Of course I know they suffer. But we all suffered. We all must suffer still. The country is healing, and that takes longer than the war itself. But these prisoners focus only on their own suffering. They ignore what our side went through. I can't get them to understand that they get more calories per day than the revolutionary soldier during the war, more than the peasants forced into refugee camps. They believe they are being victimized here, instead of being reeducated. This obstinacy shows how much reeducation they still need. As recalcitrant as you are, you are still far ahead of them. Here I agree with the commissar about the state of your reeducation. I was just talking about you with *him* the other day. He's remarkably tolerant of you. He didn't even object to being called the faceless man. No, I understand, you are not mocking him, merely describing the obvious, but he's quite sensitive about his . . . condition. Wouldn't you be? He wants to meet you this evening. That's quite an honor. No prisoner has ever met him personally, not that you are a prisoner. He wants to clarify a few issues with you.

What issues? I said. We both looked at my manuscript, its leaves neatly stacked on his bamboo table and pinned down by a small rock, all 295 pages written by the light of a wick floating in a cup of oil. The commandant tapped my pages with a middle finger, its tip cut off. What issues? he said. Where to begin? Ah, dinner. A guard was at the door with a bamboo tray, a boy, his skin a sickly shade of yellow. Whether they were guards or prisoners, most men in the camp were this shade of yellow, or else a sickly, rotten shade of green, or a sickly, deathly shade of gray, a color palette resulting from tropical illnesses and a calamitous diet. What is it?

said the commandant. Wood pigeon, manioc soup, stir-fried cabbage, and rice, sir. The wood pigeon's roasted haunches and breast made me salivate, as my usual ration was boiled manioc. Even when starving, I had to force the manioc down my gullet, where it cemented itself against the walls of my stomach, laughing at my attempts to digest it. Subsisting on a diet of manioc not only was culinarily unpleasant, it was also no fun from a gastroenterological perspective, resulting in either a painfully solid brick or its highly explosive liquid opposite. As a consequence, the inflamed piranha of one's anus was always gnawing at one's posterior. I tried desperately to time my bowel movements, knowing a guard would fetch the ammo box reserved for that purpose at 0800 hours, but the snarled firehose of my bowels erupted at will, oftentimes right after the guard returned with the emptied can. Liquids and solids then fermented for most of the night and day, a vile mixture rusting through the ammo box. But I had no right to complain, as my baby-faced guard told me. No one's picking up my shit every day, he said, peering at me through the slot in my iron door. But you're being waited on hand and foot, short of someone wiping your ass. What do you say to that?

Thank you, sir. I could not call the guards "comrade," the commandant demanding that I keep my history a secret, lest it be leaked. The commissar orders this for your own protection, the commandant had told me. The inmates will kill you if they know your secret. The only men who knew my secret were the commissar and the commandant, for whom I had developed feline feelings of both dependency and resentment. He was the one making me rewrite my confession with repeated strokes of his blue pencil. But what was I confessing to? I had done nothing wrong, except for being Westernized. Nevertheless, the commandant was right. I was recalcitrant, for I could have shortened my unwanted stay by writing what he wanted me to write. *Long live the Party and the State. Follow Ho Chi Minh's glorious example. Let's build a beautiful and perfect society!* I believed in these slogans, but I could not bring myself to write them. I could say that I was contaminated by the West, but I could not inscribe that on paper. It seemed as much of a crime to commit a cliché to paper as to kill a man, an act I had acknowledged rather than confessed, for killing Sonny and the crapulent major were not crimes in the commandant's eyes. But having nevertheless acknowledged what some might see as crimes, I could not then compound those deeds through my description of them.

My resistance to the appropriate confessional style irritated the commandant, as he resumed telling me over dinner. You southerners had it too good for too long, he said. You took beefsteak for granted, while we northerners lived on starvation rations. We've been purged of fat and bourgeois inclinations, but you, no matter how many times you've rewritten your confession, cannot eradicate those inclinations. Your confession is full of moral weaknesses, individual selfishness, and Christian superstition. You exhibit no sense of collectivity, no belief in the science of history. You show no need to sacrifice yourself in the cause of rescuing the nation and serving the people. Another of To Huu's verses is appropriate here:

I'm a son of tens of thousands of families
A younger brother of tens of thousands of withered lives
A big brother to tens of thousands of little children
Who are homeless and live in constant hunger

Compared to To Huu, you are a communist only in name. In practice, you are a bourgeois intellectual. I'm not blaming you. It's difficult to escape one's class and one's birth, and you are corrupted in both respects. You must remake yourself, as Uncle Ho and Chairman Mao both said bourgeois intellectuals should do. The good news is that you show glimmers of collective revolutionary consciousness. The bad news is that your language betrays you. It is not clear, not succinct, not direct, not simple. It is the language of the elite. You must write for the people!

You speak truthfully, sir, I said. The wood pigeon and manioc soup had begun dissolving in my stomach, their nutrients energizing my brain. I just wonder what you would say about Karl Marx, Comrade Commandant. *Das Kapital* isn't exactly written for the people.

Marx did not write for the people? Suddenly I could see the darkness of the commandant's cave through his magnified irises. Get out! See how bourgeois you are? A revolutionary humbles himself before Marx. Only a bourgeois compares himself to Marx. But rest assured, *he* will treat you for your elitism and Western inclinations. He has built a state-of-the-art examination room where he will personally supervise the final phase of your reeducation, when you are transformed from an American into a Vietnamese once more.

I'm not an American, sir, I said. If my confession reveals anything, isn't it that I'm an anti-American? I must have said something outrageously humorous, for he actually laughed. The anti-American already includes the American, he said. Don't you see that the Americans need the anti-American? While it is better to be loved than hated, it is also far better to be hated than ignored. To be anti-American only makes you a reactionary. In our case, having defeated the Americans, we no longer define ourselves as anti-American. We are simply one hundred percent Vietnamese. You must try to be as well.

Respectfully speaking, sir, most of our countrymen do not think I am one of them.

All the more reason for you to work harder to prove that you are one of us. Obviously you think of yourself as one of us, at least sometimes, so you are making progress. I see you've finished eating. What did you think of the wood pigeon? I admitted that it was delicious. What if I told you that "wood pigeon" is only a euphemism? He watched me carefully as I looked again at the pile of little bones on my plate, sucked clean of every bit of meat and tendon. Regardless of what it was, I still longed for another serving. Some call this rat, but I prefer "field mouse," he said. But it hardly matters, does it? Meat is meat, and we eat what we must. Do you know I once saw a dog eating the brains of our battalion doctor? Ugh. I don't blame the dog. He was only eating the brains because the man's intestines had already been eaten by his fellow dog. These are the kinds of things you see on the battlefield. But losing all those men was worth it. All the bombs dropped on us by those air pirates were not dropped on our homeland. Not to mention that we liberated the Laotians. That is what revolutionaries do. We sacrifice ourselves to save others.

Yes, Comrade Commandant.

Enough serious talk. He threw the jute cover back over the pickled baby. I just wanted to give you my personal congratulations on having finished the written phase of your reeducation, no matter how barely, in my opinion. You should be pleased with how far you've come, even if you should be critical yourself for the limitations so evident in your confession. As good a student as you are, you may yet become the dialectical materialist that the revolution needs you to be. Now, let us go meet the commissar. The commandant checked the time on his wristwatch, which also happened to have been my wristwatch. *He* is expecting us.

We descended from the commandant's quarters and walked past the guard barracks to the stretch of flatland separating the two hills. My isolation cell was located here, one of a dozen brick ovens where we basted in our own juices and where the prisoners tapped messages on the walls with tin cups. They had developed a simple code for communicating, and it was not long before they taught it to me. Part of what they conveyed to me was how they held me in high regard. Much of my heroic reputation came from Bon, who often greeted me through my neighbors. He and they believed I was singled out for extended isolation because of my ardent republicanism and my Special Branch credentials. They blamed the commissar for my fate, for he was really the one in charge of the camp, as everyone, including the commandant, knew. My neighbors had seen the commissar up close during his weekly political lectures, and the sight was truly horrific. Some cursed him, taking delight in his suffering. But the facelessness compelled respect among others, the mark of his dedication and sacrifice, even if for a cause that the prisoners despised. The guards, too, spoke of the faceless commissar with mixed tones of horror, fear, and respect, but never mockery. A commissar must never be mocked, even among one's peers, for one never knew when one of those peers might report such antirevolutionary thinking.

I understood the need for my temporary detention and marginal conditions, for the revolution must be vigilant, but what I could not understand, and what I hoped the commissar would explain, was why the guards feared *him*, and, more generally, why revolutionaries feared one another. Aren't we all comrades? I asked the commandant at an earlier session. Yes, he said, but not all comrades have the same level of ideological consciousness. Although I am not thrilled at having to seek the commissar's approval on certain matters, I also admit that *he* knows Marxist-Leninist theory and Ho Chi Minh Thought much better than I ever will. I'm not a scholar, but he is. Men like him are guiding us toward a truly classless society. But we haven't eradicated all elements of antirevolutionary thinking, and we must not forgive antirevolutionary faults. We must be vigilant, even of each other, but mostly of ourselves. What my time in the cave taught me is that the ultimate life-and-death struggle is with ourselves. Foreign invaders might kill my body, but only I could kill my spirit. This is the lesson you must absorb by heart, which is why we give you so much time to achieve it.

Ascending the hill toward the commissar's quarters, it seemed to me that I had already spent too much time learning that lesson. We stopped at the stairs leading up to his balcony, where the baby-faced guard and three other guards awaited. The commissar's in charge of you now, the commandant said, inspecting me from head to toe with a frown. I'll be frank. *He* sees much more potential in you than I do. You are addicted to the social evils of alcohol, prostitution, and yellow music. You write in an unacceptable, counterrevolutionary manner. You are responsible for the deaths of the Bru comrade and the Watchman. You failed even in undermining this movie that misrepresents and insults us. If it were only up to me, I'd send you to the fields for your final cure. And if things do not work out with the commissar, I still can. Remember that.

I will, I said. And, knowing that I had not yet escaped his power, I also said, Thank you, Comrade Commandant, for all you have done for me. I know I've seemed reactionary to you because of my confession, but please believe me when I say that I have learned much under your tutelage and criticism. (This, after all, was the truth.)

My show of gratitude mollified the commandant. Let me give you some advice, he said. The prisoners tell me what they think I want to hear, but they don't understand that what I want to hear is sincerity. Isn't that what education is all about? Getting the student to sincerely say what the teacher wants to hear? Keep that in mind. With that, the commandant turned and began his descent down the hill, a man of admirably erect posture.

The commissar's waiting, the baby-faced guard said. Let's go.

I gathered what remained of myself. I was three-quarters of the man I used to be, according to the commandant's scale, manufactured in the USA and appropriated from a southern hospital. The commandant was obsessed with his weight and enamored with the scale's statistical precision. Through a rigorous longitudinal study of bowel movements, sampled from both guards and prisoners, including myself, the commandant had calculated that the camp's collective bowels issued about six hundred kilos of waste per day. The prisoners collected and hand-carried this waste to the fields, where it served as fertilizer. Fecal precision was thus necessary for the scientific management of agricultural production. Even now, climbing the stairs ahead of the guards and knocking on the commissar's door, I felt the factory of my innards fashioning the wood pigeon into a solid brick that would be used tomorrow to help build the revolution.

Come in, said the commissar. That voice . . .

His quarters consisted entirely of one big, rectangular room as austere as the commandant's, with bamboo walls, bamboo floors, bamboo furniture, and bamboo rafters holding up a thatched roof. I had entered the sitting area, furnished with some low-slung bamboo chairs, a bamboo coffee table, and an altar on which sat Ho Chi Minh's gold-painted bust. Above his head hung a red banner imprinted with those golden words NOTHING IS MORE PRECIOUS THAN INDEPENDENCE AND FREEDOM. In the middle of the room was a long table stacked with books and papers, surrounded by chairs. Leaning against one of the chairs was a guitar with familiar curvaceous hips, and at one end of the long table was a record player that looked like the one I had left behind at the General's villa . . . At the far end of the room was a platform bed, draped in a cloud of mosquito netting behind which a shadow stirred. The bamboo floor was cool under my bare feet, and the breeze whispering through the open windows caused the netting to tremble. A hand parted the netting, its skin burned red, and *he* emerged from the bed's recesses, a visage of fearful asymmetry. I looked away. Come now, the commissar said. Am I really so horrible that you do not recognize me, my friend? I looked back to see lips scorched away to reveal perfect teeth, eyes bulging from withered sockets, nostrils reduced to holes without a nose, the hairless, earless skull one massive keloid scar, leaving the head to resemble one of those dried, decapitated trophies swung on a string by an ebullient headhunter. He coughed, and a marble rattled in his throat.

Didn't I tell you, Man said, not to return?

CHAPTER 20

He was the commissar? Before I could say a word, or make any sound at all, the guards seized me, gagged me, and blindfolded me. *You?* I wanted to scream, to shout into the darkness, but I could do no more than grunt and moan as they dragged me outside and down the hill, the blindfold scratchy, my arms pinioned, to a destination less than a hundred paces away. Open the door, the baby-faced guard said. Hinges creaked, and I was pushed from the open air into a confined, echoing space. Arms up, the baby-faced guard said. I raised my arms. Someone unbuttoned my shirt and stripped it from me. Hands untied the string holding up my pants and they dropped around my ankles. Look at that, another guard said, whistling with admiration. The bastard's *big*. Not as big as me, a third guard said. Let's see it, then, the fourth guard said. You'll see it when I fuck your mother with it.

Perhaps more was said, but after someone with rough fingers inserted foam plugs into my ears, and someone else placed muffs of some kind on top of them, I heard nothing more. Deaf, dumb, and blind, I was pushed down onto a mattress. A mattress! I had slept on planks the past year. The guards strapped me down with ropes around my chest, thighs, wrists, and ankles until I could do no more than wriggle my spread-eagled body. A foamy material was wrapped around my hands and feet and a silky hood was pulled over my head, the softest fabric I had felt since Lana's lingerie. I stopped squirming, calming myself down so I could focus on my breathing through the hood. Then came vibrations of feet on the rough cement floor, followed by the faintest clank of the door being shut, and nothing more.

Was I alone, or was someone watching me? I began sweating from the accumulating heat, rage, and fear, my sweat pooling under my back faster than the mattress could absorb it. My hands and feet were hot and clammy as well. A sudden sense of panic, of drowning, surged through me. I thrashed against my constraints and tried to scream, but my body would hardly move and no sound emerged except a snuffle. Why was this being done to me? What did Man want from me? Surely he would not let me die here! No! This was my final examination. I must calm down. This was only a test. I aced tests. The Oriental is a perfect student, the Department Chair had remarked more than once. And according to Professor Hammer, I had studied the best of what had been thought and said in Western civilization, its torch passed on to me. I was my country's finest representative, Claude had assured me, a natural at the intelligence game. Remember, you're not half of anything, my mother said, you're twice of everything! Yes, I could pass this test, whatever it was, devised by a commissar who had been studying me, and Bon, for the past year. He had been reading my confession, even though he, unlike the commandant, already knew most of what was in it. He could have let us go, set us free. He could have told me he was the commissar. Why subject me to a year in isolation? My calm vanished and I almost choked against my gag. Calm down! Breathe slowly! I managed to control myself once more. Now what? How would I pass the time? At least an hour must have elapsed since I was blindfolded, hadn't it? I longed to lick my lips, but with the gag in my mouth I almost vomited. That would have been the death of me. When was he coming for me? How long would he leave me here? What had happened to his face? The guards would feed me, surely. On and on the thoughts came, the thousand cockroaches of time crawling over me until I shivered in agony and revulsion.

I wept for myself then, and the tears under my blindfold had the unexpected benefit of clearing the dust from my mind's eye, enough for me to realize that I was not blind. My mind's eye could see, and what I saw was the crapulent major and Sonny, circling around me as I lay on my mattress. How did you end up here, with your best friend and blood brother overseeing your demise? said the crapulent major. Don't you think your life would have taken a different course if you hadn't killed me? Not to mention mine, said Sonny. Do you know Sofia still weeps for me? I've tried to visit her and put her at peace but she can't see me. Whereas you, who I would rather not see at all, can see me all the time. But I have to say that seeing you like this does give me some pleasure. Justice exists after all! I wanted to reply to these accusations and tell them to wait for my friend the commissar to explain everything, but even in my head I was mute. All I could do was moan in protest, which only made them laugh. The crapulent major nudged my thigh with his foot and said, See where your plotting has led you now? He nudged me even harder, and I shuddered in protest. He kept nudging me with that foot, and I kept shuddering, until I realized it was not the crapulent major but someone I could not see pushing his heel against my leg. I felt the door clang shut again. Someone had entered without me knowing, or someone had been here the entire time and just left. How much time had passed? I couldn't be certain. Had I fallen asleep? If I had, then several hours must have gone by, perhaps an entire day. That must be why I was hungry. Finally a part of me, my stomach, could be heard, groaning. The loudest voice in the world is the voice of one's own tortured stomach. Even so, this voice was still a quiet one compared to the angry beast it could be. I was not starving, not yet. I was just famished, my body having completely digested the wood pigeon that was actually a rat. Were they not going to feed me? Why was this being done to me? What had I ever done to him?

I remembered this kind of hunger. I had experienced it so often in my youth, even when my mother served me three-quarters of a meal and saved only a quarter for herself. I'm not hungry, she said. When I was old enough to see that she was denying herself, I said, I'm not hungry, either, Mama. Our staring contest over the meager helpings led us to push them back and forth until her love for me over-powered mine for her, as always. Eating her portion, I swallowed not just the food but the salt and pepper of love and anger, spices stronger and harsher than the sugar of sympathy. Why were we hungry? my stomach cried. Even then I understood that if the rich could only spare all the hungry a bowl of rice, they would be less rich but they would not starve. If the solution was so simple, why was anyone hungry? Was it only a lack of sympathy? No, Man said. As he taught me in our study group, both the Bible and *Das Kapital* provided answers. Sympathy alone would never persuade the rich to share willingly and the powerful to give up power voluntarily. Revolution made those impossible things happen. Revolution would free us all, rich and poor . . . but by that Man meant freedom for classes and collectivities. He did not necessarily mean that individuals would be freed. No, many revolutionaries had died in prison, and that seemed more and more as if it would be my fate. But despite my sense of doom, as well as my sweat, my hunger, my love, and my rage, sleep almost overcame me. I was fading when that foot nudged me again, this time in the ribs. I shook my head and tried to turn onto my side, but my restraints would not let me. The foot nudged me once more. That foot! The demon would not let me rest. How I came to hate its horned toes scraping against my bare skin and pushing against my thigh, my hip, my shoulder, my forehead. The foot knew whenever I was on the verge of sleep, returning at exactly that moment to deny me even the slightest taste of what I

needed so much. The monotony of darkness was challeng-
ing, and hunger was painful, but this constant wakefulness
was even worse. How long had I been awake? How long
had I been in what must be the examination room? When
was he coming to explain everything to me? I could not
tell. The only interruptions to mark the passage of time
were that foot and the occasional touch of hands lifting my
hood, loosening my gag, squirting water down my throat.
I never got more than a word or two out before the gag was
tightened again and the hood pulled down to my neck. Oh,
let me sleep! I could touch its dark waters . . . and then
that damned foot would nudge at me again.

The foot would keep me awake until I died. The foot
was slowly, ever so slowly, killing me. The foot was judge,
guard, and executioner. Oh, foot, have sympathy for me.
Foot, whose whole life is one of being stood upon, of being
made to walk the dirty earth, neglected by all above, you of
all living things should understand how I feel. Foot, where
would we, humanity, be without you? You delivered us from
Africa to the rest of the world, and yet so little is said about
you. Clearly you got a raw deal as compared with, say, the
hand. If you let me live, I will dedicate words to you and
make my readers realize your importance. Oh, foot! I beg
of you, nudge me no more. Stop rubbing your calluses on
my skin. Don't scratch me with your sharp, uncut nails. Not
that your calluses and nails are your fault. They are your
negligent master's fault. I confess that I am just as heedless
in the care of my feet, your kin. But I promise if you just let
me go to sleep, I will be a new man in regards to my own

feet, to all feet! I will worship you, foot, as Jesus Christ did when he washed the feet of sinners and kissed them.

Foot, you should be revolution's symbol, not the hand holding hammer and sickle. Yet we keep you hidden under the table, or shod in a shoe. We abuse you, as the Chinese do, by binding you. Would we ever inflict such an injury on the hand? Stop prodding me, please, I beg of you. I recognize that humanity poorly represents you, except for when we spend copious amounts of money in dressing you, because you, of course, cannot represent yourself. Foot, I wonder why I never thought about you before, or hardly ever. The hand is free to do whatever it pleases. It even writes! No wonder more words have been written about the hand than the foot. We share something in common, foot. We are the downtrodden of the world. If you would only stop keeping me awake, if only—

This time the hand nudged me. Someone tugged at my hood, loosened it and raised it above my ears, but kept it on my head. Then the hand pulled the muffs away and yanked the plugs out and I heard the shuffling of sandals, the scraping of a chair or a stool on cement. You idiot! the voice said. I was still in darkness, hands and feet still bound and encased, body naked and damp. Water was poured down my parched throat until I gagged. Didn't I tell you not to come? It came from far above me, somewhere in the ceiling, *his* voice, I was sure of it even in my agonized state. But how could I not come back? I blubbered. Mama told me the bird always returns to its nest. Am I not that bird? Is this not my nest? My origin, my place of birth, my country? My home?

Are these not my people? Are you not my friend, my sworn brother, my true comrade? Tell me why you're doing this to me. I wouldn't do this to my worst enemy.

The voice sighed. Never underestimate what you can do to your worst enemy. But so far as this goes, what was it that priests like your father always said? Do unto others as you would have them do unto you. That sounds good, but things are never that simple. The problem, you see, is how to know what we want to have done to us.

I have no idea what you're talking about, I said. Why are you torturing me?

Do you think I want to do this to you? I am doing my best to make sure worse things don't happen to you. The commandant already believes that I am being too gentle with my pedagogical methods, with my desire to hear your confession. He is the kind of dentist who believes toothaches can be treated by removing all of one's teeth with pliers. This is the situation you have gotten yourself into by doing exactly what I told you not to do. Now, if you have any wish of leaving this camp with your teeth intact, we must play out our roles until the commandant is satisfied.

Please don't be angry with me, I sobbed. I couldn't take it if you were angry at me, too! He sighed once more. Do you remember writing that you forgot something, but that you couldn't remember what it was? I told him I didn't remember. Of course, he said. Human memory is short, and time is long. The reason you are here in this examination room is for you to remember what you forgot, or at least forgotten to write. My friend, I am here to help you see what it is you cannot see on your own. His foot nudged the base of my skull. Here, at the back of your head.

But what does that have to do with not letting me sleep? I said. He laughed, not the laugh of the schoolboy who had enjoyed Tintin comics, but the laugh of someone perhaps just a bit mad. You know as well as I why I cannot let you sleep, he said. We must access that safe hiding the last of your secrets. The longer we keep you awake, the better chance we have of cracking that safe.

But I've confessed to everything.

No, you haven't, the voice said. I am not accusing you of deliberately withholding, though I gave you many opportunities to write your confession in such a way as to satisfy the commandant. It is you who bring this on yourself, no one else.

But what am I supposed to confess to?

If I told you what to confess to, then it would not be much of a confession, the voice said. But take comfort in knowing that your situation is not as impossible as you think. Do you remember our exams, when you would always score perfectly and I would miss a few points? Even though I read and memorized as feverishly as you, you always outdid me. I just couldn't get the answers to come out of my head. But they were there. The mind never forgets. When I looked at our textbooks again, I thought, *Of course!* I knew them all the time. In fact, I know you know the answer to the question you must pass in order to finish your reeducation. I will even ask you that question now. Answer it successfully and I will free you from your bonds. Are you ready?

Go ahead, I said, swelling with confidence. All I ever needed was a test to prove myself. I heard the rustle of paper, as if he was thumbing through a book, or perhaps my confession. What is more precious than independence and freedom?

A trick question? The answer was obvious. What was he looking for? My mind was swaddled in something soft and clammy. Through it I could feel the hard, solid answer, but what it was I could not tell. Perhaps the obvious was indeed the answer. At last I told him what I thought he wanted to hear: Nothing, I said, is more precious than independence and freedom.

The voice sighed. Almost, but not quite. Almost, but not right. Isn't it frustrating when the answer is right there but one doesn't know what it is?

Why, I cried, are you doing this to me? You are my friend, my brother, my comrade!

A long silence ensued. I heard only the shuffling of paper and the rasp of his tortured breathing. He was sucking hard to ensure the passage of even a small amount of air. Then he said, Yes, I am your friend, brother, comrade, all these things until I die. As your friend, brother, comrade, I warned you, didn't I? I could not have been any clearer. I was not the only one reading your messages, nor could I send you a message without someone looking over my shoulder. Everyone has someone looking over his shoulder here. And yet you insisted on returning, you fool.

Bon was going to get himself killed, I had to come back to protect him.

And you were going to get yourself killed, too, the voice said. What kind of plan is that? Where would you two be if I was not here? We are the Three Musketeers, aren't we? Or perhaps now we are the Three Stooges. No one volunteers for this camp, but when I realized you would be returning I demanded to be the commissar and to have the two of you sent here. Do you know who they put in this camp? The ones who chose to make a last stand, who continued to fight a guerrilla war, who will not recant or confess with proper contrition. Bon has already demanded twice to be shot by firing squad. The commandant would gladly have done it if not for me. As for you, your chances of survival would be doubtful without my protection.

You call this protection?

If it weren't for me, you would likely be dead already. I am a commissar but above me are more commissars, reading your messages, following your progress. They dictate your reeducation. All I can do is take charge of it and persuade the commandant that my method will work. The commandant would have put you on a demining squad, and that would be the end of you. But I have gotten you the luxury of a year writing in an isolation cell. The other prisoners would kill for your privilege. I don't mean that metaphorically. I've done you a big favor, getting the commandant to keep you locked up. In his eyes, you are the most dangerous of all subversives, but I've convinced him that the revolution is better off curing you than killing you.

Me? Haven't I proven myself a true revolutionary? Haven't I sacrificed decades of my life in the cause of liberating our country? You of all people should know that!

It is not me who needs convincing. It is the commandant. You do not write in any way a man like him can understand. You claim to be a revolutionary, but your story betrays you, or rather, you betray yourself. Why, you stubborn ass, do you insist on writing this way, when you must know that the likes of you threaten the commandants of the world . . . The foot nudged me awake. I had fallen asleep for one delicious instance, as if I had been crawling through a desert and tasted a tear. Stay awake, the voice said. Your life depends on it.

You're going to kill me if you won't let me sleep, I said.

I am going to keep you awake until you understand, the voice said.

I understand nothing!

Then you have understood almost everything, the voice said. He chuckled and it sounded almost like my old school mate. Isn't it funny how we find ourselves here, my friend? You came to save Bon's life and I came to save both your lives. Let us hope my plot works out better than yours. But truth be told, it wasn't purely out of friendship that I petitioned to be the commissar here. You have seen my face, or rather, my lack of one. Can you imagine my wife and children seeing this? The voice cracked. Can you imagine their horror? Can you imagine mine every time I look in the mirror? Although, to be honest, I have not looked at a mirror for years now.

I wept, thinking of him exiled from them. His wife was a revolutionary, too, a girl from our sister school of such integrity and simple beauty that I would have fallen in love with her if he hadn't first. His boy and girl must be now at least seven and eight, little angels whose only fault was that they sometimes fought with each other. They would never look with fear on your . . . your condition, I said. You only imagine what they see through how you see yourself.

You know nothing! he shouted. Silence ensued again, interrupted only by the rasp of his breathing. I could imagine the scars of his lips, the scars in his throat, but all I wanted was to sleep . . . His foot nudged me. I apologize for losing my temper, the voice said, softly. My friend, you cannot know what I feel. You only think you can. But can you know what it is like to be so horrible that your own children cry when they see you, when your wife flinches at your touch, when your own friend does not recognize you? Bon has seen me this last year and not known who I am. True, he sits at the back of the meeting hall and only sees me from afar. I have not called him in to let him know who I am, because such knowledge would certainly do him no good and probably do him great harm. Nevertheless—nevertheless I dream that he will recognize me despite myself, even if, in recognizing me, he would only want to kill me. Can you imagine the pain of losing my friendship with him? Perhaps you can. But can you actually know the pain of napalm burning the skin off your face and your body? How can you?

Then tell me, I cried. I want to know what happened to you!

Silence ensued, for how long I do not know, until the foot nudged me again and I realized I had missed the first part of his story. I was still wearing my uniform, said the voice.

The sense of doom was thick among my unit, panic in the eyes of the officers and the men. With the liberation only hours away, I hid my joy and excitement but not my worry for my family, even though they should be safe. My wife was at home with the children, one of our couriers close by to ensure their safety. When the tanks of the liberation army approached our bridge and my commanding officer ordered us to stand firm, I worried for myself as well. I didn't want our liberators to shoot me on the last day of the war, and my mind was calculating how to avoid such a fate when someone said, Here's the air force at last. One of our planes was overhead, flying high to avoid antiaircraft fire, but also flying far too high for a bombing run. Get closer, someone shouted. How's he going to hit anything flying that high? The voice chuckled. How indeed? When the pilot dropped his bombs, the sense of dread possessing my fellow officers touched me, for I could see that the bombs, instead of falling toward the tanks, were falling toward us, in slow motion. The bombs fell faster than our eyesight told us, and though we ran, we did not get far. A cloud of napalm engulfed us, and I suppose I was lucky. I ran faster than the others and the napalm only licked me. It hurt. Oh, how much it hurt! But what can I tell you besides the fact that being on fire feels like being on fire? What can I tell you about the pain except that it was the most horrendous pain I have ever felt? The only way for me to show you how much it hurt, my friend, is for me to burn you myself, and that I will never do.

I, too, had come close to death on the tarmac of the Saigon airport, and again on the set of the Movie, but neither experience was the same as being burned. At worst I had been lightly scorched. I tried to imagine that multiplied by ten thousand, by a napalm that was the very light of Western civilization, having been invented at Harvard, or so I had learned in Claude's class. But I could not. All I could feel was my desire for sleep as my self dissolved, leaving only my melting mind. But even in this buttery condition, my mind understood that this was not the time to talk about me. I can't imagine, I said. Not at all.

It was a miracle that I lived. I am a living miracle! A human being turned inside out. I should be dead but for my dear wife, who searched for me when I did not come home. She found me dying in an army hospital, a low-priority case. When she notified the powers that be, they ordered the best surgeons remaining in Saigon to operate on me. I was saved! But for what? The pain of being burned was hardly less than the pain of having no skin and no face. I was on fire every day for months. When my medication wears off, I still burn. Excruciating is the right word, but it cannot convey the feeling it describes.

I think I know what excruciation feels like.

You are only beginning to know.

You don't have to do this!

Then you do not yet understand. Certain things can be learned only through the feeling of excruciation. I want you to know what it is that I knew and still know. I would have spared you that knowledge if you had not come back. But you have come back, and the commandant is watching. Left by yourself, you would not survive under his care. You frighten him. You are nothing but a shadow standing at the mouth of his cave, some strange creature that sees things from two sides. People like you must be purged because you bear the contamination that can destroy the revolution's purity. My task is to prove that you do not need to be purged, that you can be released. I have constructed this examination room exactly for this purpose.

You don't have to do this, I muttered.

But I do! What's being done to you is for your own good. The commandant would break you the only way he knows how, through your body. The only way to save you was to promise the commandant that I would test new methods of examination that would not leave a mark. This is why we have not beat you even once.

I should be thankful?

Yes, you should. But now it is time for the final revision. The commandant will accept no less. You must give him more than what you have.

I have nothing left to confess!

There is always something. That is confession's nature. We can never stop confessing because we are imperfect. Even the commandant and I must criticize ourselves to each other, as the Party has intended. The military commandant and the political commissar are the living embodiment of dialectical materialism. We are the thesis and the antithesis from which comes the more powerful synthesis, the truly revolutionary consciousness.

If you already know what I forgot to confess, then tell me!

The voice chuckled again. I heard the shuffling of papers. Let me quote from your manuscript, the voice said. "The communist agent with the papier-mâché evidence of her espionage crammed into her mouth, our sour names literally on the tip of her tongue." You mention her four more times in your confession. We learn that you pulled this list from her mouth and that she looked at you with mortal hatred, but we don't learn her fate. You must tell us what you did to her. We demand to know!

I saw her face again, her dark peasant skin and broad, flat nose, so similar to those broad, flat noses of the doctors surrounding her in the movie theater. But, I said, I did nothing to her.

Nothing! Do you think her fate is the thing you have forgotten that you have forgotten? But how is her tragedy possible to forget? Her fate is so clear. Was there ever any fate for her that could differ from what a reader might imagine, seeing her in your confession?

But I did nothing to her!

Exactly! Don't you see how everything in need of confession is already known? You indeed did nothing. That is the crime that you must acknowledge and to which you must confess. Do you agree?

Perhaps. My voice was faint. His foot nudged me again. Would he let me sleep if I said yes?

It is time for me to rest, my friend. I can feel the pain again. The pain never goes away. Do you know how I tolerate it? Morphine. The voice chuckled. But that wonder drug only numbs the body and the brain. What about my mind?

I've discovered that the only way to manage pain is to imagine someone else's greater pain, a suffering that diminishes your own. So, remember what we learned in the lycée, the words of Phan Boi Chau? "For a human being, the greatest suffering comes from losing his country." When this human being lost his face, his skin, and his family, this human being imagined you, my friend. You had lost your country and I was the one who exiled you. I felt deeply for you, the terrible loss only hinted at in your cryptic messages. But now you have returned, and I can no longer imagine your suffering to be greater than mine.

I'm suffering now, I said. Please, just let me go to sleep.

We're revolutionaries, my friend. Suffering made us. Suffering *for* the people is what we chose because we sympathized so much *with* their suffering.

I know all this, I said.

Then listen to me. The chair scraped and his voice, already high above me, rose even higher. Please understand. I do this to you because I am your friend and your brother. Only without the comfort of sleep will you fully understand the horrors of history. I tell you this as someone who has slept very little since what has happened to me. Believe me when I say that I know how you feel, and that this has to be done.

I was already afraid, but his prescription of my treatment magnified my fear even more. Somebody must have something done to him! Was I that somebody? No! That cannot be true, or so I wanted to tell him, but my tongue refused to obey me. I was only mistaken to be that somebody, because

I was, I told him, or thought I did, a nobody. I am a lie, a keeper, a book. No! I am a fly, a creeper, a gook. No! I am—I am—I am—

The chair scraped again and I smelled the distinct, gamy odor of the baby-faced guard. A foot nudged me and I trembled. Please, Comrade, I said. Just let me sleep. The baby-faced guard snorted, nudged me once more with his horny foot, and said, I'm not your comrade.

CHAPTER 21

The prisoner had never known that he needed a respite from history, he who had committed his adult life to its hot pursuit. His friend Man had introduced him to the science of history in the study group, its chosen books written in scarlet letters. If one understood history's laws, then one could control history's chronology, wresting it away from capitalism, already intent on monopolizing time. We wake, work, eat, and sleep according to what the landlord, the owner, the banker, the politician, and the schoolmaster command, Man had said. We accept that our time belongs to them, when in truth our time belongs to us. Awaken, peasants, workers, colonized! Awaken, invisible ones! Stir from your zones of occult instability and steal the gold watch of time from the paper tigers, running dogs, and fat cats of imperialism, colonialism, and capitalism! If you know how to steal it, time is on your side, and numbers are, too. There are millions of *you* and only thousands of *them*, the colonizers, compradors, and capitalists who have persuaded the wretched of the earth that capitalist history is inevitable. We, the vanguard, must convince the dark peoples and subterranean classes that communist history is inevitable! The exhaustion of the exploited will inevitably lead them to revolt, but it is our vanguard that speeds up the time toward that uprising, resets the clock of history and rings the alarm clock of revolution. *Ticktock—ticktock—ticktock—*

Fixed on his mattress, the prisoner—no, the pupil—understood that this was the study group's final session. To be a revolutionary subject he must be a historical subject who remembered all, which he could do so only by being fully awake, even if being fully awake would, eventually, kill him. And yet if he could but sleep, he would understand better! He writhed, he wriggled, he wrestled with himself in his failed bid for sleep, and this may have gone on for hours, or minutes, or seconds, when, all of a sudden, his hood was removed, followed by his gag, allowing him to gasp and suck in air. His captor's rough hands plucked away his muffs and earplugs and, lastly, untied the blindfold chafing against his skin. Light! He could see, but just as quickly he had to shut his eyes. Suspended over him were dozens—no, hundreds of lightbulbs, planted in the ceiling and blinding him with their collective wattage, their glare radiating through the red filter of his eyelids. A foot pushed against his temple and the baby-faced guard said, No sleeping, you. He opened his eyes to the glowing hot mass of bulbs arranged in an orderly grid, their intense light revealing an examination room whose walls and ceiling were plastered in white. The floor was cement painted white, and even the iron door was painted white, all in a chamber roughly three meters by five. The baby-faced guard in his yellow uniform stood at attention in the corner, but the three others in the room stood at the edges of his mattress, one to either side and another at his feet. They were dressed in white lab coats and sea-green medical scrubs, hands behind their backs. Surgical masks and stainless steel goggles hid their faces, all six orbital lenses focused on him, who was now clearly not only prisoner and pupil but also patient.

Q. Who are you?

The man to his left asked the question. Didn't they know who he was by now? He was the man with a plan, the spy with an eye, the mole in the hole, but his tongue had inflated itself to fill his entire mouth. Please, he wanted to say, let me close my eyes. Then I'll tell you who I am. The answer is on the tip of my tongue—I am the gook being cooked. And if you say I am only *half* a gook? Well, in the words of that blond-haired major tasked with counting the communist dead after the battle for Ben Tre, confronted with the mathematical problem of a corpse whose remains included only his head, chest, and arms: half a gook is still a gook. And since the only good gook is a dead gook, as the American soldiers liked to say, it must be that this patient was one bad gook.

Q. What are you?

This came from the man to his right in the commandant's voice. On hearing this voice, the patient lunged against his ropes until they burned his flesh, the question inciting a red flare of silent rage. I know what you're thinking! You think I'm a traitor! A counterrevolutionary! A bastard who belongs nowhere, not to be trusted by anyone! The rage subsided just as suddenly into despair, and he wept. Would his sacrifices never be honored? Would no one ever understand him? Would he always be alone? Why must he be the man to whom things are done?

Q. What is your name?

It was the man at the end of the mattress, speaking in the commissar's voice. An easy question, or so he thought. He opened his mouth, but when his tongue would not move, he shrank in fright. Had he forgotten his name? No, impossible! He had given himself his American name. As for his native name, his mother, the only one who understood him, had given it to him, his father no help, his father who never called him son or by his name, even in class simply calling him *you*. No, he could never forget his name, and when at last it came to him, he freed his tongue from its gummy bed and said it aloud.

The commissar said, He can't even get his name right. Doctor, I think he needs the serum, to which the man on the patient's left said, Very well, then. The doctor brought his hands from behind his back, gloved to the forearms in white rubber, one hand with an ampule the size of a rifle cartridge, the other with a needle. With a smooth stroke, the doctor drew a clear liquid from the ampule into the needle, then crouched by the patient's side. When he shuddered and twitched, the doctor said, One way or another I'll inject you, and if you move, it will be worse for you. The patient stopped thrashing and the prick in the crook of the elbow was almost a welcome relief, another kind of feeling than the hallucinatory urge for sleep. Almost, but not quite. Please, he said, turn off the lights.

The commissar said, That we cannot do. Don't you see that you must see? The commandant snorted. He will never see, not with all the light in the world. He's been underground too long. He's fundamentally blind! Now, now, said the doctor, patting the patient's arm. Men of science must never give up hope, least of all when operating on the mind. As we can neither see nor touch his mind, all we can do is help the patient see his own mind by keeping him awake, until he can observe himself as someone else. This is most crucial, for we are the ones most able to know ourselves and yet the most unable to know ourselves. It's as if our noses are pressed up against the pages of a book, the words right in front of us but which we cannot read. Just as distance is needed for legibility, so it is that if we could only split ourselves in two and gain some distance from ourselves, we could see ourselves better than anyone else can. This is the nature of our experiment, for which we need one more device. The doctor pointed to a brown leather satchel on the floor that the patient had not noticed but immediately recognized, a military field telephone, the sight of which made him tremble again. The Soviets provided the serum that will compel our patient to tell the truth, the doctor

said. This other component is American. You see the look
in our patient's eyes? He remembers what he has seen in
those interrogation rooms. But we will not be wiring him via
nipple and scrotum to the battery terminals on the phone's
generator. Instead—the doctor reached into the satchel and
extracted a black wire—we clip this to a toe. As for the hand
crank, it generates too much electricity. We do not want
pain. We do not torture. All we want is enough stimulus to
keep him awake. Thus I have modified the electrical output
and wired the phone to this. The doctor held up a wristwatch. Every time the second hand crosses twelve o'clock,
a brief spark travels to the patient's toe.

The doctor untied the burlap sack of wadding from around
the patient's foot, and although the patient craned his neck
to see the doctor's contraption he could not elevate himself
enough to observe the details. All he could see was the black
wire running from toe to satchel, inside of which the doctor
had replaced the wristwatch. Sixty seconds, gentlemen, said
the doctor. *Ticktock* . . . the patient trembled, waiting for the
call. The patient had seen how a subject receiving such a call
answered it by screaming and flinging about. By the tenth
or twentieth such call, the subject's eyes took on the glassy
sheen of a taxidermically prepared specimen in a diorama,
living and yet dead, or vice versa, as the subject anticipated
the crank's next turn. Claude, who had taken the class to see
such an interrogation, said, Any of you jokers laugh or get
a hard-on, I yank you. This is serious business. The patient
remembered being relieved when he was not asked to turn
the crank. Watching the subject spasm, he had winced and

wondered what the call felt like. Now here he was, sweating and shivering as the seconds ticked away until a burst of static electricity made him jump, not pained but startled. See? Perfectly harmless, said the doctor. Just keep switching the wire to different toes so he doesn't get a burn from the wire's clip.

Thank you, Doctor, said the commissar. Now if you wouldn't mind, I'd like some privacy with our patient. Take all the time you want, said the commandant, heading for the door. This patient's mind is contaminated. It needs a thorough washing. After the exit of the commandant, the doctor, and the baby-faced guard—but not Sonny and the crapulent major, who observed the patient with great patience as they stood in one corner—the commissar sat down on a wooden chair, the only furnishing in the room besides the patient's mattress. Please, the patient said, just let me rest. The commissar said nothing until the next burst of static electricity jarred the patient. Then he leaned forward and showed the patient a thin book heretofore hidden from him. We found this in your quarters at the General's villa.

Q. What is the title?
A. *KUBARK Counterintelligence Interrogation*, 1963.
Q. What is *KUBARK*?
A. A cryptonym for the CIA.
Q. What is the CIA?
A. The Central Intelligence Agency of the USA.
Q. What is the USA?
A. The United States of America.

You see that I hide nothing from you, the commissar said, leaning back. I have read your marginal notes, taken account of your underlined passages. Everything being done to you comes from this book. In other words, yours is an open-book exam. There are no surprises.

Sleep . . .

No. I am observing you to see if this serum is working. A gift from the KGB, although we both know what the great powers expect for their gifts. They have tested their techniques, their weapons, and their ideas on our small country. We have been the subjects of that experiment they call, with a straight face, the Cold War. What a joke, given how hot the war has been for us! Funny but not so funny, for you and I are together the butt of this joke. (I thought *we* were the butt of the joke, said Sonny. Hush, said the crapulent major. I want to hear this. It's going to be rich!) As always, the commissar continued, we have appropriated their techniques and technology. These lightbulbs? Manufactured in the USA, and the generator that powers them as well, although the gasoline is a Soviet import.

Please, turn off the lights, the patient said, sweating from the heat generated by the grid of bulbs. Hearing no response, he repeated himself, and when he still heard nothing, he realized that the commissar had left. He closed his eyes, and for a moment he thought he was asleep, until the electricity bit his toe. I've been subjected to these techniques myself at the Farm, Claude had told the class. They work even if you know what is being done to you. He was referring to the techniques in the mimeographed *KUBARK* manual now in the commissar's hands, the required reading for the interrogation course. The patient, before he was a patient and when he was only a pupil, had read this book several times. He had memorized its plot, characters, and devices, and he understood the importance of isolation, sensory deprivation, joint interrogators, and penetration agents. He had mastered the Ivan Is a Dope technique, the Wolf in Sheep's Clothing technique, the Alice in Wonderland technique, the All-Seeing Eye technique, the Nobody Loves You technique. In short, he knew this book inside and out, including its stress on an unpredictable routine. Thus it was no surprise when the baby-faced guard came in and reattached the wire to one of his fingers. While the baby-faced guard was rewrapping his foot, the patient mumbled something even he did not understand, to which the baby-faced guard said nothing at all. This baby-faced guard was the one who had shown the patient his tattoo, BORN IN THE NORTH TO DIE IN THE SOUTH, scripted in blue ink on his biceps. As he was in the last division to march on Saigon, however, the war was over by the time he arrived to liberate the city. But his tattoo might still be prophetic. He had nearly died already from the syphilis given to him by a prisoner's visiting wife, who had paid her bribe with the only resource she had. Please, turn off the lights, the patient said. But the baby-faced guard was no longer tending to him. It was a teenage guard, delivering his food. Hadn't he just eaten? He wasn't hungry, but the teenage guard forced the rice gruel down his throat with a metal spoon. The schedule of his basic necessities must be disrupted, his feeding schedule irregular and unpredictable, exactly according to the book. Like a doctor studying a fatal disease that suddenly afflicts him, he knew everything that had happened and would happen to him, and yet it made no difference. He attempted to tell this to the teenage guard, who told him to shut up before kicking him in the ribs and leaving. The electric wire bit him again, only this time it was not clipped to his finger but to his ear. He shook his head but the wire would not release its jaws, nagging at him to stay awake. His mind was raw and chapped, as his mother's nipples must have been after he fed on them. My hungry baby, she called him. Just a few hours old, you couldn't even open your eyes and yet you knew exactly where to find my milk. And once you latched on, you wouldn't let go! You demanded it every hour on the hour. That first soupçon of his mother's milk must have been perfection, but he could not remember what it tasted like. All he knew was what it did *not* taste like: fear, the sharp, metallic tinge of a nine-volt battery rubbed on his tongue.

Q. How do you feel?

The commissar had returned, looming over the patient in his white lab coat, surgical mask, and stainless steel goggles, his hands in white rubber gloves, holding a notepad and a pen.

Q. I said, how are you feeling?
A. I can't feel my body.

Q. But can you feel your mind?
A. My mind feels everything.
Q. Now do you remember?
A. What?
Q. Do you remember what you have forgotten?

And it occurred to the patient that he did remember what he had forgotten, and that if he could just articulate it, the wire would be removed from the tip of his nose, the taste of a battery in his mouth would go away, the lights would be turned off, and he could, at last, sleep. He wept, his tears falling into the vast waters of his forgetting, and that slight saline change to the liquid constitution of his amnesia provoked the obsidian past to rise. An obelisk slowly emerged from his ocean of disremembering, the resurrection of what he did not even know was dead since it had been buried at sea. Engraved on the obelisk were hieroglyphs—cryptic images of three mice, a series of rectangles, undulating curves, a scattering of kanji . . . and a movie projector, for what had been forgotten, he now remembered, had occurred in the room they called the movie theater.

Q. Who called it the movie theater?
A. The policemen.
Q. Why is it called the movie theater?
A. When foreigners visit, the room is a movie theater.
Q. And when foreigners are not visiting?
A. . . .
Q. And when foreigners are not visiting?

A. Interrogations are done there.

Q. How are interrogations done?

A. There are so many ways.

Q. What is one example?

One example! There were so many to choose from. The telephone call, of course, and the plane ride, and the water drum, and the ingenious, scarless method involving pins, paper, and an electric fan, and the massage, and the lizards, and the spot burns, and the eel. None of them were written in the book. Even Claude did not know their origins, only that they had been practiced long before his entry into the guild. (This is going on for far too long, said the crapulent major. He's had enough. No, said Sonny. He's really sweating now. We're starting to get somewhere!)

Q. Who was in the movie theater?

A. The three policemen. The major. Claude.

Q. Who else was in the movie theater?

A. Me.

Q. Who else was in the movie theater?

A. . . .

Q. Who else—

A. The communist agent.

Q. What happened to her?

How could he have forgotten the agent with the papier-mâché evidence in her mouth? His own name was written on the list of policemen she had been trying to swallow when she was caught. Watching her in the movie theater, he was certain that she was unaware of his true identity, though he was the one who had passed the list to Man. But the agent, being Man's courier, knew who Man was. She lay in the center of the capacious room, naked on a table covered with a black rubber sheet, hands and feet roped to the table's four legs. The movie theater was lit only by overhead fluorescent lighting, its blackout curtains puckered shut. Pushed haphazardly against the walls were gray metal folding chairs, while in the back of the room stood a Sony movie projector. On the opposite wall the movie screen served as the backdrop, from where Claude watched by the projector, of the agent's interrogation. The crapulent major was in charge, but having abdicated his role to the three policemen in the movie theater, he sat watching from a folding chair, his face unhappy and sweating.

Q. Where were you?
A. With Claude.
Q. What did you do?
A. I watched.
Q. What did you see?

Later, sometime in the bright future, the commissar would play the patient a tape recording of his answer, though he had no memory of the tape recorder's presence. Many people who heard their voices on tape thought that they did not sound like themselves, which they found disturbing, and he was no exception. He heard this stranger's voice say, I

saw everything. Claude told me that this was nasty business, but that I had to see it. I said, Is this really necessary?
Claude said, Talk to the major. He's in charge. I'm just the
adviser. So I went to the major, who said, There's nothing I
can do about it. Nothing! The General wants to know how
she got the names and he wants to know now. But this is
wrong, I said. Don't you see? This doesn't need to be done.
The major sat there and said nothing, and Claude, standing
by the movie projector, was also silent. Just give me some
time alone with her, I said to the three policemen. Although
the Americans called our policemen white mice because of
their white dress uniforms and hats, none of these three were
mouselike. They were average specimens of national manhood, slim and gaunt with deeply tanned skin from riding
in jeeps and on motorcycles. Instead of head-to-toe dress
whites, they wore field uniforms of white shirts and light
blue pants, their light blue caps doffed. Just give me a couple
of hours with her, I said. The youngest policeman snorted.
He just wants first dibs. I turned red with fury and shame,
and the oldest policeman said, The American's not worrying
about this. Neither should you. Here, have a Coke. In the
corner was a Frigidaire full of soda, and the oldest policeman, who already had an open bottle in his hand, pressed it
into mine before ushering me to the chair next to the major.
I sat down and the fingers of my hand, holding the ice-cold
bottle, began to go numb.

Please, sirs! cried the agent. I'm innocent! I swear! That
explains why you got a list with all those policemen's names
on it? said the youngest. You just found that lying around

somewhere and then got so hungry you had to try to eat it? No, no, sobbed the agent. She needed a good story to cover herself but for some reason she could not come up with it, not that any story could divert the policemen. All right, said the middle-aged one, unbuckling his belt and unzipping his pants. He was already erect, his eleventh finger protruding from his boxers. The agent moaned and turned her eyes away to the other side of the table, only to find the youngest policeman standing there. Having already dropped his pants, he was pumping himself furiously with one hand. Sitting behind him, all I saw were the sunken cheeks of his naked buttocks, as well as the horror in the agent's eyes. She saw that this was not an interrogation but a sentence, written by the policemen with the instruments in their hands. The oldest, who must have been a father, was fondling the stubby length of the ugliest part of most adult male bodies. This was fully evident to me now that the youngest policeman had turned in profile, bringing himself closer to the agent's face. Come on, take a look, he said. He likes you! The three engorged members differed in length, one pointing up, another down, the third bent to the side. Please don't do this! the agent cried, eyes shut and head shaking. I beg you! The oldest policeman laughed. Look at that flat nose and dark skin. She's got some Cambodian in her, or maybe Cham. They're hot-blooded.

Let's start easy, the middle-aged policeman said, climbing up awkwardly onto the table between her legs. What's your name? She said nothing, but when he repeated the question, something primitive awoke in her, and when she opened her eyes to look at the policeman, she said, My surname is Viet and my given name is Nam. For a moment, the three policemen were speechless. Then they burst into laughter. This bitch is asking for it, said the youngest. The middle-aged one, still laughing, ponderously lowered himself onto the agent as she screamed and screamed. Watching the policeman grunting and pounding, and the other two shuffling around the table with their pants around their ankles, ugly knees exposed, it seemed to me that they were, after all, mice, gathered around a block of cheese. My countrymen never understood the concept of a queue, no one wanting to be at the end of a line, and as these three mice jostled one another and obstructed my view, all I could see were their sweaty nether regions and the agent's thrashing legs. She was no longer screaming becaus she no longer could, the youngest policeman having silenced her. Hurry up, he said. What's taking so long? I'll take as long as I please, said the middle-aged one. You're enjoying yourself with her anyway, aren't you? (Stop talking about this! cried the crapulent major, clapping his hands over his eyes. I can't look!) But we were helpless except to watch as the middle-aged policeman at last convulsed with a tremendous spasm. Pleasure of this degree should always be kept private, unless everyone was participating, as in a carnival or an orgy. Here, the pleasure was hideous to those who only looked. My turn, said the youngest, detaching himself from the agent, who was able to scream once more until the oldest took the youngest policeman's place, silencing her. What a mess, said the youngest, hiking up his shirt. He took his position on the table, undeterred by the mess, and even as the middle-aged policeman zipped up his pants over the frizzy toupee crowning his deflated self, the youngest began repeating his predecessor's motions, reaching, in a few minutes, the same obscene conclusion. Then it was the oldest policeman's turn, and when he climbed onto the table, he left me an unimpeded view of the agent's face. Although she was now free to scream, she no longer did, or no longer could. She was staring directly at me, but with the screws of pain tightened on her jaws and eyes, those screws that turned ever more, I had the feeling she did not see me at all.

After the oldest was finished, the room was quiet except for the agent's sobbing and the hiss of the cigarettes being smoked by the other policemen. The oldest, catching me looking at him as he tucked his shirt in, shrugged. Somebody else would do it. So why not us? The youngest said, Don't waste your time talking to him. He couldn't get it up to give her the treatment anyway. Look, he hasn't even touched his soda. It was true, I had forgotten the bottle in my hand. It was no longer even cold. If you're not going to drink it, the middle-aged one said, give it to me. I did not move and the exasperated policeman walked three paces to me and seized the bottle. He took a sip and made a face. I hate warm soda. He said this with malevolence and offered me back the bottle, but I could only look blankly at it, my mind as numb as my fingers had been. Wait a minute, said the oldest. No need to make the man drink warm soda when this one here needs a good washing. He patted the agent's knee, and at that touch, and at those words, she came back to life, rearing her head and glaring at us all with a hatred so intense that every man in the room should have turned to cinders and smoke. But nothing happened. We remained flesh and blood, and so did she as the middle-aged policeman laughed, putting his thumb over the bottle's mouth and shaking it vigorously. Good idea, he said. But it's going to be sticky!

Yes, memory was sticky. I must have stepped on some of that soda, even though afterward the policemen had splashed buckets of water on the agent and the table, then mopped the tile floor. (I ordered them to do that, said the crapulent major. They weren't happy about cleaning up after themselves, I can tell you that.) As for the agent, left on the table still naked, she no longer screamed or even sobbed but was dead silent, eyes closed once more, head flung back, back arched. After the policemen had flushed themselves from her, they left the drained bottle inside, buried to the throat of its neck. I can see right into her, said the middle-aged policeman, bending down to peer through the bottom of the bottle with gynecological interest. Let me see, said the youngest, shouldering him aside. I don't see a thing, he complained. It's a joke, you idiot! shouted the oldest. A joke! Yes, a very bad joke, a slapstick travesty that one understands in any language, as Claude did. While the policemen played doctor with their makeshift speculum, he came up to me and said, Just so you know? I didn't teach them how to do that. The bottle, I mean. They came up with it all on their own.

They were good students, just like me. They learned their lesson well, and so have I, so if you would please just turn off the lights, if you would please just turn off the telephone, if you would just stop calling me, if you would remember that the two of us were once and perhaps still are the best of friends, if you could see that I have nothing left to confess, if history's ship had taken a different tack, if I had become an accountant, if I had fallen in love with the right woman, if I had been a more virtuous lover, if my mother had been less of a mother, if my father had gone to save souls in Algeria instead of here, if the commandant did not need to make me over, if my own people did not suspect me, if they saw me as one of them, if we forgot our resentment, if we forgot revenge, if we acknowledged that we are all puppets in someone else's play, if we had not fought a war against each other, if some of us had not called ourselves nationalists or communists or capitalists or realists, if our bonzes had not incinerated themselves, if the Americans hadn't come to save us from ourselves, if we had not bought what they sold, if the Soviets had never called us comrades, if Mao had not sought to do the same, if the Japanese hadn't taught us the superiority of the yellow race, if the French had never sought to civilize us, if Ho Chi Minh had not been dialectical and Karl Marx not analytical, if the invisible hand of the market did not hold us by the scruffs of our necks, if the British had defeated the rebels of the new world, if the natives had simply said, Hell no, on first seeing the white man, if our emperors and mandarins had not clashed among themselves, if the Chinese had never ruled us for a thousand years, if they had used gunpowder for more than fireworks, if the Buddha had never lived, if the Bible had never been written and Jesus Christ never sacrificed, if Adam and Eve still frolicked in the Garden of Eden, if the dragon lord and the fairy queen had not given birth to us, if the two of them had not parted ways, if fifty of their children had not followed their fairy mother to the mountains, if fifty more had not followed their dragon father to the sea, if legend's phoenix had truly soared from its own ashes rather than simply crashed and burned in our countryside, if there were no Light and no Word, if Heaven and earth had never parted, if history had never happened, neither as farce nor as tragedy, if the serpent of language had not bitten me, if I had never been born, if my mother was never cleft, if you needed no more revisions, and if I saw no more of these visions, please, could you please just let me sleep?

CHAPTER 22

Of course you cannot sleep. Revolutionaries are insomniacs, too afraid of history's nightmare to sleep, too troubled by the world's ills to be less than awake, or so the commandant said. He spoke as I lay on my mattress, a specimen on a slide under a microscope, and with a shutter's smooth snick, I realized that the doctor's experiment had succeeded. I was divided, tormented body below, placid consciousness floating high above, beyond the illuminated ceiling, buffeted from my agony through an invisible gyroscopic mechanism. Seen from this altitude, the vivisection being done to me was actually very interesting, leaving my wobbly body's yolk shimmering beneath my viscous white mind. Thus simultaneously subjugated and elevated, I was beyond the comprehension of even Sonny and the crapulent major, who remained on the plane of my chronic sleeplessness, peering over the shoulders of the doctor, the commandant, and the commissar as they stood around me, no longer in lab coats, scrubs, and stainless steel goggles but in yellow uniforms with red tabs of rank, pistols holstered on their hips. While those below were human and ghost, I was the supernatural Holy Spirit, clairvoyant and clairaudient. In this detached way, I saw the commandant kneel down and reach his hand toward my subhuman self, index finger slowly extending until it pressed lightly on my open eyeball, a touch at which my poor body flinched.

MYSELF

Please, let me sleep.

THE COMMANDANT

You can sleep when I'm satisfied with your confession.

MYSELF

But I've done nothing!

THE COMMANDANT

Exactly.

MYSELF

The lights are too bright. If you could—

THE COMMANDANT

The world watched what happened to our country and most of the world did nothing. Not only that—they also took great pleasure in it. You are no exception.

MYSELF

I spoke out, didn't I? Is it my fault no one listened?

THE COMMANDANT

Don't make excuses! We didn't whine. We were all willing to be martyrs. It's only pure luck that the doctor, the commissar, and myself are alive. You simply weren't willing to sacrifice yourself to save the agent, though she was willing to sacrifice her life to save the commissar's.

MYSELF

No, I—

THE COMMANDANT and
THE COMMISSAR and
THE DOCTOR (in unison)

Admit it!

I saw myself admit it then. I heard myself acknowledge that I was not being punished or reeducated for the things I had done, but for the thing I had not done. I wept and cried without shame for the shame I felt. I was guilty of the crime of doing nothing. I was the man to whom things are done because he had done nothing! And not only did I weep and cry; I howled, a tornado of feeling causing the windows of my soul to shudder and clack. The sight and sound of my abjection was so disturbing that everyone averted his eyes from the sorry mess I had made of myself, except for the commandant, the commissar, and I.

THE COMMISSAR

Satisfied?

THE COMMANDANT

So he's admitted to doing nothing. But what about the Bru comrade and the Watchman?

THE COMMISSAR

He couldn't have done anything to save the Bru comrade and the Watchman. As for the agent, she lived.

THE COMMANDANT

She couldn't even walk when we liberated her.

THE COMMISSAR

Perhaps she was broken in body, but not in spirit.

THE DOCTOR

What happened to those policemen?

THE COMMISSAR

I found them.

THE COMMANDANT

They paid the price. Shouldn't he?

THE COMMISSAR

Yes, but he should also receive credit for the lives he took.

THE COMMANDANT

Sonny and the major? Their pitiful lives aren't even equal to the agent's injuries.

THE COMMISSAR

But is his father's life equal?

My father? What was this? Even Sonny and the crapulent major, appalled at the harsh evaluation of their lives and deaths, paused in their agitation to listen.

THE COMMANDANT

What did he do to his father?

THE COMMISSAR

Ask him yourself.

THE COMMANDANT

You! Look at me! What did you do to your father?

MYSELF

I didn't do anything to my father!

THE COMMANDANT and
THE COMMISSAR and
THE DOCTOR (in unison)

Admit it!

And looking down on my weeping, yolked self, I did not know whether I should laugh or cry in sympathy. Did I not remember what I had written to Man about my father? *I wish he were dead.*

MYSELF

But I didn't mean it!

THE COMMISSAR

Be honest with yourself.

MYSELF

I didn't mean for you to do it!

THE COMMISSAR

Of course you did! Who did you think you were writing to?

I was writing to the revolutionary who was on a powerful committee and who knew, even then, that he might one day be a commissar; I was writing to a political cadre already learning the plastic art of making over the souls and minds of men; I was writing to a friend who would do whatever I asked; I was writing to a writer who valued the force of a sentence and the weight of the word; I was writing to a brother who knew what I wanted more than I knew it myself.

THE COMMANDANT and
THE COMMISSAR and
THE DOCTOR (in unison)

What did you do?

MYSELF

I wanted him dead!

The commandant rubbed his chin and looked doubtfully at the doctor, who shrugged. The doctor only cracked open bodies and minds; he was not responsible for what was found.

THE DOCTOR

How did his father die?

THE COMMISSAR

A bullet in the head, listening to his assassin's confession.

THE COMMANDANT

I wouldn't put it past you to make up this story to save him.

THE COMMISSAR

Ask my agent. She arranged the father's death.

The commandant gazed down at me. If I could be guilty of doing nothing, shouldn't I also be deserving of wanting something? In this case, my father's death. This father, in the commandant's atheistic mind, was a colonizer, a dealer in the opiate of the masses, a spokesman for a God for whom millions of dark-skinned people had been sacrificed, supposedly for their own salvation, a burning cross lighting their hard road to Heaven. His death was not murder but a just sentence, which was all that I had ever wanted to write.

THE COMMANDANT

I'll think about it.

The commandant turned and departed, the doctor obediently following, leaving Sonny and the crapulent major to watch as the commissar slowly settled into the chair with a grimace.

THE COMMISSAR

What a pair we are.

MYSELF

Turn off the lights. I can't see.

THE COMMISSAR

What is more precious than independence and freedom?

MYSELF

Happiness?

THE COMMISSAR

What is more precious than independence and freedom?

MYSELF

Love?

THE COMMISSAR

What is more precious than independence and freedom?

MYSELF

I don't know!

THE COMMISSAR

What is more precious than independence and
freedom?

MYSELF

I wish I was dead!

There, I had said it, sobbing and howling. Now, at last, I knew
what it was that I wanted for myself, what so many people
wanted for me. Sonny and the crapulent major applauded
in approval, while the commissar drew his pistol. At last!
Death would hurt only for a moment, which was not so
bad when one considered how much, and for how long, life
hurt. The sound of the bullet loading into the chamber was
as clear as the bell of my father's church, which my mother
and I heard from our hovel every Sunday morning. Looking
down on my self, I could still see the child in the man and
the man in the child. I was ever always divided, although
it was only partially my fault. While I chose to live two
lives and be a man of two minds, it was hard not to, given
how people had always called me a bastard. Our country
itself was cursed, bastardized, partitioned into north and
south, and if it could be said of us that we chose division
and death in our uncivil war, that was also only partially
true. We had not chosen to be debased by the French, to be
divided by them into an unholy trinity of north, center, and
south, to be turned over to the great powers of capitalism
and communism for a further bisection, then given roles
as the clashing armies of a Cold War chess match played
in air-conditioned rooms by white men wearing suits and

lies. No, just as my abused generation was divided before birth, so was I divided on birth, delivered into a postpartum world where hardly anyone accepted me for who I was, but only ever bullied me into choosing between my two sides. This was not simply hard to do—no, it was truly impossible, for how could I choose me against myself? Now my friend would release me from this small world with its small-minded people, those mobs who treated a man with two minds and two faces as a freak, who wanted only one answer for any question.

But wait—what was he doing? He had put the gun on the floor and knelt by my side, untying the sack around my right hand, then untying the rope binding it. I saw myself holding my hand before my eyes, scored with the red mark of our brotherhood. Through those subhuman eyes and through my supernatural gaze above, I saw my friend place the pistol in my hand, a Tokarev. The Soviets had based their design on the American Colt, and while its weight was not unfamiliar, I could not hold the pistol upright on my own, forcing my friend to wrap my fingers around the grip.

THE COMMISSAR
You are the only one who can do this for me. Will you?

And here he leaned forward, pressing the muzzle between his eyes, his hands steadying my own.

MYSELF
Why are you doing this?

As I spoke, I cried. He, too, wept, tears rolling down the hideous absence of a face that I had not seen this close in years. Where was the brother of my youth, vanished from everywhere except my memory? There, and only there, his earnest face remained, serious and idealistic, with high, pronounced cheekbones; thin, narrow lips; an aristocratic, slim nose; and an expansive brow hinting at a powerful intelligence whose tidal force had worn away the hairline. All that was left to be recognized were the eyes, kept alive by tears, and the timbre of his voice.

THE COMMISSAR

I'm crying because I can hardly bear to see you so afflicted. But I cannot save you except to have you afflicted. The commandant would not have it otherwise.

At this I laughed, although the body on the mattress only trembled.

MYSELF

How is this saving me?

He smiled through his tears. I recognized the smile, too, the whitest I had ever seen among any of my people, befitting a dentist's son. What had changed was not the smile but the face, or the lack of it, so that this white smile floated in a void, the horrible grin of a Cheshire cat.

THE COMMISSAR

We are in an impossible situation. The commandant will let you leave only when you redeem yourself. But what about Bon? And even if he can leave, what will you two do?

MYSELF

If Bon can't leave . . . neither can I.

THE COMMISSAR

And so you will die here.

He pressed the barrel of the gun against his head even harder.

THE COMMISSAR

Shoot me first. Not because of my face. I would not die for its sake. I would only exile myself here so that my family need never see this *thing* again. But I would live.

I was no longer my body or myself, I was only the gun, and through its steel came the vibrations of his words, signaling the impending arrival of a locomotive that would crush us both.

THE COMMISSAR

I am the commissar, but what kind of school do I oversee? One in which you, of all people, are reeducated. It is not because you did nothing that you are here. It is because you are too educated that you are being reeducated. But what have you learned?

MYSELF

I watched and did nothing!

THE COMMISSAR

I will tell you what cannot be found in any book. In every town, village, and ward the cadres deliver the same lectures. They reassure those citizens not in reeducation of our good intentions. But the committees and the commissars do not care about remaking these prisoners. Everyone knows this and no one will say it aloud. All the jargon that the cadres spout only hides an awful truth—

MYSELF

I wanted my father dead!

THE COMMISSAR

Now that we are the powerful, we don't need the French or the Americans to fuck us over. We can fuck ourselves just fine.

The glare above my body was blinding. I was no longer certain whether I could see everything or nothing, and under the heat of the lights my palm was slick with perspiration. My grip on the pistol was slippery, but the commissar's hands held the barrel in place.

THE COMMISSAR

If anyone besides you knew that I had spoken the unspeakable, I would be reeducated. But it is not reeducation that I fear. It is the education I have that terrifies me. How can

a teacher live teaching something he does not believe in?
How do I live seeing you like this? I cannot. Now pull
the trigger.

I think I said that I would rather shoot myself first, but I could
not hear myself, and when I tried to pull the gun away from his
head and turn it toward my own, I did not have the strength.
Those relentless eyes stared down at me, now dry as bones, and
from somewhere deep inside of him came a rumble. Then the
rumble burst forth, and he was laughing. What was so funny?
This black comedy? No, that was too heavy. This illuminated
room allowed for only a light comedy, a white comedy where
one could die from laughter, not that he laughed that long. He
stopped laughing when he let go of my hand, my arm dropping
to my side and the pistol clattering on the cement floor. Behind
the commissar, Sonny and the crapulent major stared with
longing at the Tokarev. Either one would have been happy to
pick it up and shoot me if he could, but they no longer possessed their bodies. As for the commissar and I, we had bodies
but could not shoot, and perhaps that made the commissar
laugh. The void that had been his face still loomed above me,
his hilarity having passed with such rapidity I was not sure I
had heard correctly. I thought I saw sadness in that void, but
I could not be certain. Only the eyes and teeth expressed any
emotion, and he no longer cried or smiled.

THE COMMISSAR
I apologize. That was selfish and weak of me. If I died,
you would die, and then Bon. The commandant can't

wait to drag him before the firing squad. At least now
you can save yourself and our friend, if not me. That I
can live with.

MYSELF

Please, can we talk of this after I sleep?

THE COMMISSAR

First answer my question.

MYSELF

But why?

The commissar holstered his pistol. Then he tied my free
hand down once more and stood up. He gazed down on
me from a great height, and perhaps it was because of the
foreshortened angle, but I saw in his absence of a face something else besides horror . . . a faint shadow cast by madness,
although perhaps it was merely an ocular effect created by
the glare behind his head.

THE COMMISSAR

My friend, the commandant may let you go because you
wanted your father dead, but I will let you go only when
you can answer my question. Just remember, my brother,
that I do this for your own good.

He raised his hand to me in farewell, and on his palm blazed
the red mark of our oath. With that, he left. Those are the
most dangerous words you can hear, Sonny said, sitting
down on the vacated chair. The crapulent major joined him,
pushing him aside for room. "For your own good" can only

mean something bad, he said. As if on cue, the speakers mounted high in the corners clicked and hummed, the ones I had only noticed when the commissar played for me my own stranger's voice. The question of what would be done to me was answered when somebody began screaming, and while Sonny and the crapulent major could clap their hands over their ears I could not. But even with ears protected, Sonny and the crapulent major could not endure this screaming for more than a minute, this shrieking of a baby in torment, and in the blink of an eye they, too, vanished.

Somewhere a baby was screaming, its suffering shared with me, who needed no more. I saw myself squeeze my eyes shut, as if that could also squeeze my ears shut. It was impossible to think with the screaming in this examination room, and for the first time in a very long time I wanted something more than sleep. I wanted silence. Oh, please—I heard myself crying this aloud—stop! Then another click, and the screaming ceased. A tape! I was listening to a tape. No baby was being tortured in some nearby chamber, its howls piped into mine. It was just a recording, and for a few more moments I only had to worry about the unceasing light and heat and the rubber band snap of the electric wire against my little toe. But then I heard the click again, and my body clenched in anticipation. Somebody began screaming once more. Somebody was screaming so loudly that I not only lost track of myself, I lost track of time. Time no longer ran straight as a railroad; time no longer rotated on a dial; time no longer crawled under my back; time was infinitely looping, a cassette tape repeating without end; time howled in my ear, screaming with laughter at the idea that we could control it with wristwatches, alarm clocks, revolutions, history. We were, all of us, running out of time, except for the malevolent baby. The baby who was screaming had all the time in the world, and the irony was that the baby did not even know it.

Please—I heard myself again—stop! I'll do anything you want! How was it that the most vulnerable creature in the world could also be the most powerful? Did I scream like this at my mother? If so, forgive me, Mama! If I screamed, it was not because of you. I am one but I am also two, made from an egg and a sperm, and if I screamed, it must be because of those blue genes gleaned from my father. I saw it now, that moment of my origin, the Chinese acrobat of time bent impossibly back on itself so that I could see the invasion of my mother's womb by my father's dumb, masculine horde, a howling gang of hel-meted, hell-bent nomads intent on piercing the great wall of my mother's egg. From this invasion, the nothing that I was became the somebody that I am. *Somebody was screaming and it was not the baby.* My cell divided, and divided, and divided again, until I was a million cells and more, until I was multi-tudes and multitudes, my own country, my own nation, the emperor and dictator of the masses of myself, commanding my mother's undivided attention. *Somebody was screaming and it was the agent.* I was packed tight into my mother's aquarium, knowing nothing of independence and freedom, witness by all my senses except the sense of sight to the uncanniest experience of all, being inside another human being. I was a doll within a doll, hypnotized by a metronome ticking with perfect regular-ity, my mother's strong and steady heartbeat. *Somebody was screaming and it was my mother.* Her voice was the first sound I heard when I emerged headfirst, thrust into a humid room as warm as the womb, seized by the gnarled hands of an unimpressed doula who would tell me, years later, how she had used her sharpened thumbnail to slice the tight frenulum holding down my tongue, the better for me to suckle and to talk. This was also the woman who told me, with glee, of how my mother pushed so hard she expelled not only me but also the waste from her bowels, washing me onto the shores of a strange new world in a maternal effluence of blood and excrement. *Somebody was screaming and I did not know who it was.* My leash was cut and my naked, smeared purple self was turned toward a throbbing light, revealing to me a world of shadows and dim shapes speaking my mother tongue, a foreign language. *Somebody was screaming and I knew who it was.* It was me, screaming the one word that had dangled before me since the question was first asked—nothing—the answer that I could neither see nor hear until now —nothing!—the answer I screamed again and again and again—*nothing!*—because I was, at last, enlightened.

CHAPTER 23

With that one word, I completed my reeducation. All that remains to be told is how I glued myself back together, and how I found myself where I am now, preparing for a watery departure from my country. Like everything else of consequence in my life, neither task was easy. Leaving, in particular, is not something that I want to do but is something I must do. What in life is left for me, or any of the other graduates of reeducation? No place exists for us in this revolutionary society, even for those who think of ourselves as revolutionaries. We cannot be represented here, and this knowledge hurts more than anything done to me in my examination. Pain ends but knowledge does not, at least until the mind rots away—and when would that ever happen for me, the man with two minds?

The end of pain, at least, began when I spoke that one word. In retrospect the answer was obvious. So why did it take me so long to understand? Why did I have to be educated and reeducated for so many years, and at such great expense to both the American taxpayer and Vietnamese society, not to mention considerable damage to myself, in order to see, at last, the word that was there at the very beginning? The answer was so absurd that now, months later and in the temporary safety of the navigator's house, I laugh even as I reread this scene of my enlightenment, which itself devolved—or is it evolved?— from screams to laughter. Of course I was still screaming when the commissar came to turn off the light and sound. I was still screaming when he unbound me and embraced me, cradling my head against his breast until my screams subsided. There, there, he said in the dark examination room, silent at last except for my sobbing. Now you know what I know, don't you? Yes, I said, sobbing still. I get it. I get it!

What was it that I got? *The joke.* Nothing was the punch line, and if part of me was rather hurt at being punched— by nothing, no less!—the other part of me thought it was hilarious. That was why, as I shook and shuddered in that dark examination room, my wailing and sobbing turned to howls of laughter. I laughed so hard that eventually the baby-faced guard and the commandant came to investigate the cause of the commotion. What's so funny? the commandant demanded. Nothing! I cried. I was, at last, broken. I had, at last, spoken. Don't you get it? I cried. The answer is nothing! Nothing, nothing, *nothing!*

Only the commissar understood what I meant. The commandant, flustered by my bizarre behavior, said, Look what you've done to him. He's out of his mind. He was not so much concerned with me as he was about the camp's health, for a madman who kept on saying nothing would be bad for morale. I was mad that it had taken me so long to understand nothing, even though my failure, in hindsight, was inevitable. A good student cannot understand nothing; only the class clown, the misunderstood idiot, the devious fool, and the perpetual joker can do that. Still, such a realization could not spare me from the pain of overlooking the obvious, the pain that drove me to push the commissar away, to beat my fists against my forehead.

Stop that! said the commandant. He turned to the baby-faced guard. Stop him!

The baby-faced guard struggled with me as I beat not only my fists against my forehead, but my head against the wall. Finally, the commissar and the commandant themselves had to help him tie me down again. Only the commissar understood that I had to beat myself. I was so stupid! How could I forget that every truth meant at least two things, that slogans were empty suits draped on the corpse of an idea? The suits depended on how one wore them, and this suit was now worn out. I was mad but not insane, although I was not going to disabuse the commandant. He saw only one meaning in nothing—the negative, the absence, as in *there's nothing there*. The *positive* meaning eluded him, the paradoxical fact that nothing is, indeed, something. Our commandant was a man who didn't get the joke, and people who do not get the joke are dangerous people indeed. They are the ones who say nothing with great piousness, who ask everyone else to die for nothing, who revere nothing. Such a man could not tolerate someone who laughed at nothing. Satisfied? he asked the commissar, both of them looking down on me, sobbing, weeping, and laughing all at the same time. Now we have to call in the doctor again.

Call him in, then, said the commissar. The hard part's done.

The doctor moved me back to my old isolation cell, although now the chamber was unlocked and I was not shackled. I was free to go as I pleased but was reluctant to do so, sometimes needing the baby-faced guard to coax me out of the corners. Even on those rare occasions when I emerged voluntarily, it was never into sunlight, but only the night, a conjunctivitis having rendered my eyes sensitive to the solarized world. The doctor prescribed an improved diet, sunlight, and exercise, but all I wanted was to sleep, and when I was not sleeping, I was somnambulent and silent, except for when the commandant came. Is he still not saying anything? the commandant asked whenever he dropped by, to which I said, Nothing, nothing, nothing, a grinning simpleton huddled in the corner. Poor fellow, said the doctor. He is a little, how shall we say, discombobulated after his experiences.

Well, do something about it! cried the commandant.

I'll do my best, but it's all in his mind, the doctor said, pointing at my bruised forehead. The doctor was only half right. It was certainly all in my mind, but which one? Eventually, however, the doctor did hit on the treatment that put me on the slow road to recovery, its end the reunification of me with myself. Perhaps, he said one day, sitting on a chair next to me as I huddled in the corner, arms folded and head resting on them, a familiar activity might help you. I peered at him with one eye. Before your examination began, your days were occupied by writing your confession. Your state of mind is such that I don't think you can write anything now, but perhaps just going through the motions may help. I peered at him with both eyes. From his briefcase, he extracted a thick stack of paper. Does this look familiar? Cautiously, I unfolded my arms and took the stack. I looked at the first page, then the second, and the third, slowly thumbing my way through the numbered sheaf of 295 pages. What do you think that is? said the doctor. My confession, I muttered. Exactly, dear fellow! Very good! Now what I want you to do is to copy this confession. Out came another stack of paper from his briefcase, as well as a handful of pens. Word for word. Can you do that for me?

I nodded slowly. He left me alone with my two stacks of paper, and for a very long time—it must have been hours—I stared at the first blank page, pen in trembling hand. And then I began, my tongue between my lips. At first I could copy only a few words an hour, then a page an hour, and then a few pages an hour. My drool dotted the pages as I saw my entire life unfold over the months it took to copy the confession. Gradually, as my bruised forehead healed, and as I absorbed my own words, I developed a growing sympathy for the man in these pages, the intelligence operative of doubtful intelligence. Was he a fool or too smart for his own good? Had he chosen the right side or the wrong side of history? And were not these the questions we should all ask ourselves? Or was it only me and myself who should be so concerned?

By the time I finished copying my confession, enough of my senses had returned for me to understand that the answers were not to be found in those pages. When the doctor next came to examine me, I asked for a favor. What is it, dear fellow? More paper, Doctor. More paper! I explained that I wanted to write the story of those events that had happened after my confession, in the interminable time of my examination. So he brought me more paper, and I wrote new pages about what had been done to me in the examination room. I felt very sorry for the man with two minds, as would be expected. He had not realized that such a man best belonged in a low-budget movie, a Hollywood film or perhaps a Japanese one about a military-grade science experiment gone terribly awry. How dare a man with two minds think he could represent himself much less anyone else, including his own recalcitrant people? They would never, in the end, be representable at all, regardless of what their representatives claimed. But as the pages mounted, I felt something else that surprised me: sympathy for the man who did those things to me. Would he, my friend, not also be tortured by the things he had done to me? I was certain he would be by the time I finished writing, by the time I concluded with me screaming that one awful word into the bright, shining light. All that remained after the certainty was to ask the doctor to let me see the commissar once more.

That is a very good idea, the doctor said, patting the pages of my manuscript and nodding with satisfaction. You are nearly done, my boy. You are nearly done.

I had not seen the commissar since the examination's conclusion. He had left me alone to begin my recovery, and I can only think that it was because he, too, was conflicted over what he had done to me, even though what was done to me had to be done, for I had to come to the answer myself. No one could tell me the solution to his riddle, not even him. All he could do was speed up my reeducation through the regrettable method of pain. Having used such a method, he was reluctant to see me again, reasonably expecting my hatred. Meeting him in his quarters for our next and last meeting, I could see that he was uneasy, offering me tea, tapping his fingers on his knees, studying the new pages I had written. What do a torturer and the tortured say to each other after their climax has passed? I did not know, but as I sat watching him from my bamboo chair, still bisected into myself and another, I detected a similar division in him, in the horrible void where a face had been. He was the commissar but he was also Man; he was my interrogator but also my only confidant; he was the fiend who had tortured me but also my friend. Some might say I was seeing things, but the true optical illusion was in seeing others and oneself as undivided and whole, as if being in focus was more real than being out of focus. We thought our reflection in the mirror was who we truly were, when how we saw ourselves and how others saw us was often not the same. Likewise, we often deceived ourselves when we thought we saw ourselves most clearly. And how did I know that I was not deluding myself as I heard my friend speak? I do not. I could only try to understand whether he was fooling me as he skipped the pleasantries of inquiring about my dubious health, physical and mental, and announced that Bon and I were leaving both camp and country. I had assumed that I would die here, and the finality of what he was saying startled me. Leave? I said. How?

A truck is waiting for you and Bon at the gates. When I heard you were ready to see me, I wanted to waste no more time. You are going to Saigon. Bon has a cousin there, who I am sure he will contact. This man has already tried twice to flee from this country and been caught both times. This third time, with you and Bon, he will succeed.

His plan left me in a daze. How do you know that? I said at last.

How do I know? His void was without expression, but his voice was amused and, perhaps, bitter. Because I bought your escape. I've sent money to the right officials, who will make sure the right police officers look the other way when the time comes. Do you know where the money comes from? I had no idea. Desperate women will pay any price to see their husbands in this camp. The guards take their portion and leave the rest to the commandant and myself. I send some home to my wife, I pay my tithe to my superiors, and I used the remainder for your escape. Isn't it remarkable that in a communist country money can still buy you anything you want?

It's not remarkable, I muttered. It's funny.

Is it? I can't say I laughed in taking the money and gold of these poor women. But you see, while a confession may be enough to free you from this camp, given your revolutionary background, nothing less than money will free Bon. The commandant must be paid, after all—a considerable sum, too, given Bon's crimes. And nothing less than a great deal of money will ensure that the two of you can leave our country, as you must. This, my friend, is what I have done to these women out of friendship for you. Am I still the friend you recognize and love?

He was the faceless man who had tortured me, for my own good, for the sake of nothing. But I could still recognize him, for who but a man with two minds could understand a man with no face? I embraced him then and wept, knowing that while he was setting me free, he himself could never be free, unable or unwilling to leave this camp except through death, which at least would be a relief from his living death. The only benefit from his condition was that he could see what others could not, or what they might have seen and disavowed, for when he looked into the mirror and saw the void he understood the meaning of nothing.

But what was this meaning? What had I intuited at last? Namely this: while nothing is more precious than independence and freedom, *nothing is also more precious than independence and freedom!* These two slogans are almost the same, but not quite. The first inspiring slogan was Ho Chi Minh's empty suit, which he no longer wore. How could he? He was dead. The second slogan was the tricky one, the joke.

It was Uncle Ho's empty suit turned inside out, a sartorial sensation that only a man of two minds, or a man with no face, dared to wear. This odd suit suited me, for it was of a cutting-edge cut. Wearing this inside-out suit, my seams exposed in an unseemly way, I understood, at last, how our revolution had gone from being the vanguard of political change to the rearguard hoarding power. In this transformation, we were not unusual. Hadn't the French and the Americans done exactly the same? Once revolutionaries themselves, they had become imperialists, colonizing and occupying our defiant little land, taking away our freedom in the name of saving us. Our revolution took considerably longer than theirs, and was consideraby bloodier, but we made up for lost time. When it came to learning the worst habits of our French masters and their American replacements, we quickly proved ourselves the best. We, too, could abuse grand ideals! Having liberated ourselves in the name of independence and freedom—I was so tired of saying these words!—we then deprived our defeated brethren of the same.

Besides a man with no face, only a man of two minds could get this joke, about how a revolution fought for independence and freedom could make those things *worth less than nothing*. I was that man of two minds, me and myself. We had been through so much, me and myself. Everyone we met had wanted to drive us apart from each other, wanted us to choose either one thing or another, except the commissar. He showed us his hand and we showed him ours, the red scars as indelible as they were in our youth. Even after all we had been through, this was the only mark on our body. We clasped hands and he said, Before you leave, I have something to give you. From beneath his desk he retrieved our battered rucksack and our copy of *Asian Communism and the Oriental Mode of Destruction*. The last we had seen it, the book was nearly falling apart, creased deeply at the spine. The binding had finally torn apart, and a rubber band bound the book's two halves. We tried to refuse it, but he slipped the book in the rucksack and pressed it on us. In case you ever need to send me a message, he said. Or vice versa. I still have my copy.

Reluctantly, we took the rucksack. Dear friend—

One more thing. He picked up our manuscript, the copy of our confession and everything after, and motioned for us to open the rucksack. What happened in that examination room is between us. So take this with you, too.

We just want you to know—

Go! Bon is waiting.

So we went, rucksack over our shoulders, dismissed for the last time. No more pencils, no more books, no more teacher's dirty looks. Silly rhymes and childish wordplay, but if we had thought of anything more serious we would have fallen down under the weight of disbelief, of our sheer relief.

The baby-faced guard escorted us to the camp gates, where the commandant and Bon stood by an idling Molotova truck. We had not seen Bon in a year and many months, and the first words he said were, You look like hell. Us? What about him? Our disembodied minds laughed, but our embodied selves did not. How could we? Our poor friend stumbled before us in patchwork and rags, a puppet in an alcoholic's hands, hair thinning and skin a sickly shade of decayed jungle vegetation. Over one eye he wore a black patch, and we knew better than to ask him what had been done to him. A few meters away, behind barbed wire, three other haggard men in shambolic clothing watched. It took us a moment to recognize our comrades, the Hmong scout, the philosophical medic, and the dark marine. You don't look like hell, the Hmong scout said. You look worse. The philosophical medic managed a grin with half his teeth missing. Don't pay him any attention, he said. He's just jealous. As for the dark marine, he said, I knew you bastards would get out of here first. Good luck to you.

We couldn't say anything, only smile and raise our hand in farewell before climbing into the truck with Bon. The baby-faced guard raised the hatch and locked it. What? the commandant said, looking up at us. You still have nothing to say? In fact, we had many things to say, but not wanting to provoke the commandant into revoking our release, we only shook our head. Have it your way. You've confessed your errors and there's nothing more to say after that, is there?

Nothing indeed! Nothing was truly unspeakable. As the truck departed in a cloud of red dust that made the baby-faced guard cough, we watched the commandant walk away and the Hmong scout, the philosophical medic, and the dark marine cover their eyes. Then we turned a corner and the camp disappeared from view. When we asked Bon about our other comrades, he told us that the Lao farmer had vanished in the river, trying to escape, while the darkest marine bled to death after a landmine sheared off his legs. At first we were quiet on hearing this news. What cause had they died for? For what reason had millions more died in our great war to unify our country and liberate ourselves, often through no choice of their own? Like them, we had sacrificed everything, but at least we still had a sense of humor. If one really thought about it, with just a little bit of distance, with even the faintest sense of irony, one could laugh at this joke played on us, those who had so willingly sacrificed ourselves and others. So we laughed and laughed and laughed, and when Bon looked at us as if we were crazy and asked what was the matter with us, we wiped the tears from our eyes and said, Nothing.

After a numbing two-day journey over mountain passes and crumbling highways, the Molotova deposited us on Saigon's outskirts. From there we shuffled along sullied streets populated by sullen people toward the navigator's house, our pace slowed by Bon's limp. The muffled city was eerily muted, perhaps because the country was once again at war, or so we were told by the Molotova's driver. Tired of the Khmer Rouge attacks on our western border, we had invaded and seized Cambodia. China, to punish us, had raided our northern border earlier in the year, sometime during my examination. So much for peace. What bothered us more was that we had not heard even one romantic song or snatch of pop music by the time we arrived at the home of the navigator, Bon's cousin. Sidewalk cafés and transistor radios had always played such tunes, but over a dinner only marginally better than the commandant's meal, the navigator confirmed what the commandant had implied. Yellow music was now banned, and only red, revolutionary music was allowed.

No yellow music in a land of so-called yellow people? Not having fought for this, we could not help but laugh. The navigator looked at us curiously. I've seen worse, he said. Two stints in reeducation and I've seen much worse. He had been reeducated for the crime of trying to escape the country by boat. On those previous attempts, he had not taken his family with him, hoping to brave the dangers alone and reach a foreign country from where he could send money home to help his family survive or flee, once the route was proven safe. But he was certain that a third capture would lead to reeducation in a northern camp, from which no one had so far returned. For this attempt, then, he was taking his wife, three sons and their families, two daughters and their families, and the families of three in-laws, the clan living or dying together on the open sea.

What are the odds? Bon asked the navigator, an experienced sailor of the old regime whose expertise Bon trusted. Fifty-fifty, the navigator said. I've only heard from half of those who fled. It's safe to assume the other half never made it. Bon shrugged. Sounds good enough, he said. What do you think? This was addressed to us. We looked to the ceiling, where Sonny and the crapulent major lay flat on their backs, scaring away the geckos. In unison, as they were now wont to speak, they said, Those are excellent odds, as the chances of one ultimately dying are one hundred percent. Thus reassured, we turned back to Bon and the navigator and, with no more laughter, nodded our agreement. This they interpreted as a sign of progress.

Over the next two months, as we waited for our departure, we continued working on our manuscript. Despite the chronic shortages of almost every good and commodity, there was no shortage of paper, since everyone in the neighborhood was required to write confessions on a periodic basis. Even we, who had confessed so extensively, had to write these and submit them to the local cadres. They were exercises in fiction, for we had to find things to confess even though we had not done anything since our return to Saigon. Small things, like failing to display sufficient enthusiasm at a self-criticism session, were acceptable. But certainly nothing big, and we never failed to end a confession without writing that nothing was more precious than independence and freedom.

Now it is the evening before our departure. We have paid for Bon's fare and our own with the commissar's gold, hidden in my rucksack's false bottom. The cipher that we share with the commissar has taken the gold's place, the heaviest thing we will carry after this manuscript, our testament if not our will. We have nothing to leave to anyone except these words, our best attempt to represent ourselves against all those who sought to represent us. Tomorrow we will join those tens of thousands who have taken to the sea, refugees from a revolution. According to the navigator's plan, on the afternoon of our departure tomorrow, from houses all over Saigon, families will leave as if on a short trip lasting less than a day. We will travel by bus to a village three hours south, where a ferryman waits by a riverbank, a conical hat shading his features. Can you take us to our uncle's funeral? To this coded question, the coded answer: Your uncle was a great man. We, along with the navigator, his wife, and Bon, clamber on board the skiff, we carrying in our rucksack our rubber-bound cipher and this unbound manuscript, wrapped in watertight plastic. We glide across the river to a hamlet where the rest of the navigator's clan will join us. The mother ship awaits further down the river, a fishing trawler for 150, almost all of whom will hide in the hold. It will be hot, warned the navigator. It reeks. Once the crew battens down the hatches of the hold, we will struggle to breathe, no vents to alleviate the pressure from 150 bodies locked into a space for a third that number. Heavier than depleted air, however, is the knowledge that even astronauts have a better chance of survival than we do.

Around our shoulders and chest we will strap the rucksack, cipher and manuscript inside. Whether we live or die, the weight of those words will hang on us. Only a few more need to be written by the light of this oil lamp. Having answered the commissar's question, we find ourselves facing more questions, universal and timeless ones that never get tired. What do those who struggle against power do when they seize power? What does the revolutionary do when the revolution triumphs? Why do those who call for independence and freedom take away the independence and freedom of others? And is it sane or insane to believe, as so many around us apparently do, in nothing? We can only answer these questions for ourselves. Our life and our death have taught us always to sympathize with the undesirables among the undesirables. Thus magnetized by experience, our compass continually points toward those who suffer. Even now, we think of our suffering friend, our blood brother, the commissar, the faceless man, the one who spoke the unspeakable, sleeping his morphine dream, dreaming of an eternal sleep, or perhaps dreaming of nothing. As for us, how long it had taken us to stare at nothing until we saw something! Might this be what our mother felt? Did she look into herself and feel wonderstruck that where nothing had been something now existed, namely us? Where was the turning point when she began wanting us rather than not wanting us, seed of a father who should not have been a father? When did she stop thinking of herself and began to think of us?

Tomorrow we will find ourselves among strangers, reluctant mariners of whom a tentative manifest can be written. Among us will be infants and children, as well as adults and parents, but no elderly, for none dare the voyage. Among us will be men and women, as well as the thin and lean, but not one among us will be fat, the entire nation having undergone a forced diet. Among us will be the light skinned, dark skinned, and every shade in between, some speaking in refined accents and some in rough ones. Many will be Chinese, persecuted for being Chinese, with many others the recipients of degrees in reeducation. Collectively we will be called the boat people, a name we heard once more earlier this night, when we surreptitiously listened to the Voice of America on the navigator's radio. Now that we are to be counted among these boat people, their name disturbs us. It smacks of anthropological condescension, evoking some forgotten branch of the human family, some lost tribe of amphibians emerging from ocean mist, crowned with seaweed. But we are not primitives, and we are not to be pitied. If and when we reach safe harbor, it will hardly be a surprise if we, in turn, turn our backs on the unwanted, human nature being what we know of it. Yet we are not cynical. Despite it all—yes, despite everything, in the face of *nothing*—we still consider ourselves revolutionary. We remain that most hopeful of creatures, a revolutionary in search of a revolution, although we will not dispute being called a dreamer doped by an illusion. Soon enough we will see the scarlet sunrise on that horizon where the East is always red, but for now our view through our window is of a dark alley, the pavement barren, the curtains closed. Surely we cannot be the only ones awake, even if we are the only ones with a single lamp lit. No, we cannot be alone! Thousands more must be staring into darkness like us, gripped by scandalous thoughts, extravagant hopes, and forbidden plots. We lie in wait for the right moment and the just cause, which, at this moment, is simply wanting to live. And even as we write this final sentence, the sentence that will not be revised, we confess to being certain of one and only one thing—we swear to keep, on penalty of death, this one promise:

We will live!

ACKNOWLEDGMENTS

Many of the events in this novel did happen, although I confess to taking some liberties with details and chronology. For the fall of Saigon and the last days of the Republic of Vietnam, I consulted David Butler's *The Fall of Saigon*, Larry Engelmann's *Tears Before the Rain*, James Fenton's "The Fall of Saigon," Dirck Halstead's "White Christmas," Charles Henderson's *Goodnight Saigon*, and Tiziano Terzani's *Giai Phong! The Fall and Liberation of Saigon*. I am particularly indebted to Frank Snepp's important book *Decent Interval*, which provided the inspiration for Claude's flight from Saigon and the episode with the Watchman. For accounts of South Vietnamese prisons and police, as well as Viet Cong activities, I turned to Douglas Valentine's *The Phoenix Program*, the pamphlet *We Accuse* by Jean-Pierre Debris and André Menras, Truong Nhu Tang's *A Vietcong Memoir,* and an article in the January 1968 issue of *Life*. Alfred W. McCoy's *A Question of Torture* was crucial for understanding the development of American interrogation techniques from the 1950s through the war in Vietnam, and their extension into the American wars in Iraq and Afghanistan. For the reeducation camps, I made use of Huynh Sanh Thong's *To Be Made Over*, Jade Ngoc Quang Huynh's *South Wind Changing*, and Tran Tri Vu's *Lost Years*. As for the Vietnamese resistance fighters who attempted to invade Vietnam, a small exhibit in the Lao People's Army History Museum in Vientiane displays their captured artifacts and weapons.

While those fighters have been largely forgotten, or simply never known, the inspiration for the Movie can hardly be a secret. Eleanor Coppola's documentary *Hearts of Darkness* and her *Notes: The Making of Apocalypse Now* provided many insights, as did Francis Ford Coppola's commentary on the *Apocalypse Now* DVD. These works were also helpful: Ronald Bergan's *Francis Ford Coppola: Close Up*; Jean-Paul Chaillet and Elizabeth Vincent's *Francis Ford Coppola*; Jeffrey Chown's *Hollywood Auteur: Francis Coppola*; Peter Cowie's *The Apocalypse Now Book* and *Coppola: A Biography*; Michael Goodwin and Naomi Wise's *On the Edge: The Life and Times of Francis Coppola*; Gene D. Phillips and Rodney Hill's *Francis Ford Coppola: Interviews*; and Michael Schumacher's *Francis Ford Coppola: A Filmmaker's Life*. I also drew on articles by Dirck Halstead, "Apocalypse Finally"; Christa Larwood, "Return to *Apocalypse Now*"; Deirdre McKay and Padmapani L. Perez, "Apocalypse Yesterday Already! Ifugao Extras and the Making of *Apocalypse Now*"; Tony Rennell, "The Maddest Movie Ever"; and Robert Sellers, "The Strained Making of *Apocalypse Now*."

The exact words of others were occasionally important as well, in particular those of To Huu, whose poems appeared in the *Viet Nam News* article "To Huu: The People's Poet"; Nguyên Van Ky, who translated the proverb "The good deeds of Father are as great as Mount Thai Son," available in the book *Viêt Nam Exposé*; the 1975 edition of *Fodor's Southeast Asia*; and General William Westmoreland, whose ideas concerning the Oriental's view of life and its value were given in the documentary *Hearts and Minds* by director Peter Davis. Those ideas are attributed here to Richard Hedd.

Finally, I am grateful to a number of organizations and people without whom this novel would not be the book that it is. The Asian Cultural Council, the Bread Loaf Writers Conference, the Center for Cultural Innovation, the Djerassi Resident Artists Program, the Fine Arts Work Center, and the University of Southern California gave me grants, residencies, or sabbaticals that facilitated my research or writing. My agents, Nat Sobel and Julie Stevenson, provided patient encouragement and wise editing, as did my editor, Peter Blackstock. Morgan Entrekin and Judy Hottensen were enthusiastic supporters, while Deb Seager, John Mark Boling, and all the staff of Grove Atlantic have worked hard on this book. My friend Chiori Miyagawa believed in this novel from its beginning and tirelessly read the early drafts. But the people to whom I owe the greatest debt are, as ever, my father, Joseph Thanh Nguyen, and my mother, Linda Kim Nguyen. Their indomitable will and sacrifice during the war years and after made possible my life and that of my brother, Tung Thanh Nguyen. He has been ever supportive, as has his wonderful partner, Huyen Le Cao, and their children, Minh, Luc, and Linh.

As for the last words of this book, I save them for the two who will always come first: Lan Duong, who read every word, and our son, Ellison, who arrived right on time.

The Refugees

Viet Thanh Nguyen
Winner of the Pulitzer Prize
for Fiction 2016

'A powerful antidote to all the fearmongering and lies out there . . .
never has a short story collection been timelier'
Independent

'Nguyen's eight heart-wrenching and hopeful stories ought to be
required reading for every politician in this era of wall-building
and xenophobia'
Guardian

'Beautiful and heartrending'
Joyce Carol Oates, *New Yorker*

'[A] superb collection . . . exquisite stories . . .
Nguyen crafts dazzlingly lucid prose'
Observer